I0549368

STEPPING ON THE DEVIL'S TAIL

A Mystery Thriller

R A U L   H E R N A N D E Z

ISBN: 0692461604
ISBN 13: 9780692461600
Library of Congress Control Number: TXu001907066
Santa Barbara, California

ABOUT THE AUTHOR

Raul Hernandez has been a journalist for more than 30 years. He has worked at the El Paso Herald-Post, the El Paso Times, the Press Enterprise in Riverside County, California and the Ventura County Star in California.

He worked as a court reporter for more than 18 years and is currently the publisher of the website American Justice Notebook — www.cjnotebook.com

And if you gaze for long into an abyss,
the abyss gazes also into you. — **Friedrich Nietzsche**

PREFACE

Jack Fuentes, a burned-out newspaper reporter, stumbles into a diabolical plot just when he's about to hand in his resignation and put newsrooms in the rearview mirror of his life.

His girlfriend Emily has left him, and his close relationship with his father is crumbling.

The newsroom's loose cannon packs up his belongings and plans to head to the West Coast. He wants to put as much distance as possible between him and his personal demons, deadlines and demanding editors.

But he doesn't have enough money to leave town. So Jack bets city editor and fellow pool hustler, C.J. Cortez, a thousand dollars that he can get quotes from Mickey Madrid for the drug kingpin's obituary. Mickey is in the hospital close to death from a two-pack-a-day, cigarette habit.

C.J. thinks Jack's wager is insane, but he sees the bet as easy money. C.J. knows Mickey hates reporters and all his grieving relatives are also at the hospital, including his beautiful daughter Sierra. She can't stand Jack because of the stories he has written about her father whose clandestine drug-smuggling routes that the DEA has been unable to shut down.

Late at night, Jack weasels his way into Mickey's hospital room. He gets the quotes, beats a late-night deadline, and Mickey dies that night.

The next day when he is about to hand in his resignation, everything changes. Jack is surprised by what else is on the recorded interview. What Mickey Madrid's feeble lips revealed.

When Jack starts asking questions about who will takeover Mickey's prized narcotics pipeline, he finds himself staring into the throat of an unsuspecting monster — an unholy trinity of drug cartels, criminal street gangs and jihadists.

The search for answers leads to an old artist's studio in a small Mexican town with Sierra who is searching for her brother's killer.

Soon, Jack and Sierra are running for their lives.

By Raul Hernandez

They say that in Mexico even the devil is packing heat because he's afraid of the cartels. I don't know about that. I know about the Mickey Madrid story, and some would argue that Mickey is the devil himself.

The story took on a life of its own, as though it had a soul.

It followed me like a phantom with a mean streak long after it had elbowed its way and lingered on the streets. I chased the story for weeks, and the weeks turned into months, and months into years.

Soon, the questions and the notebooks just kept piling up. But it all went nowhere. All I got were fragments about what happened, bits and pieces.

This is what I know: Two heavy hitters from Bogota came looking for Mickey. Well-scripted, the Colombian *sicarios* had a plan to lure Mickey and his bodyguard Bazooka to a meeting and kill them after a briefcase full of cash was exchanged.

It was a simple plan. But Mickey complicated things. He always complicated things. That was his style.

Mickey was raised on the streets and learned to live by his wits. So the plan didn't go as intended, and what evolved was a dark side that turned intrigue into an obsession. Obsession that stands on its tiptoes and looks down into an abyss.

Most who would say anything about what happened would only do so off-the-record and all of them did so with apprehensive eyes or spoke with back-alley whispers. Still, I kept pursing every tip, every clue, every hunch, every morsel of information.

Until one day, the trail of breadcrumbs blurred before it slowly began to fade. Then, like some Gothic ghost with a taunting smile, the story disappeared. I finally decided to bury this thing way in the back of my mind.

Days after I walked away from the story, it managed to crawl out, found its legs again, and came knocking on my door. This time more like pounding, pounding hard with a pigheaded fist.

The phone rang.

"Newsroom."

"Jack."

It was a source. A DEA agent named Nick Roper who had a cadre of snitches on speed dial.

"What's up, Nick?" I said.

"The Mickey Madrid story."

"Yeah, what about it?"

"You still interested?"

"Yeah, hell yeah. Of course, I am. Why?"

"I found it. The whole thing."

"Found it where?"

"Inside a box marked evidence."

"Are you bullshitting?"

"No. It was on the wire. One that Indio wore," he said.

"A wire? That would have been the last place on the planet where I would have looked. Is it solid?"

"It's there, all there. Some real sweet details, everything. I read the transcript. It's thick."

"Indio's dead," I said.

"No, shit. He was my CI."

"Who else is on the wire with Indio?"

"Tecolote."

"Bazooka's cousin?"

"Yeah."

"How would Tecolote know what happened?" I said.

"He was there."

"What happened to him?"

"Your guess is as good as mine."

"I heard he found Jesus in Altiplano, the Mexican prison where they housed Chapo, and is now driving cabs in Cancun."

Nick laughed.

"No way. Nobody retires. One of my snitches said his charred remains are in the desert near the Juarez airport with the rest of them," Nick said. "Anyway, the wire was part of the evidence we were gathering to make a case against Jose Alberto Perez Cuevas, a.k.a. *El Pinguino*. DEA shut down the investigation after *Pinguino* disappeared in Piedras Negras."

"Sinaloa Cartel snatched him up?" I said.

"That's what our people say."

"So, did Mickey know about the FedEx thing? Now, that's bat-shit crazy."

I waited anxiously for him to say something else, anything. But there was only a long, awkward pause, a gesture conveyed by silence. A signal I immediately picked up that said that he didn't want to tell me anything else over the phone. That this story, the Mickey Madrid story, suddenly had piercing clearness and more.

"See you at the House?" I said.

"Okay, text me when you leave the newsroom," he said.

"I will."

CHAPTER 2

The Ice House is a raucous dive that sat at the edge of El Paso since the 50's. It's got bad lighting and equally bad service. The scuffed-up dance floor is surrounded by dozens of tables and a few booths. Much of it smells like days-old booze with hints of urine. The roof sags and from a distance, it looks like it's about to cave in.

But the watering hole also has the coldest beer in town, mouth-watering chicken tacos, and in the summer, the temperature inside rivals a Chicago meat locker. And, the best part, it's secluded, near the base of the Franklin Mountains, a mile before the city limit. The place is encircled by a poorly lit parking lot where sometimes addicts do lines of coke or get high on meth inside cars and pickup trucks.

It's a great place to meet people who you wouldn't be seen with in a mall or downtown El Paso, like a DEA agent. We usually sat at a corner table, sipped slow beers and gabbed about what is going on in the streets, sometimes about our lives and once in a while, what we planned to do on weekends.

Nick got to the Ice House first. I arrived a short time later. We ordered a couple of Coronas and got the usual complimentary bowl of peanuts put on top of a wobbly table.

We always began our conversations talking about trivial stuff, shuffling around a few hard statistics and suspect player trades in the NFL. That night, we also talked about the downpours of the recent late summer rains that caused a lot of flooding on Interstate 10, sometimes flooding the highway.

Shortly after our beers arrived, my ears began to itch. I was euphoric, the way a newspaper reporter feels when he is about to be handed all the missing puzzles to an investigative piece, a great story. The Mickey Madrid story was different. It kept me flipping through my notebook at the kitchen table, going through interviews and searching for one quote or remark that would steer me in the right direction.

I put my elbows on the table and closed some of the distance between Nick and I.

"So, how did it all go down?" I finally asked.

"I swear, you couldn't find this in a Hollywood script," he said. "It's incredible."

Nick took a sip of his beer and scooted his chair forward and looked me straight in the eye, making sure he had my complete attention. Nick was a master storyteller and always began his stories in good spots, great spots. Places reserved for a seasoned newspaper reporter, one who understood how to grab his readers' attention by the testicles.

Always, Nick's lips moved at the pace of a slug going up a rusty drain pipe. Then, his narrations gradually galloped like a white stallion cutting through a fog. But tonight, his gallop would be hindered by annoying and unexpected stops and starts by the time he finished telling the story.

"The Colombians were handpicked and sent by a Cali Cartel boss. They arrived in downtown Juarez and were armed with two pocketsize cannons," said Nick. "They worked as a team, methodical and deadly like a pair of killer whales on the hunt for fat California seals."

Nick took a long gulp of his beer, glanced at the bar and scratched the back of his head before he continued.

"Between the two of them, they had killed dozens, including a priest who was inside a confessional booth."

"A priest? Why?"

"He was a part-time courier for the Beltran-Leyva Drug Cartel."

"Any witnesses?"

"Only one. A boy, a street kid, 10 years old, who unfortunately saw what happened, and ran. He got shot in the back of the head halfway down the aisle of the church."

"That's cold."

"It's business, cartel business," Nick said. "This kid would go to church in the morning to pray and light a candle to Saint Jude before he hit the streets to shine shoes. He believed the prayers. The candles brought him luck and more tips to help support his family."

"Saint Jude, the patron saint of the impossible."

"Yeah, I guess he was out to lunch that day," Nick said dismissively with eyes fixed on the label on the beer bottle. He huffed and slowly shook his head as though he had a sudden gleam of insight.

"On the surface, the two Colombians, Fernando and Topo, looked like a couple of tourists who had just stepped out of a Carnival cruise ship," Nick said. "But they were in a league of their own. Let me put it this way, if there's a Narco Hall of Fame, they'd be in it and have their faces plastered on trading cards."

Nick glanced at his cell phone that lit up and buzzed. He poked it. The phone stopped buzzing.

"Who was this Topo guy?" I said.

"He was half Chinese, half Colombian. He had a deformed ear and scraggly Fu-Manchu. And, one green, glass eye and walked with a slight limp. He hid his nefarious side behind a big, Sunday-morning smile, Ray-Bans, and a morbid, sick sense of humor."

"That's weird," I said.

"Fernando, he was a big son of a bitch with a goofy looking smile," he said.

"The Colombian odd couple."

Outside the Ice House, a heavy downpour beat on the roof like hundreds of tiny hammers. It was the middle of the week, and the bar was nearly empty. On Fridays, it turned into a different place. It was packed and rowdy. A rock band shook the walls while brash, blue-collar patrons, social oddballs, outlaws, parolees, construction workers and biker types crowded the tables or dance floor or hugged the L-shaped bar.

On weekends, bouncers kept the violence in check.

Nick and I sat at a table under the soft glow of a neon beer sign and near a peeling 60's poster of actor Steve McQueen on a motorcycle that had been sloppily glued on a wall.

An old jukebox with its flashing laser lights played an Eric Clapton classic loud enough to keep our conversation from spilling into a nearby table where two bearded bikers with booming laughter, talked and shared a couple of pitchers of beer with their aging women, one who had a silver ring on a mangled, flat nose. The other had unshaven armpits and flaming red hair.

Just as he was about to open his mouth after taking two long swallows of beer, Nick's phone vibrated, again. He wiped his lips with the back of his hand, read the message, frowned and slipped the phone back into his pocket.

"Where was I?" he said.

"The Colombians, one was huge," I said.

"Oh yeah. Anyway, they were well-scripted, stone-cold killers," he said.

"Mickey would be dead after they got a briefcase with the cash, right?" I said.

"Right. And then, they'd smoke Bazooka."

"What about the FedEx thing and Mickey? Cut to the chase."

"Whoa. Slow down, okay? I'm getting there. Patience, Kemosabe."

Nick knew I was savoring every word of the story. He was toying with my impatience.

Light from the neon sign softened Nick's hard hazel eyes, his cop hardness, highlighting a smooth, square jaw and high cheekbones. I was convinced that Nick's memory was cluttered with facts, details, times and places. Much of it was useless stuff, and other times, a treasure trove.

Long seconds passed, as I anxiously waited for him to return to the story. All the time, I fought the urge to reach inside my coat pocket, whip out a notebook and start writing. But there was no way I would do this, not at a bar where AT&T had taken out its pay phone decades ago because of drug dealing problems.

The music stopped. Nick flung his eyes toward the jukebox. He got up and put a few dollar bills in its maw so the music would camouflage our conversation and keep it on a short leash. A thirsty, grease-stained, grungy crew of junkyard workers from across the highway had just sat down on two nearby tables and ordered two pitchers of beer.

Before Nick could utter another word, a bolt of lightening lit up the outside, followed by booming thunder that rattled the roof. It made bar patrons flinch, followed by some oooohhs. Neon lights flicker and then, the electrical power stuttered, gasped and went out.

Curse words. Cigarette coughs. Groans. Snickers. The jukebox stopped dead in its tracks. The bar was nearly pitch dark.

It got quiet for a few seconds.

Jittery female laughter followed, then, some gabbing, a few more curse words along with playful put downs aimed at the bar owner, wondering out loud if he had paid the bar's light bill.

Silence flooded the room before someone took out a cigarette lighter so another patron could aim a beer pitcher without spilling a drop of alcohol.

A minute went by before the lights went back on and Eric Clapton's loud vocal cords leaped out of the jukebox like a leopard and gobbled up the quiet with his baritone lungs. Nick sat back in his chair, calm and reflecting, as though he was reorganizing his train of thought that was temporarily derailed by the lightening and thunder, as though nothing had happened.

He continued the Mickey Madrid story after tossing a handful of peanuts down his throat, running his tongue across his teeth and washing the remaining peanuts down with a swig of beer.

"Anyway, Indio was wired when he went to meet Tecolote at a park near the downtown library in El Paso to set up a big drug deal," he said. "We had eyes on him. Two agents were parked a couple of blocks away with a pair of binoculars. Watching their every move like hawks. We knew things could go wrong real quick. Indio would give the signal, and we'd swoop down."

Nick said everything went smooth.

"Indio and Tecolote sat on a park bench like two downtown pigeons, cooing away and watching the world go by," said Nick. "Tecolote bragged how easy it was to smuggle cocaine. He said 'Mickey's underlings could smuggle a Russian tank across the border through the Santa Fe Bridge.'"

"There is no shortage of mind magic and creativity in Mexico when it comes to hiding shit from the Customs," I said.

"Get this. Tecolote said he once used a 60's Volkswagen van to smuggle cocaine inside some hidden compartments. The van had a bad transmission, bald tires and a fading church sign on the side of it."

"Yeah, yeah, but what does that have to do with the two Colombians and Mickey Madrid?"

"Wait, alright, I'm getting to that."

Nick used his hand to emphasize the church sign across the van, *La Vida Eterna Iglesia*," he said. "Mickey's boys stuffed the van with some Mexican Bible-thumping church members. Mostly, old ladies and children who didn't have a clue that they were sitting on 40 pounds of cocaine hidden inside the floor panels every time they crossed the border, singing Jesus songs. They were going to a four-day religious revival in El Paso. Tecolote drove church members there. Then, he drove the van to a stash house, they took out the coke, and Tecolote drove back to the revival."

"Mickey's organization hired a lot of low-life weasels to smuggle his dope," I said. "But there was never any shortage of creativity with that group."

"Well, listen to this. All of a sudden, out of the blue, Tecolote bragged to Indio that the church van had once been used to load two bodies at a restaurant parking lot in Juarez."

"The two Colombians?" I said.

"Yeah."

"Did Indio pick up on all of this?" I said.

"Like a magnet. But first, he stroked Tecolote's ego and laughed at his lame jokes. Then, he patiently and carefully coaxed him for more details."

"Indio? This is the same snitch whose ice-picked body was found in the dugout by a Little League coach."

"Yeah," Nick said and slowly shook his head. "That was such a waste of a good CI. He was my prized informant. The Mikhail Baryshnikov of snitches. When Indio wore a wire, nobody was safe. I swear to God, he was so good he could get you to talk about your grandmother's hemorrhoids."

Nick's cell phone buzzed again. He glanced at the text message, mumbled to himself, and shut it off. He rolled his eyes up and shook his head.

"Some dude who we flipped. A real pain in the ass," He said. "He's a whining little shit. Wants to earn DEA merit badges and work off some jail time by becoming a snitch for us."

He frowned after glancing at the cell phone and poking some buttons on it.

"Anyway, where was I? Oh, yeah, Fernando and Topo checked into the Palacio the night before."

"El Palacio? El Palacio del Rey, the four-star hotel in downtown Juarez that was near the Plaza de Los Toros?"

"Yeah."

"There are a lot of political heavyweights that stay there, a lot of money."

"Right, so they had to be inconspicuous. That requires a special kind of alertness, almost animal instinct," said Nick. "But Mickey knew that Fernando and Topo were in town as soon as they stepped through the hotel doors. So, Mickey sent two high-end whores and a bottle of Remy Martin cognac up to their room. The prostitutes left early the next morning. They told Mickey that the Colombians had *quetes* with silencers. They also saw a street map of Juarez with side streets all marked up with a red felt pen."

"Marking up quick exit routes out of town," I interjected.

"Correct," Nick said. "Fernando laid a line of bullshit on Mickey. He told him that the Colombia bosses were tapping new cocaine pipelines straight through Mickey's corridor, promising big profits."

"Who sent the Colombians?"

"Jorge Alvarez Cantu. One of Pablo Escobar's right-hand henchmen before Pablo got taken out on the rooftop by Colombian commandos," Nick said. "But Mickey had already been tipped off that Alvarez Cantu and his Colombian henchmen wanted him dead."

"Why? Mickey's drug routines are nearly invisible."

"Word was that Alvarez Cantu was fed up that Mickey was doing little side deals with the Juarez Cartel," said Nick. "Topo set up a meeting with Mickey the following day at a restaurant on the outskirts of Juarez, El Sol de Azteca restaurant."

"Near the Avenida de las Americas?"

"Yeah, you've heard of it?"

"Oh, yeah. Took a date there, years ago. Excellent service, nice cuts of meat," I said.

"The ambiance alone is worth the trip to Juarez," Nick said. "I loved the fountain. The lights and the whole mystic thing around the Aztec temple as you walk into the place. Remember that old guy that looked like Geronimo's grandfather. He was dressed like an Aztec sitting by the fountain playing this flute?"

"I don't remember. It was quite a ways back."

I anxiously waited for him to finish his annoying restaurant review and continue with the Mickey Madrid story. But he kept talking about the restaurant.

"What did you order?" Nick said.

"What did I what?"

"On the menu, what did you order?"

"I don't recall. I think, maybe, I had the prime rib, and she had the fish tacos or she had the prime rib and I had the fish tacos. I don't remember," I said with a testy voice. "Like I said, it's been years.'"

He looked pensive.

"Excellent choices. Next time, try the marinated rib-eye steak with the ranchero sauce. Have you ever had the flan?" Nick said.

"The what?"

"The flan."

"No."

"Ohhh, man, you've got to go back. I'm serious. Go back and order the flan. I swear to die for."

"I'll do that some day," I said impatiently. "So, what happened to the Colombians?"

"I'm getting there."

Nick finished his Corona and belched. He raised the empty beer bottle high up, shook it and caught the attention of the bartender with a graying beard, red suspenders, pug nose and crooked teeth named Leon who ambled over and put two more beers on the table and left.

Nick put his elbows on top of the table and to my frustration and dismay; he hijacked the conversation to another direction, again. This time he took it to a place that I didn't want it to go, a real sore spot. I hoped he wouldn't go there, and if he did, maybe after I had a few beers and was nice and numb. But that wasn't going to happen, it never did.

"Hey, before I finish, I need to ask you something," he said.

"What?"

"I heard you're leaving the newsroom," he said.

"Who told you?"

"Sources. I got my sources," he said, winked.

"I'm going to resign."

"Seriously? You're serious this time."

"Oh, yeah. I'm done. Period."

"I don't get it. You have front-row seats to this spook show, and you want to leave just when it's getting good. Just when the shit is about to fly?"

Nick's prodding and provoking could get irritating, condescending.

"You're a hell of a reporter. I bet that God even reads your stuff on the Web."

"Why? Why would God read my stuff?" I said, knowing he was just piling up the sarcasm.

"The words you use are like finely-tuned razors, the sentences crisp, and the way you use the talents that God gave you, amazing. I bet he's as proud as punch."

He flashed his teeth and snorted, trying to keep a straight face.

"Are you through slinging the bullshit?" I said.

He busted out laughing. I fumed. He gradually stopped laughing.

"Hey, don't get all puffed up. I'm just messing with you," he said. "Seriously, though, why are you leaving? Quitting isn't in your DNA, never was."

I stared at the entrance of the bar to mull over what I was going to say. I knew the reason. It swirled in my head but I never really had to explain it to anyone because I didn't know how it would sound once the words left my mouth, once I heard them.

"The newsroom," I said and paused. "I went to work early one morning, I mean really early. It was still dark. I stared at the rows of computer screens, the empty desks. It looked surreal in a way, and right then and there, I realized that almost overnight, management had turned the place I loved into this digital Disneyland. We are catering to kids with bouncy houses inside their heads, smart phones glued to their hands and with the attention span of Rhesus monkeys."

"It's the world of Twitter and Twilight, my friend. Learn to embrace it."

"Embrace what? Entertainment is masquerading as journalism. CNN and others assigned reporters to the Justin Bieber beat to chase after this adolescent asshole. That's news?" I said. "Pit bull journalism is dying, going by way of buffalo nickels. We're chasing after subscribers with butterfly nets."

I took a couple of gulps of beer and looked across the table where the bikers and their old ladies had been sitting. It was empty.

"It was nice while it lasted," I said with a nostalgic smile.

"You're really serious this time."

I nodded.

"The bonfire, it's nearly out."

"The what fire?"

"Bonfire. The passion. It's gone. It's like one-by-one, these mealy-mouth editors lined up and pissed on the passion, the bonfire. Years later, the flame is barely flickering. They just wear you out."

"It's that new editor, right? What's his name?"

"Ricardo Scott," I said. "No, he just made it easier to leave."

"So where do you go from here?"

"Seriously? I have a few plans but in all honestly, I don't really have a clue," I said. "Everything is on the table, *todo*."

"How are you going to pay the rent?"

I shrugged.

"Don't tell me that you're going to bank on your pool-stick hustle to pay the bills?" Nick said.

"If I'm short of cash and need rent money, why not?"

"Are you and C.J. still tag-teaming people down at the pool hall?"

"Hustling, my friend, is an under-appreciated art form."

"You'll be stopping in Chicago, right?"

"Why would I do that?"

"To see Emily," Nick said.

I laughed. "No way. She dumped me. Took her half of the furniture, the good pots and pans and Knuckles. I was at work when she was doing the packing. I never saw it coming."

"She took your dog too, wow?"

"Yeah. Knuckles was a birthday gift. I told her I loved bulldogs. Our family had a bulldog named Cisco. Him and me were buds growing up. My dad loved that dog. Cisco and my dad sometimes split a six-pack. Got the dog drunk, which pissed off my mom."

"I told Emily about Cisco, and how much he meant to me when I was a boy, and she went out and bought this bulldog puppy for my birthday, a year ago. She wouldn't let him have a sip of my beer. She said one drunk in the family was enough."

"Ouch. So she took the dog and the good pots and pans?"

"Well, yeah, but I was okay with it. She kind of bonded with Knuckles while I was in the newsroom or pool hall. After a while, the dog only chased the ball when she threw it. He practically ignored me. Ain't that a bitch?"

"Being ignored by your own dog. That's cold."

"It bothered me, you know, but I didn't take it personal. A dog is a dog."

"You still have that crazy-ass cockatiel? What's his name? She didn't take him too did she?"

"Dexter," I said. "No. The bird and I have been really tight since he flew down from my roof eight years ago."

"I thought you and Emily had big plans. That it was serious."

"In the beginning, we did. She was pretty level headed, and understood deadlines and pool halls. Then, it's like she changed overnight, started making demands like we were married."

"Bossy?"

"Naw, not really. But once in a while, she'd yell about my drinking and pool playing, and slam doors for emphasis. Then, I'd get the silent treatment for days. That was worse than the yelling. I hated when she wouldn't speak to me. I'd ask her a question, and she'd say, 'figure it out' or point at stuff without saying a word when I asked her where something was."

"She probably grew tired of covering your half of the rent after C.J. cleaned your clock."

"C.J., on a hot streak is unstoppable."

"You still have feelings for her. I can tell. I bet if she walked through that door right now, your eyes would spin, and you'd spit out quarters."

"It's like this. She's not coming back, ever. Game over. So just drop it."

"She is one gorgeous lady. Waaay out of your league."

"Shut-up, *bofo*," I said.

After the jukebox took another short respite, I anxiously cajoled Nick into continuing the Mickey Madrid story.

"Can we just stop, okay? Just stop here and rewind here? Please. Let's go back. So what happened? Did Mickey Madrid show up?"

"Everybody showed up, the Colombians, Mickey and Bazooka. They all sat at a corner table in the back of the restaurant," said Nick. "Ordered a fancy meal."

Nick said a spiffy, droopy-eyed waiter named Chapulin waited on them. Mickey recommended the prime rib.

"A $140 bottle of 2003 Carlos Pulenta Vistalba wine soon graced the dinner table, compliments of Mickey," Nick said.

"Nice touch," I said. "Mickey loves wine. I heard he owned a vineyard in Sonoma, California. Heard he had his own wine cellar at his house."

"Who knows? I never get invited to family gatherings," Nick joked. "Rumor has it that you and Mickey were on the same bowling team, and he let's you date his hot, little psycho daughter, Sierra."

"I can neither confirm or deny," I said with a grin.

Nick knew Mickey hated my ass because I had written a pile of stories about his alleged ties to drug cartels, often putting Mickey's Madrid's name on the front pages. The newspaper once ran a front-page photo of him walking out of the courthouse with a smirk and his lawyers along with Bazooka in tow after Mickey got acquitted of drug smuggling.

After she read the story, his daughter Sierra threatened to cut off my manhood. Then, there was the story that linked her father to a Mexican beauty queen who was caught in a big drug bust, and later, she turned up dead in a Tijuana alley. Word had it that she was given a bad batch of black-tar heroin.

Furious, Sierra called C.J., cussed him out and threatened to sue the newspaper.

Nick said Mickey was relaxed at El Sol de Azteca with the Colombians.

"Smiles everywhere, plenty of compliments and glasses of wine as the conversation bounced from one topic to the next. It was all over the map," Nick said. "Fernando was pissed that his bosses ordered him to deliver a Nike gym bag full of cash to a Cancun hotel room."

"Who got the gym bag?"

"This Mexican army general named Oswaldo with a receding hairline and a big forehead. Behind his back, his troops called him *El Pelon*. Fernando wanted to put a bullet in this guy's head after he made him pay for room service that included the three whores who were servicing the general."

I cracked up.

"I hate those out-of-pocket expenses," I said.

"Topo told the story about how he snuck a pipe bomb under a rival's Lincoln Town Car and detonated it with a cell phone. Get this, he's sipping a Frappuccino three blocks away at a downtown Starbucks in Mexico City when he detonated the bomb," said Nick. "Topo bragged that he was able to rig up the bomb with parts he bought at Radio Shack. Topo had everybody laughing. Even Bazooka cracked a smile."

"Bazooka smiled? No, shit? Seriously?"

"Yeah, and he's not the Zen Master," said Nick.

While everybody stuffed their faces and guzzled wine, Topo told them the story on how he tracked down a Sinaloa *asesino*, a towering man nicknamed "El Vaquero," who had dispatched dozens of cartel people, Nick said.

"Up to that time, we wondered what happened to El Vaquero after he fell off our radar screen. Topo beat us to him," Nick said. "Vaquero was legendary in Mexico. He was hiding at a house in middle-class, barrio in Chihuahua when Topo nailed him. Vaquero made a big mistake. He got hungry and went to Carl Jr.'s."

"Topo was waiting at the Carl Jr.'s?"

"Oh, yeah. Vaquero was a tightwad. He had a habit of using the credit cards of people he killed. But he never used one of the cards more than twice. The rule was to use it once or twice. That was his downfall. He used one three times."

"A credit card was his demise?"

"Yeah, American Express to boot. Who uses American Express? Apparently, Mexico has its own version of PayPal, and the cartels use their bank connections to tap into credit card information. Vaquero wasn't familiar with Mexico's vastly improved banking system. A banker tipped off a cartel lieutenant who passed it to Topo who staked out the Carl's Jr. Two days later, Vaquero, returned to the Carl's Jr. and ordered a one of those loaded burritos. He loved them. He sat there and ate it with cups of black coffee. Topo patiently waited and was parked a block down the street. He had been waiting two days. He followed Vaquero to his house. Vaquero was sitting on the can with his headphones on, pants down to his ankles, holding up an old Victoria Secrets catalog, a cigarette dangling from his lips bobbed as he jerked off. Topo slowly cracked open the bathroom door and snuck up on him. Vaquero turned his head and there was Topo with this big, shit-eating grin. '*Buenas, cabron*,' Topo told El Vaquero."

"Ooooh, shit." I said.

"Yeah. El Vaquero froze like a kitchen cockroach. Topo fired. Vaquero's brains went one way and his cigarette another. It landed on a pile of dirty clothes. The place, Vaquero and all the evidence went up in flames."

"Did Mickey give the Colombians the briefcase inside the restaurant?" I said.

"I'm getting there. Fernando assured Mickey that his boss Alvarez Cantu was pleased with the way Mickey was handling things. Fernando patted Mickey on the back and whispered something to him. Mickey turned toward Bazooka and said '*Vete*, go pull out the briefcase.' Bazooka headed for the door. As soon as they got the money, they planned to kill Mickey and Bazooka and make a quick exit. Mickey motioned to Chapulin who rushed over from the other side of the large room. 'Get my friends a bottle of Don Julio,' Mickey told Chapulin."

Chapulin left and quickly returned with the Tequila. He handed it to Fernando who took a few seconds to admire the bottle.

"*Gracias*," Fernando said.

"My pleasure," Mickey told Fernando and winked. "For your trip back home."

Nick said Mickey then pulled out a wad of money and put it on the table. Chapulin saw the money, and his eyes almost popped out.

Nick stopped talking long enough to take a few gulps from his beer.

"As the trio walked toward the entrance, Mickey's cell phone went off. He glanced at the number, stopped, and excused himself to talk to the caller. '*Un cliente*,' Mickey told the Colombians. '*Una carga de cocaína*.' Mickey was cautious. Any slight signal or nuance in the normal flow of things, and everything would go south and go deadly really fast. 'The briefcase is outside. Bazooka will give it to you,' Mickey told Fernando. 'I got to go take a leak. Make sure you count the money.' Fernando and Topo grinned and walked outside.'"

"Bazooka was waiting?" I said.

"Yep. As soon as they stepped out the door, the two spotted him. He waved them over and opened the trunk of the car. The Colombians walked toward him. Bazooka pulled out a briefcase and slowly raised it up to his chest. As soon as they got close, Bazooka slammed the trunk shut. It was a signal. An ambush was sprung."

"In the middle of the parking lot?"

Nick grinned and nodded.

"Nino and Sombras popped up from behind the back of a pickup truck. Kneeling, they unloaded two shotgun blasts, and it was over. The shots tore through their torsos, knocking them back. The bottle of Don Julio shattered into a million pieces. Blood was everywhere. Fernando was dead by the time he landed on his back.

Topo flopped around for a few seconds like a sand shark on a boat. He made gurgling sounds, long, excruciating moans like a bellowing rabid cow. Nino went over, took out a gun, stood over Topo fired two slugs in his chest. Bazooka fired four more times into the bodies."

"Were there witnesses?"

"A couple of female restaurant customers saw what happened, screamed and ran. A van screeched from around the corner."

"The *Vida Eterna Igelsia* van."

"Bingo, and guess who was driving?"

"Tecolote."

"Tecolote and two guys wearing baseball caps. The two guys hopped out of the van and tossed the bodies in the back of the van and sped off."

"What happened to the bodies?" I asked, expecting to get Nick's trademark grin followed by a shrug and a *"Quien sabe."*

But that didn't happen.

"Topo and Fernando were decapitated. Their bodies torched in the desert," Nick said matter-of-factly.

"What about the FedEx thing? Were the heads FedExed to Bogota?"

He shrugged, arms extended outward and palms up.

"That's what Tecolote told Indio at the park. It's on the wire," Nick said. "But nobody knows for sure, only Mickey and Bazooka, and Mickey is on his deathbed. Good luck talking to Bazooka about it."

"Where did Tecolote say the heads were shipped to?"

"To Jorge Alvarez Cantu in Colombia," Nick said.

"Wow. That's some mind boggling, brain-busting shit. I'd hate to open that package."

"The drug cartels are simply lifting a page from the Romans' playbook."

"What?"

"Yeah. Hundreds of years ago, the Romans were masters at beat downs and mayhem. Terror was their calling card. They had crucifixions down to a science," he said. "When Roman commanders wanted to punish mutinous and cowardly units, they'd divide soldiers into groups of ten and drew lots. Those soldiers who got the unfortunate lot were stoned or clubbed by the nine others."

"That's brutal."

"Yeah. That's where the word decimation or decimate come from, the Romans. It's Latin meaning the removal of a tenth," he said. "Brutality gets compliance. It's a simple formula. First, use reason in making mandatory compliance bearable. Then, resort to terror to make noncompliance unimaginable. The Mexican cartels are the modern-day masters of beat-downs, brutality, mayhem and terror. Those Middle East terrorist ragheads are Cub Scouts compared to the south-of-the-border, cartel savages who use chainsaws to behead people."

"Who tipped off Mickey that he and Bazooka were going to get smoked?" I asked.

"*Quien sabe.* But the rumor is that the devil, himself, has Mickey's cell phone number. So it could have been Lucifer for all I know," he said and laughed. "Nobody saw Mickey leave the restaurant that night. He simply vanished. Like some *espanto.*"

Nick dropped his somber eyes, raised them. He shook his head, a smirk.

"Chapulin the waiter, he left town. He had enough of the big city and went back to his pueblo *en* Zacatecas."

"I bet he left that night."

"The next morning," Nick said and chuckled. "He packed two bags and got on a bus heading south."

Nick and I finished our beers, got a good, respectable buzz and left. There were still a lot of questions out there.

Many years after the Colombians checked into that Juarez hotel, Mickey Madrid ended up on the third floor of a hospital. His enemies' bullets didn't send him there. A two-pack-a-day cigarette habit did. He was dying of lung cancer, barely clinging to life.

The long and mysterious shadows Mickey left behind would probably be boxed up and buried with him. How did he elude the DEA and FBI for so long, not even a parking ticket? Who would be calling the shots, and most of all, how did most of Mickey's big loads make it through the fenced, heavily patrolled border that is wired for sight and sound?

Mickey would probably take everything to the grave, and his life was now hanging by a thread.

Word has it that the family had already snuck a priest up to his room to give him last rites and sprinkle holy water on his drug-dealing ass

I wasn't going to stick around to find out. I had plans. I was on my way to the West Coast to work on my cousin's fishing boat. Work on the boat and on my days off, hang out at the beach, watch the waves, play pool and bang bikini-clad tourists at downtown nightclubs in Santa Barbara.

From there, who knows? I'd probably end up in Seattle or Portland if I got tired of California.

Little did I know, however, that everything would change. Soon, I'd be looking down the monster's throat - the abyss.

CHAPTER 3

I didn't go up to the third floor blindfolded, or to quell some primal journalistic high-priest calling, or to appease the newsroom gods or some strange vision, either. This really wacked-out illusion, a far-fetched aspiration that landing an interview with Mickey Madrid would put me on some short list for a Pulitzer Prize for journalism.

It was none of that. It was never about the chest thumping either. It was simple. I went up there to win a bet, a one-thousand-dollar wager with a pair of balls.

I needed enough cash to get out of town. But what is crazy about the whole thing is how it all came together as I sat on a bar stool at a pool hall, of all places.

Some might say it was fate or some supernatural thing like an avenging angel that took me up to Mickey's room on the third floor. This divine messenger that came down from the heavens after God reached into a cosmic grab bag and plucked out my name to settle some celestial score.

In the strangest part of my mind, however, I'd like to think that I was picked because of my boyish good looks and my confident, shit-eating grin and the dimples under a dark brown mane, parted down the middle.

And, maybe, this spirit being or whatever it was also wanted a reporter who can sling newspaper ink with the best of them and write in tight sentences with words that pack a wallop.

But I really don't believe in avenging angels or spooks or black cats or Friday the Thirteenth or stuff like that. Simply put, I'm in control. I'm the master of my own destiny, and it's always been that way, and always will be.

Why it all went down like it did, I'll never really know. I can only guess.

But it all happened one night at the Painted Lady pool hall. The air was thick that night with the usual smell of hotdogs, nachos, beer, pool-cue chalk and heavy doses of after-shave clung to the air. But there was also an eerie aura of uncertainty and unpredictability. I couldn't put my finger on it.

The Painted Lady is where C.J. and I sometimes hung out after work, hustled and guzzled beer. It was our gold mine. A place where we would milk braggadocio suckers with pool sticks and wads of cash. C.J. and I loved to fleece the sheep that fancied themselves as pool sharks. We drain their wallets and send them home drunk, dejected and broke.

Earlier in the day, C.J. and I had planned another night of flawless hustle.

The night started out an odd note. C.J was late. He was always on time, and in hustling, timing and opportunity go hand-in-hand. It's everything. That's the golden rule. C.J. never broke the golden rule until tonight.

I waited, kept an eye on the door and sat on a bar stool, gripping the top of the pool stick, occasionally, taking peeks at my watch. My back leaned against the bar with two elbows resting on top of it. I looked like some vigilant Chinese nobleman guarding the entrance to the emperor's palace, guarding the virgins, and protecting an ancient family name and all its secrets.

Inside, the Painted lady, the crowd of people was thin, mostly amateurs who dropped by for a few beers and a few games of pool.

The Painted Lady is at a strip mall near Interstate 10 in El Paso. It is usually fast-paced and in a rambunctious state-of-mind with the clicking of pool balls rising and receding like the tide and often competing with the chatter. But a cold, hard steady rain had kept many players, the ones with thick billfolds, away.

Still, the waitresses flashed warm smiles, flirting, showing plenty of cleavage and meandering through the maze of pool tables, working even harder to get tips from a thin crowd.

Wet, C.J. finally showed up. He dried off with bar napkins, ordered a beer and bought me one. He looked haggard.

"You're late," I said, staring straight ahead.

"Ricardo, was on my ass all day," he said. "I finally left. He was still up at the newsroom."

"That prick got there at 5:30. He should get a life."

"Apparently, he's giving you competition," C.J. said. "You two need matching company-logo tattoos on both of your asses."

"I got one on my left nut. Wanna see it?" I implied.

"I believe you," he said and gave the place a somber scan. "Where is everybody?"

I shrugged.

"This rain just pissed on our parade," he said. "This whole night is a bust."

After scanning the place with the rows of idle pool tables, we knew that the fat fish - wanna-be pool hustlers with custom cue sticks and plump wallets, our two-legged ATMs – were no shows.

"When is this rain going to stop?" He said.

"I'm heading west soon. It's been sunny on the West Coast."

Irritated at my remark, he knew what I was going to say before I opened my mouth.

"With a little more money —" I started to say.

"And, I blow this town.' I know the line. You're always leaving, always needing 'a little more cash' to go to some pie-in-the-sky gig somewhere. You're stuck here, fool. You're stuck with me. You're stuck with this rain," he said, took a sip of his beer. "Where are you going to go? To the Magic Kingdom to live with Donald, Mickey and Goofy? Dance with Snow White?"

I laughed.

"Just watch," I retorted.

C.J. "Mush Mouth." Cortez was a steeled city editor that loved the newspaper business and enjoyed making politicians squirm by politely asking bruising questions, tough, probing questions. We became close friends after we both found out we also loved beer, pool halls and the ladies. C.J. had gone through two marriages. I had problems hanging on to meaningful relationships.

A few months after C.J. walked into the newsroom, reporters gave him the nickname "Mush Mouth" because when he got drunk, he mumbled as though he was trying to filter words through a mouthful of marbles. Nobody understood most of what he said. But it didn't matter. His pool stick did all his talking, and the stick's voice was always loud and always clear.

He was a pool hustler's hustler. His uncle, a legendary East Los Angeles pool shark whose pool-hall moniker was "Vision," taught him the game. He soon mastered the angles and later, the art of the hustle.

C.J. had both down to a science.

Uncle Vision took him down to all the pool halls in downtown Los Angeles when he was 12 years old. The beer guzzling and the dabbling in online day trading came much later in his life.

Since Ricardo walked into the newsroom, life for reporters and editors had been miserable. C.J., who had a reputation of a consistently grumpy editor, was now having mood swings outside the newsroom.

Morale was at a low point. Resignations began trickling into Ricardo's office.

Before Ricardo became editor, life was sweet, the staff was on cruise control and morale was high. We busted our asses, got things done and got awards, including coming razor-thin close to winning the Pulitzer Prize twice with stories about the Mexican drug cartels.

One day, the newspaper was sold to some East Coast media corporation that owned two other newspapers and a string of TV stations. After we were sold, the new bosses began to turn our world inside out. New faces sent to roll back the darkness arrived, and one of them was Ricardo Scott, a pudgy little package of a man. He had been the assistant managing editor at the Miami Herald.

He, along with the new managers and yes-men, was sent by the new corporate pricks to fix our newspaper, pump up subscriptions, resurrect its content and give us a new, vibrant look, a jolt of energy and a new facelift.

I drank more. Stayed at the pool hall longer. And that got me in trouble with Emily.

Outside the Painted Lady, the rain had eased up. C.J. stared at the pool hall's entrance, still harboring hard, angry eyes as though he expected Ricardo to walk inside the pool hall. He was uptight. If Ricardo were to walk into pool hall, I believe C.J. would wrap his hands around his neck and not let go.

"Ricardo's renting space inside your head," I said. "Relax. Just play his game, and humor the prick."

"This morning, the *bofo* shows up at the editors' meeting, upset and stands there, fuming. He rips up the newspaper, crumbles it and throws it in the trash."

I laughed.

"And, let me guess, he flashes his gorilla glare, right?" I asked.

"Oh yea, and out of nowhere, he digs up Elvis."

"The King of Rock and Roll?"

"Yeah. He looked around the room, and then, he says, 'mediocrity has parked its fat ass smack in the middle of the newsroom for too long,'" C.J. said. "'Elvis and mediocrity have just left the building, and some of you are fixing to follow suit if his mundane bullshit continues.'"

I held up two fingers to get the bartender's attention at the end of the bar.

When there were no easy marks at the pool tables to hustle, C.J. and I would play against each other. It often became a war. The competition was fierce, often brutal but I usually came out on the short end of the pool stick.

C.J. took no prisoners. He was a pool-playing virtuoso who loved clearing a pool table, watching jaws drop while doing it.

In the newsroom, I swore that C.J. used a meat cleaver to butcher sentences underneath my newspaper byline. But with a $650, silver-plated Predator 2 ultra-wrap pool stick, C.J. could part the Red Sea.

There were nights, rare nights when C.J. seemed to have some sorceress spell on the pool balls and had mastered perfection. His style was silk, pure silk on every bank shot. He had mastered the cut shots, the impossible angles.

When he beat me, he talked trash, a lot of trash.

Sometimes, C.J. would even whistle and flash his trademark, hyena grin, which he hung under an arched eyebrow, and strut around the pool table like a cocky, bantam rooster.

After Emily left, I waded through an emotional swamp. My pool game went to the dogs.

"Rack 'em up, *cabron*," he'd say and tease. "Take out the rent money. Emily is gone. So you can play with the rent money."

That touched a raw nerve. The rent money is what got me into trouble with Emily, the final straw.

The issues I had with Emily over the rent came to a head one winter after C.J. racked up one win after another. I lost my half of the rent money twice. That pissed off Emily, my then live-in girlfriend. She never understood the game of pool, and stopped trying to understand the deadlines, frequent visits to the pool hall and drinking.

"I'm not covering your bets anymore!" she'd say, walk into the bedroom and slam the door.

"I swear, sweetheart, this is my last time!" I said. "As God is my witness!"

"What!? Do you think I am that naïve!? Stupid? Or what!" She'd reply. "God doesn't believe you, and neither do I, and I'm not covering your pool hall bets anymore! Maybe, He can!"

One night, I came home, and she had moved out.

With $400 in my wallet from beating C.J. during a short-lived winning streak, I walked into the house with a smile and a pizza. But the smile collapsed after I looked around the rooms. Most of the furniture was gone, the good stuff including a hand-carved, antique bookshelf, which Emily had bought at a yard sale.

I cursed, thinking we had been hit by burglars who also took my bulldog Knuckles. I went into the bedroom, and the bedspread was gone. They even took the good sheets. My head was racing. I walked into the kitchen and confirmed my worst fears. I found the note. It was taped to the microwave: <u>"I love you very much but I am done. Knuckles is okay. He is safe with me."</u>

I was so bummed out. I drank for two straight days, missed work and was nearly fired. C.J. persuaded management to give me another chance. He begged them even after they rattled off my past transgressions, and there were plenty.

"You owe me. Big time," C.J. joked.

As much as I wanted, it was hard to forget Emily. She was a sweet lady with full lips and round, hazel eyes. At first, she understood the long hours and deadlines. It was who I was, and Emily accepted it. She also learned to live with the occasional, after-work trips to the pool hall.

Sundays, however, was our time together. We'd sit on the balcony, eat breakfast and watch the sunrise, read newspapers, books, lay around and just share intimate moments, conversations, and plenty of laughs.

But what I miss are the lipstick messages. She'd sometimes leave those on the bathroom mirror before she headed off to work.

The very last one stated: "Hey Boyfriend, I Luv U madly!"

I though our relationship would never end. But it did. It was my fault.

I knew I had made a mess of things, and I was torn up inside, emotionally devastated the first weeks Emily had moved out. I tried calling, but she didn't return my calls. I gave up. I thought I'd give her some space, and maybe, she'd call.

A couple of months after we split up, Emily moved out of town and went back to Chicago. She went to work at her father's thriving real estate business.

The day before she left, she called and asked if I could give her and Knuckles a ride to the airport. I tried to sound upbeat. But it was so hard to do. I could tell by her voice that there was more that she had to tell me. I was right.

"Want me to pick you up when you return?" I asked with eager eyes.

"I'm not coming back," she said, voice starting to crack with emotion.

"I understand," I said and kissed her cheek.

"Take care of yourself," she said.

"I will," I said.

My heart sank as I watched her go through the metal detector at the airport. I knew that I'd probably never see her or Knuckles again. After she left town, I spent a lot more time at the pool hall. Eventually, it became easier to go there without Emily's guilt trips festering over my head and spoiling my concentration when I angled for a do-or-die, big-money shot.

As hard as I tried, Emily was hard to shake from my mind, especially on Sundays when I found myself alone on the balcony staring into oblivion, hoping she was doing fine. Thinking about the lipstick messages, the pecan-colored hair that smelled like green apples.

Emily would be successful whatever she decided to do. I knew she was selling a lot of houses in Chicago with that vivacious and magnetic personality.

Outside the Painted Lady, the rain had stopped. People came inside, slowly the place filled up. The sweet sound of eight balls crashing into racked balls picked up but not by much.

C.J. and I sat on bar stools looking like a pair of iguanas sipping Coronas, anxiously waiting for the jungle to cough up some winged thing, a fat and crunchy six-legged thing. One that would dare come close enough so one of us could snag it with our tongues.

We weren't saying much. Occasionally, we'd chew on some pretzels or slip into worn-out conversation about basketball games or stocks that were soaring, which were C.J.'s favorite things to talk about.

C.J. then decided to rattle my mental testicles.

"Let's play," he said. "Take out the rent money."

I looked at him with a scowl as he got off the bar stool to take a leak. He chucked as he walked away.

Then, it hit me, out of nowhere.

It struck me hard like an 18-wheeler. This heavy-metal monster zooming down a moonlit desert highway at 100 mph, and shaking up the roadside scrub brush and scattering jittery jackrabbits.

A bet, oh hell, yeah. If I win, I walk. I go into Ricardo's office, give him my letter of resignation, and I'm on the road heading west. Nirvana.

I looked around the room before I laid out the bait, trying to be as inconspicuous as possible about my motives.

C.J. ambled back and racked up the balls on the pool table.

"Ready to lose some rent money?" he said.

I took out my wallet and pulled out four $100 bills. I slapped the money on top of the bar. I looked C.J. in the eye. He rubbed his long nose with his finger and groaned.

"Wow," he said. "Rack 'em up."

"This ain't about pool."

He looked down, and turned his head to the side, walked up to me and grinned. "Speak to me."

I pointed at the four hundred dollars on the bar.

"See that $400?" I said.

"Yeah, and?"

"It's talking, and it's saying that I can get an interview with Mickey Madrid."

C.J. laughed and beer came out of his nose and mouth. He coughed violently while wiping the beer from his nose and mouth.

After catching his breath, he grimaced and raised an eyebrow.

"Are you insane? An interview with Mickey, yeah, right. He's on death's door."

"I'm serious," I said. "I can sneak into the hospital and get some quotes before Mickey dies. Either way, I'm writing his obit for the front page and quotes would spice it up. Quotes from Mickey while he's on his deathbed."

"The beer is talking. You know damn well that Mickey hates reporters. He's never done an interview. We're snakes. All reporters are snakes in his eyes. And you, you're snake shit. The worst."

"Exactly. So that makes this bet just a tad more interesting."

He reached inside his potato chip bag took out a handful of chips, and stuffed them into his large mouth. He slowly crunched them, washing them down with beer.

C.J. blew out a long, disgusting burp. He checked his watch and snickered.

"Word has it that Mickey will probably be dead by tomorrow night. Which means that Mexican barbwire is already strung around his bed," he said. "Grieving relatives wailing away."

I took a sip from my beer. The bartender put a fresh bowl of popcorn in front of us. He left and went over scooped up a five-dollar tip from a customer who sat at the end of the bar.

Before C.J. could utter another word, I reminded him that the fire-breathing troglodyte would be at the hospital. His ears perked up.

"Oh, yeah, Sierra Madrid," he said. "Mickey's psycho daughter can't stand your ass."

"That complicates things. So it's easy money for you."

I was slowly tightening the noose around his pencil-thin neck. As soon as I saw C.J. peer at the money, I tugged on the line, pulled a bit harder.

I put another $200 on top of the bar. C.J. peered at it cautiously.

"You've got to be crazy," he said.

"Confident," I said. "Here's the bet. I get some quotes, put them in Mickey's obit, and I win. He dies, no quotes, you win. It's that simple."

C.J. looked at the money and looked at me, expecting that I'd burst out laughing and tell him that I was joking and just wanted to see his stunned face.

Instead, I reached into my pocket, took out two twenties and laid them on the bar counter.

"I'm all in," I said. "Rent money and all I've got."

C.J. playfully patted the money and nodded.

"Let me get this straight," he said. "Mickey gives you quotes, you win. No quotes, and I win."

"Exactly," I said.

I paused and looked around, pretending that I was having serious thoughts about backing out. All the while my heart did cartwheels and pirouettes. I strongly believed that I could pull it off. I scratched the back of my head.

"An even thousand?" I said.

He looked at me, briefly looked down at the money, glanced at the clock and grinned, a cocksure grin.

"Sure. Why not? I'm in," C.J. said. "An even thousand. This is a slam dunk."

"Where's your money?"

"I'm good for it. I'm always good for it. My stock picks have been right on the money, lately."

"It's on," I said and stuck out my hand.

He shook it.

CHAPTER 4

I walked through the double-glass hospital doors with a partially mangled Bible tucked under my armpit. The Bible was for props. I bought it at yard sale a few years back for another story. The Good Book would help me get up to the third floor of the hospital, get just enough quotes from Mickey to include in his obituary story, leave quickly and go and collect $1,000 from C.J.

Timing and perception were everything. So I bought flowers from a roadside vendor and wore a Polynesian-style shirt that was a gift from my mother after she and my dad returned from a Hawaiian vacation. I never wore the shirt unless it was for a cookout in my parent's backyard in New Mexico.

The clothing and Bible were all to ward off suspicious, long, hard looks. The Bible came in handy a few months ago. I had it on my lap when I sat for a few hours at the downtown Greyhound bus station, working on an investigative piece about teen-aged runaways, and a pimp ring preying on them. The roving eyes of a pimp would have blown my cover and possibly, put me in danger.

My heart was pounding as I neared the hospital elevator while scanning the faces in the building, making sure I didn't bump into Mickey's family or friends.

It was late, and haggard adults and fidgety children shuffled out of the hospital.

The elevator doors dinged and opened. I was about to step inside when someone tapped my shoulder. Blood rushed to my head. I turned.

It was a middle-aged, for-hire security cop with breasts the size of pillows and a double chin. She stood a few feet in front of me. She dipped her head and gave me a disapproving look.

"Are you a visitor?" she said.

"Yes."

"Twenty minutes," she said flatly, pointing to a large clock in the hallway. "Visiting hours are over in twenty minutes."

"I understand," I said, and quickly changed the subject. "Did Mr. Mickey Madrid pass away?"

"Who?

"Mickey Leopoldo Madrid. He is in very bad shape, in critical condition."

"Oh, yeah, Mr. Madrid. I can't say anything. He's still upstairs, barely. Third floor. Check the nurse's station. They can tell you what you need to know."

I thumbed the elevator button to keep the doors from closing.

"Are you family?" She said.

I immediately raised the Bible, dodging the question.

"Prayer. Mr. Madrid needs prayer," I said with my best set of phony, mournful eyes. "What about you? Do you need prayer?"

"No. I'm busy," she said quickly and pointed at a large clock in the lobby. "Twenty minutes."

"I understand."

The Bible, the shirt and flowers along with the offer to pray for her had worked so far.

The elevator whisked me up, and seconds later, spat me out in front of the nurses' station. Two nurses looked at each other after glancing at me. One kept her eyes on me while the other wrote on a piece of paper pinned to a clipboard and entering notes into the computer.

"Excuse me, ma'am, Mr. Madrid, what room can I find him at?" I asked.

"Down the hall. Room 334," said the nurse who had lowered the clipboard to her side.

"Thank you," I said and smiled.

The walk down the hallway was long and went by the visitors' room. I glanced inside. Some of Mickey's relatives sprawled throughout. Some slouched on the sofas and chairs staring at an overhanging TV watching the news. There was a newspaper and a couple of magazines on the floor.

Mickey's son, Emilio was slumped on a chair reading a book. Mickey's daughter Sierra was asleep in a large sofa chair, curled like a cat with a thin blue blanket on top.

As I kept walking down the hall, I knew that Sierra, a twenty-four-year-old beauty, with long, curly, auburn hair and dainty nose turned slightly upward, would pounce like a leopardess if she saw me anywhere near her dying father.

Sierra was one tough woman who had attended Catholic private schools and was close to her mother, who was demanding and strict. She grew up riding horses on her father's cattle ranch that sat on a high mesa 60 miles northwest of Chihuahua.

Sierra was twelve years old when her mother, Julia, died of a brain aneurism. She cried for days. After her mother's death, Sierra and her father became very close.

Her grades were good enough to get her into Stanford University where she got a degree in business administration.

But life changed for Sierra when a craggy face servant named Juanita told her that she had a stepbrother named Emilio. Emilio's mother, Clara Ruiz, a shy beauty with raven-colored, shoulder-length hair, was one of Mickey Madrid's teen-aged maids who worked at his ranch in Mexico. Years before Mickey's wife's death, he lured Clara, then a 19-year-old into his bedroom and raped her. She left the ranch. Nine months later, she gave birth to Emilio, and Mickey gave Clara's family a small fortune to keep their mouths shut.

Mickey knew his son through photographs and often wrote to Clara. Emilio grew up to be a tall boy with a soft oval face. He never knew who his father was until Sierra went to visit him one day and told him. His jaw nearly dropped, and he turned pale.

After telling Emilio what she knew, she angrily confronted and blamed her father for not keeping an eye on him or telling her about her stepbrother.

Sierra and Emilio grew close and both confided in each other. Sierra was very protective of her younger brother. Mickey reconciled with Emilio. They were close and were always seen together, often hunting at the family ranch. Clara never told Emilio about the rape. She simply dismissed the violent sexual encounter as the bad judgment of a teenaged girl and never blamed Mickey.

As I got close to Mickey's hospital room, I glanced over my shoulder. The long hallway was empty. I went by Mickey's room and made sure he was inside and alone. A chalk-white bony foot stuck out of the sheet. On the other end, a baldhead caused by chemotherapy reflected the light. His cheeks sunk deep.

I wasn't sure it was Mickey lying on that bed.

Two doors later, I ducked into a dimly lit room. A woman with thick white hair was asleep. Her mouth open slightly and her forefinger twitched as though she was pointing at an invisible tormentor standing in the corner of the room.

I stuck my head out into the hallway. It was still empty. I waited a few seconds, took a deep breath and slipped into Mickey's room.

As soon as I walked in, a large sandalwood-colored stuffed teddy bear with two, round black eyes greeted me. It had a cartoonish grin and slumped on a corner table. Two rosaries, a blue and white one, dangled around its neck. There were nearly a dozen get-well cards near the bear and a splay of red, pink and white roses.

I read the names of the card senders. A couple of signatures I recognized from federal drug indictments. Another signature bore the name of a city councilman who represented Mickey's district in West El Paso.

I laid my flowers on the windowsill, looked around the room, making mental notes.

Mickey Madrid, or what was left of him, lay close to the bear whose goofy grin was starting to become very annoying.

Mickey was asleep and almost unrecognizable, a mere skeleton. A few layers of skin barely held his bones intact. A weak chest rose and quickly collapsed. His dry, cracked lips briefly quivered.

The powerful drug dealer's wrists were tied to the bed rail by white-cloth restraints to keep him from yanking tubes out of the purple veins on his arms. The tattoos of his youth had faded.

A fire-spewing dragon tattoo on his right arm looked like a frail lizard, harmless and old. The ink etching of the Virgin de Guadalupe on his upper shoulder barely peered out from under the sheet. Her dour eyes sagged and looked tired.

Sweat, nervous perspiration, went down the side of my head. I had to wake him up. I had to get my quotes fast. My eyes darted around the room as I collected my thoughts.

Hospital disinfectant and hints of old vomit lingered in the air. The room was full of annoying little clicks coming from the heart-monitoring machine with the small green screen. A plump IV bag hung from a tall, thin metal pole.

I paused to make more mental notes of the room.

My head jerked up after I heard footsteps, then voices, approaching.

I froze. The footsteps continued. It was probably a nurse making her rounds. I peered out the door. The hallway was clear. The nurses' station at the end of the long hallway was quiet.

I glanced at my watch. Five minutes had gone by.

Mickey moved. His lips parted slightly, and then wider. He closed them. His body jerked once, then twice. His eyes barely opened for a few seconds, flickered and closed.

Time was running out, and I needed to get my quotes and get out.

I shook him a bit. He stirred but barely. His breath smelled like sour milk. I shook him harder, stopped, and shook him some more. Shook him hard.

"Come on, Mickey," I said above a whisper. "Wake up. Give me a lousy, *pinche* quote. Just one. Come on. Don't die. One measly quote, that's it and I'm gone, and you can go back to dying in peace. Come on."

I waited. Nothing. I shook him again. Nothing. I got close to his ear. "Mickey. Mickey. Wake up." Nothing. I was too late. His drug-induced coma had a strong grip on him, I surmised. Frustrated, I decided to leave. But I tried one more time. "Mickey. Hey. Mickey." His eyes popped open. We were nearly eyeball-to-eyeball. He stared at me and blinked. I swallowed hard.

"It's me, Jack. Jack Fuentes. The newspaper reporter."

He didn't say a word, but kept looking at me as though he was trying to clear the fog in his head, trying to shake off the pain medication. I hope he recognized who I was.

"I'm Jack. The reporter who wrote stories about you," I said, desperate to break through the medication-induced sedation.

His glassy eyes stared for what seemed to be the longest time. Finally, he barely said, "Jack."

"Yeah, yeah, Mickey. Jack. The reporter. It's me. I want to talk to you. Can we talk?"

He moved his parched lips.

"Water. I need water. Ice. Get me water. Ice water."

"Sure. No problem."

I poured a little water from a white pitcher into a red plastic cup. I lifted his head a little and watched him sip, slowly at first before he gulped down the water and gasped.

"Slow down, Mickey."

He coughed loudly as saliva ran down the side of his mouth. I wiped it away with the corner of his blanket. He drank another cup of water and wanted more. I poured more water into the cup, and he gulped that down.

He asked for more water and I kept pouring it down his throat. Soon, it was like I was putting a sprinkler in the middle of the Mojave Desert. He finished drinking and stared at me.

"Get out," he said, taking short breaths. "Out. Now."

"Wait, okay. Just wait. I'm not going to bullshit you. I'm writing an obituary, yours. I guess, by now, you know that you're dying so I am not telling you anything new."

He said nothing, slowly blinked, looking at me as though I wasn't there. As much as I wanted, I couldn't lie to someone on his deathbed. It wouldn't be right. I had to be straightforward.

"Talk to me, Mickey," I said.

Mickey slowly blinked. I pulled out my recorder from my pant pocket, and put it a couple of inches from his lips, hoping and praying that he wouldn't drift back to his drug-induce sleep. I had no doubt that the recorder would save my ass. If I got the quotes, there would be angry denials by his relatives after he died and the newspaper ran my story. No question, they'd say that I never interviewed Mickey, that he was in a coma and heavily medicated when I walked into his room. So there was no way he could have talked to me.

While Mickey's dying eyes were getting smaller, I clicked on the recorder. The battery was low. The red light flickered. The power was failing.

"Awww, shit," I muttered. "Damn."

I smacked the recorder with the palm of my hand. The tiny, light stopped flickering but it was weak. The recorder's microphone was near his dry lips.

"Any regrets, Mickey?"

"Water," he said. "My throat is dry. I'm burning up, Jack."

"You're about to come face to face with God. What are you going to tell him, Mickey?"

"No regrets," he said with his tongue peering out his mouth like a cautious pink snake. "Water. Please. Please."

Tiny specks of dry blood clung to his nose hair, a few on the edge of his chin.

"No regrets? None?"

In frustration, he finally said, "I said, no regrets, Jack. None. Give me water."

Great, I got my quote. I should have left, walked out of that room, down the hallway and out of the hospital as soon as I got Mickey on the record and won the $1,000 bet. I should have just left it like that and walked away.

But I didn't. Curiosity cemented my fate. I wanted to know more, I wanted to know whether the story was true. The story that almost drove me batty, kept me up at night flipping through notebooks.

"The two Colombians, Fernando and Topo. Their heads went to Bogota?

44

"It was business."

"So, the two heads were FedExed to Bogota?"

"I never said that."

"What are you telling me? That it's all bullshit?" I said, stirring the pot.

I wasn't disappointed.

His eyes suddenly bulged. It was as though he was given a shot of adrenaline. His breathing went haywire. The machine monitoring his heart went haywire. He tried to raise his body, and used every ounce of energy to jerk his hand up to grab my throat. I leaned back. He missed.

Thank God for hospital restraints, I thought.

"Relax, Mickey."

"Get out," he said with flamethrower eyes. "Don't call me a liar. Get out, now."

"Take it easy."

I gently pushed his chest down.

"Relax."

I turned off the recorder and poured more water down his throat. I turned the recorder back on and glanced at my watch. It was 8:45: p.m.

With the recorder's light blinking erratically, I went for broke and asked the question.

"Who helped you smuggle drugs?" I asked.

He didn't say anything. I gave the recorder a good smack. The light stopped flickering.

Footsteps, slow moving and purposeful were heading my way.

"How'd you get tons of drugs across the border?"

Nothing.

The footsteps were getting closer. The recorder's red light went off. I wanted to scream. Hands shaking, I picked up the recorder and took out the batteries. Blew hot air on them, hoping to get a little more electrical juice. I dropped a battery on the floor, quickly picked it up and put both of them back into the recorder. I turned it on. The red light was on but flickering. I laid the recorder back on the pillow, closer to Mickey's lips.

"Who is helping you smuggle drugs? Who, Mickey?"

He mumbled something. I hurried to the doorway and stuck my head out of the room. I locked eyes with a nurse who was down the hallway. She walked toward me. I yanked my head back inside the room. Mickey mumbled some more, stirred a bit and moaned, stopped and moaned some more. The footsteps were fast approaching with purpose and in my direction.

I hurried and grabbed the recorder, turned it off, and shoved it inside my pocket. I grabbed my flowers and the Bible. I opened the Bible and placed it on a small table next to a sofa chair. When the nurse came into the room, she saw me holding up the flowers.

"I was looking for a vase for the flowers. I don't see one," I said.

"Visiting hours are over. Why are you still here?" she demanded to know.

"Mickey Madrid needs prayer," I said, smiled and held out my hand with the flowers. "And, I need a vase."

"Sir, you need to leave. Please go, now."

I got up and leaned over Mickey and stroked his hair as though I were Gabriel the Archangel, as though I really cared about a cancer-ridden drug kingpin. I just wanted some quotes. I just wanted to make some money to leave town. That's it. I didn't care about Mickey, and I was certain that had he been in good health, I would have gone through the plate-glass window. But I had to pretend to care and hope that the nurse didn't ask more questions. Hopefully, she didn't call security or worse, alert Mickey's relatives.

"Goodbye, Mickey," I said and inconspicuously mouthed *thank-you* and slipped him a wink.

His lips were opened. He barely moved his jaw.

"Water, Jack. I need a little more water," Mickey said. "Please."

The nurse glanced at the pitcher and scowled. I headed toward the door.

"Sir," the nurse said with a stern face, holding up a plastic pitcher.

I stopped and turned.

"Yes?"

"You didn't give him water, did you? He's not supposed to have any liquids. None."

"Why would anybody do that?" I said as innocently as possible.

Mickey bellowed. The machine monitoring his heart went crazy like it was about to payoff in quarters.

Then, all hell broke loose.

Mickey went into shock. His bucking and contorting triggered a code blue emergency.

I left the room, stepped up my pace as I walked down the long hallway and flew past the waiting room. Behind me, I could hear Mickey's relatives hurriedly heading toward his room.

A middle-aged doctor with large eyeglasses who moments earlier had passed me in the hospital lobby also rushed by me and into the room.

As I walked onto the hospital parking lot and into the fresh air, I felt like clicking my heels, raising my fist high and dancing.

I won the bet. I was a thousand dollars richer, and I could now see light at the end of the deadline tunnel. Freedom was around the corner.

When I got to the newsroom, I called the hospital and talked to a nurse who said Mickey Madrid had died. The tape recorder's batteries also went dead. So, I wrote Mickey's obituary with the few quotes I remembered and beat a 10 o'clock deadline.

Thirty minutes after I hit the send button on the computer, I sat on a bar stool at the Blue Note Bar, a few blocks from the newspaper building, to have a few beers and mull over the rise, demise and death of Mickey Madrid.

In a strange way, I was going to miss Mickey, miss writing about the little cat-and-mouse game he had going with the feds. They never nailed him, and he taunted them with his arrogance and high-priced lawyers.

I used by cell phone to click on the newspaper website: My story was online: BREAKING NEWS: Alleged Drug Dealer Dead: "No Regrets."

What I hadn't realized was that there was a lot more on the recorder with the dead batteries. More than I could have imagined.

CHAPTER 5

My cell phone bleeped. My eyes opened. A block of fresh sunlight leaped from a bay window and landed feet first on my eyeballs. Its piercing light stuck its finger inside my bloodshot eyes and sluggishly stirred my hung-over cells and nerves, igniting an implosion of red dots and blue streaks, all of which were bounding off the walls of my cranium.

The piercing pain of bright light was excruciating.

Ohhhh, God, I thought. I'm going blind too.

I closed my eyes to shield them from the light and gradually tried to open them, squinting at first. Smells, hot greasy ones, nudged my nostrils. The smell of chorizo, scrambled eggs, sausage, and warm tortillas saturated the place.

I couldn't get up, not just yet. My brain-busting hangover pinned me down on my back to a red vinyl booth. I stared at the whirling ceiling fan at Rodrigo's Café.

As the haze began to lift from inside my head, the fan seemed to pick up speed, making my stomach queasier. I started to feel nauseated.

The cell phone gained momentum, bleeping bolder and louder.

Someone was desperate to get a hold of me, and I didn't give a damn. It was 6:45 a.m. on a Friday. I ordered something to eat, dozed off, took a catnap and woke up with a monumental hangover.

I remembered parts of the night before. I celebrated getting the quotes and looking forward to writing my last story. I had found my way to the Blue Note Bar and stayed there until the place closed.

My legs felt weak. The phone continued it's bleeping. I sat straight up, yawned, a long yawn. My tongue was dry like it had cactus needles stuck at the tip. My blood felt thick, thick as syrup, and barely circulating, making its way up to my brain and down to my toes.

The cell phone kept ringing. I wanted to answer it but I didn't feel like talking to anyone, not this early, not before breakfast.

I was hours away from walking out the newsroom, and whoever was at the other end could wait.

My head felt like it was about to explode into a thousand pieces. On wall, a dime-store oil painting of a sad clown with a red ball at the end of his nose, holding up some colorful balloons hung on the wall. The painting seemed to punctuate my life.

The phone kept ringing.

Dana Olivas, the almond-eyed waitress, walked up to me with the food I had ordered before I fell asleep.

The phone begged to be answered.

She put things on my table: a green bottle of hot sauce, a plate of huevos rancheros and bacon. Toast. A side order of pancakes. Two neat slices of butter, and an ice-cold Corona with a slice of lime dangling from its glass mouth that anxiously waited to kiss my dry, hung-over lips.

Dana neatly arranged everything near a folded morning newspaper. The phone suddenly turned into a screaming Banshee.

Her eyes went from my phone to me and back while she dipped her hand inside a large Kangaroo-pouch-size pocket on her waitress apron and pulled out a new plastic bottle of ketchup. She set it on the table.

The cell phone kept bleeping.

Looking at the phone, she yelled, "Damn it, Jack, answer the damn phone!"

Customers' heads turned in our direction. I nodded and reached over, picked up the phone and squeezed the bridge of my nose.

"What?" I said and yawned.

It was C.J. I moaned.

"Were you up?" he said.

"Yeah, I'm grabbing a bite to eat. What's up?"

"There's a dead guy in the alley near Five Points. Cops are everywhere looking for two suspects who were seen running toward the railroad tracks. I need a reporter out there, and you're it."

"Okay," I said, and quickly changed the subject. "I was looking for you last night, called you several times, and you never called back."

"I probably had my cell phone turned off," he said.

"Yeah, whatever," I said impatiently. "You've got today's paper, right?"

"Got it in front of me, right here."

"Good. So, I got the Mickey quotes, and you've got my money, right?"

Pause, a long pause. I heard him inhale and slowly exhale. It didn't sound good.

I repeated, "I said, 'you have my money, right?"

"Most of it," he said.

"Most of it is not all of it. That's not what I want to hear."

"I'll get it, alright? I just had a few bad day trades. I need to pawn a few more things but I'll have all of it by tomorrow."

"Perfect. Don't disappoint me. I get my money, put things in my car and I'm on I-10."

"I'm good. Bank on it."

Yawning, I gave my tie a few tugs, sat straight up and forked my eggs. I gave Dana a salacious wink. She shot back a look of disgust mixed with pity before walking away, shaking her head.

"So, what's going on in the alley?" I asked C.J.

C.J. gave me a few bits of information about the homicide and what he heard over the newsroom's police scanner. A frantic hunt was taking place for two men in white T-shirts, blue jeans who were seen jumping rock-wall fences and running toward the railroad tracks.

C.J. said Benny, the newspaper photographer, was there. Benny told him that the victim was apparently on his way to work when he was ambushed and stabbed by the two suspects.

"It's wild, Benny told me that 'the dead guy's sack lunch is all over the alley.' Two burritos, bag of chips, an apple, and discarded cupcake wrapper lying several yards from the body. Cops laid yellow markers throughout the alley to tag and photograph the evidence.'"

"A cupcake wrapper?"

"Discarded cupcake wrapper. A half-eaten cupcake," C.J. said.

"The killer probably bit into the victim's cupcake?"

"Yeah. Looks that way. Benny is trying to get a better shot of the victim."

"Did Benny say it was a Little Debbie Cupcake?" I said.

"What?"

"Little Debbie. Was it a Little Debbie cupcake?"

"Who cares? Who knows? Why is that important?"

"Details. Readers love details. They spice up a story."

"Sure. Whatever. Benny will give you what he has when you get there."

While I listened to C.J., I could hear the police radio in the background going wild with activity, Dana walked over and poured more orange juice into my glass. She put the pitcher of juice on top of the table and started scribbling, putting the finishing touches on my check.

Dana was a pretty lady with reddish-brown hair and enough firm curves to confuse a season Nascar racecar driver.

When she jotted down orders on her notebook, Dana would tilt her head slightly and lean on one leg, hip sticking out just a tinge. That little body slant highlighted a perky ass and muscular thighs.

Dana laid the check near the edge of my table. C.J. finally shut his yap.

"I'll be there in fifteen minutes," I told C.J.

Just before he hung up, C.J. gave me the bad news.

"Ricardo wants to see you as soon as you get here," said C.J.

"About what?"

"The Mickey Madrid story. The interview."

"What about it?"

"His loved ones, they read your story, and they're pissed. Pissed as African bees on crack. The narco-princess Sierra was screaming at Ricardo this morning, threatening to sue the newspaper."

"For what?"

He laughed. "For invasion of daddy's privacy."

"Mi importa madre," I said.

"Well, Ricardo's pissed, *guey.*"

"Today is my last day. After I write about the dead guy in the alley, I hit the send button, walk into Ricardo's office, hand in my resignation, put my stuff in a cardboard box, walk out the door and live happily ever-after."

"You're always saying that."

"I'm serious. I'm done."

"Sure. Wait a minute."

C.J. briefly stopped talking, and I could hear papers being shuffled as a police radio revved up what was happening at the crime scene.

"Hey, a helicopter is circling the area. They're asking for another K-9 unit. Get out there now," he said and hung up.

I knew I'd have to go see Ricardo and let him know how I got Mickey to give an interview on his deathbed. He wasn't the only one who wanted to know. So did Dana.

She walked up to the table, picked up my newspaper, glanced at it and put it down.

"How'd you do it?" she said.

"Do what?" I said.

"Get Mickey to talk?"

Dana read everything I wrote, every line, every word, every sentence, and was one of my biggest fans and worst critics.

"Didn't you know? Mickey and I are pals," I joked. "We're on the same bowling team. Both Gemini and elders at our temple where I'm a Shinto High Priest."

"You're such a smart ass, Jack," she said. "Seriously, did Mickey really say that?"

"Say what?"

"You know, the no regrets comment?"

"That's what he told me."

I really made an effort to gently lay Mickey's quotes at the beginning of his obituary. Lay his remarks across the story as though I was wrapping a pearl necklace around the smooth neck of a long-legged, New York City model.

Under my byline, I wrote: "Even near death, Miguel "Mickey" Leopoldo Madrid, the target of several narcotics investigations, said he wouldn't change anything about his life.

"Shortly before taking his last breath, and with cheek bones protruding from his face as a result of a short battle with lung cancer, Madrid said he had no regrets about anything he did in his life."

"Law enforcement officials say Madrid's death could mean the start of a drug war for control of drug trafficking routes."

Dana read the entire, front-page story that jumped to the inside section of the paper. She wanted to know all the little details about the drug war that was brewing, even other things that didn't appear in my story.

"A drug war sounds serious," Dana said.

I nodded.

"It's going to get real nasty, real quick."

Dana frowned, closed her eyes and slowly shook her head.

"Frightening," she said.

"Oh, yeah, frightening like a spook house," I teased. "A real 'Night of the Living Dead.'"

"Shut up, wiseass,"

I reached into my shirt pocket and took out the two aspirins. I tossed them into my mouth, crushed them and washed them down with long swallows from my beer.

"That's disgusting," she said.

"Well, I got to go. I got a stabbing to cover. C.J. needs quotes," I said.

"Quotes, quotes, and more quotes," Dana quipped. "The beast needs to be fed. Give me quotes. Feed me, Jack. Feed me."

Dana glanced at the food, which, for the most part, was untouched. "Aren't you going to finish your breakfast?"

"Naw. I just lost my appetite, and my head is about to explode," I said, glancing at my watch. "Why can't these assholes kill themselves at a decent hour. It's always really early in the morning or very late at night. Always. Seldom in between. Hey, I've got a life too. Why can't they appreciate that?"

Looking down at the cup of black coffee, I saw my tired reflection. I gulped down the coffee, knowing that I'd shortly be dealing with grouchy detectives who'd probably start mumbling curse words as soon as they saw me coming.

I took out a handful of crumbled bills, pulled out a $20 bill and put it on top of my check. I gave her an eight-dollar tip. Hell, I was on my way to collect a thousand dollars from C.J., and this would be the last tip I'd probably leave on the table for Dana.

When I stood to put on my wrinkled navy-blue blazer, Dana walked over. She thanked me for the big tip. I ran my fingers through my hair a few times and tugged on my crumpled tie.

"How do I look?" I said, expecting a compliment in exchange for leaving a fat tip.

It wasn't going to happen. She rolled her eyes.

"Like a homeless campsite," she said. "You drink like a fish, play too much pool and hardly sleep."

"I'm still grieving," I said, yawned and stretched.

"Grieving for who? Sad for what?" She said with an incredulous look.

"Emily is gone," I said rubbing my forehead.

"Oh, good God, Jack," she said with her bitchy tone of voice; the one I hate, the one that felt like eagle claws gripping my balls.

"She left," Dana continued. "The woman didn't die. She left and is living in Chicago. They all leave, and they leave for obvious reasons."

"What's so obvious about the reasons?"

"Look in the mirror. If they closed this place and the pool hall and unplugged all the vending machines in the city, you'd starve to death."

"What does this have to do with diet?"

"You're this pathetic, newsroom junkie."

"I'm a wordsmith. A writer. A reporter."

"Who can't pay the rent."

"I admit. I sometimes struggle to pay the rent."

"Have you heard from Emily?"

"No. I hope she is happy though."

"She was sooo sweet," she said and shook her head. "Everything you touch turns to crap."

"Ouch." I said.

Dana looked down on my tie, frowned, dipped the tip of a cloth into a glass of water, and handed it to me

"What?" I said.

"Egg. You've got egg on the tie."

I looked at the tie. I lifted the tie, licked and sucked it to remove the thin streak of egg.

"Gross," she said and twisted her mouth.

"Look at you," she said whining again.

"What?" I yawned.

"Never mind."

"I'm leaving town. What do you say we have dinner before I go?"

"You've been leaving this town for years."

"I'm really leaving this time. I'm dead serious. So what do you say? Dinner and a movie, and maybe a late night drink, some light, uncluttered conversation. Harmless stuff, no commitments."

"No. It's not a good time."

"Ryan, right. Listen, you've got to get over Ryan. Time to move on."

"Who are you to tell me to move on?" she said. "I grieve my way, and you grieve yours."

"Sorry, okay. You're right. That wasn't cool what I just said." I meekly added, "Forgive, me?"

Dana gradually smiled, "Go. Go on. There's a dead guy in the alley. Another stupid story, another dumb deadline, another dead guy. It's what you do best. Go talk to your cop friend, the homicide detective, what's his name?'

"Leo."

"I'm sure Leo's already there. As soon as Leo and his cop pals see you coming, they're going to be doing cart wheels."

"I hate cops," I said and yawned.

"Well, that's who goes to homicides."

"Well, I'd prefer to see a marauding band of Mongols on horses with badges working crime scenes. They'd be easier to deal with, to talk to."

As she walked away, I felt bad about the caustic comment I made about Ryan. Dana was crazy about Ryan, and he thought the world of her.

A year earlier, Dana had been engaged to an up and coming stock broker named Ryan Sanderson who had a bright future until a drunk driver slammed into his Porsche and killed him. Ryan had just dropped Dana off after a weekend in Santa Fe.

The two were making plans to get married and move to Portland, where Ryan would work with a large financial firm as an executive officer.

The tragedy crushed Dana, who called me that night and begged me to call the medical examiner to make sure it was Ryan at the morgue. She believed it was a case of mistaken identity.

"He's not dead, Jack. They made a mistake. It's not Ryan," she said, sobbing loudly on the phone. "It can't be."

I called the county medical examiner, who was a source, and went to look at the body. Half of Ryan's face was crushed, and a jawbone stuck out of the side of his head. There was no way his body would be viewed at the funeral.

When I got home, I called Dana. "I'm so sorry," I told her.

With her voice cracking, she said thank you above a whisper and hung up before I could say anything else.

As I was leaving Rodrigo's restaurant to go to the homicide, I looked back. Dana waited on two men with nicely cut suits who studied the menu like they were about to lay some serious money on some racetrack ponies. She stood over them with her hands behind her back. She swept her eyes my way, a serious look that mushroomed into a beautiful smile.

"Be careful," she mouthed.

My grumpy, hung-over ass raised a thumb up and mouthed back, "I will." As I left, I wondered who'd kill someone and take a bite of his cupcake, especially one the victim was saving for lunch.

That seemed so cold. So brutal. So thoughtless. But this wasn't my first murder. However, I hoped it would be the last and I'd bang out one hell of a murder story.

Still, I couldn't help but wonder if it was a Little Debbie cupcake. It made for good newspaper copy: The victim was repeatedly stabbed. He died in a Central El Paso alley with his sack lunch - a burrito and a half-eaten, Little Debbie cupcake - spilled around his blood soaked body as detectives hovered around it.

A divine little detail of what my story might look like. I hope it was a Little Debbie cupcake. That little gem of information, if true, would be somewhere at the top of my story.

CHAPTER 6

When I arrived at the crime scene, there were cops everywhere. Witnesses reported suspects running to a nearby park.

Patrol cars lights flashed everywhere, and one cop with a shotgun walked briskly down the sidewalk. Two other police officers jumped over fences. A police helicopter made low passes just above the treetops and telephone poles. The thudding blades made some rooftops shake, and the tree branches bend.

Cops searched backyards, alleys, and rooftops.

A few residents stood on their front porches or edges of their yards watching the cops. A man with a crying child in his arms held up his cell phone high to video record the action. Television crews started to arrive and unpack equipment.

A block away, a second K-9 dog took a short leaped out of the back of a patrol car and onto the asphalt. A few minutes later, the animal picked up a scent. The dog and the cop handler with two other officers in tow hurriedly rounded a corner and disappeared.

I walked down the sidewalk. In the distance, I spotted an elderly woman wearing a blue robe and puffing on a cigarette while she watered the grass near a large tree on her front yard.

The stabbing took place in a long alley right behind her house. I pulled out my notebook from the back of my pocket, making notes of the images and noises spawned by a stabbing.

Years of experience and dozens of cop stories, I knew how to work a crime scene. It taught me this much: Stay away from cops as much as possible. Cops at crime scenes hold their cards close to their vests and are suspicious of reporters and won't say much, if anything at all.

Next, find old ladies or youngsters on bicycles. They know what went down. And, if they didn't see anything, they probably know who did and point out where they live. Kids will take you to the houses where witnesses or the victims' families live. Old ladies will give you a rundown on the barrio, the comings and goings, a short history of its residents.

Most of all, kids and old ladies also tend to be friendly to reporters rummaging crimes scenes for quotes and details.

But the trick is to shake down people for information as fast as possible or some high-brow cop who has a hard-on for reporters will spook witnesses by telling them to shut up because criminals read newspapers, have long memories and hate snitches.

It's all bullshit.

The cops don't want reporters to nail down an interview before they do. It complicates things, they say. But it's really because I've seen some reporters, the good ones, will often work crime scenes better than some homicide detectives.

The truth is most cops hate reporters. But they can't live without the media, and the media can't live without them.

All the neighborhood youngsters were in school so the old lady with the water hose was all I had to work with at the moment. She leaned forward slightly while holding her fingertip on the mouth of the hose to make the water jet out further. A cigarette barely clung to her lips. She kept one wary eye on me as I approached.

Wind chimes hung on a large wooden beam that ran across the front of her house tinkled as a breeze swept through.

"*Buenos dias, senora*," I said.

The woman's wrinkles on her forehead dug deep like farm-road ruts. She squinted, pruned back her lips and showed me her false teeth.

"Good morning, *mijo*," she said.

"A lot of action, huh?"

"Oh, yes. I'm very nervous."

"Are you a detective?" she said.

"Detective?" I said, surprised she would ask that. "*Senora*, do I look like a homicide detective? Look, no cheap suit or a big back side or gut."

The woman laughed so hard that her dentures came loose. Red-faced, she lowered her head and turned it to one side to hide and quickly fastened the fake teeth back into her gums.

"I'm sorry. I didn't have time to put my teeth in right this morning with all the commotion. I was so worried. That's why I'm out here."

I held up my notebook like a badge and bent the corners of my lips skyward as far as they could go.

"I'm a reporter," I said. "Jack Fuentes with the El Paso Daily News."

I handed her my business card, and she pressed it near the tip of her round nose that had a mole on one side.

"I don't have my glasses, *mijo*," she said, and handed back the card.

"You can keep it," I said.

"Thank you," she said.

"Did you see what happened?"

"No, just heard the dogs, then shouting. Men yelling cuss words and screams. Then, it stopped. The noise, except the dogs, and before you knew it there were police everywhere."

I wrote down what she said.

"How long did the screams last?"

"Seconds, less than a minute. I thought it was probably, bums."

"Bums?"

"Oh, yeah. Those homeless bums. They hop off the freight trains and sleep in the alley sometimes. They make a lot of racket back there when they get drunk and start fighting."

She dropped her cigarette onto the sidewalk and smashed it with her foot.

"What are you writing down? I'm not going to get in trouble?"

Nervous cackling punctuated her concern.

"Naw, it's a free country. Why would you get into trouble?"

"You never know."

She told me that her name was Lucy Ramos. But requested that I not use her name because the killers might come back and get her.

I promised that I wouldn't use her name or print where she lives.

"Just don't get me in trouble."

"I won't."

Lucy pointed with her chin in the direction of a salmon-colored brick house a block away.

"There's where the Hallelujahs live," she said.

The house had a picket fence around it and a white, small wooden cross that read, "Jesus is Lord. Praise His Name."

"Hallelujahs?"

"Yeah, those born-agains. They live in the house on the corner," she said. "The dead man lived with them. He was a Hallelujah."

"How do you know that he lived there?" I asked.

"We use to see him going to work every morning. My neighbor, Mrs. Perez, also knew that he lived there."

"Where does Mrs. Perez live?"

"Two doors down. But she isn't home. She went out into her backyard after her dog, Malo, kept barking and barking. She told me she opened the door and looked down the alley. *Y hay estava tirado el juven.*"

"A young man was lying in the alley? Was he dead?"

"She said 'he looked dead. But he started moaning. His shirt was soaked in blood.' He always walks through the alley to get to the bus stop. *Pobrecito.* His sandwiches were scattered everywhere. Mrs. Perez said she saw two guys running away."

"What did they look like?"

"Mexicans with a lot of tattoos."

"She ran to my house, and I called police."

"Where is Mrs. Perez?" I said.

"The cops took her away to interview her, I guess."

I closed my notebook after asking a few more questions about the neighborhood, thanked the woman, and walked down toward the end of the block.

The so-called Hallelujah house where the victim lived was an alcohol and drug halfway house named Christ is the Light. When I got there, a man who said his name was Assistant Pastor Johnny said they had no comments and refused to say anything else, even verify that the dead man lived there.

"The police said not to talk to anyone about this because it could hurt their investigation," Johnny said.

When I started to ask another question, he said, "no, no, no. I'm sorry. God Bless you," and gently shut the door.

Walking down the sidewalk, Tex-Mex *musica* from a Spanish-speaking station barely came out of a two-story beige apartment building where a young mother sat on the steps and doted over a toddler who played with toy cars on the dirt while keeping an eye on the police comings and goings.

At the entrance to the alley, Benny, the newspaper photographer, was on one knee, angling his body to get a good shot of the dead guy. The body was stretched out in the middle of a long alley. The sides of the alley were blocked off by yellow crime scene tape. He looked up at me. I partially closed my eyes to shield them from the bright sun.

"I'm screwed. I can't get a decent shot from here," Benny said and frowned. "The dumpster is in the way. This is as close as I can get."

The dead man's black work boots that he was wearing barely stuck out from the side of the dumpster. Detectives were working the crime scene, looking at it like a bloody chessboard and trying to figure out how all the pieces of evidence got to where they found them.

I had an idea to get closer to the body.

"Come on, I think this might work," I told Benny.

We walked over to Lucy's house as a cop stood across the street and beside a patrol car parked with its red lights flashing and kept a wary eye on us.

I could tell he recognized Benny or me from previous crime scenes or he would have stopped and questioned us. We walked a few more houses down before I stopped at Lucy's house. She was still in the front yard and smoking another cigarette, sitting on the front steps of her porch.

I introduced her to Benny, who dropped a few well-placed grins mixed with bits of Spanish about the cop commotion.

"It's been a crazy morning, huh?" Benny said.

"Yes, I'm still a little bit shaky," she replied.

When I felt she was at ease talking to Benny, I asked her, "Can Benny go to the back of your house? We can't go into the alley because we might step on the evidence and get in the cops' way."

"I guess," she said. "Is it okay? The police won't mind? I don't want to get them mad at me."

"Naw. Cops love to see themselves in the newspaper," Benny said.

"*Bueno, si, passele,*" she said. "Go ahead."

As I walked into the backyard, I told Benny to be as quiet as possible. I cracked open the wooden door to a high, cinder block fence that ran parallel to the alley.

I could hear the voices, some gruff and raspy, of two homicide detectives methodically working the crime scene, describing the body and sizing up the evidence.

I pressed my finger against my lips.

I looked through a thin crack on the fence. The cops were about twenty yards away, comparing notes and one squatted to get a better angle of the crime scene.

Hovering over the dead body, I recognized Leo Saenz, a detective who was working homicides when I was trying to manage high school zits and get the courage to ask a cheerleader named Rosie Limon to the prom.

Leo was a Texas tough cop who always had this cool aura. His calm demeanor said I-am-in-control at the crime scene no matter how macabre it might be. He sat on the back of his heel inspecting the dead man. His neck craned forward to get a clear look at the body while he pulled back the cover. He looked like a hunter inspecting the carcass of a deer. Another cop bowed close to the asphalt and checked for any marks, traces, stains or small objects that were made or dropped by the killers around the crime scene, a paved alley with weeds, a dumpster and battered trashcans lined on its sides.

I motioned to Billy to come close and look through the crack. He did. I put my lips within inches of his ear.

"Quick. As soon as I crack open the door, click away," I said very softly.

He nodded and made rapid adjustments to his camera.

"Ready?" I asked.

Benny looked up, nodded several times, and carefully positioned himself like some well-trained sniper. He took a deep breath. I slowly cracked the door open. Its rusty hinges creaked. Benny put his finger on the camera's trigger and clicked away. The cops turned in our direction. Startled at first, the detectives looked at us like skittish deer caught in the cross hairs of a telescope mounted on the hunter's rifle.

Surprise turned to outrage when they saw Benny snapping photographs. They pulled out guns, pointing them in our direction and started yelling. Billy was still snapping away.

"Hey!" Leo said.

"Whoooaa! We aren't armed!" I said. "Leo, it's me, Jack."

"Put the guns away," Leo said to the other detectives.

"What are those two assholes doing there?" another detective named Bert with a flat forehead and wearing rubber gloves said.

"You two are busted," said Manny, another detective with broad shoulders and a tight-fitting coat. "Both of you are under arrest."

Benny kept shooting photographs.

The detectives then charged like old, lumbering elephants. We meekly tried to close the door and walk away. But they tore the frail door nearly off its hinges. They grabbed fistfuls of our shirts, pushed and pinned us against the cinder block wall in the yard, both our cheeks pressed hard against cold, cider blocks while our arms were twisted. We moaned.

"I have a mind to shove that camera up your ass," Burt said within inches from Benny's ear. "Sideways."

"Get off me!" I said. "Off! Let go!"

"Don't break my camera. Don't break my fucking camera," Benny said.

"Shut up!" said Manny.

Leo waved back two detectives who were manhandling us and raised his palms toward them to keep them at bay.

"Hold on," he told them.

"You two are charged with impeding an investigation," said Burt.

"And, contaminating a crime scene," said Manny. "You two piss-ants are in big trouble."

Poking my forefinger toward the ground a few times, I said, "We were standing on private property, and we've got permission from the owner to be here."

Pointing toward the alley entrance, I continued.

"So, we're not interfering with shit or impeding shit. By law, we can be here, all day. We are reporters gathering information for a story. The Supreme Court says we can."

"We're the *pinche* law, here," said the Manny.

"This whole block is now a crime scene," Leo said. "So leave or we're going to charge you with contaminating a crime scene and impeding an investigation."

Leo looked at me, and I looked at Burt and Manny who stood like a deranged crew from the Gambino Family and were ready to bounce and break bones.

"We're leaving," I said.

As Benny and I started to leave, I stopped and glanced at the body when the county coroner approached it. All eyes were now on the body and the corner who had just arrived.

"Why would anyone want to spoil his day?" I said, pointing at the dead man.

"No comment," Leo said. "Get out."

"Right. But can I at least get the name of the dead guy?" I said.

"Yosemite Sam," Burt said and sniggered.

"Is Yosemite spelled with two TTs?" I said with a smirk, pretending to write something on my notebook.

"Get the fuck out!" Leo said.

CHAPTER 7

A few minutes after Benny and I coughed up $30 to pay Lucy for the broken backyard door, I called in some notes about the homicide to the city desk so the story could be slapped on the newspaper's website.

I drove to the newsroom to make more calls and continue writing on my story, flipping through my notebook while banging on the computer keys. After I finished the story, I tapped the send button hard, took a deep breath and spread my lips, stretching them as far as they could go.

"I'm out of here," I mumbled.

My days of reporting were minutes away, 20 minutes at the most, I thought as I watched my last news story disappear. Sucked up into this electronic abyss with an endless appetite that devoured stories.

"Story's in," I shouted to the city editors.

On a blank document on the screen, I wrote my resignation addressed to Ricardo Scott and with two words: "I Quit." I printed a copy, signed it and neatly folded the original into my shirt pocket.

I was ready to end my journalism career with a billion butterflies tickling my stomach. I ambled toward Ricardo's office. I made up my mind to bite my lip, keep my cool and let Ricardo finish his rant about the Mickey Madrid interview. One that I was sure would singe my eyebrows.

I chuckled. Before the morning was over, the whole newsroom opera with all its politics, gossip, quarks, power trips, chit chat, warped humor, dark jokes and the endless jockeying for news holes with other reporters would be in the rearview mirror of my life.

Sweeeeeet.

I would miss some of the reporters but, for the most part, I was looking forward to some new career, new opportunities, new challenges and new friendships.

The walk to Ricardo's office meant that reporters went through the eye corridor, the peering eyes of other journalists and editors from behind computers or high piles of newspaper, stacks of books. The fired, fatigued, feisty and frightened went through the corridor on the way to the Deadline Dragon's Lair.

But it never bothered me, not one bit.

As I walked by education beat reporter Cristina Langley, she had a smirk.

"Sierra called Jack. She wants your *huevos* on a silver platter," she joked. "The narco-princess is so pissed. Daddy is dead, and you're about to be torched by Puff the Magic Dragon in the corner office."

I winked and gave her a rigid thumbs-up. I didn't care. My gait was purposeful and proud. Head held high. That's the way I wanted to go out. Sierra Madrid and her family would just be a bad memory after I left the building with my stuff in a cardboard box.

Emancipation Day felt great, the light at the end of the tunnel was getting brighter as I got closer to Ricardo's office. I would no longer have o put up with the newsroom's Hannibal Lector, and his tirades and mood swings and deadline demands.

I had this all figured out. After Ricardo got through with his ass chewing, I'd give him my biggest, shit-eating grin and flippantly toss my resignation on his desk.

"Read 'em and weep, prick. I am out of here," I'd say with the cocky precision of a drum major.

But first, I'd looked at him square in the eye and calmly tell him what I thought about his crimped management style. What I thought about his sorry ass, his unreasonable demands and his tantrums. Why I thought the newspaper was losing its spunk, its balls, and its character and why morale was low.

Before I went to see Ricardo, I walked up to C.J.'s desk and stood next to him while he edited a story. He looked up at me and continued editing a story.

"Do you have my money, *cabron*," I said above a whisper.

"I'm still working on it. Don't worry," he said without taking his eyes off the computer screen. "I'll have it soon."

"Soon? What does soon mean?"

"Soon means I'll have it, okay." He said, annoyed at my question.

"Work hard, real hard. Don't throw a *pinche* monkey wrench on my plans. I want to pack up and fly down I-10 this weekend. I've got most of my stuff packed up."

"Giving Ricardo your two-weeks notice?"

I plucked out my resignation from my shirt pocket and waved it in his face.

"My resignation starts today. After I resign, I'm putting my stuff in a box, saying my goodbyes and I'm out the door," I said.

"You're going to bust up our tag-team hustle?"

"You'll do alright by yourself."

He shrugged.

"Work on getting my money. I need to blow this place as soon as possible," I said.

"I got it. I'll have it by the end of the day."

"Good."

I left and went and knocked on Ricardo's door. His gruff voice immediately told me to come in. I entered the lair.

"Sit down," he barked.

I did. He seethed. His jaw muscles locked. I was calm and determined to keep this conversation as briefly as possible.

"How did you get Mickey Madrid to talk to you?" Ricardo asked.

"Simple. Went up to the hospital and asked him questions."

Ricardo leaned back his chair, tossed his pen on the desk in frustration, looked up at the ceiling, and back to me. He huffed as though he was expelling one of his demons. One who would grab my throat with its claws and shake my head.

"Madrid's family called. They're angry, very angry. Sierra Madrid threatened to sue the newspaper."

"For what?"

"Invasion of privacy."

"Mickey's dead. Dead people don't have privacy issues. Did you tell her that? Any third-rate lawyer will tell you that."

"Sierra Madrid said you made it up, and that her father was in a coma. He couldn't have talked to you."

"Bullshit. We talked. The stuffed bear in that room with the white and blue rosaries is in the obit. I also wrote that there were nearly a dozen get-well cards and splay of roses in the room. I wrote some of the names on those cards. How would I know that?"

"So, why the clown suit? The palm tree shirt and white pants? What was that about?"

"To get me past the nurses station," I said. "All the time I was up there nobody bothered to ask who I was. I never told them. But Mickey knew who he was talking to."

Ricardo's eyes were like flamethrowers.

"You've got one foot out the door," he said.

I kept my cool, giving myself a few more minutes before I tossed my letter of resignation on his desk, give him a piece of my mind and waltz out the door. First, I had to get a few things off my chest.

"I got an interview with a drug dealer who, for years, outfoxed the FBI, the DEA and every cop in the city," I said. "They couldn't even get this guy on a parking ticket. And, I've got one foot out the door?"

Just as he was about to open his mouth, I pulled out my digital recorder with fresh batteries from out of my coat pocket and held it up high.

"I also recorded some of Mickey's comments before the batteries went dead. It's all here. Mickey's last words. The quotes I used in my story."

I clicked on the recorder and turned up the volume. There was a short pause before Mickey's anemic breathing could be heard. At the end of the short conversation, almost a minute of labored breathing and just as I was about to click the off recorder's button, Mickey said in a clear voice: "Ward. Sheriff Ward."

I was stunned but tried to hide my emotions.

This had been Mickey's reply when I asked him who was helping him smuggle drugs across the border? Who'd be calling the shots after he was gone? He clearly said, "Ward, Sheriff Ward."

Then out of the blue, he barely said something odd. "Chihuahua Charlie" and mumbled something else, something incoherent about Chihuahua.

Ricardo only heard Mickey say the sheriff's name. He didn't hear my question, but his curiosity made him lean forward with eyebrows lowered.

"Ward? He said something about Rick Ward, the sheriff. What did he say?"

With a racing heart, I paused, looking straight at Ricardo. I was numb from what I had just heard. Maybe, this was just Mickey's pathetic stab at humor one last time on his way to the grave. His way of getting payback on my ass for all the negative ink I gave him.

But Mickey had just confirmed what one of my sources had said about Sheriff Ward. That he was in the thick of things. But who or what was Chihuahua Charlie?

My curiosity soared. Ricardo raised his voice, and I snapped out of my semi-trance.

"Why is Mickey talking about Ward?" He demanded to know.

"Mickey believed everybody was out to get him, including Ward. He hated Sheriff Ward," I said dismissively.

Before he could ask me another question, I changed the subject, quickly dismissing my plans to resign. This was the closest I had been in linking Sheriff Ward to the drug trade, to Mickey and all this came out of Mickey's lips

"My DEA source said, off the record, that a narco war is brewing. The Colombians along with the Sinaola Cartel are also making bold moves to take over the La Plaza from the Juarez Cartel. Mickey did business with the Juarez Cartel. So the whole show might spill over to this side of the border. I want to do the story. I need a little time to ferret it out," I said. "I need six weeks."

"What Plaza?"

"La Plaza is just Mexican slang meaning turf." I said, realizing that Ricardo didn't have a clue about the inner workings of the Mexican drug trade.

He had been a sports editor before working himself up to city editor and then, managing editor at the Miami Herald.

Ricardo's chin rested on his thumbs. His eyes were hard while he sized up my intentions before he said another word.

"You've got three weeks," he said. "That's it."

"Four. Please, I need at least four weeks."

"We're short reporters. I can't have a reporter working on any story for that long."

"This story has legs. It's big. Four, four weeks. That's it."

"Four and you're back on the court beat."

The ends of my lips almost touched my ears.

"Thanks."

I got up and took a few steps toward the door.

"Hold on," he said. "There is a rumor floating around."

I turned around and shoved my hands into my pants' pockets.

"What rumor?"

"Rumor about a pool hall bet. The rumor that you won a grand from your newsroom pal and that writing Mickey Madrid's obituary had something to do with it."

Before I could reply, he said, "I don't care who you two hustle or how you win bets. But if it involves this newspaper and money exchanged hands and I find out, you two are fired. Got it?"

With a pink tinge in my face, I said, "Yeah."

As I walked out the door, I knew I could kiss the thousand dollars goodbye.

I took out my letter of resignation, tore it up and tossed it in the trashcan. I went by C.J.'s desk.

"You tell him about our bet?" I asked him.

"Oh hell, no," he said. "I have most of your money"

He opened a drawer to show. I believed him. C.J. wasn't some unscrupulous street thug. He had helped me out in tight spots, and I trusted him. He was always good on his promises and paid off the bets he lost. Still, I felt someone had just popped my balloon.

"Keep it for now," I told him.

"Okay," he said, and returned to his editing. "How did it go in there?"

"He ranted and raved, and I've got work to do."

"What about you leaving for the West Coast?"

"That's on hold."

I walked to my desk and stared at a blank computer for a few minutes. I muttered obscenities at my gray reflection as I banged on the desk with the side of my apprehensive thumb.

I fumed. I was out a thousand dollars for now, and stuck in the newsroom with a four-week deadline.

This had set my plans to leave town back a few weeks.

But I was anxious, really antsy, to find out where all this was going and if powerful drug cartels were fixing to light up downtown Juarez over who would control La Plaza.

After I cracked opened some of my emails and checked my phone messages, I played and rewound Mickey Madrid's deathbed confession a few times.

It was sincere, and it seemed as though Mickey wanted to make things right before he checked out. But being a reporter, I was cynical. Who knows what's going on inside a dying man's head?

As I finished putting the last of my mental notes of the conversation with Detective Leo into my computer, Benny walked up. He dropped a few photographs of the crime scene on my desk.

"Check it out," he said.

"Nice," I said. "The details, the light, the angle, everything, perfect."

The photo showed Detective Leo kneeling over the body, looking over his shoulder, staring into oblivion as though he's expecting the grim reaper to walk into the alley at any minute to scoop up the corpse, put it over his shoulder and swagger away.

The photo was suspended and surreal, leaving a person wondering what the dead man's last thoughts were as his soul was leaving his body, as he gulped his last breath on earth. But there is definitely no sweet state of surrender when a person is being butchered to death in an alley. There was only terror, terror in the eyes; cemetery terror as two-legged predators carved him up with knives.

As I looked closer at the photograph, I spotted something that sent a cold shiver up my spine. My eyes widened and I turned to Benny.

"Did you see this?"

"See what?" Benny said.

"The tattoo in his arm. Check it out. Tell me what you see."

Benny picked up the photo and held it close to the tip of his nose.

"See it?" I asked.

He nodded. "Yeah. An L and part of what looks like a C."

"Part of a black rose petal."

"Oh, yeah." He said. "I see it. Los Carnales. They're out of Houston."

"A prison gang hit or the Juarez Cartel might be recruiting more prison muscle, which means that the Colombians are making a serious move to take back their old drug routes now that Mickey's dead," I said.

"We need to check out the tats real close. That would be a crown jewel to your story, make my photo pop out," Benny said.

"Let's go see the Walrus," I said. "What do we got?"

"I've got two tickets to The Grind concert next week."

"That'll get us in?"

"Oh, hell yeah. It's an up and coming band. They've just re-leased an album that's climbing the charts."

"Great."

As the police radio in the newsroom cracked with activity, Benny and I walked out the door to see the Walrus after I called him to say we were on our way.

CHAPTER 8

I pushed the doorbell to the county morgue, glanced at my watch, banged on the door with a closed fist and looked back at Benny who looked bored.

Finally, the tiny red security button on the overhead camera blinked. We were being eye balled. It was nearly 7 p.m.

The intercom crackled, Benny and I looked up at the camera. The jovial voice of the county medical examiner Paul Kelly, aka the Walrus, came through the intercom.

"Hi kids," he chimed. "Sorry, but we are out of trick or treat candy."

"Open the *pinche* door," I said, in no mood for his dark humor.

The Walrus burst out laughing.

"I'm in the office," he said,

There was buzz, a loud buzz. Benny and I walked inside and down a long hallway, taking long confident strides. The steel door slammed shut behind us, the sound of the metal striking metal echoed in the long hallway.

Immediately, there was a very, pungent smell of ammonia and alcohol, which meant someone had just finished performing an autopsy. Benny had his camera bag strapped on his shoulder, a notebook stuck out of my back pocket.

It wasn't our first time at the county morgue but each time, we felt its cold morbid embrace as soon as we entered the building.

The morgue, in the middle of the week, was usually quiet and empty. Except for an occasional nursing home stiff or a homeless man found inside a box with a blown liver, there wasn't much going on.

On weekends, it was a different story. It got busy with dead drunken drivers, gunshot victims, suicides or drug overdoses.

At the end of the hallway, we took a few steps and made a quick right and walked into a small office. There sat the Walrus behind steel-framed desk. He had his back toward us as he faced the wall, dictating into a recorder, reading from a file filled with colored autopsy photographs. He stopped dictating, swirled the chair around and smiled.

"Sit down, guys. I'm finishing up here," he said.

On his desk, there was a sandwich with thick slabs of ham shavings waving from the bread edges. He made a few more medical remarks on a recorder and put it down. He tossed the file on his desk and bit into the sandwich.

Benny and I briefly locked eyes, amazed that he could eat in place where the strong, lingering stench of decaying corpses that were in a refrigerated storage room. An unforgiving smell that can sometimes bore through the nostrils lingered in the air. The Walrus' sense of smell was probably immune from this rancid assault or his nostrils were probably coated with Teflon.

"What do you got?" said the Walrus through a mouth full.

Benny tossed two complimentary concert tickets on top of the desk.

"Third row seats," he said.

Walrus looked at the tickets as he moved the wad of food down his windpipe with a long sip from his diet soda.

RAUL HERNANDEZ

"The Grind?" he said. "Never heard of these folks."

"Heavy-metal," Benny said. "They cracked Billboard's Top Ten Chart last year."

"Well, quite frankly, I don't care if it's Puerto Rican mambo or a Polish polka band," the Walrus replied. He slipped the tickets inside the pocket of his white shirt with the short sleeves, exposing his hairy arms.

"I need to get my girlfriend's teen-aged daughters out of the house while I hump their mama," he said. "She's got custody of the girls this weekend. Dad is on a golf trip in Florida with his hot secretary."

"The Grind is a rock band," Benny said.

"Good," Walrus said. "I want some alone time with mama. The woman is looking fine. She dropped twenty on that South Beach or East Coast or West Coast diet or some diet de jour. It tightened her ass some. For her birthday, I got her a bikini wax job, and for the first time in a long while, I look forward to banging her. That took some doing and a lot of imagination before she dropped the weight."

I grinned. Benny remained somber. He disliked the Walrus.

"The body you were asking about arrived several hours ago," Walrus told me. "I hadn't had time to work on it but it's basically a no-brainer. A lot of punctures in vital organs. Definitely, homicide."

He took another bite from the sandwich.

"I could have told you that over the phone," he said.

"We want to see the guy's arms, torso," I said.

"Sure, no problem," the Walrus said.

Just under 260 pounds, with short arms, the Walrus had a slight hunch, short, powerful squat legs, and he wore large rectangular-shaped eyeglasses. His hair, dark brown, was combed back,

82

with a white square patch just above the middle of his forehead. His upper lip held up a prominent mustache that looked like a hairbrush. He moved slowly, thus, the name Walrus.

The Walrus snuck us into the morgue to allow us to get a good gander at a murder victim or get some inside information, for a price, usually concert tickets, sometimes, boxing tickets, basically, just comp tickets the newspaper got for these events, hoping we'd send a reporter to write a story about it. Reporters weren't allowed to use these complimentary tickets. It was against newspaper policy. The newspaper bought tickets for reporters covering an event to avoid any conflict of interest. So we usually had extra event tickets from promoters we couldn't use.

Benny and I used them to get inside the morgue from time to time.

The Walrus was good at what he did. He read dead bodies like a good mystery book. He could find clues that other medical examiners missed, the murky stuff that even baffled detectives.

But without fail, he gave us the standard don't-touch-the-dead warning because he didn't want our DNA or fingerprints on the bodies. This was in case detectives came back to dust the body for fingerprints or to lift DNA. That had never happened.

"Wear gloves. You touch, you wear gloves," the Walrus always said. "I don't want you two pawing or getting too close to Exhibit A, the dead man."

"We know the drill, and we've never touched shit around here," Benny grumbled.

The Walrus grinned. "Well, just in case you get curious."

Benny looked around, shook his head and said, "I've never gotten that curious."

Minutes later, we were standing next to a steel table with a sheet over the homicide victim. Like some pompous magician-clown,

Walrus had to put on a show. He yanked the sheet on top of the corpse, exposing a naked dead man. His mouth was opened. He looked like a dead rat waiting to be filleted and fed to a giant cat. Benny and I sat stone-faced. We were used to the show, and the antics.

"This gentleman is Alfredo Mendoza-Sanchez, lovingly remembered by his prison gang buddies by his moniker, Chino."

"How did you get his moniker?"

"Cops at the crime scene. Shoulder tattoo."

The Walrus slipped on some rubber gloves.

"Alfredo, we have visitors," the Walrus said, pretending to speak to the corpse. "Mr. Jack Fuentes here and the guy with the camera is his photographer."

"Benny, my name is Benny," he said and glared at Walrus.

"Excuse me, Alfredo. This is Benny," Walrus said harmoniously. "The photographer."

"Enough with the bullshit, please," I said.

Our attention turned to Alfredo, a thin man whose body was scarred, tattooed and sliced up probably by knives. He had an old appendix scar, cigarette burns on the web of his hand and ugly prison tattoos, mostly of serpents, a pair of dice, snakes and saints, all over his upper body.

Alfredo looked like a walking billboard for some third-rate, back-alley tattoo shop in downtown Nogales.

Walrus held up one tattooed arm, then the other like a haughty China Town butcher showing a duck to a customer.

"See anything?" I asked Benny.

"There, there it is," he said and pointed at the tattoo on Chino's forearm.

"Bingo," I said. "Los Carnales' *placa*. A tattoo of two hands clutching a black thorny rose and dagger wrapped in barbwire. The letters L.C. below the rose."

Then, I spotted it, a small tattoo of an impression of a black dagger on the left side of the chest, dripping with red blood.

"This tattoo tells me that he was a heavy hitter for a prison gang," I said. "A clubhouse assassin."

I spotted his gang moniker tattooed on his left shoulder, "Chino."

Benny got close to Alfredo's body and started taking photographs of the tattoos. The Walrus got upset.

"Hey!" he said. "What are you doing?"

"Relax," I said. "We are just taking photos of Alfredo's tats. Proof, we need proof."

"I swear if the photos show up on Facebook, me, you and Benny are done. Got that?" he said with a raised voice.

"Have we ever burned you? I don't burn sources. Never have, never will. And, these photos will never see the light of day. We just need them to verify that they exist and Benny and I saw them. That's all. That's it."

Walrus calmed down. Benny kept clicking away.

The Walrus turned Chino's head to one side, then to another, checking behind the ears. While checking Chino's oily scalp for head wounds, the Walrus suddenly looked up at Benny and me as we studied his intensity.

"How many holes?" I asked.

The Walrus shrugged.

"I'm guessing. This is a ballpark figure, but I would say about thirty-six puncture wounds," he replied, and casually added, "Haven't flipped him over yet. I suspect there are a few more in his back."

"Anything in the blood?" I asked.

"Don't know yet. Toxicology results usually take a few weeks. At first glance, he seems to be clean. No fresh needle marks."

85

"Classic prison-ordered hit. Overkill. Broad daylight," I said. "It's either the prison gang cleaning up its own outside the walls or he was taken out by rivals."

After leaving the morgue, I went to the newsroom, wrote a story, and rummaged through my new phone messages. There were three, one from Lucy Ramos, the older woman whom we had talked to that morning.

She said she remembered Chino talking to some fat, friendly man with a tattoo on his neck who approached Chino on the sidewalk two days before he was killed. Chino kept calling this man "Whale," Lucy said in her message.

"Another man waited in the car. I just remembered that. Maybe that will help you," Lucy said. "Goodbye."

The second message was my landlady who wanted the rent money. The last message was from Mickey's daughter Sierra.

"You twit bastard. Stay away from my family," she said, paused, heavy breathing. "I mean it, prick, or you're going to hear from me and my lawyer. You better hope it's from my lawyer."

Click. She hung up.

CHAPTER 9

Detective Leo Saenz was munching on an egg, cheese and chorizo burrito and washing it down with a cup of black coffee when I walked into his office early the next morning. He was behind a desk with his nose buried in the sports page. He lowered the newspaper when he glanced up and saw me standing a few feet from his cluttered desk.

"How do you find anything with all that debris on your desk, Leo?" I said. "How do you sift through it?"

"I've got a card catalog inside my head. Now, get out, and don't let the screen door hit you in the ass," he said with his deep voice. "Out."

"Before I leave, have you guys ID'd, the dead guy in the alley?"

He raised the newspaper up and continued reading it while he recited the usual cop-press mumble jumble.

"We are not releasing his name pending notification of next of kin. No arrests, no suspects, no comment," he said and slurped his coffee. "Leave. I'm busy."

"Who is Whale?"

Leo lowered the newspaper. He had a frown.

"What did I say? No, comment."

I put out a large envelope with a half dozen, large photographs inside, on top of Saenz's desk. His attention quickly went from the envelope to me and back to he envelope.

"What's this?"

"Open it."

He took a gulp of coffee and put the newspaper away. Suspiciously picking up the envelope, he carefully took out the crime scene photographs. While thumbing through them, his somber expression changed, and he smiled as he thumbed through the photographs.

"From yesterday's crime scene," I said. "Compliments of Benny and I, mostly Benny."

Leo scoffed and became impatient.

"Thanks. But nothing has changed. No suspects, no arrests, no comment. The investigation is ongoing. Now, leave."

"Give me this much. This one will be a hard to solve," I said.

He ignored my remark while he looked closer at the photographs, soaking up the haunting, minute details of a body lying near a dumpster.

"Check out my wingtip shoes next to Chino's head? Nice," Leo said. "And the apple by Chino's feet. That intensity on my face is powerful. This could be a poster for every crime scene in America."

"Benny's got an eye for details, knows how to use light," I said. "Is Chino's murder connected to the cartels? Mickey's death?"

"Maybe it's connected," he said. "In homicide, we sort murders into two categories. Those that matter and misdemeanor murders. This is a misdemeanor murder. The killing of a scumbag by other scumbags. We work our asses off to solve it just to get it off the books. But most of these prison homicides end in cold case files."

"Chino's untimely death is a misdemeanor murder?"

"I didn't say that."

He finished his coffee and poked at the newspaper several times with his finger.

"I read your story, and heard how you got the interview with Mickey."

"And?"

"I'm impressed. You should work homicide. Word of caution."

"What?"

"Sierra Madrid. She's pissed, and she's ruthless and vindictive."

Leo's eyes lit up when he saw a photograph of himself lifting the blanket covering Chino to get a better look at the body as he knelt next to it. No doubt, these were strong images. In that photograph, Leo Saenz looked like he was in some holy communion with what was a malevolent and tortured soul.

"Like that one, huh?" I asked.

He snapped out of a short-lived trance and blinked.

"What?"

"The photographs? What do you think?"

"Benny does really nice work," he said. "Nice stuff."

Leo, who had flecks of gray hair, worked most homicides like he owned them, like they were his personal jigsaw puzzles to figure out. Sometimes, the pieces were intricate and didn't fit. Sometimes, the pieces came together quickly, neatly and timely.

Leo, however, had no use for reporters but for some reason, he put up with me. He once told someone that he liked the pit bull running through my veins when I clamped onto a story.

"Benny said they're yours to frame."

"Thank Benny for me, will you?" he said.

"I'll do that."

"These things will be put on my shelf in my den," he said, holding up the photograph. "Right next to my city softball trophy and my daughter's college graduation photo."

"Good spot for it."

I looked around the room and stopped at a large wall next to Leo's police academy graduation certificate. I saw an opening, a vulnerability spot I could exploit.

"If you ask me, I'd put it next to your cop-school diploma up there," I said. "The photos and diploma will complement each other like salt and pepper."

"Think so?"

"Most definitely."

He leaned back in his chair, turned his neck to look up at the wall that was full of years of awards, cop trophies and diplomas. He nodded and grinned, still admiring his image on the photographs.

"Yeah, you're right," he said.

Resigned that I wouldn't get anything from this hard-nose detective but satisfied that I had racked up some PR points, I ended my probing and headed for the door.

"Enjoy the photos, later," I said.

"Jack."

Great! I thought.

"What?"

He mouthed for me to close the door. After I did, he motioned for me to come closer.

"Off the record?" He said in a low voice.

"Yeah."

"I mean totally off-the-record."

"Of course, off-the-record."

"We lifted some DNA from a cupcake wrapper and a partial fingerprint that's linked to a guy whose moniker is Whale and that led us to Rengo."

"Why was Chino green lighted?"

"He was ordered to do a hit. Take out a Colombian shot caller named Maximo. He didn't do it."

"Apparently, Chino recently found God. That's what his neighbors, two old ladies, said," I said.

Leo rubbed his forehead and grimaced.

"Really? And you believe it?"

"That's what I was told."

"You know the game as well as I do," he said and sighed. "These guys parole out and use Christian halfway houses as cover. They say they've found Jesus and some continue committing crimes."

"Maybe, Chino really had a religious conversion," I said with a sardonic grin. "Saw the light."

"Sure, maybe he did, and maybe you and I will bump into him in heaven," Leo said. "Up there at the big pool table in the sky."

"What happened to Maximo?"

"Disappeared. Presumed dead," he said. "That's all I can say."

"Thanks, Leo. I really appreciate your insight and all your help," I said with a cynical emphasis on "all."

As I walked toward the door, he said, "Hey, numb nuts. Come here."

I ambled over and stood in front of his desk, yawned and shoved both hands into my pant pockets.

"What?"

"The Juarez and Sinaloa cartels are recruiting in prison, going after some of the heavy hitters. The most violent and hardcore career criminals with a lot of *cora*. A lot of heart and balls."

"They've always done that."

"Not in these numbers that we are seeing. Apparently, they're gearing up for something big, really big," he said. "We believe the new recruits will be used to hunt down and kill rivals on both sides of the border."

"Mickey's death touched off a power struggle, right?"

"If it didn't, it stirred things up. The feds are intercepting more weapons heading south of the border including rocket propelled grenades, grenades, armor-piercing bullets. The feds stopped a guy heading to Mexico with two light anti-tank weapons."

"Holy shit. The cartels are about to light up downtown Juarez."

"Also sales of La Santa Muerte statues are up."

The cult of Santa Muerte, the Holy Death, had millions of followers in Mexico. She is the patron saint of the dregs of society, prostitutes, robbers, thieves and drug dealers. They pray to La Santa Muerte for success. Drug dealers build altars to the Santa Muerte in their homes.

"That's a good sign that a war for La Plaza is in the works," I said.

"All this is off the record. Totally off the record," he said.

"Thanks, Leo," I said and turned to leave.

"Hey," he called me back.

"What?"

"I see a word in print having to do with our off-the-record conversation, and I swear, me and you are done with a capital D."

"I've never burned a source, never."

"I'm just making sure you know where I'm coming from."

I smiled and nodded.

He raised the newspaper and returned to his burrito, coffee and the Sports page.

CHAPTER 10

Two weeks after I talked to Leo, SWAT lobbed a stun-grenade through an open window. The grenade bounced off the wall, exploded and temporarily dazed the two Los Carnales prison gang members, Willie Jacquez, aka the Whale, and Tomas Estevez, whose nickname is El Rengo, which means the crippled one.

Just before SWAT showed up, the two were sitting on the couch and eating cereal and watching reruns of the World Wrestling Federation's grudge matches.

The cops then burst into the door, pointed guns at the two stunned suspects and shouted commands. The cops swarmed the house, thundering past its lopsided and decaying front porch.

Whale was momentarily dazed but he got up, cursed and was hit in the head by a SWAT rifle butt. He was struck again after he took a few steps towards the kitchen where a loaded shotgun was on top of the table next to a bag of cocaine.

Finally, several cops tackled him and gave him a little thump therapy, mostly with boots. All this while Rengo was a handcuffed and hogtied by other cops. He was carried away and thrown in the back of a patrol car.

The two were traced by Rengo's DNA and a partial fingerprint left on the cupcake wrapper. The two were from Houston and had recently moved to El Paso.

My DEA source Nick also said Los Carnales' generals were farming out contract hits to their members and associates to do hits on Juarez Cartel rivals, the Sinaloa Drug Cartel members who had partnered with Colombian drug dealers.

The Colombians and the Sinaloa Cartel assassins, in turn, were cruising the cities searching for Juarez Cartel targets, the DEA guys said.

Nick later put things into perspective and said that whoever came up on top after the gun battles would have to deal with the person who was now the new drug kingpin of the Mickey Madrid drug-smuggling ring.

"The drug lord that comes out on top will be much stronger and deadlier, and it'll be nearly impossible to launder all the drug profits," said Nick.

Three days after their arrests, Whale and Rengo were arraigned in a crowded courtroom with nearly a dozen sheriff's deputies and heavily armed plainclothes detectives strategically spread around the courtroom, along the courtroom corridor, and around the building.

Only a few people were in the courtroom.

Four days later, Whale died from a mysterious heroin overdose in the jail.

A week later, I would learn about Rengo's fate at the Blue Note Bar, the downtown bar attracts a large crowd of young professionals on a Friday night.

I was there one night having some drinks after work with Benny, C.J. and two newspaper reporters, Chico Redmond and Sarah Cummins.

We had a full-blown bitch session going.

Lately, the grumblings centered on Ricardo and his newly created, ironclad edict: deadlines are sacred. No one misses a deadline unless he or she is laid out in the morgue with a toe tag – no exceptions. First offense, verbal reprimand. Second offense, written reprimand. And third violation, the reporter is fired.

As the booze took its toll, one-by-one, we fell into a sweet state of alcoholic bliss. Our cares and concerns all but evaporated as shit-faced smiles and silly grins surfaced beneath glassy eyes.

After Benny ordered another round, he told a newsroom joke.

"How many editors does it take to change a light bulb?" he asked.

After the head shaking and mellow grins, Benny said, "Only one, but first they have to rewire the whole goddamn building."

A roar of laughter followed shrilling whistles and applause.

"Here's one?" C.J. said. "A better joke. How many Ricardos does it take to change a light bulb?"

Everybody looked at each other, nobody replied.

"Ricardo doesn't change light bulbs. He assigns Jack to do it and afterwards, he'll send him home for fucking it up."

"Ohhhhhhs," followed by chortling and snickering.

I had a nice buzz going from three beers so I wasn't upset.

"Funny, asshole. Really funny," I said. "That's some really lame shit."

My cell phone buzzed. I took it out of my pocket and checked the number. It was a source, a jailer named Russell.

"Rengo is dead," Russell said. "He hung himself. They found him an hour ago."

"What's the unofficial version?"

"His *compadres* beat and hung him from a bed sheet. One left a shoe imprint on the side of his head from the beat down," he said.

"Thanks," I said.

I hung up, finished my beer, put on my coat and headed out the door.

"Where are you going?" C.J. said.

"Rengo hung himself at the jail," I said as I headed for the door. "I got to go get the details."

"Damn," said Sarah. "Your boys are dropping like flies."

CHAPTER 11

After I left the bar, I went to the newsroom and finally tracked down Vincent Nieves, the PR flak for the Sheriff's Department. Upset that I woke him up, he berated me for not calling the night-shift cop commander.

"You know the rules," he said.

"If I wanted the usual 'no-comment, it's under investigation' quotes, I would have called the nightshift commander," I replied. "I'm beyond that."

During a short pause, I heard the groggy voice of a woman telling him to hang up. He loved to screw the television reporters. I figured one of them had already pumped him for information about Rengo's death. So I would get beat on this story.

Vincent hushed her up and returned to our conversation.

"What makes you think I know anything about this death?" he said.

"I don't care what you know or don't know. I want to find out how Tomas Estevez, a.k.a. El Rengo, died. Make some phone calls and find out. That's how it works."

He mockingly laughed.

"Off the record, I'm not jumping out of bed to find out how some scumbag hanged himself and saved taxpayers money," Nieves said. "On the record, 'no comment. This is an ongoing

investigation. We will issue a press release in the morning.' How's
that? Huh?"

I could almost feel his disdain.

I had little use and much less patience for this supercilious
buffoon.

Nieves was usually good for a few useless quotes. He made police
gibberish into fine art. He loved the television cameras, and loved
female television reporters even more. He felt comfortable standing
in front of a large El Paso Sheriff's Department concrete sign dressed
in snazzy suits, donning a somber expression, and wearing stiff, but-
toned-down shirts.

I was in a foul mood and not interested in playing public relations
patty cake with this PR prick, especially with a mysterious jail death
hanging in the air and a big drug war about to erupt across the border.

"Listen, clown, my *pinche* patience is on a very short leash tonight.
Very short," I said. "I want to know what these two dead guys were all
about and why they were killed?"

"Who in the hell do you think you're talking to, Fuentes? I'm
calling your editor first thing in the morning and tell him about our
conversation. You're way out of line and unprofessional."

Then, he took a cheap shot that sent a hot, upward rush of anger.

"I also heard that you already have one foot out the door with
Ricardo," he said. "I bet if I make a call, you'll be lucky if you get a
paper route."

"I could give a rat's ass who you call, and you know why?"

"Why?"

"Receipts. I got receipts in my desk. These are charges you ran up
on the city's credit card for the last conference you attended. A receipt
from Prince Town Entertainment. Sound familiar?"

I could feel his adrenaline rushing up to his head.

98

"I believe they own The King's Cuties Gentlemen's Club. The receipt is for $368. I venture to say that some of it might be for some stripper to whirl her ass in front of your face. Lap dances. Oh, there's a $35 room fee for adult movies you rented. I bet if I try real hard, I can get the titles. Do you understand where I'm going with this?"

Dead silence.

While he put his hand over the phone speaker, again, he said something to the female who was apparently in his bed wide-awake now. As soon as he took his hand off the speaker, I heard the woman say above a whisper, "That lowlife prick."

Nieves quickly covered the phone speaker again to tell the woman to shut up. He cleared his throat and resumed our conversation.

"Look, I'll call you back," he said reluctantly.

"When?"

"Give me a few hours."

"Don't disappoint me."

Two hours later, I stared at El Rengo's tattooed body laid out on the metal table at the morgue. The rubber-gloved Walrus stood beside me as we both looked at Rengo's remains. Walrus wasn't happy that he had to come down to the morgue.

"I should give you a key," he said, heavy-eyed.

"That'd be nice," I said.

My tired eyes stood over another dead tattooed corpse. This one had a goatee and a wiry, muscular body, probably from the weight lifting in prison. One side of his face was badly swollen. His knuckles were bruised and cut as though he'd fought hard before he died. There were the old prison scars on his body put there by shanks, wounds on top of wounds. A partial and fresh shoe print was on the side of his head. Rengo had been stomped.

"What's the official verdict?" I asked without taking my eyes off the body. "I'll take a wild guess. He was stomped to death."

"I don't want to be quoted," he said.

"I never come in here looking for quotes."

"It'll be hard for the Sheriff's Department to put a happy face on this one," he said. "Let me look at a couple of more things."

After briefly moving Rengo's limbs like he was working a large batter of dough and positioning Rengo's oily head in various angles, Walrus looked up at me.

"It's obvious. He was beaten and strangled," he said. "Head trauma, abrasions on the right cheek and right shoulder and around the wrist. Homicide by asphyxia by strangulation associated with craniocerebral trauma."

"That's a nice way of saying, 'he was stomped to death while being strangled.'"

"Yeah, that would be the condensed and unofficial version of the cause of death."

I thanked him and hurried out the door. I drove to the newsroom where my fingers danced on the computer keys: "According to sources, Rengo's cellmates beat and strangled him to death at the county jail."

I wrote about Rengo's criminal past and his unexpected demise at the county jail.

I finished and hit the send button.

The story was immediately put up on the newspaper website.

In the morning, Vincent called. He prefaced what he was about to say with, "This is all I know. I swear, and it's all off the record."

Then, he gave me the run down on Whale and Rengo.

"Word has it that they were about to rat out who gave the order to kill Chino to avoid death row," Vincent said. "Detectives suspect that Whale was given a hot-dose of heroin in his jail cell.

Rengo had help hanging himself. Los Carnales are suddenly busing their assassins to the border with lists of Sinaloa cartel targets. That's all I know. The drug war is heating up."

"Thanks," I said.

I went home, tried to sleep but couldn't. I had left so many questions unanswered, and those questions kept nudging a REM-less sleep.

I was back to work at 5:30 a.m. The cop reporter, a young intern named Lesa, was on the telephone making early-morning cop calls to check if anything had occurred overnight that was worthy of some ink.

A few hours later, the place would be bustling with activity, early morning clacking of computer keys began to rise as reporters with cups of coffee, cream-cheesed bagels and egg burritos cracked opened gray screens. Editors held meetings to pick stories that would land on the front page and to spread others throughout the newspaper.

The police radio sat close. Lesa was already squelching out the a.m. fender benders and a slew of minor crimes, mostly petty crimes like shoplifting.

My mind, however, was a thousand miles away struggling to make sense what I had found out so far and make sense of the evil converging on the border.

I needed a lot more time sorting this whole thing out, and I would need Ricardo's approval to do this. That was one of his edicts. He makes the final deadline extensions on investigative stories.

CHAPTER 12

The next two days, I spent hours calling my sources, trying to milk them for any tips, clues or hints, anything, about who had risen to the top of the Mickey Madrid's drug dynasty.

Who's calling the shots?

I had no luck. Nobody knew anything and if they did, they weren't saying a word or making any wild speculations.

I was desperate. I even went to Mickey's funeral, keeping a good distance from the gravesite. I had a good vantage point and a pair of binoculars. From there, I glassed the comings and goings, making notes, trying to read the body language of those standing near the coffin.

In the murky world that Mickey had left behind, posturing and positioning at a funeral are good ways to gauge who is in power and who has fallen from grace. But it all turned out to be a bust. Nothing credible surfaced.

One night, I worked late and left the building after checking my voicemail.

There were a few messages. The first message was from my landlady who was unhappy, complaining that I was late on my rent again. Then the dentist's receptionist said I was overdue to get my teeth cleaned. And the remaining calls were insignificant or anonymous or both, including a tormented soul who said he wanted me to investigate his neighbor's barking dogs because they kept him up at night.

The last message was from my older sister Susan. She left one of her guilt trips on my phone. The funny sister turned mom and businesswoman was now second runner-up in the laying of guilt trips in our family. In first place was my mother who taught Susan well.

My eardrums fastened their seatbelts as Susan revved her whine.

"Jack, you are such a shit for a brother," she said. "Your niece wants to know if her Uncle Jack is still alive or have the bad guys made him go with God."

A second heaping of guilt followed grunts and huffing.

"Are you coming to mom and dad's anniversary? Mom expects you here. Dad, well, Dad is Dad. Jack, you and dad need to patch things up. He's not getting any younger, and if something happens to him, God forbid, you'll regret it for the rest of your life. Wait, someone wants to talk to you."

A long silence was interrupted by background babbling and then, a child's giggle. The recording ended. I was relieved. But Susan's wasn't done, not just yet. She called back and left another message, continuing the mea culpa.

"Jack, sorry. We got disconnected. Anyway, here's Jessica."

My six-year-old niece and one of the joys in my life, who my sister was apparently grooming in the Fuentes' Women School of Laying of the Guilt Trips on Vulnerable Men, grabbed the phone.

"Hi, Uncle Jack. How are you? I love you," she said, followed by a pause. "Oh, yeah, and can you please come to see us? Pretty please. Pretty, pretty, pretty please."

Obviously, Jessica was being coached. I could hear mother and daughter whispering.

"Oh, yeah," Jessica said, through the gap in her front teeth. "Grandpa and Grandma miss you too. Bye. Here's mom."

My sister picked up the phone again.

"Satisfied? You act like such a jerk sometimes. Think about what I just said. Patch things up with Dad and come up and visit us," Susan barked, and mercifully ending the recording.

The estranged relationship with my father started months ago after I trashed these far-fetched plans he had for me, and they were big plans too. Plans that he never bothered to run past me.

When I was a boy, he wanted me to be a Marine just like him. When that didn't happen, he said that as soon as I got a business degree, I could take over his barbershop and manage his rental property. Out of nowhere, he asked if I ever thought about clipping hair for a living.

"Not really," I replied, not telling how I really felt. "Nope."

I hated barbershops because I spent so much time in them. They smell like my father. The manly talc and aftershave and cologne scents sometimes enter a room before he does.

All his life he talked about cutting hair like it is some noble lost art, a sacred trade. He always reminded me that my great-grandfather had a shop in Taos, New Mexico and cut the mayor's and police chief's hair.

My father talked about haircutting as though there is a Barbershop Museum, always saying that he knew all the great barbers, rattling out their names Reynosa Ruiz, Shorty Montes, Eddie Quintana, Eddie Rendell, Blackie Denton and Chuco Luna. And, he knew all their stories that my grandfather and great-grandfather passed down to him.

I was dragged into this business when I was ten years old, mentally kicking and screaming. I had no choice. So for many summers afterwards, I was held hostage there, sweeping up tons of hair that fell on the floor, making sure the magazines were in a neat and alphabetical order on the rack.

Or, he'd have me running errands for him and the other two barbers, a portly and balding man named Ruben and a smallish guy whom people called *Perico* or parrot because of the shape of his nose. He talked a lot, too.

After all the trips to the store to get packs of Marlboro Lights or change for my dad or to Senora Perla's restaurant for beacon and egg burritos, I swore off smoking and breakfast burritos along with barbershops.

The barbershop gibberish was also annoying, and in the summer months, it usually revolved around how hot it was outside or how hot it was getting or whether it was going to rain or if the sun would get hotter the next day.

Weather talk was endless.

The yakking would occasionally shift to building up or dismantling car engines, and of course, the usual allegations about corruption or conspiracy at city hall, deer season or hunting rifles.

During hunting season, braggadocio ran amuck. I was convinced that at a young age, the whole world has a "clean shot" at this mystical eight-point buck standing two or three football fields away. But the animal always dodges the bullet.

Some of the best times I had, however, were with my father when I was boy, and we were out in the woods, chasing after deer or quail.

During our hunting trips, he taught me my lessons of life, how to be a man, a Fuentes man. The rules were simple: Roll with life's punches and if you get knocked down, pick yourself up, dust yourself off and keep going.

One thing, he said once that I never forgot.

"Never put a for-sale sign on your dignity and self respect," he said.

I don't think I ever disappointed my father until I made a decision to become a journalist. He said I'd waste my time pursuing *puro chismes* or pure gossip with other notebook prima donnas who, he said, love to wallow in scandals.

We argued back and forth and soon we drifted apart after I got a degree in journalism and landed my first job as an intern for the Dallas Morning News more than 10 years ago. I don't think he's ever read one of my stories. Never asked about any of them, not one. I've written hundreds of stories.

But that's my father.

The last message I got was from the Walrus. It made my ears perk up.

"Jack, Sheriff Rick Ward from Marfa called. Wants a copy of the Rengo's and Whale's autopsy reports. Thought you might want to know that."

The name Rick Ward sent an icy tingle down my spine. But that could have all been bullshit what Mickey said about the sheriff, and he was just getting a last laugh before checking out. Still a lump dropped down my windpipe when I heard the message from Walrus.

Why would Sheriff Rick who lives in Hudspeth County want copies of the autopsy reports of two dead prison gang thugs who died in the El Paso County jail?

I needed to find out.

CHAPTER 13

I pulled into my driveway. It was odd.

There was a strange stiffness in the air. Black and white shadows from the television splashed and danced on the ceiling of the dark room. Gray TV shadows appeared to flutter against the white curtains, sweeping them across the ceiling like ghosts being spewed out from the TV screen. Inside the room, the shadows flew, tumbled around like gray and dark-gray clothes inside a dryer.

I was probably half-asleep that morning when I left for work and forgot to turn off the TV, I thought.

I ambled up to the door with my carrying case dangling from my shoulder, clutching a bag of warm greasy, barbecue wings. As I got closer to the house, I waited for my cockatiel Dexter to start shrieking and chirping. The bird would always do that as soon as he heard the car door slam.

It didn't happen.

Maybe the hours of TV images flashing in the room scared the bird. I checked the mailbox. No bills, just junk mail. I went to open the door, and there was a note scotch-taped high up.

It was from the landlady telling me that the rent was past due: Pay up or move, she had written with a large red marker. She put three exclamation marks at the end of the pay-up sentence and underscored the words pay up.

I shook my head, crumbled and stuffed the note into my pocket. Then, I stepped inside and flipped on the lights. The room was empty. On the television, a shrink interviewed disgruntled couples who had issues with the in-laws. In the corner, Dexter, who usually flapped his wings, was quiet. The bird had its back toward me. That was strange.

I tried to stir him up by greeting him, whistling, and calling him by his name. The bird was unresponsive, barely managing a few weak tweets.

"What's up, Dexter? Bummed out, huh? Do you miss Knuckles? Emily?"

He barely chirped.

"I do too."

The bird stood perfectly still.

I sniffed the air. There were hints of sandalwood and fresh flowers. I stood in the middle of the room for a few moments, waiting to hear a sound while trying to figure out where the sweet odor was coming from, nothing.

I sniffed at my clothes, nothing.

Oh, well.

After flopping down on the sofa chair, I grabbed the TV remote control and started channel surfing until I got ESPN. I leaned to one side to put the bag of chicken wings on the floor.

Blood rushed up my head when I saw a wine glass. The glass-rim was slightly smudged with lipstick, a light red color.

I slowly picked it up, put it under my nose, and raised it against a lamp's light to get a closer look. There was some white wine inside the wine glass.

I figured Dana had dropped by to visit Dexter and dropped off some take-out food on the kitchen table from the restaurant. I looked around for a note on the television set where she usually left it. Nothing. I sat back down.

I reached into the bag and grabbed a chicken wing. I took bites of the chicken and started channel surfing. Suddenly, I felt an overpowering presence of a body, standing behind me. I dropped the chicken. My heart took off like a racehorse at the starting gate. I stiffened my body, trembled, locked my jaw, and waited.

I had no doubt my brains would soon be flying across the room.

The sound of a gun trigger being pulled back filled the whole room. Dexter fluttered his wings.

"Move and your brains will be in that bag with the *pinche* chicken," the female voice said.

I thought I recognized the voice, but I didn't want to blurt out a name or get this female intruder pissed off.

"I got two twenties. Take it. It's in my wallet. That's all I have," I said. "You saw the note from my landlady. I'm struggling financially."

"Shut up!" the voice demanded. "Get up."

I did and slowly turned. It was Sierra. I was in a state of stunned incredulity. She was in a rage. A forest fire burning in her eyes, she had her hand straight out and holding a gun that looked like a cannon. She flashed a snarl, one a Doberman Pincher would envy.

"You sneaky bastard," she said.

"What are you talking about?"

"Shut up!"

"Get that gun out of my face. It could go off."

"If you don't shut up, it will."

"Okay. Okay. Relax."

The barrel of the gun seemed to be getting bigger by the minute.

"You showed up at my father's funeral, of all places!" she said. "You *pinche* idiot. You have no respect for anything living. No one, do you?"

"What's this about?"

"Oh, God. Don't even go there or I swear —"

"Okay, okay."

I glanced at Dexter. The feathers on his head were up. Sweat came down the side of my head, my Adam's apple slid down my throat and felt like it dropped to my ankles. My heart was ready to leap out of my chest and dash out the door.

"I had a hunch that you'd show up," she said. "Did you see the shovel?"

"What shovel?"

"The one next to the tree. The tree you climbed up with the binoculars?"

"Yeah," I said.

"That was the cemetery groundskeeper letting me know where you were," she said. "For a nice finder's fee. I knew your sorry ass would show up. You couldn't stay away."

"I'm a reporter and it's my job to—"

"Shut up. Get on the floor, now! Hands on your head, spread your legs and if you make any sudden moves, you're so dead."

I did as I was told and tried to calm her down, pleading for her to put the gun down.

"Look, I needed to find out who went to your father's funeral and who didn't. All hell is fixing to break loose in Juarez. Three parolees are already dead."

"I couldn't care less about dead parolees or any of your other bullshit."

She grinned, calmly took two steps toward me, and put the gun in the back of my neck. My face turned ashen.

"This is from me and my family," she said.

I whimpered and closed my eyes tight and prepared to be hurled into the great beyond.

In a flash, she rammed the tip of her high-heeled shoe into my balls. A jolt from the pain felt like it was going to shoot through my skull. I doubled up, and curled up in a fetal position, moaning, gasping for air.

"Put that in your story. By the way, my family still has no comment," she said sternly

Cooley, she lowered herself down, her mouth close to my ear. She pressed the cold gun barrel hard on the side of my head.

She pulled the trigger. I jerked. She pulled again, and again. I whimpered, again.

She whispered in my ear, "It wasn't loaded, *idiota*."

Laughter, cruel laughter, as cold as an Arctic blast, blanketed the room. I heard her heels walking out the door, stop halfway there, turn and softly chime, "Bye, bye, Dexter. You're a cutie. You know that?"

Dexter barely chirped once, as if to say he didn't know me and didn't see anything. He fluttered his wings as if to shake off some of the tension inside the room.

Bastard bird, I thought. He is just looking out for his own feathery ass.

Sierra slammed the door. The living room window shook. I moaned for a few minutes, cupping my swollen balls.

After much of the pain finally left me, and an hour after Sierra was long gone, I sat in the bathtub soaking my aching testicles, going through my mind and wondering why Rick Ward would want a copy of the autopsy.

The sheriff never returned my calls. So I decided to take a trip to Hudspeth County to pay a visit to Sheriff Rick and ask him some questions.

CHAPTER 14

The next morning, I got on Interstate 10 and headed east of El Paso when the sun was barely boring through a fading night canopy. I was on my way to Marfa to see Sheriff Rick Ward.

Sheriff Rick was the head of the West Texas Narcotics Task Force, a tight conglomeration of state, federal, and local law enforcement agencies put together to stop drug smugglers along the border.

I wanted to know why he wanted an autopsy report on the jail deaths in El Paso. I also couldn't shake Mickey Madrid's last words about Sheriff Rick. I had to go see the sheriff to ask some questions.

As I drove down the desert highway, anemic sunlight began to gently push away most of the grayness of dawn. Powerful heat blasts sent temperatures soaring to what could turn out to be another 100-degree-plus day at West Texas desert.

Images flew by as I drove down the desolate highway to Marfa: endless clumps of scrub oak. A few jack rabbits tearing through the desert floor. The towering mountain ranges with ragged edges, and one lone coyote in the distance with its head hung low, sniffing for rabbit trails.

On the way there, I passed a couple of rustic West Texas towns barely clinging to life.

I pulled into the parking lot and parked beside a patrol car. A sheriff's deputy with muscular brown arms sat behind the wheel. He glanced my way before he continued to write on a piece of paper on a clipboard.

Marfa was just a tad over 2,000 faces, and I wasn't a familiar one. I climbed the old courthouse steps, looked back and caught the deputy glaring at me.

The deputy probably figured that I was another blue-jeaned stranger on my way to the clerk's window to pay traffic ticket, or perhaps, a backpacking tourist who stopped to use the restroom and get directions to some obscure hiking trail.

On the second floor, the sheriff's office was empty. His secretary was gone. A hot cup of coffee on her desk told me she was nearby. I went into his office after politely knocking on the half-open door, just in case he was tucked away in some unseen corner of the room.

"Sheriff?" I said. "Hello. Anybody here?"

The room was a museum to his life and accomplishments: An oil painting of the sheriff, arms folded and standing next to a saddle, hung on the wall facing the door.

Sheriff Rick could have been cast in a Gary Cooper western film. A tall and rugged West Texas mountain man, he had rough, cactus-dry hands that were as large as bear paws. A silver belt buckle looked like a large serving plate.

The oil painting didn't show the physical blemishes: a gap between his tobacco-stained teeth, a small insignificant chin, and a brown mole near the tip of his nose took away from the western mystique.

In the corner of the room were a pair of $500 Tony Lama boots with a Lone Star flag stitched on alligator and ostrich hides.

Only the humming of the ceiling fan stirring up the cool morning air rose above distant voices, probably of court clerks and others, arriving for work. Along a dark-oak paneled wall, a few rows of photographs were nailed, mostly people with happy faces and cowboy hats showing off rifles or kneeling or standing beside dead creatures, fish, ducks, deer and a wide-eyed moose head. Above the rows of photographs was a larger picture of the sheriff grinning. Flanked by the governor and two congressmen, whom I recognized for their work with narcotics task forces and the U.S. Border Patrol.

Next to that was a black-and-white, signed photograph of John Wayne, standing tall and holding a Winchester rifle with a prideful look as though he was standing guard over Sheriff Rick's green-carpeted office. On the corner of a large wooden desk, a photograph of the sheriff with his blonde-haired wife Karen and their two teen-aged daughters, Amanda and Roberta.

Three neat stacks of paper were also on top of the desk. On top of one pile was Rengo's autopsy report. Someone had redlined a couple of paragraphs on the page and circled a couple of words.

After I had arched my torso and back and angled my neck to try and get a better read on the highlighted words, a booming voice yanked me back.

"Hey, who the hell let you in here?"

It was the sheriff. He was fuming.

"What are you doing in my office?" he said.

Red-faced, I said, "Came by to see you."

"Why are you snooping around?"

"Curiosity got the best of me about what's up on the walls. I didn't mean to snoop."

"Get out. I have nothing else to say. *Comprende?*"

"I'm a reporter with the El Paso Daily."

"I know who you are."

He tossed keys on top of his desk, took his hat off and hung it on a coat hanger, sat behind his desk and looked up.

"I don't recall putting up a sign outside saying that I was having an open house today," he said.

"Nobody was out at the front desk, so I figured you were in the office working."

"Vasquez, my deputy, ran your plates after he saw the notebook sticking out of your back pocket and gave me a heads up that you might be here."

I plucked out my notebook from my back pocket.

"I'm doing a story and I was just curious. You asked for a copy of Tomas Estevez's and Willie Jacquez's autopsies. Why are you interested in two prison parolees who died in the El Paso County jail?"

"That is a law enforcement matter. It's none of your business. I have no comment."

The sheriff glared at me while he leaned his chair back and put his two boots on top of his desk. The two boots made thuds that punctuated an awkward silence.

"I heard Los Carnales are moving muscle to the border for the Juarez Cartel."

"I clearly said, 'I have no comment.' *Capeesh?*"

He shoved a cigarette between his lips, lit and puffed on it while his eyes shot darts my way.

"Heard Mickey Madrid got help from well-placed people on this side of the border. What do you hear?"

"Show's over. Get your ass out of here. Leave. I've got work to do," he barked.

I took out my business card, put it on his desk, and slid it toward him.

"If anything comes up, give me a call."

He scooped it up, glanced at the card, crumbled and tossed it in the trashcan.

"Sure," he said flatly. "You're the first person I'm going to call."

I chuckled.

As I walked out the door, I spotted a photograph near the door that caught my eye, the sheriff grinning, showing the gap on his teeth. He stood next to a lake with his shirt off and holding a catfish the size of a small shark.

"Nice fish," I said. "Fat and healthy. I bet he was smothered in onions and a little butter as he was being fried."

The sheriff said nothing. I continued talking.

"Look at those eyes. Full of defiance. Full of fight."

The sheriff's leather swivel chair creaked a bit. I kept pushing his buttons.

"I bet this big cocky fish swam around the lake without a care in the world. It never occurred to him that one day someone would snag him, and it was you of all people," I said.

I turned around and saw the sheriff's jaws tighten. He took a long puff from his cigarette and smashed it in the ashtray, avoiding eye contact.

Just then, his secretary, a thin middle-aged woman with long, straight, strawberry-dyed hair and slightly bow-legged walked in. She saw me standing there, and looked at the sheriff's angry eyes. Her half smile vanished.

"How did you get in here?" she asked me.

"Door was open. I knocked politely and walked in," I said.

"He was snooping around when I walked in," the sheriff said.

"I was admiring, looking at the artifacts on the wall, the photographs, and all the awards and hunting trophies."

The secretary shifted into an indignant posture and tone.

"That can't be. No sir, we have some sensitive material in this office, reports and other confidential papers," she said.

Her eyes bounced off the sheriff and me. She had disgust stamped on his face.

"Show his ass out, Margaret," the sheriff told the secretary.

"Gladly," she said. "Let's go. Out!"

As we walked out, Margaret said, "I'm sorry this happened, sheriff."

"I am too, sheriff," I said.

I stopped and looked toward the photograph of the sheriff holding the fish.

"Call me, sheriff, if you catch another giant catfish," I said sarcastically. "I'll splash that story on the front page with a big, old headline."

I used my hand for emphasis: "Sheriff from Marfa Catches Giant Fish."

"That's all you're good for, fish stories and slinging bullshit for that rag you work for," the sheriff fired back. "You would have been a good, parking-lot attendant at a Tijuana fruit stand."

I laughed, "Hold that thought."

"Out!" Margaret said.

I walked down the steps while Margaret frowned, making sure I drove away.

Defiantly, I winked and flashed my notebook at Deputy Vasquez who was still sitting in patrol car pretending to ignore me. I sped down the highway, heading back to El Paso. The air conditioning and radio were in full blast.

The music was interrupted: "We have breaking news. A powerful explosion just rocked a Rim Road neighborhood. What we know is that a car bomb exploded, sending fireball twenty feet up. One man is dead. The bomb squad and emergency crews are responding. The neighborhood has been evacuated," the news-caster said.

A few minutes later, my cell phone went off. It was C.J. He repeated what the radio newscaster had said, adding a chilling twist.

"We think the Colombians took out Mickey's Madrid's kid, Emilio," he said.

"Who? Why?"

"He was heir to the throne, I guess. Who knows?"

I told him I was on my way.

A few hours later, I was standing among a group of people with the usual blank expressions and wary smiles. Everyone stood behind a couple of police cars three blocks away from where the blast occurred. Police had already set up a mobile command post where FBI, ATF agents and other cops congregated.

A bomb-sniffing dog worked the crime scene, sniffing between bushes and around parked cars. An emergency medical technician sat behind the wheel of an ambulance, eyes fixed straight ahead. Firefighters gathered near the fire trucks, waiting for the bomb squad to finish so they could clean up gasoline spills.

The newspaper's crime reporter Jacob Young and Benny were there. Benny snapped away using a long lens, kneeling in the middle of the blocked-off street to get a good shot of a burned and shredded 2012 BMW.

Jacob said he interviewed a dozen people, including some residents who lived close to where the explosion occurred. They told him that the blast sent fragments of glass flying in all directions and blew out some windows. One of the car doors ended up being ripped off the vehicle and sliding a block down the street.

"The coroner and cops aren't going near the car until the bomb squad clears the area," Jacob said. "Body parts were strewn on the street."

Bomb-squad experts dressed in what looked like space suits concentrated near the BMW. I wondered whether Sierra knew that her stepbrother was dead.

"Have Mickey's relatives shown up?" I asked Jacob.

"Haven't seen them," he replied.

Benny finished snapping photographs, walked over.

"I venture to say it was the Colombians," he said.

"Yeah," I replied.

CHAPTER 15

Two days after Emilio's death, the police had made no arrests. The bodies were piling up in Juarez, and my story wasn't going anywhere. I had placed dozens of calls and nothing, not even a rumor to chase

The newspaper published stories about Emilio and whether Mickey's stepson had been targeted. There were questions about whether some of this cartel violence had already spread into El Paso. Those who went on the record only offered dilettante speculation.

People were afraid, demanding answers. More federal agents were sent to the border.

In Juarez, the Sinaloa Cartel left its calling card. Two pipe bombs exploded inside downtown nightclubs, sending metal, fragments of glass and body parts flying into the streets.

After I left the newsroom, I drove down Interstate 10 and watched the downtown lights on my rearview mirror get smaller.

A cool breeze ran its fingers through my hair. It felt good. I turned on the radio and kept going through my mental notes over and over again, searching for something that would help jump start my story and take it in a fresh direction.

I got on the on-ramp heading east on I-10 when I felt an eerie presence. I glanced up, and two eyes, two-catlike eyes deep inside a dark hoodie stared at me from the backseat.

I yelled and froze. The car swerved as a jolt of adrenaline shot up my spine. My thumping heart felt like it was about to spread my ribcage to get out and run down the freeway.

"Please, don't shoot," I said.

The dark figure shoved a gun on the side of my neck.

"Shut up."

It was Sierra.

"This one is loaded," she said.

She pulled the trigger back.

I cursed, pinned the gas pedal against the floorboard, hoping and praying that she wouldn't fire the weapon.

A bullet through my skull would send the speeding car tumbling, twisting and turning as it went out of control and barreled down the highway, smashing everything in its path.

"Slow down!" she yelled.

"Put the gun away! Now! Put it away!"

"No!"

The speedometer read 100 mph, as I zigzagging past cars as rage-filled horns blasted.

Sweat ran down my forehead as street lights, roadside neon and billboard signs flashed by. I swerved to keep from hitting some metal barriers. I slammed on the brakes. The car screeched and skidded sideways down the center lane.

Sierra screamed as she was slammed against rear-passenger door.

"Stop, prick, or you're dead!" she said.

Sierra fired. The bullet blew a hole through the car roof.

"I mean it," she said.

Disheveled, Sierra popped straight up.

I kept the gas pedal down. I hoped that scaring Sierra would give me the edge and she'd put the gun away.

"Pull over!" she said, pressing the gun hard against my head. "Now!"

I could feel the Chimera's blazing breathe, her flames about to singe the hair on the back of my head.

"I count to ten and if you don't slow down, I'll blow your head off, I swear, and we'll both die."

I didn't let up on the gasoline pedal.

"One, two, three, four, five, six, seven, eight."

"All right. Put the gun away," I shouted.

I took my foot off the pedal and gradually stepped on the brakes. The car dropped speed. She took the gun barrel was off my throbbing head.

I was pissed.

She smacked me hard in the back of my head.

"Ouch!" I said.

"You almost got us killed! Prick!"

Sierra told me to drive past the city limits and into the desert. A dusty fog left by car tires smudged the clear night.

About a mile into the desert she told me to slow down.

"Stop," she said.

Angrily, I slammed the brakes. Sierra landed on the floor. Just as I was about to bolt out the door, Sierra sprang up and fired the gun. The bullet blew another hole in my car roof.

I shook and gripped the steering wheel.

"You did that on purpose!" Sierra said.

I wanted to strangle her but I didn't dare look back, say anything or make any sudden moves. There were goose bumps on my goose bumps.

"Turn the motor off. Now! I mean it," she said. "The lights, too."

The motor, then the lights went off. It got quiet for a few seconds, the dust settled.

"Get out," she said.

As I got out of the car, I thought that I was going to die. She was going to shoot me in the head. But I wondered where were the flashbacks? Where were the near-death haunts to early childhood days, faces of dead relatives, the regrets and the longing to say goodbye to loved ones?

None of that was rummaging through my mind as I stood in front of the car hood. She ordered me to step back. She turned on the headlights. The brightness assaulted my eyes. I squinted and didn't move.

I took a few steps back, lowered my head slightly and put my hand over my eyes to adjust to the bright light.

Sierra took a deep breath, probably mulling over whether to kill me now and quickly drive away or play some sick little, cat-and-mouse head game before she pulled the trigger.

Silence, a long silence. I could hear my heart pounding.

Sierra stood beside the car. Her hoodie was down, and her arms stretched outward as she gripped the gun with both hands. She looked down and around.

"Are there rattlesnakes out here?"

I couldn't believe what she asked but I calmly replied to try and defuse the situation.

"Yeah. They come out at night to eat rats," I said as calmly as I could.

As soon as I said that, the car lights went off. I swallowed hard. I was about to bolt but my feet were chained to the desert floor by fear. Then, she asked this strange question.

"Who killed my brother?"

Stunned, I replied, "Who killed your brother?"

"Yeah."

"How in the hell would I know?" I said raising my voice.

"Your sources, some of them are cops. They know."

"They don't know a damn thing. Neither do I."

She fired straight up in the air. Startled, I threw my shoulders up.

"This isn't a game!" she screamed.

"Relax, okay, just relax."

Sierra took a few steps toward me, perhaps to get a better aim. I closed my eyes, again, tightened by body and waited.

Her breathing picked up, and she began to sob, sobbing loud.

"My brother is dead," she said.

"I'm sorry," I said. "Are you okay?"

"No," she said.

"Put the gun down. Just put it down. We'll talk."

"Those bastards killed my brother."

I swallowed hard. My heart pounded. I stretched out my hand.

"Please. Give me the gun. Let's talk," I said in a soft voice.

She took a few steps and handed me the gun. I snatched it from her hand. Tossed the weapon and wrapped my arms around her tightly. She screamed. We tumbled on the ground. I pinned her down while her screams clawed my eardrums.

"Shut up!" I said. "Just shut up!"

"Let go of me."

"I should just squeeze your neck until your evil, little eyes pop out and take a shovel and bury your dumb ass out here."

"Get off me," she said, pushing my chest. "Get off!"

I got up, swore, found the gun, threw it further into the desert, and briskly walked to the car.

"I hope the snakes bit your ass," I said.

Frightened about being left behind in a desolate place, she jumped up and followed. I started the car, she hopped inside, and I sped away.

"You open your mouth, and I swear, I'll toss you out of the car," I said.

"Just drive," she said, and muttered a curse word.

She turned on the radio as though nothing had happened and raised the volume.

The car raced through the desert, kicking up clouds of dust. I kept swearing. Sierra and I bounced on the seat as we hit clumps of sand and rock along the way.

We said nothing. The car finally left the desert road and got back on Interstate 10. We drove ten minutes on the highway. She kept staring out the side window, wiping the tears with the palm of her hand, still sobbing. Sierra turned off the radio and let out an annoying huff.

"Turn the radio on," I said. "I don't want to hear your bullshit or brat whining."

She turned on the radio and immediately, and turned it back off.

"I know things," she said. "I can help you."

"You don't know shit."

"I do."

"About what?"

"Who visited my father and talked to him. Faces, names, places. I've got names," she said. "So you need me, asshole. Got it, you need me."

It got quiet for a few seconds before I pulled the car off the freeway and drove into an alley behind a lamp manufacturing company surrounded with a high razor fence. My car faced the side of a railroad boxcar two blocks away. I turned off the engine.

"I'm listening."

"That scum bag in Marfa with a badge. He's heavily involved in drug trafficking," she said.

"Prove it." I said.

"Tell me who they suspect killed my brother, and I'll tell you how I know. Drop me off downtown near the museum."

The ride seemed too long and too quiet but I saw the moment as an opportunity to try and pump her for information.

"Did your father do business with the sheriff?"

"Yeah."

"How? When?"

"My father kept notes. He hid them. I found some. You have sources. I don't. Sources at the DEA, on the streets and on the other side of the border. They tell you things. I know that. I read the stories you wrote about my father. Your sources are solid."

"I don't know who killed your brother or why?"

"But you will know, and when you find out, I want to know. You help me. I help you."

"I need to see what you have."

I stopped the car. She got out.

"Talk to your people. Your sources or whoever you talk to. I'll be in touch soon," she said.

"When?"

"Soon," she said and closed the door. "I'll call you."

"Wait."

She ignored me.

I watched her get into her car, a block away and drive off, thinking that I was now in an unholy alliance with a she-devil. She probably wouldn't hesitate to snuff out my life if she felt I was no longer any use to her.

CHAPTER 16

Tommy Rubio was late.

The morning air was crisp at Concordia Cemetery, an old graveyard beside a busy street. I waited there for him. I had met him there a few other times so there must be a good reason why he wasn't on time.

Tommy, an undercover cop, who knew the drug scene, was a listening post on the streets. He could rattle the names of drug dealers, pimps, prostitutes, gangsters, street thugs and other assorted vermin.

He was a good source who was solid.

I wanted to ask him about Emilio's death and what he's heard on the streets. But the more I waited, the more impatient I got.

Where in the hell is Tommy? I wondered.

A river of iron-grey clouds kept the sunlight thin, hazy. Birds bickered nosily over choice tree limbs.

Tommy was a tough cop who had a reputation on the streets for meting out "thump therapy" as he described it to suspects who gave him lip or thought they could outrun him.

"I am the Lion King, and I tune people up," he'd say.

His cop tactics had racked up a lot of enemies. There were also other cops who didn't like him. Some of his former girlfriends who preferred that he simply drop dead.

Tommy was an intimidating tank-of-a-man who was not quite six-feet tall. His hawkish eyes crowned a pronounced jaw line. Powerful forearms and granite shoulders gave away the time he spent at the gym sweating and moving metal.

The top of his left pinkie was missing and spoke of his days with Army Special Forces. Tommy Rubio and his Green Beret pals were sent to Iraq and dropped off in the middle of the desert behind enemy lines. They went on a secret mission to gather intelligence, destroy targets and prepare for the U.S.-led invasion.

Before the Iraq War, there had been other secret missions to Haiti, Panama and Afghanistan and other Third-World countries.

He spoke about these incursions on a few occasions. Once he mentioned something I found disturbing about captured prisoners of war.

"They're like extra luggage when you're on a mission, so you lighten the load," he said. "Nobody is going to pull out a claim ticket on a dead terrorist."

I never asked him to elaborate. I didn't want to find out whether these were war stories or whether he was a cold-blood murderer.

Occasionally, Tommy and I would meet at the edge of Concordia Cemetery where the headstones dated back decades, some to the early 1900s. The cemetery ran out of places to bury people, so there weren't many funerals held there anymore. Weighty ivy was draped on a high chain-link fence that surrounded the cemetery. The made the graveyard a perfect place to meet a maverick cop like Tommy Rubio.

I glanced into the rearview mirror. No Tommy.

I was about to leave when a man lazily walked toward my direction. He caught my eye. He was quite a distance away and near the entrance of the cemetery.

The lanky man with small shoulders slightly pinned back had a swagger. He wore a white construction hard hat, grey work pants and a green, checkered shirt, hugging something inside a paper bag close tucked underneath his armpit.

My eyes scanned a row of marble grave markers. A bird flew onto a flat headstone, hopped across it, chirped and flung itself toward some elm trees.

I glanced up again at the rearview mirror. The man was getting closer, still walking in my direction.

He zigzagged through some headstones and got on the small cemetery dirt road. He picked up the pace as he walked toward me. I surmised that he was going to visit a dead relative or was heading home from his job and taking a shortcut home.

As he came closer, I adjusted my rearview mirror.

My gut feeling told me not to let this guy out of my sight, not for a second. The bad vibes I got paid off. Out of nowhere, he whipped out a gun from the brown, paper bag, stretched out his arm, and pointed the weapon at me. He had a sinister grin on his face under a thick mustache.

His eyes hid behind dark sunglasses.

He fired the gun, once, twice, and a third time. The back windshield shattered and another shot tore into metal. He fired again. A bullet went through the car and went through the front windshield.

Shaking, I ducked and tried to turn on the ignition. The car keys fell on the floor. I swept the floor with my hand, found them, and tried again to start the car.

Another bullet shattered the passenger-side mirror. Glass fragments showered the inside of the car.

I started the engine and put the car in gear and the gears jammed.

I couldn't go straight because of the high gravestones in front of me. I put the car in reverse when he was just fifty yards away.

I heard the armed stranger laughing, troubling laughter, and evil laughter. He saw the top of my head and fired.

I ducked.

The shot zinged near my head. I threw open the driver's door, lowered my body, poked my head out of the side of the car and put my foot onto the gas pedal.

I yanked on the gearshift as hard as I could. The tires finally spun. The car sped in reverse. A grayish-white spray of burning rubber mixed with dirt hit my face.

The car ran over several flat headstones on the side of the road, scraping the undercarriage of the vehicle and causing my head jerk up.

The gunman fired and jumped out of the way, but not before the car clipped his leg and sent him spinning in the air. He landed hard on the ground and moaned. He cursed, staggered up and looked for the gun that had been knocked out of his hand by the impact.

I slammed the brakes on the car and sat ramrod straight.

We made eye contact. His face was full of rage, torment. He limped while searching for the gun. I put the car into drive. I tore out of the cemetery into the street, nearly causing an accident with a motorist who slammed on his brakes and swerved to avoid hitting my car.

I heard two more gunshots as I fishtailed the car out of there.

CHAPTER 17

I sat at a booth at Rodrigo's restaurant, gulping down a beer and trying to shake off the jolt of terror that had just ravished my body. A cut on the back of my hand bled. The flying bits of glass caused by the gunfire cut my hand when I reached for the car keys.

Dana brought me another beer. I started gulping it down.

"Slow down," she said softly.

I licked my wound.

"What did you expect? You're dealing with extremely violent and crazy animals," she said, sounding like a cranky mom scolding a 5-year-old.

"What do you want me to do? I'm not backing down." I said. "Never."

"Sure, go ahead. End up at the morgue."

"That's my job to ask questions, poke around and piss people off."

"You have the pissing-people-off-thing down to a science."

Dana sat across the table while I finished the beer. The shaking began to subside. Thanks to the alcohol.

"Did you call the cops?" she said.

"To tell them what?" I whispered. "That I was there to meet one of their undercover cops who tells me what goes on in the streets along with all the illegal and unethical shit that goes on at the police department?"

Dana raised her eyebrows high and smirked.

"What?" I said.

"Well, on the bright side, your car's got year-around air conditioning." She giggled.

"This is a joke to you? I almost left my brains on somebody's headstone, and you find humor in it?"

"Since, I've known you, I've learned to put everything you do into two categories, crazy and insane. But there is a third category after today: mind-boggling insanity."

"Thanks for the pep talk," I said and forced a smile.

"You're welcome," she chimed and ambled away.

Halfway through the third beer, I eased into the alcohol-induced calm. The shakes had subsided. Still, I was angry, upset that Tommy Rubio didn't show up. He could have fired back at the gunman.

His cell phone was either off or he wasn't answering it. I checked my cell phone. There was a text message from Tommy. It stated: "Sidetracked, sorry. Got picked at the last minute to do security for the president."

The President of the United States was in El Paso on a brief visit to talk about the perils of drug smuggling along the Mexican border. The President would be stopping for a photo-opt at the El Paso Intelligence Center, a large agency run by the DEA and U.S. Customs that is located within a military base.

I asked Dana to click on the television.

We watched the news coverage of the President. He was telling the country about the drug problem in Mexico, and how Mexican authorities were clamping down on the drug lords. We were not impressed by his speech.

"This is going to make a huge dent on the war on drugs," she said in a cynical tone. "A pep rally and photo op."

Dana turned her head and looked right at me, suspicious eyes sitting on awkward silence. She knew I was going to say something unpleasant.

"What?" she said bluntly.

I didn't disappoint her.

"I need a favor."

"What?" she said.

"I need to borrow your car. Just 'til I fix mine," I pleaded.

"No way," she said. "I need it for school, and I'm teaching aerobics classes. And, I just got it painted. So I don't want bullet holes on it."

I brushed off her snide remark and resorted to begging.

"Please, just for two days until I get my car back," I said and held up two fingers. "Two days. Just two. Please, I'm desperate. Please, do me that favor."

"Absolutely not. I got to go to library in a few hours. Finals are next week. There's no way in hell. So just forget it. No, Jack."

CHAPTER 18

The inside of Dana's car smelled like mint julep when I opened the door. The black leather seats and dashboard were spotless. The expensive speaker system sounded crystal clear when I turned it up. Not one smudge throughout the car. No window streaks or a piece of paper or lint on the floor. It had been waxed, polished hard. The new paint job looked like glass.

Nice.

As I drove it, I was convinced that Dana was this obsessive-compulsive basket case, a squeaky-clean freak who probably had arranged the Campbell's soup cans inside her pantry in alphabetical order.

A sneeze snuck up on me. I hurriedly rolled the window down, stuck my head out, and let out a violent expulsion of air. There was no way that I was going to spray the dashboard and windshield.

Before I left the restaurant, I walked outside and two blocks down to a pay phone near a drugstore where I called Tommy Rubio. He didn't pick up. I left him a message, deeply disguising my voice: "Meet me at six. Be there at five. One is up."

A few minutes later he texted from an untraceable cell phone: "10-4." He got my message.

The text messages between Tommy and me had numbers, numbers only he and I understood. The meaning of the numbers was often changed. It was simple and left no electronic footprint in case there was ever an investigation on who was leaking information to the media.

Meeting at six meant the place would be at Album Park on the eastside of town. There were ten locations in all, which we numerically shuffled around from time to time, depending on the day of the week.

Five meant 5 p.m.; subtract three, always three hours. So we'd be meeting at 2 p.m. One is up meant that it was urgent. Two up meant that we just needed to talk. Three was recreation time. We would then hook up at a certain location, a set time, and sometimes at this bar near the New Mexican border. There we'd shoot pool and drink beers. Tommy would fill me in on the latest comings and goings on in the streets.

He would often change the numbers in case somebody figured it out. He'd type the new codes on a piece of paper and give them to me. Also I used a prepaid cell phone when I talked to Tommy or some of my other sources. I knew that law enforcement always subpoena phone records during an investigation.

Tommy was a great source, always reliable, always careful and cunning.

One day, his superiors suspected that someone was giving me inside information. They suspected Tommy. They tailed him. It was an exercise in futility. Tommy could spot a tail a mile away and lose it in an instant. He had schooled me on what he knew like the best way to lose a tail or how to do surveillance without being spotted. I was a grateful student, hanging on his every word as though he was a Harvard professor.

Before meeting Tommy, I drove to the newsroom, booted my computer and did some Internet searches. The place was a mad house. Everybody was banging the computer keys, writing the-President-is-in-town stories. Phones rang often and hard.

Reporters were making last minute calls. Editors were demanding stories. The deadline gods needed to be appeased. I could sense by the glares of a couple of reporters when I walked into the newsroom that they were not happy that I didn't have to be part of the pool of newsroom journalists who were assigned to cover the president.

I didn't care whose feathers I ruffled. I was determined to take this story as far as I was able.

As I checked my email, one caught my eye. It was from Maxon's Funeral Home. I thought it was spam but decided to open it when it listed my name, Mr. Jack Fuentes along with my mother's maiden name, Carrillo, on the subject box.

That was a bit of information that very few people had, very few.

The email stated that a loved one had submitted my name for a preplanned funeral, inviting me to call the funeral planner.

Blood rushed to my head. Who would do this? A friend pulling a cruel practical joke? Dana wouldn't do this. None of my friends would, and I couldn't think of any one of my enemies who would stoop at pulling a high school prank like this.

I called the funeral salesman, and spoke to a guy named Rodney. He didn't know who had suggested that I might want to know the details about preplanning my funeral.

"We have brochures here explaining our pre-planned services in our office, people are free to take one, fill them out and mail them back with contact information," said Rodney.

He put me on hold so he could check out who filled the preplanned funeral card. Five minutes later, he came back.

"Sir?" he said.

"Yeah."

"The signature is printed with large letters."

"Letters?"

"Yeah. R-I-P-M-F."

I softly said, "rest in peace, motherfucker."

"What?"

"Never mind. Take my name off your mailing list."

"Yes, sir. I apologize for the inconvenience. But if the need arises—"

I hung up before he could finish his sales pitch. My face was white. Someone patted me on the back. I twitched, looked up and over my shoulder. It was C.J., quietly standing behind me. I was irritated.

"Are you planning an early departure?" he said.

I ignored his question. His eyes were on my computer screen. C.J. read my e-mail, probably heard my conversation with Rodney.

"Why are you sneaking around and reading shit on my screen?" I asked.

"I'm not. But I'm curious. Why would you be shopping for a funeral?" he said. "Just in case somebody wants to punch your ticket?"

"I'm not," I said, deleting the email. "It's some sick prick's idea of a joke."

C.J used his head to point toward Ricardo's office.

"I got bad news. This is straight from the corner office. Ricardo said, 'you've got three weeks to work on this project. Then, you're back on the assembly line like the rest of the reporters, pumping out dailies."

"He gave me four weeks," I said, holding up four fingers.

"Changed his mind."

"Are you serious?"

"Yeah, I'm, serious," said C.J.

"Can't you talk to him? This story has legs. It's big. It takes time to gather the facts. Nobody is going to dump them on my lap. Talk to Ricardo, tell him I need more time."

"It's a waste of my time," said C.J. "He'll just say that advertising revenue is down, and we just lost twenty-three employees, five of them were reporters. We don't have the luxury any more to give remaining reporters weeks to work on investigative pieces."

"I know the box score. He doesn't have to tell me that. I got the memo," I said with a raised voice. "That's the one with the corporate quote, 'necessary action to realign our operation' unquote. Total bullshit. Cut managerial salaries and bonuses, cut managerial perks. How can you call yourself a newspaper and let five reporters go when we've already down to the bare bones? It's crazy."

I took off my glasses and flung them on my desk in frustration. Bored, C.J. glanced at his watch.

"Are you done preaching to the choir, Billy Graham?" he said. "I've got an editors' meeting in about five minutes."

I tightened my jaw as C.J. headed for the conference room to discuss what stories would make tomorrow's front page, and probably how to shuffle around the news beat coverage.

As I scrolled down my email list, I glared toward Ricardo's corner office. His office door opened he walked out and headed to the conference room where C.J. and the other editors were waiting.

Smiling, Ricardo greeted everyone inside and closed the door.

"Asshole," I muttered.

CHAPTER 19

With my brain on overload, I desperately needed to talk to Tommy Rubio. He'd know the latest rumors and *chisme* on the streets. Did Tommy have a hunch, even a slight inkling on who shot at me? Who might want me dead? Did somebody want to punch my ticket?

If Tommy didn't know, he might point me in the right direction.

Stress was taking its toll; I looked over my shoulder more often. I waited for Tommy, parking Dana's car beneath a tree at an eastside park facing the park entrances. It was 1:50 p.m.

I took quick peeps at the rear view and the side mirrors of the car, hoping another gunman wouldn't appear and finish what the first one he started.

My thumb repeatedly hit the top of the steering wheel. I adjusted and readjusted the rearview mirror. I started humming, occasionally glancing to my right and then left.

A handful of children played on a slide and swings at the far edge of the park. Parents sat on park benches near a baby stroller and gabbed with each other.

Tommy Rubio always said to never do business near dogs or children. Dogs bark, and children notice strangers sitting in a car, often pointing in their direction or walking up to them.

A lone male at the park sometimes raised suspicions among alert moms with cell phones.

Tommy arrived in a six-year-old green Chevy truck with big tires. He drove slowly until he realized it was I inside someone else's car. He waved. I walked outside the car with a sack full of fast-food fries and a hamburger, clutching a soda.

As I walked toward a park table, I met Tommy halfway there. We shook hands and talked briefly about the heat.

I put the fast food and soda on the table, and Tommy put a chessboard on it. The chessboard was camouflage. When we first met, we'd use it mostly as props to ease the apprehensions of anyone who might be watching.

Tommy, whose hair was in a ponytail, stroked his goatee. Without asking, he lifted some of my fries, laid them on a napkin and emptied a packet of ketchup on them. He licked his fingers and then set up the chess pieces.

"Want half my burger?" I asked.

"No, just some fries," he said.

While Tommy laid the chess pieces on the board, he occasionally scanned the park. I felt better being with someone who was accustomed to looking over his shoulder every so often, someone with a badge who also carried a concealed gun holstered above his ankle. Tommy almost always hid his eyes behind some dark sunglasses, always poking, probing and getting a read on a person's body language.

"So what's up?" he asked.

I took some gulps from my drink and leaned forward a bit and told him what happened at the cemetery, giving him all the little fine points. He took off his sunglasses putting them beside the chessboard.

"Wow," he said. "Damn. Did you get a good look at the gunman?"

"I couldn't identify him. I was focused on getting the hell out of there."

"Are you okay?"

I nodded.

"Did you call the cops?"

"Are you kidding? What would I tell them I was doing in the graveyard? Waiting for you to show up?

"You weren't tailed were you?"

"No. I did what you told me to shake off surveillance."

"Good."

He looked over at Dana's car, gave it a once over.

"Whose ride?"

"Dana. She let me borrow it," I said.

"The waitress at Rodrigo's?" he said.

"Yeah," I replied. "My car is in the shop. They're patching up the bullet holes and replacing the windshield."

Tommy loaded his mouth with fries.

"Who'd want to bust a cap on your ass?"

"Off the top of my head, a dozen or so people. Probably, drug dealers. That's why I'm here. Can you shake down some of your sources for some information?"

"Yeah, no problem. I'll ask around. But since Mickey died a lot of people have clammed up. There are some dark days ahead."

"Yeah, I know."

We continued playing the game. Tommy made five moves on the chessboard and it was over.

"Checkmate," he said, then proceeded to rub it in. "And in record time, too. Stick to pool halls."

I ignored his remark as he reached over and helped himself to more fries. I wasn't in the mood for games. I steered our conversation to the death of Emilio and the way he was killed.

"It seemed to have the earmark of Colombian hit?"

"Naw. Colombians aren't dime-store cowboys. That was the work of an amateur bomb maker who's sloppy and stupid. A pro, a heavy-hitter, would have shot him in the head and left town before his body dropped to the ground."

Tommy put some more fries in his mouth and glanced at his phone.

"It's the work of some mid-level mental midget who probably works for low-level drug dealers."

"Why would they kill Emilio?"

"The Madrid drug empire. Rumor has it that Emilio got the keys to Mickey's narco kingdom."

Tommy set up the chessboard again and quickly cornered my queen. Game over. My concentration was worse than our first game, and I could have been playing Tic-Tac-Toe. It didn't matter. I wasn't even trying to win.

"That move," he said. "That is a classic, Ruy Lopez. That medieval chess master had a pair of balls when he played the game. He quickly destroyed his opponents."

"He's your hero, huh? You've studied all of his chess moves."

"Ruy Lopez was brilliant," he said. "The guy was pure mental finesse. He would have been a good cop, a detective, methodical and clairvoyant, staying two or three moves ahead of the competition."

He said Andy, an army sniper, told him about the medieval chess master.

"Andy also was a top-notch chess player. He won a high school state chess tournament."

Tommy once bragged about Andy's accuracy with a sniper's rife when he found a target.

"He could get a head shot from a thousand yards," Tommy said. "If he had you in his crosshairs, you're dead."

Tommy said his friend once waited for a target to finish having lunch and described what happened.

"This rag head was sitting on a large rock eating a goat sandwich or something, and Andy waited until the guy finished eating and took a piss before sending him to Allah heaven to be with his virgins," said Tommy. "I thought it was a nice gesture, dispatching him to Allah with a full stomach and an empty bladder. Andy was so considerate."

Tommy said Andy had a nickname in the Special Forces unit.

"Everybody called him Numbers," Tommy said. "Andy loved doing mental gymnastics, solving algebraic equations. It helped him relax and concentrate when he took his kill shots."

Andy's father was a guy named Charles Foxman, a high-powered architect who designed a lot of the building in Chicago, Tommy said.

"Andy wanted to be an engineer, and he had corporate connections. His uncle Gregory Foxman was an executive at Hewlett Packard in Seattle," said Tommy. "Andy said to look him up after I was discharged. His uncle knew all the suits at Hewlett Packard."

"You ever call Andy's uncle?"

"I don't want a desk job, and the last time I spoke to Andy, he was offering his sniping skills to a mercenary group. I heard he plied his skills in Somalia and Yemen or some other African shithole. We had brief stints in Iraq, Panama, Malaysia and some desert villages in Afghanistan that aren't even on the map yet."

"A lot of war stories," I said.

"It was a job. One adrenaline rush after another. Once, we watched a group of Taliban fighters going into a cave," he said.

"Pointed the laser at the cave and watched a hell-fire rocket from a drone make its way inside the cave and spoil their day. Andy then picked off a couple of rag heads that staggered out of the cave."

After we finished another game and talked briefly about who was being promoted and demoted at the cop station, we parted ways.

CHAPTER 20

I sat up in bed gasping for air and sweating. The nightmare was all too real. In the reoccurring dream, a gunman kicks open the front door to my house. He blasted away with an assault rifle. As I bolt out the door, he keeps firing and chasing me down the block.

In the dream, I keep looking over my shoulder as I run on a dirt road and into a cemetery, passing graveyard headstones. The gunman is closing the distance fast. Keeps firing.

There was nowhere to hide. I keep running. He keeps firing. I rounded the corner, cross the street and dash behind a building. There he is, standing a few yards away. He lifts his rifle to shoot, I try to yell but no words came out of my mouth. I can't run.

Each time, I'd wake up my heart thumped. I wait until it slowed down before I'd roll out of bed

One night, I was shaken from the nightmare at 4:30 a.m. The cell phone's ring-tone woke me up. I grabbed the phone. It was an unfamiliar number.

I cursed at the cell phone and poked the green on-button.

"What?" I said.

"Jack."

It was Sierra, and I was now in a grumpy mood but grateful that the nightmare was over.

"Yeah?"

"I found some things."

"It's 4:30."

"I know. It's good stuff."

"What did you find?"

"Old newspaper clippings. I found them in my father's safe."

"You call at 4:30 to tell me that you found old newspaper stories?"

"I found them with notes clipped to them."

My interest peaked.

"Notes from who?"

"My father. Yeah. The stories are about Sheriff Rick's tax problems with the IRS?" she said. "And that's not all."

Hurriedly, I cut her off, "Wait. Wait. Just wait. Don't say anything. Not another word."

"Why?"

"The phone. It might be tapped."

"Are you serious?"

"Yeah, I'll tell you about it later."

We agreed to meet at a shopping mall parking lot near the interstate at 9 a.m.

I hung up.

I drove into the mall parking lot just before the stores opened and quickly made some mental notes. How many cars were already parked there? Who looked out of place?

I left the parking lot and drove slowly around nearby streets looking for vans or people sitting in parked cars. I took some side streets, and went through alleys to make sure I didn't have a tail. Then, I stopped my car a block from the mall and waited for a while.

Then I retraced the streets and alleys that I had just driven through, making sure the same vehicles I had seen were still there.

Tommy Rubio taught me to do this. He taught me well.

I kept looking in the rear-view mirror. Since the cemetery ambush, the rear-view mirror and I had become best buddies.

I couldn't rule out that Sierra might be setting me up and was behind the cemetery shooting. She had a strong motive to kill me.

I wrote down a few license plate numbers of cars in the parking lot, studied some faces, including a man reading a newspaper while sitting behind the steering wheel.

None gave me any good reason to worry. But my eyes and ears worked overtime feeding my antsy brain.

Fifteen minutes after I got to the mall, Sierra showed up.

I stuck out my hand and waved. She spotted Dana's Honda, one of only a dozen early-morning cars in the parking lot. I turned my headlights off and on. She parked next to me and rolled down the window. She wore a sports cap over a ponytail and trendy white-framed sunglasses.

She got into the Honda, looked around, and immediately came to the same conclusion about the car's mint julep smell and its squeaky-clean interior as I had.

"Who's car?" she said.

"A friend."

"It's smells like peppermint or something," she said and looked in the backseat. "You could take out somebody's appendix in the backseat?"

"My friend, she hates smudges. Smudges, grime and thumbprints. When a thumbprint or smudge appears on shiny surfaces, she wipes them off right away. You should see her apartment."

"Pass," Sierra said as her eyes scanned the car roof. "Is she on meds to control her obsessive compulsive disorder?"

"She's a nice lady, alright. She let me borrow her car."

Sierra opened the glove compartment and quickly closed it to satisfy her curiosity.

"Where's your wreck?"

"In the shop, getting body work done. So where are the newspaper clippings and notes?"

She dug into her purse, took out an old envelope and handed it to me. It had old newspaper clippings and some scrawling on a fading piece of yellow paper with thin blue lines. The newspaper article had notes clipped onto it.

The stories were written by a reporter named Andrew Lockhard, and were about Rick Ward. They were published in 1972, when I was still in grade school. Ward was a sheriff's deputy and was in trouble with the Internal Revenue Service. He owed back taxes for 1969, 1970, and 1971, and they were threatening to take his small ranch. He owed $38,000.

The feds had put a lien on his property. Lockhard did his homework and apparently interviewed Ward for his story. Ward blamed his accountant and said he'd pay the debt by borrowing money from relatives.

I read the note that had words scrawled with a pencil: <u>Para San Pedro.</u> The amount of $50,000 was circled. Nothing else.

"Who's San Pedro? A charity?" I asked.

"I guess it's a nickname for a person."

"Why do you say that?"

"My father once told Bazooka that San Pedro was running out of fish and needed more bait, worms."

"What did he say, exactly?"

"*San Pedrito quiere mas gusanitos.*"

As soon as she said that, images flooded my mind, images of fish and fishing poles and fishing trophies that were scattered throughout Sheriff Rick Ward's office.

I held the newspaper clippings and the note and knew it was the first link connecting Mickey Madrid and Rick Ward.

These were gold nuggets. Hunches, a note and newspaper clippings still proved nothing other than it allegedly belonged to Mickey Madrid.

"Something wrong?" Sierra asked.

"Huh?" I said, raising my head. "Oh, no."

She seemed to know, however, that the note and newspaper story had unlocked a door, maybe, a big one. She was right but I had to dig some more. I had a long way to go.

"I'm leaving. I'll call you later," I said.

"When?"

"Soon."

I left, called the office and spoke to C.J.

I asked him to go to the copy desk and quiz some of the older copy editors, ask if they remember a cop reporter by the name of Andrew Lockhard. I told him I needed to find Lockhard in a big hurry.

"If someone knows where the guy is at, get me an address and phone number. Check the stories this guy wrote when he worked in El Paso."

"Something big?" he asked.

"Yeah. I'll tell you about it later. I need to find him."

Twenty minutes later, I got my call returned.

"Lockhard also interviewed Ward about a mysterious death in his jail in Marfa that was ruled a suicide," C.J. said. "There were two old stories about the jail death. It didn't go anywhere."

He said there were a couple of stories about sheriff's problems with the IRS. Ward was then an up and coming deputy who had made a name for himself by being involved in a gunfight with two robbers, killing one.

"Where does Lockhard live?"

"In a monastery."

"What?"

"He was living in a monastery in New Mexico. The Benedictine Monastery in Pecos, New Mexico. It's a five-hour ride, one way. He's probably still there."

"Are you serious?"

"Yeah, that's what I found out."

CHAPTER 21

I woke up at dawn the next day, took a quick shower and drove off to find Andrew Lockhard. It was going to be a long day, a hot day.

After nearly five hours on the road, past miles of New Mexican mesas, mountains, ridge tops and rugged deserts, I found myself tapping on the office door of Abbot Alexander at the Benedictine Monastery in Pecos, New Mexico.

It's nestled next to the Pecos River in a mountain range that is 25 miles east of Santa Fe. It's a place where monks and nuns live simple lives and make delicious bread to sell and spend countless hours in prayer, meditation, solitude and silence.

It would be the last place I would expect to find a former and aging newspaper reporter who once owned a Harley and had a reputation for getting into political squabbles and fist fights at downtown bars. Reporters said he was a drunk and known for the ass-chewings meted out to young reporters when he was hung-over.

Andrew Lockhard was now resigned to a life of 24-7 prayer, peace and solitude.

He had exchanged this numbing quiet for a place that never seems to sleep, tire or run out of breath, where the constant pecking of computer keys rivals the continuous squawking of a police radio, where rows of overworked computers sit atop cluttered desks. He left behind a deadline factory that makes constant demands and where sentences are bent, reshaped and polished so they can fit in tight spaces on newspapers.

Andrew Lockhard found a niche of paradise on earth.

As I scanned the beautiful surroundings, in an odd moment, I wondered if God ever took a break from listening to the endless fluttering of lips, billions of problems, and the constant pelting of prayers.

The monastery seemed to be void of evil and wicked men.

I tapped on the thick oak door harder.

Footsteps approached, and a man with frail gray, curly hair, and large, light-green eyes opened the door.

"Welcome my friend," he said. "May I help you?"

He offered a calm demeanor, smiled and extended a smooth hand. I shook it.

"Yeah, father. Uh, my name is Jack Fuentes. I'm looking for a monk by the name of Brother Andrew Lockhard."

He grinned, a relaxed grin.

"Well, first of all, I'm not a priest. I am the Superior of the monastery," he said. "I'm the Abbot of the monastery. Abbot Alexander."

"Sorry, I, uh —"

"Oh, no, no problem. Visitors always seem to be promoting me," he said. "Are you related to Brother Andrew?"

"No, he worked in El Paso at the newspaper. I work there now, and I want to talk to him about a story he wrote years ago."

I explained to the abbot that I had driven all the way from El Paso just to talk to Brother Andrew.

"The story was about a sheriff in Marfa, Texas, and I need to ask him about it," I said.

"He left all that, the writing and editing, years ago. He's serving God, now," said Abbot Alexander. "He works for the Lord."

"I know that. But it's important. I drove a long way just to see him. I'll only need a few minutes of his time. That's all."

The Abbot sensed the desperation in my voice.

"Wait here," he said. "If he's not in prayer, I'll see what I can do."

"I appreciate it. Could you tell him that I've got a deadline? He'd understand."

The abbot lowered his eyebrows, paused for a moment and left. I sat on a bench near the hallway, underneath a painting with soft, thick strokes, of the Virgin Mary, smiling and holding up a plump and happy Baby Jesus.

Minutes later, a robust nun walked into the room with a large glass of cold lemonade and a plate with half a loaf of bread along with two thick slices of butter. On the plate was a butter knife.

She eased into smile and urged me to try some of the bread.

"The abbot said you might be a little hungry after the long drive up here," she said. "I think you will like our bread. We make it here and sell it to the community."

"Thank you."

She left as I broke the bread, put a square of butter on it, and sank my teeth into it. It was so delicious. While I chewed, I could hear a lone hard breath of wind outside barely shaking some oak trees and sending a flock of birds flinging themselves into the sky.

I doubted if Brother Andrew missed the newsroom.

The silence in the room was interrupted from the clanging of the plate as I put the knife down after spreading more butter on another slice of bread. I was hungry.

In the corner, Christ hung on a wooden cross on the wall next to the hallway, beside a perfectly square window that framed the red hills and brush-stroked hazy clouds.

154

It was nice to chew some heaven-made bread and look out the window, if only for a few minutes.

Footsteps approached from a long, dim hallway. I turned my head and saw a tall man donning a flowing garb walking toward me, a slow, purposeful pace. Bright light from an arched window in the distance and at the end of the hallway, reduced this person's being to a large flowing, moth-like shadow.

When he stepped into the light in the room, his pecan-colored hair shined and looked like a hairy reef around a balding spot. His hooded, brown Monk's robe with his large sleeves highlighted his ruddy face and thin, graying beard.

A jovial Brother Andrew smiled. He stuck out his bony hands and wrapped them around my hand and shook it.

"Welcome to our humble home, Jack," he said.

"Thank you."

He had apparently shed the suspicion and caution of years of working as a reporter and editor. He was friendly. The jaded negativity that comes from years of working in a newsroom was gone from his eyes.

We had a lively conversation, chatting about El Paso and all the haunts. He even knew the reporters favorite watering holes, some were long gone and others barely surviving. They had been replaced by new, hot spots that attracted younger crowds, mostly college students.

It was getting harder to believe. Brother Andrew, who was fifty-something, had once been a part of the newsroom brethren, the few, the proud, the lame. I wondered how he exorcised the newsroom demons? I was convinced that his religious conversion was nothing short of Lazarus being raised from the dead.

After swapping a few more names and newsroom stories, he invited me to go outside for a stroll.

"The beauty of the day should never be wasted indoors," he said.

We casually walked down a sidewalk alongside some of the buildings. We went across a small field and into a cluster of pine trees within a stone's throw from the abbot's office. We sat at one of the oak tables next to the overpowering shadows of tall eucalyptus trees.

As soon I sat down, I asked, "How did you end up here?"

He smiled and cast his eyes down, staring briefly at the ground to gather his thoughts.

"Years ago, I was a broken-down alcoholic with a motorcycle, living in a newsroom. I rode my bike to escape the deadlines, the rat race and quite frankly, to run away from myself," he said.

"You decided to be a monk?"

"No, I had no clue what a monk was or what they did. I didn't even know this place existed. One day, I hopped on my bike and rode through the back roads. I smelled the bread lingering in the air as I went by here and stopped. I became friends with the abbot. I left but kept coming back. I decided this is what I wanted. I became a monk, and here I am. I plan to die here." He waved a finger across the pine trees, the hills and the mountain.

"All this beauty. It's simply frosting on the cake," he said.

"No second thoughts?"

"At first, oh yeah, plenty. I thought, maybe, I made a big mistake. Hated it. As the days slipped by, and the years followed, this is home. This is my spot in the world. I was fortunate to find it before alcohol robbed me of my life, my zest."

"Did you know that only one or two people in the newsroom know you're here?"

Andrew laughed. "I kept that a secret, for the most part. And, sad to say, I've forgotten most of the stories I wrote."

"Mickey Madrid. Do you remember interviewing him?"

He took a long breath, folded his hands and put them on top of the table.

"The hair on the back of my neck still stands up when his name comes up. He inflicted so much pain and suffering on others."

"Well, he's dead. Died recently from a two-pack-a-day habit, cancer."

"Sad."

"Actually, it depends on who you ask."

"He did, for the record, do a lot of things for the poor. Good things. Schools. Houses. Soccer fields. A hospital in Chihuahua."

"Never heard that."

"He never said much about it," he said. "May God have mercy on his soul."

"I interviewed him just before he died. He said something about a Chihuahua Charlie. Did that ever come up in any of your stories? Chihuahua Charlie, that name?"

He became pensive before shaking his head.

"No, I can't say that it did," he said. "Is it a person? Code words? What?"

"Your guess is as good as mine. What do you know about Sheriff Rick Ward?"

Andrew's mood turned sour, then angry.

"That's a mean streak with a badge," said Andrew. "Violent and dangerous. There are stories, countless stories, about people taken to the desert and beaten. Never heard from again. Mostly poor, ignorant Mexican migrants. One of the stories I wrote was about his problems with the IRS."

"In the eyes of many, he's a crime fighter, a frontier hero, a mythical John Wayne. But I strongly suspect he's a player in Mickey's drug operation."

"Believing is one thing. Proving it, another."

"The jailhouse death of Jose Martinez Leon in Marfa. Do you recall that story?"

"That will always stick out in my mind until the day I die. Jose Martinez Leon was as meek and mild as they come. He died in the jail. It was ruled a suicide. His front teeth were knocked out. A lacerated testicle. Swollen face. Bruises. I guess he beat himself up before he hung himself."

"Hung himself in jail?"

"Yes. That's the official version. I never believed it."

"Why was he in jail?"

"For being drunk and resisting arrest."

"What about his family?"

"A wife and young daughter. They were scared and left Marfa after Jose was killed."

"Where did they go?"

He lapsed into a long pause before he asked, "How serious are you about this?"

"Dead serious."

Brother Andrew carefully pressed his fingertips together, formed a temple, and rested his chin on his thumbs. He closed his eyes as though to say a quick prayer. I watched and wanted to say something, but thought it would be best just to keep quiet for the time being.

Finally, he dropped his hands, his eyes boring through mine. I knew he was sizing me up, trying to determine whether he could trust me, whether he could tell, by experience, that I was consumed by this unexplained compulsion to find the truth. Or, whether he was dealing with some hotshot reporter who merely wanted to slap something together so it could be put on the front page with his pulsating byline and win some kind of a writing award to put on his wall, slap on a resume.

I hope he understood that this story had me in its powerful and mesmerizing grip.

Brother Andrew leaned forward. I could tell that a flood of doubt was rising within him about my motives.

"If I told you where Maria lives, her life could be put in danger if they know she is talking to a reporter," he said. "So I'll be frank. Don't bullshit me, okay? She's a good woman."

"Look, I've been threatened and shot at. So I've shaken things up and pissed some people off. But I'm here, still standing, still digging for information" I said. "I came all this way because I need to find where all this is going. I need to know."

An approving smile surfaced, as the hardness in his eyes softened. He slipped his hand into his pocket, took out a pen and asked for a sheet of paper. I took out my reporter's notebook from the back of my pocket and tore out a piece of paper.

Brother Andrew scribbled something on it, folded it and pushed it with his forefinger to my side of the table. I picked it up.

"Jose Leon's widow. Maria Leon's address. She lives near Mesilla. She doesn't have a phone," he said.

Brother Andrew told me that after her husband's death, she became a bit of a recluse.

"We kept in touch after I wrote the story about his death," he said. "Two years ago, she wrote and said her daughter had been killed in a traffic accident. A drunken boyfriend struck a tree on the highway. Maria's gone through hell. So handle with care. She is fragile. Tell her that Brother Andrew sent you. That will get you in."

"I appreciate it."

I slipped the paper inside my shirt pocket.

A strong, unannounced cool wind that swept down from the mountains made us squint and lower our heads, turning them sideways as bits of dry leaves and grass hit our faces like hard confetti.

Before I left, I asked how I'd be able to get a hold of him, again, if I needed to do so. He asked for another piece of notebook paper and wrote on it.

"My cell phone number," he said. "The cell phone lets me take peeks at the world through CNN, New York Times and other sources."

I nodded.

"Thanks."

His low voice turned somber.

"It's sad but there are those who live in dark places like rats and cockroaches. Who embrace evil and are driven by greed. Men who kill people like they are barnyard flies. A world where God doesn't exist. Where rage and revenge run rampant."

There was silence while he looked at my face as though he was studying a map. With his fingers, he slowly slid the piece of paper with his phone number toward me. I picked it up.

"Call me if I can be of help but don't abuse the privilege," he said.

"I won't. You've got my word."

"Like you, I've written about these drug traffickers. So I know what you are up against, and I know you know what is out there. So, just be careful, very careful because it's dangerous, very dangerous to step on the devil's tail."

"I'm in for the long haul."

We both stood up. He pulled me toward him, smiled and gave me a bear hug.

"Go," Brother Andrew said. "Go write your stories and shine some light, a blinding light on some of that darkness."

"I will try to do that."

"God be with you. I'll pray for you."

"Thank you. I need all the help I can get."

As soon as I left, I felt energized by a holy man. One who was familiar with the Deadline Druids and the never-ending, daily grind of banging out one story after another. Most of all, we shared this fourth-estate kinship, and this newsroom bond.

CHAPTER 22

Half an hour later, I raced down Interstate 25, heading toward Mesilla, near Las Cruces, a city about fifty miles northwest of El Paso. When I approached the Organ Mountains, I pulled over on the side of the freeway to gulp down a soda, eat a couple of convenience store hotdogs, and munch on a bag of potato chips.

Before I drove off, I studied a map, tracing the roads to Maria Leon's address with my fingers. It was in the middle of the desert, in the middle of nowhere. A gravel-laden dirt road lined with scrub brush and thorny mesquite was the main road to her home. The land was bone dry, fiercely hot in the summer. Temperatures sometimes dropped to below freezing at night.

In March, the winds whip up the sand so bad it's hard to cross the street in some desert towns, and when the rains come, large mud puddles dot the road, making it impassable in some places.

I drove off the highway and stopped in front of a rustic sign with spray-painted letters pointing the way to the desolate community of San Miguelito.

In the distance, a cluster of weathered-roofs on fading gray and brown houses looked like gigantic desert tortoises spawned by the blazing heat. The farther into the desert that I traveled, the more I wondered whether the Honda's spare tire and jack were intact and whether a tow truck driver would even bother to come and pull me out of the gravel surfaced road.

Nearly two miles later, a young woman in blue jean-overalls wearing a floppy green hat caught my eye. She stood in the back yard of a wooden house, tending to a small patch of a garden with a hoe as she listened to a portable radio on the wooden deck of her trailer.

As soon as I stopped the car, she slowly walked over toward the chain-link fence. She was probably used to giving directions to strangers. She approached as two dogs walked behind her, wagging their tails and dangling their tongues.

She smiled.

"*Buenos tardes, senora,*" I said.

"*Buenas tardes.*"

"*Donde vive senora* Maria Leon? *Cual casa?*" I asked.

She pointed to Maria Leon's old brick house with a green-tile roof about half a mile away. I drove slowly, parked the car. A large German Sheppard, clumsily walked toward me, sat on a rock pathway, cocked its head as far as it could go, and barked, a booming bark, dripping with dog slobber. I beeped the horn.

The door opened. A woman stood behind a screen door. There wasn't enough light in the doorway to make heads or tails of what she looked like or anything else.

The dog barked louder at full throttle. He went up to the brown wooden fence and put his paws on top of it. Ears perked up, he growled and occasionally barked.

"Cantinflas!" the woman yelled at the dog.

The dog got down and rollicked toward the house with its tail wagging.

"*Senora,*" I yelled.

"*Si.*"

"My name is Jack Fuentes, and I'm looking for Maria Leon."

"*Yo soy Maria Leon.*"

"I am a newspaper reporter from El Paso. I want to talk to you about your husband."

"He's dead."

"I know," I said, paused. "I want to know about what happened. How he died."

Quiet.

I thought she was going to slam the door, refuse to say another word and leave the dog outside to make certain that I didn't knock on her door. But she opened the screen door, and the dog went inside the house.

"My husband's death is old news, *senor*," she said.

"*El monje* Andrew gave me your address. Said you'd talk to me about what happened."

"The past is gone. Leave it alone. I don't have anything more to say about it."

"*Por favor, senora.* Just a few questions. I came from the monastery where Brother Lockhard lives."

She didn't say a word, and just when I thought she was about to close the door, I pleaded.

"*Por favor.* It is important. I need to know the truth."

Minutes later, Maria and I sat at the kitchen table, and I sipped a cup of coffee while Cantinflas looked at me with a keen eye. I wrote in my notebook as Maria recounted the death of her husband.

"My daughter, she was a just child when he died. She never got over it. Grew up angry, rebelled, and ended up with this boy. A troubled boy who got drunk a lot. They had that car accident, and now, she is dead, too," she said, wiping away a tear.

"I'm so sorry, *senora*," I said. "How did your husband die?"

"Rick Ward killed him."

Maria looked down at the red checkered tablecloth like it was a puzzle, and she was trying to solve it. She lifted her head quickly, as though she got a jolt of memory.

"Jose was out of work," she said. "It was a bad time. Two mouths to feed and no money.

Rick offered him a job. All he had to do was drive to the Greyhound bus station in El Paso and pick up boxes, return to Marfa, and give them to this man in a pickup truck at different parking lots downtown."

"Who was this man?"

"*Quien sabe.* Jose called him Limon. My husband said he always wore a starched white shirt. Always in a hurry. Always complaining."

She said that he did this for six months and got paid $300 for each trip.

"They told him the boxes had Mexican serapes, sombreros, table cloths, and Mexican dresses for tourist stores in South Carolina and Chicago," she said.

"How many boxes did he pick up on each trip?"

"Four, sometimes five a month," she said. "Rick told him it was okay. Everything was legal. He said he was doing it as a favor for gringos who owned the tourist stores, selling Mexican souvenirs."

She said her husband was a simple man and could barely write

"He believed Rick, everything the sheriff said," she said. "Rick was a sheriff. Why wouldn't my husband believe him."

"When did he suspect something wasn't right?"

"One day, Jose dropped a box. It tore open. Inside the wall of the cardboard box, white powder. Limon was in a rage. Cursed and threatened to kill him if he said anything about the boxes."

"The white powder. Cocaine?"

"Yes."

She slowly shook her head, eyes moist and swallowed hard.

"Jose didn't want any part of this anymore. My husband was a good man, an honest man. When Sheriff Rick called him to go to El Paso, Jose made all kinds of excuses why he couldn't go. Days went by. Weeks. Jose thought it was over. That Rick would not call again. We both did."

The sun began to sink. Its light still pierced through laced curtains on the kitchen window, crawled up the wall and got tangled in Maria's hair. It reflected from her light brown eyes and gently stroked the side of her face, wedging into the tiny wrinkles near her mouth. She let out a deep breath.

She dropped her head and sobbed.

"I don't want to say no more," she said. "It still hurts."

"Senora, I understand it's very painful. You've been through so much. But I need the truth. This man still has a gun and badge. He is very powerful."

She stopped sobbing and gently rubbed the top of the table.

"One night, Rick came in the patrol car," she said. "He was drunk. He ordered Jose to put his shirt on. Jose went to kiss our daughter who was sleeping. He said he'd return soon. But his eyes, his sad, desperate look told another story. I will never forget those eyes. That look. Never."

Maria wiped away some tears. She gazed out the window toward the sunset. The sun's rays, now peach and gold, rested on the mountain peaks.

An uneasy quiet settled briefly between us.

I pretended that I was writing something meaningful in my notebook. But all I did was scribble dozens of circles, loops, waves, and curls. I patiently waited for her to say something.

When her dignity eased her back to our conversation, the glassy-eyed woman cleared her throat.

"The next morning, the sheriff banged on my door. His face was pale. I knew it wasn't good. He said that Jose had hung himself in his cell. I screamed, cursed at him and told him it was a lie, that he killed Jose."

"What did Sheriff Rick do?"

"His face was twisted. Hatred and rage filled his eyes. He snarled, pulled my hair, and slapped me. I yelled at him, *asesino!* He grabbed me by the throat and pinned me against the wall. He put his mouth next to my ear and said, 'if you ever say anything, I'll rape you and your daughter, cut your throats, pour gasoline on you, and light a match.'"

As she spoke about the violence, her hands quivered. Angry blood rushed to my head but I had to remain calm and hide my feelings, stifle my outrage.

"My daughter saw it all. She screamed and cried. She was barely eight years old. But she always remembered that morning," Maria said. "That man is a black-hearted demon."

"When did you leave Marfa?"

"A few weeks later. We buried Jose, and three days later, Sheriff Rick showed up at my house.

He gave me a large envelope. I opened the envelope. It was Jose's wallet and his personal belongings," she said. "A rosary he wore that my daughter gave him."

She briefly cried.

"He took out another envelope and tossed it on the table. He said it was $2,000. He told me to 'use the money to get out of Marfa with my daughter.'"

Her eyes were smoldering with anger.

"I told him that I wasn't going to take his filthy drug money."

Maria made a tossing motion to show me how she flung the envelope with the money on the wall. "He laughed, picked up the money, and left. I never saw him again. I sold all my furniture. My daughter and I left Marfa on a bus."

Maria went into the living room. She returned with a wedding photograph of her and Jose standing in front of a fountain. They stood there under a bright blue sky next to a priest who married them outside a Catholic church in Marfa. They were in their late teens and wore smiles, wide smiles. Jose, a lanky man with light hazel eyes and dark skin, had his arm wrapped around his new wife. His puffed, prideful chest made his face glow with joy. Maria's sweet spirit and tender smile showed itself on the photo that sunny day.

"We were supposed to return to the fountain when we were married 50 years and renew our vows. When you are young, you always believe that life will last forever. But sometimes, everything changes. The fountain, well, it's still there. Jose, he'll never return, and I will always remember that look of sadness, desperation that night," she said. "My daughter would have been alive had her father been around. I believe that with all my heart. *Pobrecita.* She never got over his death."

I talked to Maria another hour, asking many more questions, dozens of questions, writing on my notebook.

It was dark when I left. The moonless night made the driving slow. A sharp rock or dry mesquite branch could puncture a tire. I'd be stuck in the dark, moonless desert.

A mile from her house, my car's lights bounced off a pair of glowing eyes hidden in the distance behind some bushes. The eyes glared in my direction. I gripped the steering wheel tightly and prepared to slam my foot on the gas pedal and cut a new path through the desert.

The strange eyes were on top of a sand dune and followed my every move. I stopped the car and looked in the rearview mirror, again. I decided it would be best to slam the gear in reverse and try to maneuver the Honda backwards instead of risk boring through the desert and getting stuck in the pile of sand pits.

I began to worry about an ambush. This would be a perfect spot for it, in the middle of nowhere. A burst of gunfire from an M16 rifle would puncture metal, send glass flying and rip flesh. The assassin would dash back onto the highway, jump into a waiting car, and tear out of the area and vanish.

My hands sweated on the steering wheel.

Suddenly, the eyes emerged from behind the bushes, as I got closer.

It was a coyote, with its large mouth wrapped around a bloody jackrabbit's neck. He trotted across the dirt road. The jackrabbit, still alive, violently shook its leg. Utter terror consumed the rabbit's eyes as it was carried into the darkness. The animal couldn't escape and was about to be eaten alive.

I exhaled a chunk of air, letting out some of my jitters with it.

I glanced at the rearview and side mirrors just to make sure nobody was standing behind the car donning a hard hat and aiming a gun at the back of my head. Relieved, my shoulders fell. I gripped and massaged the back of my neck where some of my hairs were still standing. I took a long, deep breath.

As I got closer to the highway, car lights appeared like large fireflies traveling in a straight line, heading west.

CHAPTER 23

It was nearly 10 p.m. when I got home. There were three messages, one from Sierra and two from Dana that I had purposely ignored until I sat on my kitchen table with a small box of pizza. Dana's last message summed up the last two. She was very pissed: "Damn you, Jack, answer my calls!? Where is my car!? You owe me for cab fare! I should have known better!"

Sierra's message was curt: "Call me. I've got a photograph of an old Mexican artist who my father knew. The guy knows things."

I wasn't in the mood to talk to Dana about her car or Sierra about some old Mexican artist who might or might not know something that could shed light on my story.

I sat on the edge of my bed, finishing the last two pieces of cold pizza, washing it down with a beer.

Minutes after my head hit the pillow, a numbing sleep came free of bad guys and deadline Druids.

Hours later, I was awakened by cold water tossed on my head. I gasped for air and jerked out of bed. I stood next to the bed with my fists in a tight ball, ready to absorb a blow or a bullet by some sadistic hit man.

For a few seconds, there was nothing but blur but as I shook the water off at the end of the bed, a familiar figure, Dana. Her eyes bulging, crossed arms and ramrod straight.

Suddenly, she grabbed and flung a bucket at me. I ducked. The bucket knocked a lamp off the nightstand and onto the floor.

"Hey!" I protested. "Are you crazy? Stop! What the hell is wrong with you?"

She stabbed the air with her forefinger aimed at my head.

"You. You ignorant, shit-for-brains prick! What did you do to my car!?"

Red-faced, she stood there wearing dark-blue, Nike shorts, white tennis shoes, and a tight white sweater, her hair held back by two wide metal clips. Dana looked great. But I had no doubt that she would have used a chainsaw if there was one in my room.

"Calm down," I said, wiping my hair with a dry portion of the sheet. "Relax."

"Calm down?" she said. "Half the desert is on my car. All over my $1,000 paint job!"

"I was going to run it through a carwash before I returned it," I said. "Give it a nice smell again, get it detailed."

"Where did you drive it!?"

Looking around the room, I didn't say a word, hoping she'd calm down a bit before I told her. No such luck.

"Where?" she demanded to know. "Where!?"

"I had to go interview this lady. She lives in the desert, near the mountains in Mesilla, and —"

Dana bellowed. "Over the mountains?"

"Not over. Near. The mountains were nearby."

She whimpered, both hands on top of her forehead, head cocked back.

"Through the *pinche* desert?"

"Just two miles into the desert."

"Just two miles in. Two miles?" she said. "You imbecile, dirt-bag moron! What were you thinking!?"

"I had to talk to her."

"I don't ever want to see your stupid face again!" she said.

As she turned to leave, I straightened the lamp.

"How'd you get in here?" I asked.

She stopped in the middle of the hallway.

"Who takes care of Dexter when you go to Vegas? I've got a key, idiot!?" she shouted as she continued toward the door, stopping briefly only to chime at Dexter, "Poor little bird living with a two-legged, *pinche* jackass. Your life must be a bitch."

Outside, Dana turned on the water hose, spraying water to wash the dust off the car. With a raised voiced, she flung threats and obscenities.

I didn't dare go outside.

CHAPTER 24

After Dana drove off, I showered and opened Dexter's cage. The bird climbed out of the cage and stood on top of it. Then, without warning, he leaped into the air and flew in circles around the room, chirping loudly.

He landed on the large light fixture on the ceiling. He liked it up there. I figured it was because the iron-scroll-arm design of the light fixture that looked like curled branches.

"Get in the cage," I demanded. "Get in! I've got a lot of work to do."

Dexter loved to fly around the room twice and go back into his cage and eat. Not this time. The bird didn't budge. So I got the stepladder, climbed it, lifted my arm, and stuck my finger out so he could get onto it. The bird moved back, opened his beak wide, and hissed. In bird language, that meant to back off.

As I inched my finger closer, Dexter swooped down to his cage. I felt a wire that didn't belong there. I grabbed it with my two fingers. I felt the device. The wire was attached to an antenna, which was taped to the light fixture.

A bugging device. My face turned pale. I couldn't believe what I was looking at as I examined it closer. It was a listening device, simple but effective.

Oh, God, I thought. My house was bugged. My conversations were being recorded on an open mike.

I wanted to take the recording device, open the door, and fling it outside to let anyone who might be out there watching know that I wise to them.

I didn't, however. I just stood perfectly still for a moment, looking around the room, searching for a video camera or another recording device.

Who would bug my house and why? What did they want to know?

I quickly stepped down from the ladder, pretending that nothing was out of the ordinary. I didn't want anyone to know I had found the recording device.

After Dexter finally made his way back to his cage, I praised him loud enough to be picked up by the tiny microphone in the light fixture. "Good bird. Good boy, Dexter."

The phone rang.

The sound sent a bolt of adrenaline that jerked my body.

It was C.J., telling me that Ricardo wanted to talk to me as soon as I got to work.

"Fine. I'm on my way to work," I said. "Be there in twenty minutes."

Making quick mental notes, I grabbed a baseball bat in my bedroom and quietly looked inside the closets. I stood in the middle of the room with the bat by my side, trying to pick up the slightest noise, trying to determine whether an intruder was inside my house or if there was another bugging device.

After making sure the doors were locked, I got dressed and said goodbye to Dexter, and called a cab. Before I left, I slowly walked around the house, noting in my mind where every piece of clothing, every object was located to make sure I would know if anything was disturbed while I was gone.

The cab ride to the body shop to pick up my car went smooth. The cab driver smiled and didn't pick up on my edgy behavior. As he drove, my eyes darted everywhere, checking to see if any face or car around my neighborhood was out of place, if any unusual vans were parked a block or two down the street.

This whole thing made me leery of my surroundings. I felt I wasn't safe anywhere, anymore, not even in my own home. As the cab went down neighborhood streets, I talked to the cab driver, smiling and pretending that the device I found in my house didn't shake me.

I kept looking back to make certain we weren't being tailed.

When I got to the body shop, I saw my car parked near the entrance. It looked brand new. No visible bullet holes. The car almost looked showroom new. The shiny new coat of dark blue paint made my confidence level rise.

As I began to drive away, the body shop foreman named Jerry McDermont stopped me, holding up a transmitter with an antenna that stuck out like a toothpick on a green olive.

"I found this," he said.

He waited for me to react. I didn't. It was his way of probing, finding out whether I was a cop investigating chop shops or crooked businesses. He leaned down and handed me the bugging device.

"It's a bug. It was under the dashboard," he said. "A girlfriend, maybe?"

"No. Look, I'm just a writer. A reporter. In my business, you piss off a lot of people. Who put it there and why? I don't have clue."

Jerry said nothing. I handed him my business card to assure him that I wasn't a cop. He looked at it with a somber expression, nodded and didn't ask another question.

As I drove off and headed down the road, I stopped three blocks later at a dead-end street. I turned up the radio and lowered my head under the dashboard to see if there was another bugging device there, sliding my hand across the bottom surface several times to check for an loose wires or foreign objects.

For a long time, I checked the back seats and in the trunk, everywhere. Nothing. But I was enraged. This latest find made me even more suspicious of what other bugging devices might turn up.

When I walked into the newsroom, C.J. motioned me over. He logged off his computer, wanted to talk to me outside the eavesdropping, roving reporters and mid-managers whose ears were always dipped into someone else's business, the latest newsroom gossip.

A few minutes later, we sat at a far corner table near a big window in the snack room.

"Ricardo needs an update on the Mickey Madrid story."

"I just got started," I said. "What does he expect? Talk to him."

"I did. He's not budging. He feels this story has no legs. Wants you back covering the courts. We're short of reporters. Big trials are coming up."

"I know but I need more time. I haven't connected the dots yet," I said.

C.J. was in no mood to hear me bitch.

"I'm just telling you what he said."

Minutes later, I sat in front of Ricardo. He scratched the back of his head and kept staring out a window at the traffic going down the highway. He was deciding my story's fate, and I was thinking about my next move, deciding whether I would clear my desk, walk out the door, keep going with my investigative story and freelance it. Sell it to some magazine.

I had given Ricardo just a few bits and pieces about what I had learned. Just enough to pique his interest and keep him off balance. I didn't tell him about the graveyard or Sierra. I had to leave that out or else he'd probably assign another reporter to help me because, he'd say, I was now part of the story, so I could lose my objectivity.

Bullshit!

I had a stake in this story. I almost lost my life. This was my story. I would manage it, work it and write it. It was mine. I'm not giving it away to some dickhead reporter who probably sucks up to Ricardo and gives him a day-to-day rundown about what I was doing. He'd probably do it to get on Ricardo's good side.

No doubt, this story was beginning to consume my soul like some forest fire feeding on a mountain of bone-dry pine trees. There were too many questions still dangling and begging for morsels of sunlight.

Just as my frustration was about to boil over and I was about to get up, hand in my letter of resignation, and walk out the door, Ricardo peered over his eyeglasses. He groaned before he tossed his glasses on the table.

"What have you found out? Where are you with this story?"

"Making progress. It's slow, but it's progress," I said.

"We need something soon."

"I'm working hard, talking to people. There are too many things out there and not enough answers."

"Three weeks, that's what we agreed, and you're back on the court beat. You can work on it when you aren't working on court stories," he said.

"Okay."

I muttered curse words as I walked back to my desk.

Finishing this story in a few weeks would be next to impossible. This story kept getting bigger and bigger. It seemed to have a life of its own with its odious smell of evil on its black, forked tongue.

After I left his office, I checked a phone text marked urgent: "I have the photo of this Mexican artist. Call me — Sierra."

CHAPTER 25

Sierra handed me a grainy photograph of a stout, white-haired man sitting in front of an easel, in deep thought as though as he was trying to figure out some ancient cryptic message scrawled on an art canvas.

Two cups of coffee sat on our table.

"Who's this?"

"Francisco Avila, a Mexican artist."

The waitress at the coffee shop asked if we wanted a menu. We both shook our heads.

"Just coffee," I said.

She nodded and left.

In the photograph, Francisco wore a sweat-stained, gray cowboy hat with a tiny orange feather on its side. His brooding eyes on a rugged face looked tortured. A three-day stubble accented a face carved out by a lifetime of living hard.

She said her father told her that he was in a hotel in Zacatecas ten years ago when he spotted Francisco's paintings in the lobby. He found out that Francisco lived in the little Mexican town, Calera, about fifteen miles from Zacatecas.

"Years later, my father got Francisco to go to the family ranch in Chihuahua to paint a family portrait of my father, Emilio and me," she said. "He never went to the ranch to visit. Never."

"That's nice," I said, a bit annoyed. "I don't get it. What does a harmless old man who lives in some obscure Mexican town and paints portraits have to do with this *desmadre*?"

I glanced at the photograph, unimpressed by an old painter who looked uneducated and clueless.

"What does he know?" I scoffed. "An old man with a paint brush. What can he tell us? What? That he's got a map where an Aztec treasurer chest is buried?"

Her caustic stare put my impatience in check

"You want to hear the rest of this or not? I can leave."

"I'm listening."

Her seething eyes bore through my skull. Sensing she was about to rip into me with her tongue, I apologized and softened my approach.

"Look, I'm sorry, alright? Things have gotten to a bad start," I said. "I'm hitting dead ends, and I have this editor breathing down my neck."

"I understand," she said, paused until she calmly collected her thoughts.

Pointing at Francisco's photograph, she continued.

"This man, Francisco, visited my father a couple of times. The last time, he pissed my father off, big time. My father threw him out of our house. Days later, Adelia, our housekeeper, told me that she heard Francisco say something about San Pedro, appeasing San Pedro."

It dawned about the note she had given me days earlier, the one that had words scrawled with a pencil: <u>Para San Pedro.</u> The amount of $50,000 was circled.

Before I said another word about it, she read my thoughts.

"Yeah, San Pedro. The note with the $50,000 circled." Sierra said.

"She didn't say who she believed this San Pedro was?"

Sierra shook her head.

"Any hint as to who it was? Anything?" I said.

"No," she said. "Adelia also said Francisco told my father that a group was offering protection. My father apparently figured out someone or some group was trying to muscle into his business or blackmail him. He got angry and threatened to kill Francisco if he ever came back with another offer like that."

"Who? Who were these people? This group?"

"Adelia said she heard Francisco say something about 'Los Zetas.'"

My blood took a roller coaster ride to the bottom of my feet and zoomed back up.

"Are you sure?"

"Yeah. Absolutely."

The Zetas are a deadly, powerful and vicious group of disgruntled Mexican army soldiers. Some trained as elite commandos in the United States by the Green Berets to fight the drug war. They became frustrated, saw an easy way to tap into the narcotrafficking billions, and decided to switch sides. Many of them deserted and hooked up with drug dealers. Rumor had it that they were quietly recruiting adobe-hut peasants in Mexico who were hungry, broke, out of jobs, and angry with the government.

The Zetas criminal syndicate muscled their way into the drug cartels' businesses, including the rival Gulf Cartel, and leaving a trail of dead and often mutilated bodies.

Mexicans had captured Miguel Angel Trevino who authorities said ran the Los Zetas drug gang with such viciousness that he sometimes boiled enemies alive in grease.

I also knew Los Zetas were in the protections racket and offering their services and muscle to mom-and-pop drug smugglers who had connections to Mexico and Colombia. They probably got wind of Mickey's problems with Colombians.

"Are you sure, positively sure, that it was Los Zetas?" I asked Sierra.

"Yeah. That's what Adelia heard."

I gulped down the coffee and glanced at my watch.

"I got to go," I said and picked up the photograph of Francisco. "I need to borrow this."

"Where are you going?"

"Calera. Visit Francisco."

"Really?" she said. "You think that Francisco is going to talk to a nosy reporter? You'll be signing your own death warrant. You can't be that stupid. These people live on cat-like wits. He lives in a barrio where strangers are easily spotted. I can get in the door. He knows me. If he thought we were engaged, and we wanted a portrait of us, it might work. We gain his trust and slowly loosen his tongue."

"Are you serious? I run all that by my editor and he'd laugh right after he threw me out of his office."

"Screw the editor. You're sitting on this incredible story, and you're worried about what some editor thinks? Grow a pair."

"They've got rules. They own the printing press, so I follow protocol to make sure this story sees the light of day."

"Good luck," she said, hurriedly picked up her things and walked away.

"Wait," I said, but she kept walking. "Sierra!"

CHAPTER 26

I walked into the newsroom and felt as though I was being fol-lowed by desperation's dreary shadow. With a straight face, I lied. I told C.J. that an ailing, great grandmother in Zacatecas had one foot in the grave. She'd be dead in a day or so, I said.

I didn't have a great grandmother in Zacatecas or relatives in Mexico. C.J. didn't make lying easy.

"You have relatives in Mexico?"

"A great grandmother on my mother's side."

"Go. I've got your back. Try and get back as soon as you can." He said. "Sorry about your grandmother."

Feeling awful, I nodded, faked a sad-eyed expression.

"Thanks, man."

Sierra was right. Ricardo would never approve a trip south of the border on the company's dime, especially for the sole purpose of trying to siphon information from an old painter who did busi-ness in a run-down studio and rolled his own cigarettes and who might not have anything meaningful to say. Then, he could be the key to unraveling this story, which now seemed to have its own mind and leading and pulling me to places where I never dreamed of going.

The story Sierra dropped on Francisco was that she and I were engaged and wanted him to do a portrait of us before our wedding so we could use it on our wedding invitations.

We would be willing to lay down some serious money for the portrait. But we needed the portrait as soon as possible.

Sierra had been at Francisco's studio several times with her father and knew some of his neighbors, so that was to our advantage, a big advantage. It would have been dangerous to walk into a poor Mexican barrio by myself asking questions and searching for Francisco's studio.

The last thing I wanted to do was to arouse unwanted suspicion, especially in a Mexico. If they found out I was a Norte Americano reporter asking questions about the drug business, I'd probably disappear, and end up in some shallow grave and years later, my bones would be dug up by dogs.

Sierra told me that Francisco was somewhat of a recluse, a distrustful man to the point that he seldom allowed anyone inside his studio. It was where he spent countless hours painting portraits for rich clients or he'd sell his painting to private collectors.

Sierra's credit cards and cash financed most of our trip. I used money I had saved to pay the first and last month's rent after I left the newsroom. I would use most of that.

After I met Sierra at the airport, we sat in the terminal and waited for a late night flight to Zacatecas with stops in Houston and Mexico City. There was a light mist and the tarmac shone like glass in the night rain. On the flight, Sierra read women's magazines one right after the other while I read the newspaper, flipped through some of my notes, and caught up on some lost sleep.

We rented a car at the Zacatecas Airport and drove to the city about five miles away.

Sierra drove the car through the cobblestone streets in Zacatecas that were steep, narrow, and meandered past colonial buildings and ancient architecture. She drove like a pro on the streets' hairpin turns that came with plenty of motorists leaning hard on car horns.

We stopped in the parking lot of Quinta Real Zacatecas Hotel. She slipped on a wedding ring that belonged to her mother, looked in the rearview mirror, ran her fingers through her hair and licked her full lips.

"That is my engagement ring," she said lifting her finger up to my face. "Let's get a room."

"Gladly," I said and eased into a smile.

She frowned.

"This is business, idiot. That's all," she said. "So don't forget that."

The Quinta Real Zacatecas Hotel was constructed around the remains of a 140-year-old bullring and an ancient stone aqueduct. When we walked into the lobby, it was bustling with people checking in and out and hotel employees working the counter or moving luggage.

After checking into the hotel as Mr. And Mrs. Fuentes, Sierra changed into tight blue jeans and a light-yellow blouse. I went downstairs and found the bar with a timber-thin waiter who began practicing his English on me. I didn't mind. I needed a drink to unwind.

Ten minutes after I sat on a bar stool, sipped on a beer, and struck up a conversation with the waiter, who said his name was Juan, Sierra walked up.

Her frigid glare chased the waiter to the far end of the bar.

"Seriously, Jack? A beer? Really? We're not here to drink beer, sightsee, or strike up conservation with waiters or strangers," she said. "Got it?"

"Chill, alright? One beer. No harm, no foul."

We drove to Calera about half-an-hour away without saying a word. Sierra found a radio station. Salsa music was played. It made the drive whisk by along a four-lane highway. The road ran near the mountain ranges. There were long, straight stretches of asphalt and a few curves.

We entered Calera through the older barrios. The city looked frail. Some buildings and houses on the edge of town would probably crumble if the earth shook hard. Closer to the downtown municipal square, an old church cathedral dominated the landscape. Calera was smack in the middle of Mexico, about twenty miles from the city of Zacatecas, the capital of the mountainous and rich-mining state also named Zacatecas.

The town of 30,000 was busy on a Friday morning when we arrived. Cars drove down the lone main street, Calle Cino De Mayo, with its two traffic lights and decaying side streets filled with hundreds of potholes and cracked sidewalks.

Francisco's art studio was a rock house with a circular rock tower that stood near the edge of town. A pile of poorly laid stones made it look like a cheap, Mexican imitation of a Gothic castle. It was surrounded by a grimy neighborhood with battered cars on paved roads, miles of weathered black and white wrought iron or wooden fences and banged-up pickup trucks with balding tires.

The art studio had a couple of cracked windows and scattered patches of tall backyard weeds.

It looked empty, deserted.

Nobody would have known it was an art studio if it didn't have a small, old sign, hanging lopsided, that stated: "*Studio Artistico*," the letters carefully brushed on in Spanish with white paint.

Sierra knocked on the front door that had a plastic cross with Jesus looking down, keeping a wary eye on those who walked up.

She knocked again. Nobody answered. No noises from inside the house. Thick, dust-laden curtains kept anyone from peering inside.

Sierra kept tapping on the door, calling out Francisco's name.

Curiosity got the best of me. I walked to the side of the house to snoop around.

At the back end of the house, I found a discarded soda pop wooden crate. I put it below a high window on the side of the house. I laid it flat and lifted myself on my tiptoes.

A sliver between the curtain and the edge of the window let me peek inside.

On the floor stood a can of linseed oil and glass jars full of paintbrushes with wooden handles. There were tubes of bright-red, vivid-violet, lush-green, and bright yellow paint. Paintings were stacked against the wall of sombreroed Mexican men on horseback, aging, plump women in bright colored dresses making bread and a lanky Mexican bullfighter swiping his reddish cape across the black, muscular mountain of a ferocious bull's back.

This was Francisco's Mexico, a mystic land of bright colors and powerful images of brown people. A land savaged and turned into a gun-blazing country by the drug cartels who were carving up turf, killing each other and leaving the blood of innocents and others on the streets, alleys and deserts.

Sierra kept pounding on the door, calling out to Francisco.

Suddenly, a blur of gray pant legs from inside the house flashed by my peephole. The legs returned, stopped in front of me, and put a stepladder on the floor.

The man with the gray baggy pants went up to the last step on the ladder. I heard him raise a panel in the ceiling. He came down, removed the stepladder, and hurriedly walked toward the door.

Steel, cold steel suddenly pressed against my lower jaw, pressed on it hard. I froze. A gun cocked. I was dead or so I thought. My eyes shifted. I saw the barrel gun. It was huge.

A sunbaked hand held the gun.

"Okay, okay, okay," I said heart thudding. "*No dispares.*"

Pale, sweating and sucking gulps of air, I started to speak again. No more words came out.

"*Bajate cabron,*" the man said in Spanish. "*Pinche ladron.*"

"I'm not a thief," I replied in Spanish.

I stepped down only after he took a step back. The man had a thick neck, protruding teeth and lion-like facial features, a pronounced round nose, scraggly beard. His long brown, unwashed curly hair was combed back. He had a few crumbs near his mouth as though I interrupted his breakfast. He smelled like onions and alcohol. He stared at me, an iceberg stare.

Backing away farther, he pointed the gun a few feet from my face. The whites of his light-brown eyes were raging red, a hard edge to them. He was ready to send a bullet through my skull. Wrestling with a kernel of conscience, perhaps, about whether he should kill me or let me go after giving me a good beating. He snarled. His chest rose and collapsed. He spat and wiped with the back of his hand the saliva that clung to his beard.

"Jack," I said. "*Me llamo,* Jack."

"*Mi importa, madre, pendejo,*" he said.

"*Busco a Francisco? Donde esta, Francisco?*"

There were tattoos on the man, a scorpion protruding from a skull inked on a large forearm stood out along with a hairy chest and brown teeth, a chipped tooth. A scar, just beneath his eye, broke up the hardness in his face. I knew that he'd have no qualms about cutting my throat and going back to finish a breakfast.

"*Quin eres, cabron?*" he said.

Then, a whistle, a shrill whistle, sliced the warm air. The gunman's ears perked up.

"Zamora!" a booming voice called out from the back of the house. A shrill whistle.

"*Donde andas?*"

"*Aqui*, Don Franciso," he replied without taking his eyes off me. "*Con este bofo.*"

Zamora lowered his gun, but only slightly. The rattler inside his eyes made the hair on my arms stand up. I swallowed hard.

Francisco's laughter sliced the tension in the air. He raised his voice and said in Spanish, "Bring the caballero. Sierra is here, too. Mickey Madrid's daughter."

Zamora's eyes softened. He grinned, a jittery grin. He understood the weight that Mickey Madrid's name carried even in death, even in this part of Mexico.

"*Pasenle*," Zamora said, now forcing a smile. "*Por favor.*"

He put his gun away and extended his hand. I shook it.

"Welcome to Don Francisco's studio," he said in Spanish. "I'm his security guard. Luis Ignacio Rincon Zamora. Please to meet you. I thought you were a thief."

As soon as Zamora and I walked into the house, Francisco smiled and shook my hand. Zamora stood behind him. Sierra sat on a chair, pretending to smile at me. When Francisco and Zamora weren't looking, she shot an angrily look my way and mouthed, "*Idiota.*"

Sierra quickly slipped back into the role of a bashful bride-to-be and formally introduced me as her fiancé who was a fledgling law student.

My heavy breathing slowed once Sierra wrapped her arm around my waist.

"The idea for the portrait is my fiancé's," she said, looking at me with submissive eyes. *"Verdad, mi amor?"*

"Claro," I said. "It will be for our wedding invitations, and many years later, a portrait for our children and grand-children."

Leaning down, I gave her a soft peck on the lips.

"Yes, a portrait for our children," she said, appearing to be lost in my eyes.

"Our two beautiful children, *mi vida,*" I said.

I kissed her, again, hard. Francisco beamed. It worked. I enjoyed it. Sierra angry eyes bulged out when Francisco turned his back.

"Stop," she mouthed.

I smirked.

It didn't matter. We had fooled him with our bogus display of affection.

Francisco ordered Zamora to go outside.

"Vete afuera," he told him.

Zamora left with his gun stuffed inside his waistband, then squatted under the shadow of a cinderblock wall behind a wrought-iron gate near the side entrance. Francisco would spot anybody entering the property with his junkyard dog, Zamora. He casually took out a bag of pistachios from his pocket, began cracking the shells and eating the nuts. The shells landed near his feet. Francisco stood near the open door. He gave Zamora a long, pathetic look.

"I apologize for Zamora," Francisco said. "He's not right in his head. But he's fearless, though. Very fearless and will tangle with the devil if he has to."

Francisco lightly tapped the side of his head with two fingers.

"Sometimes, Zamora sees spirits. Spirits of dead people who he's killed," said Francisco. "Other than that, he does his job."

Francisco took off his sweat-stained fedora. The deep cracks on his forehead had a thin sheen of perspiration. He took out a red bandana, wiped his forehead, and complained about the weather.

"Let's talk about this painting, Senorita Madrid," he said.

He motioned for us to sit on a nearby bench and offered us coffee. We declined, but accepted cold sodas, which he got from a small, dented oil-smudged refrigerator. Sierra told the old man about her father and brother, how a violent explosion had taken her brother's life.

"His killer is still out there," she said.

Francisco expressed his sorrow.

"*Que aye descanso y paz en los Brazos de Jesus Cristo,*" he said, making the sloppy sign of the cross.

When he did this, I saw right through his insincerity. My intuition said this guy was a man with many, murky secrets and little room for compromise.

We stayed long enough to negotiate a price and make an appointment to come back early the next day so Francisco could do his magic with a paintbrush and oils.

CHAPTER 27

Sierra was quiet when we drove out of Calera toward Zacatecas. Then, she turned off the radio and erupted.

"Damn, you," she said, a forest fire blazing in her eyes. "Don't ever do that again!"

"Do what?"

"Kiss me, again, ever. Got it!?"

"Hey, you concocted this cute, little, love story. Wrote the script, now, you own it. This is just theater for me," I said. "'Strictly, business,' as you said."

"You loved it."

I burst out laughing.

"Quite frankly, I'd rather kiss a gargoyle's ass."

"*Pinche* moron."

"Sticks and stones," I chimed.

"Shut up."

She stared out the passenger window. I turned the radio back on. The sun started to dip its face behind a plateau. Its peach-colored glow split and cloaked the mountainous range.

Inside the rented car, the air conditioner blasted away. I adjusted the rearview mirror. The singer Andrea Bocelli was on the radio. I turned it off. She turned it back on.

"Another thing, I'm not paying for the painting," I said. "I can't afford it."

"Right," she said curtly. "I'm paying."

"This has become an obsession with you. Finding your brother's killer."

"Closure, okay? I want closure," she snapped. "And the painting is nothing more than a business expense. I buy it, take it home, toss it in the fire place and delight as it goes up, up in flames."

Sierra then insisted I stop by El Gallo liquor store near downtown Zacatecas and buy a bottle of expensive Tequila.

"Francisco loves Tequila," she said. "I'll use it to lubricate and loosen his tongue."

Afterwards, we went to the hotel. Sierra changed clothes, freshened up, and left. She went shopping. I emptied all my mental notes about what happened at Francisco's studio, including my encounter with Zamora, onto my laptop

I copied the notes on the computer, pasted them in an email, and sent it to my computer in the newsroom. I deleted the notes on my laptop in case someone stole it. Any and all mention of the Mexico trip was also deleted.

Fifteen minutes later, my eyes grew heavy. I was exhausted. I snuck a peek at the clock. It was 5:35 pm. I put my head on top of my arms that were resting on a table, and fell asleep.

The door opening woke me. I jerked my head up and saw Sierra enter the room clutching two light-brown plastic bags on two hangers. She also had two bags of McDonald's hamburgers and fries. It was 7:15 p.m. She tossed me a bag with a hamburger and fries. I snatched them in mid-air. She removed the plastic bag to reveal a black mariachi suit with gold embroidery and gold buttons.

"It's yours. You wear it. I wear the dress," she said.

"Hell no, I don't wear clown suits."

She gave me a stern look, one reserved for an uncooperative and defiant child at a grocery store.

"I'm not wearing it," I said.

"Look, if Francisco suspects for one second that you and I are a threat to him, it'll get very nasty, very quick. The tequila loosens his tongue. The costumes ease his suspicions. The suspicion you raised by snooping around yesterday," she said. "By the way, *idiota*, I caught Francisco motioning to Zamora with his eyes not to stray far from the house."

Her words sliced like a box cutter. She had my attention.

"He's barely buying into our bullshit. These people's lives rely on primitive intuitive power to survive, and you didn't help today," she said. "So wear the damn *charro* suit, and shut up about it."

Grudgingly, I picked up the mariachi outfit. I turned to Sierra, and before I spoke, she had already anticipated what I was about to say.

"It fits. So do the cowboy boots and sombrero in the car," she said and curled her fastidious lip.

"Fine, if this helps get inside Francisco's head, I'll wear it."

"Good."

After we ate, she took a shower, changed into some pink and white pajamas, and fell asleep on one of the twin beds. I stayed up another hour wrapping up my notes for that day. I left my cell phone in the newsroom in case it was stolen or taken from me in Mexico.

By the time I finished, Sierra was in a numbing sleep.

I slept badly, tossing and turning on the other twin bed. In the morning, I sat up in bed, stretched, turned, and saw that the bed next to mine was empty. As soon as my feet hit the floor, my hotel phone rang.

"Hello?"

"I'm downstairs having breakfast. Hurry up and take a shower. We need to get going. Put on the outfit. And remember, Franciso sees you as a harmless idiot. Don't disappoint him. See you in twenty minutes," Sierra said.

She hung up before I could say a word. I fumed. She started to take control of my story. It began to bug the hell out of me. For now, I'd play the game, hoping it would pay big dividends, hoping I could write a solid investigative piece.

I needed to get this done, and time was running out.

CHAPTER 28

On the ride to Francisco's studio, Sierra was talkative, recalling the three trips she made to the studio, twice as a little girl and once as a teenager.

She said her father would buy one or two of Francisco's paintings. He'd stay an hour or so in the studio and always brought his bodyguards, Nino, Big Rafa and of course, Bazooka who made her laugh.

"When I was a little girl, Bazooka would get on his hands and knees, and I would get on top of him and pretend that he was an elephant," Sierra said and giggled. "He would trumpet like an elephant."

Her father never traveled in Mexico without his bodyguards, Nino, Big Rafa and of course, his most trusted bodyguard, Bazooka, a giant with thick fingers.

"He was like an uncle. He taught me how to fish when I was a little girl," she said.

Once, Bazooka didn't go on the trip to Francisco's studio with her father. She snuck out to go play with another little girl, Cecilia, who lived a few blocks away.

She was gone more than an hour; her father went on a frantic search for her with Nino and Big Rafa.

Her father finally found her sitting with Cecilia on the street curb near a store five blocks away. The two were eating potato chips and drinking soda pop when her father and Big Rafa walked up and frightened Cecilia. Sierra's newfound and barefooted friend bolted after she looked up and saw Big Rafa and never looked back.

Sierra said her father thought she had been kidnapped and yelled at her. It scared her so much that she wrapped her arms around her head, trembled and held on tightly.

"I began to cry. My father hugged me, wept and kept saying, 'I'm sorry.' Over and over again," Sierra told me. "He made me promise that I would never wander off again or tell my mother what had happened. I never did."

She stared out the window. It came as a surprised when I heard that Mickey was capable to squeezing out a single tear, capable of any human emotion other than hatred and rage.

"My father hid his emotions from everyone except my mother and I," she said. "To the world, he was cold and private and had a dark presence. But at times, when no one was looking, he would strum his guitar, sing love songs to my mother and I. Beautiful songs of lost loves and better days that were always on the other side of tomorrow. He learned those songs on the streets and played his music in bars when he was 12 years old."

I was astonished to hear her telling me all this. I wanted to hear more. But she didn't say another word about another side of Mickey Madrid that I never knew existed.

"I miss my father, my mom and my brother, very much," she said.

A few seconds later, she tried to be inconspicuous when she swatted a few tears away.

"Stick to the plan," she said near the city of Calera.

"I will."

When we got to the studio Francisco had prepared the canvas and had scooted a bench close to the light, near the blank, heavy cloth that sat on a creaky easel.

He clapped his hands with delight when he saw us in our Mexican outfits. Then, he waved his arms like wands in childlike fashion to describe what blend of soft earth tones and splashes of color he was going to use to highlight our faces, our costumes.

Sierra cheerfully handed Francisco her gift, the $50 bottle of Anejo Tequila wrapped in blue paper with a yellow ribbon.

"In keeping with my father's tradition," she reminded him.

She knew he would open the gift right away. He always did this. Sierra said Francisco would always offer her father some Tequila and take out two, crystal and gold trimmed shot glasses he had kept in the cupboard. She said her father had also given Francisco the shot glasses on one of his visits.

Francisco didn't disappoint. He unwrapped the gift and grinned, exposing a silver-capped tooth.

"*Gracias*," he said.

We quietly stood back, hoping the alcohol would slowly begin to massage and loosen his tongue. Hoping that Francisco would begin telling us what he knew, and most importantly, what Mickey had told him about the drug trade and its key players.

Francisco kept admiring the bottle of Tequila as though it were a newborn baby that had just been gently put on his lap. He insisted that the three of us sip some Tequila before he started painting our portrait. Sierra politely refused. I was hospitable. That didn't please Sierra.

Francisco went to a cupboard in the kitchen and brought out two coffee cups, one was cracked. Both had brown coffee stains on the bottom.

I wondered what happened to the crystal shot glasses that Mickey had given him but I didn't dare ask or it would have made him very suspicious.

As soon as Francisco turned his back, Sierra shot a disapproving look my way and angrily mouthed, "*estupido.*"

"*Shut up,*" I mouthed back.

Francisco took a few sips of Tequila, mixed blue and white colors and spread the paint before he returned to mixing blue and white colors, just enough to spread a light aqua backdrop on the canvas.

Francisco momentarily left the room to clean a paintbrush. Sierra quickly leaned her lips close to my ear.

"Don't screw this up, moron. I mean it."

"Lighten up," I said through my teeth.

Francisco stepped back into the room. He stepped behind the easel and immediately paid Sierra a few compliments.

"You have your mother's vivacious eyes and father's dimples," he said.

"Thank you," she said, turning sideways, looked up and faked some adoring looks.

I put both my hands on her head, looked down at her bulging eyes and kissed her lips for the longest time. She turned red and managed to smile.

"Both of you will be blessed with beautiful children," Francisco quipped. "All beautiful girls."

We laughed.

This guy was a good salesman and bullshit artist, I thought.

When Francisco turned to pour a little more tequila in his coffee, Sierra suddenly reached down and pinched my thigh hard. I closed my eyes and grimaced as the sharp pain went through my leg. I had it coming, and she had warned me. But it was worth it.

Francisco started to let his guard down a bit.

Sierra patiently began to dismantle his cautious distrust while the tequila slowly loosened his tongue. He whistled occasionally and smacked his lips after sipping some of the alcohol.

Francisco shifted into a pensive mode, appearing to mentally thumb through images, visions, and poses that he then juggled in his head to find the right one.

When he plucked it out, he took a few more steps from the canvas, leaned his head sideways and turned somber. He used wide brushes to soften the backdrop with earthy high-key colors from his kidney-shaped palette to generate a feeling of warmth and spontaneity. He manipulated the oil into strong vigorous shapes as his eyes blazed with intensity, shifting from Sierra and me to the canvas.

Sierra sat on a bench with her dress fanning out, legs crossed and hands resting on top of her thighs. I stood behind her, sombrero on my left hand and my right hand gently nesting on her shoulder. It felt good to touch her silky skin.

The kiss was worth the pain, and I was getting to know a feminine side of Mickey Madrid's daughter that she hid. The fragrance coming from her hair and skin was a blend of green apples and vanilla. It was sweet, alluring and sexy.

It was Sierra at her beautiful best, and I loved it.

Ten minutes after Francisco started painting, he began to talk. He told us about the best Mexican summer resorts, the best places to shop for leather goods and purses, and the city's ancient architecture worth visiting.

Francisco was well read and knew Mexico backwards and forwards, even the names of Aztec kings. He talked about the unrest in Mexico because of the drug trade.

After an hour, Francisco, now glassy-eyed from the expensive alcohol, suddenly whistled and shouted, "Zamora!"

The man-brute eagerly appeared like a clumsy mutt, anxious to lick his master's hand. Zamora also had tiny bits of peanut shells around his mouth. Francisco told him to go to El Toro Rojo, a local Mexican barbecue place.

Francisco was hungry, and so was I. Francisco suggested to Sierra and me that we all try the *carnitas* with the red salsa and fresh corn tortillas.

He was beginning to slur his speech. I figured it would be a good time to let Sierra use her charm and her father's friendship with Francisco to try and pry information from him.

I told Francisco that I would go with Zamora.

She told me about a rocky meeting with her father a few years ago that ended with Francisco being cursed at and told to get out of the house.

I had to be careful. Zamora wasn't through sizing us up, however. With a wary eye, he looked at Sierra and me. He then whispered something to Francisco, who motioned for him to leave.

"*Vete*," he said, reassuring him that he would be fine.

CHAPTER 29

Zamora and I drove toward downtown to El Toro Rojo, about two miles away. I felt like I was sitting beside a mangy Rottweiler with loaded gun while Sierra tried to charm a wily old cobra.

The restaurant with its domed entrance and twelve tables was busy. The mouth-watering aroma of barbecued beef and freshly made corn tortillas went beyond its doors, nearly a block down the street. All the meat was cooked in an outdoor, wood-burning adobe oven.

As soon as we walked into the place, we were greeted by a fast-paced rhythm of brown hands clapping dough into thick, round shapes to be sliced in two and stuffed with potatoes, chilies, beans, cheese and meat. The place was unpretentious and simple, painted bright yellow and green. A mural of a cockfight with feathers flying was on the most spacious wall. A large menu was also on the wall. I ordered four platters of fajitas, along with chicken mole, knowing that it would take longer to get us out the door, knowing that it would give Sierra time to get Francisco's tongue wagging.

Zamora said little, keeping a vigilant eye on the entrance, sizing up anyone who walked into the eatery. On his waistband and under his shirt was the outline of the pistol he kept tucked away. Zamora had no qualms about whipping it out and firing if he saw someone whom he felt was a threat.

His menacing stare kept strangers at bay. I turned toward the door in time to see two musicians walk into the place. One sported a big grin, exposing a silver tooth. The other had a knotted nose that had seen one too many fists. Both were sunburned, wore dark sunglasses, faded blue jeans, and hadn't shaved in days.

The two *musicos* looked haggard, as though they had played thousands of songs in countless bars and hundreds of restaurants throughout Mexico. For some reason, as soon as they arrived, the musicians quickly aroused Zamora's suspicion.

I followed Zamora's watchdog eyes.

The tall, slim one with the grin politely approached people, strumming a few inviting musical notes. He had hairy arms and crusty hands. His head cocked back slightly, hair greased back, gray-plaid unbuttoned shirt and a gold crucifix dangling from a gold chain around his neck.

The other had wide shoulders and meaty hands that casually flirted with the guitar strings. He quietly scanned the restaurant and walked up to customers with a toothy grin, hoping to shake some money in exchange for a tune or two. But they weren't having any luck. Nobody was interested. Some seated at tables at the far corners ignored the musicians.

Zamora's hand slowly slipped down to his waistline. He didn't recognize the musicians. He trusted no one, especially two disheveled strangers living on the streets. He shot them a glare that had the punch of an alpha gorilla.

A man with a bright sheen on his reddish cowboy boots and chewing on a burrito was busy talking with a woman sitting at his table near the door. His woman had layers of flab on her face and arms. She munched her food with her mouth open and licked her fingers.

A ceiling fan swirled fast and stirred the hot air. Sweat soaked the musicians' armpits. The clatter of plates like the restaurant voices rose and fell.

Nobody was in the mood for music. Growing tired of being turned down, the musicians started to leave. Then, the slim musician locked eyes with me, nodded politely, and leisurely walked to our table. The second musician walked two steps behind.

Zamora leaned back in his chair. He sensed something and grew alert. His darting eyes told me that he was ready to kick the table and blast away.

The tall musician introduced himself. His name was Mateo. He laid a gentle smile and easy eyes on Zamora who snarled, hung up a contemptuous look.

"A song?" Mateo said in Spanish. "Two songs for one price. We need money for our trip north."

Zamora shook his head and waved a dismissive hand for them to leave. His eyes blazed with alertness. Obeying his instincts, he followed their every move. The two musicians didn't appear fazed by Zamora's intensity.

The other musician, who called himself Ernesto, looked straight ahead. His Spanish was slow and drawn out. The accent and slow tongue sounded like it came from Yucatan.

"And, you, *senor.* A song while you wait?" Ernesto said.

"Sure," I said. "Why not?"

I wasn't going to let Zamora believe that I was his punk, his lapdog or buying into his paranoia, suspicions. I was in control, not him.

Zamora wasn't going to be sidestepped that easy, however. He knew the town, most of the faces, and these two and their Spanish weren't native to the area. He wanted to know more.

"*De donde, son, cabrones?*" he questioned, demanding an answer.

"Oaxaca," said Mateo. "We're going to Houston, working the bars and restaurants there. We need to pay a coyote to smuggle us across."

"Here, life is very cruel, very hard. Impossible, and sometimes, hell, pure hell." Ernesto said. "There is no work, nothing to keep us in Mexico."

Mexico was hemorrhaging from its soul, simmering with rage from its people who were collectively pointing accusatory fingers at the gringos in the United States.

In the good days, America welcomed the cheap labor for centuries even if it came via the back entrance. Now, they weren't welcomed, not wanted.

In Calera, as elsewhere in Mexico, the poor blamed the Mexican government for being forced to leave home to find work. The government, they'd say, was only good in cranking out corrupt officials, political visionaries, those who clogged up the economy with more taxes and more bureaucracy

In many places, especially along the border, the tourists stayed away. The drug cartels scared many of them away with the headless bodies, indiscriminate shootings, and endless blood flow. Fear crippled much of the country, tearing apart its economy.

Houston spelled hope for the two musicians where they believed that if they hustled enough, they could make money to send home to feed their families.

"Mexico is a miserable wasteland of poor souls and empty promises," said Mateo. "It's a tinderbox ready for the flames. Ripe for a revolution to consume the country."

For a moment, nobody said a word as Ernesto lazily ran his fingers through his hair and then, his guitar strings. But a fire burned in Zamora's eyes fueled by impatience, disdain for the two musicians and their stories.

"Play your *pinche* songs," he told them in Spanish. "And then, take your *pinche chisme* and problems somewhere else."

"What song do you want us to play?" Ernesto said and pretended he didn't hear Zamora.

"Something about lost loves. I've had plenty of those," I said.

They strummed two Mexican songs, one about God finding a place for lovers in paradise; the other was about better days, better times, and better places that were always so far away.

The music made heads turn our way. Its beautiful melody, and the sad words of the songs nearly silenced everyone in the restaurant.

The *musicos* were applauded.

I gave them $20. Mateo couldn't thank me enough for the generous tip.

"*Buena suerte*," I said.

Mateo took the money and grinned. He quickly made a haphazard sign of the cross over the $20, hoping God would multiply his blessings.

"*Que Dios lo bendiga, senor*," said Ernesto.

"*Gracias*," I said.

As he was about to leave, Ernesto suddenly pulled out a handful of Michael, the Archangel medallions inside a handkerchief.

"We sell these medallions for five dollars. Archbishop Antonio Salas Paz Delgado in Vera Cruz blessed them. It helps pay for our trip north. I'm going to give you one to protect you while you're in Mexico."

"I'll buy one," I insisted.

"No, no, no," said Mateo. "It is a gift from us. You have a good heart. When you wear it, Michael the Archangel will guide and protect you while your are in Mexico."

"Gracias, e*sta bien*," I said.

Ernesto slipped it around my neck.

"Now, an angel will surround and guide you," he said and smiled.

I lifted the polished medallion up to my face. The impression on the metal showed muscular Michael the Archangel with his omnipotent wings spread, his foot rammed on the devil's chest and about to thrust a sword in a growling Lucifer's face.

"Wear it and God will bestow his protection against demons," Ernesto told me.

"I will," I said.

Zamora wasn't impressed with religious mumble, prophecies, poets, or two ragtag musicians' pipe dreams to go to Houston to play their instruments. Zamora trusted no one other than Francisco.

As they walked out of the restaurant, Ernesto glanced back. He winked when Zamora wasn't looking, followed by a sturdy smile and a rigid thumb's up.

This was odd, very odd, to say the least. I've never had a Mexican *musico* use these kinds of Anglo-Saxon hand gestures to me or anyone else. It made me wonder about those two. What brought them to the small town of Calera with few restaurants and bars?

A few minutes later, Zamora and I headed back to Francisco's studio. We were lugging two greasy brown bags with fajitas, chicken, along with rice, beans, and avocado inside along with cans of soft drinks.

On the way back to Francisco's studio, Mateo's words about Mexico slowly crumbling haunted me as we drove down Calle Cino de Mayo.

Zamora said nothing, slumped down in his seat and muttered a few obscenities as we hit two large potholes before turning onto the main street.

The Third-World landscape in certain parts of the town suddenly took on dark luminous shadows after listening to Mexican musicians.

The apocalyptic signposts became more evident as we drove by a second time: young unemployed men standing on corners, glaring at strangers driving by, baseball caps hanging low, and dull T-shirts and baggy pants wrinkled and dirty.

Near a corner, a Mexican-Indian woman in native garb toted a baby on her back with dirty barefoot children and snotty noses running in tow, approaching people walking on the sidewalk with an outstretched palm and pleading eyes. She got turned down several times. The children, oblivious to their mother's desperation, seemed to make a game out of begging for money. A few steps behind their mother, they laughed and shared a handful of candy that one of them pulled out of his pant pocket.

A few blocks later, an old man with a long, soot-stained white beard and tattered oversized coat pushed a crumbling wheelbarrow with all his worldly belongings. He had a loaf of bread, an old aluminum pot, and a large plastic jar full of water on the wheelbarrow.

Yet, amid the crushing poverty, there were contradictions, signs of an economically vibrant city where the second-largest Corona brewing plant in Latin America is located. There were satellite dishes on rooftops, many busy shops, young people in immaculate jogging suits poking at cell phones while walking down the street, and three downtown banks.

There was the hustle and bustle of downtown Calera.

I wondered if this prosperous economic landscape would one day collapse entirely, go down under the tremendous burden of too much corruption, drugs and many hungry mouths, no jobs, and angry poor folks taking their rage into the streets.

CHAPTER 30

Sierra sat near the corner of the room. The frustration in her eyes deflated my smile, doused any hope that Francisco had coughed up a secret or two, a clue or a hint to jump start my story, help find her brother's killers.

In another room, Francisco mixed paint. After Zamora left the room with the bags of food, Sierra closed her eyes and slowly shook her head.

She mouthed, "Nothing."

I muttered a curse word. This trip was going to be a complete bust, a complete waste of time, and it nearly emptied my bank account. Francisco's tongue, even with generous shots of tequila and a pretty woman's soft voice, hadn't loosened a tiny bit to give up any information about Mickey Madrid's drug dealing days or how for decades his drug-smuggling routes had gone undetected by the feds and all their electronic safeguard strung along the border.

I began to wonder if Francisco knew anything to begin with.

"Play hardball," I said in a low, demanding voice.

"He's not going to say anything. *Nada*," she said.

"Turn up the charm. Sling the bullshit. Get tough. Do it," I said.

Her eyes fired darts in my direction.

"Do I look like your bitch? Shut up."

"I should have never listened to you."

"We can pull the plug on this right now. Is that what you want?"

I shook my head.

As soon as Francisco walked into the room, we clammed up. The ends of our lips headed south at the same time.

Francisco said nothing. He stood near the portrait, hips on his shoulders, a cigarette dangling from his lips and bloodshot eyes. With contemplative silence, he took a few steps back from the painting and turned his head from one side to the other before he meticulously went over some lines with a fine brush dipped in an eggshell white paint.

"Beauty has its own time to come out of its shell. It takes patience and gentle coaxing," he said.

"'Patience and gentle coaxing. Beautifully said," Sierra said, putting spunk in her words. *"Verdad, mi amor?"*

"Yes, of course," I said.

I reached inside my shirt pocket, pulled out and showed Sierra the medallion.

"Check this out," I said.

She brought it within inches of her nose.

"How much did you pay for the good luck charm?" she said coldly.

"I got it from a couple of *musicos*. They gave it to me, and said 'the medallion was recently blessed by the Archbishop of Vera Cruz,'" I said.

"And you believed it?" she scoffed.

"Why not? I mean who knows? The archbishop is probably friends with the pope who is close to God," I said with all the cynicism of a hardened reporter. "So I'm, sort of, hooked up and in the God loop. I bet if I had given them another five bucks, I would have gotten the Pope's cell phone number. "

Francisco laughed.

"It's a souvenir," I said. "Who knows it might ward off vampires and werewolves too."

Sierra looked at the medallion, Francisco and back to me.

"Maybe, just maybe, it will improve your pool game, *mi amor*," she said sarcastically.

Without taking his eyes off the painting, Francisco said.

"You play pool?"

"Strictly for beers. It helps me relax," I said, flashing a dopey grin.

I pretended to be amused by Sierra's snide remarks. But it was obvious that she was getting payback for the lip I gave her along with the unwanted kiss.

Taking a deep breath, Francisco walked into the other room and summoned Zamora. Zamora shuffled back into the room, looking like a mangy dog waiting for scraps from the master's table. Francisco tossed him two burritos. Zamora sniffed the burritos, chortled and left, but not before peering at Sierra and me.

"Creepy," she whispered.

Zamora scraped his wooden chair across the concrete to put it in its rightful place. He sat beside a small window facing the entrance and munched on his burritos, hiding his face behind the thick curtain from anyone who dared to walk up to the studio unannounced and uninvited. This time, an AK-47 leaned against Zamora's chair. His gun buried in his waistband.

The assault weapon made me uneasy. Sierra's eyes widened when she saw it. Francisco returned and immediately followed my line of sight that was fixed on the weapon. He offered some reassurance.

"The weapon discourages thieves," he said. "In Mexico, even the devil is packing heat."

Sierra and I nervously chuckled. Everybody popped open the cans of soda and started eating lunch.

Once in a while, we could hear the old chair creak as Zamora positioned his body to pull the curtain back slightly when he heard the slightest noise, imagined or real.

As soon as Zamora began clacking and smacking his lips after biting his burrito, Francisco doused the irritating noises.

"*Parale*," Francisco shouted at Zamora. "*Eres un Marano.* We have guests."

He stopped the lip smacking. I figured that he and Francisco had this strange working relationship. Both of them were holding closely guarded, ugly secrets, festering secrets.

Time was running out along with my patience.

When Francisco went to the restroom to take a leak, I leaned over and whispered to Sierra.

"Now. Do it now. Go for the throat," I said. "We need something."

When Francisco returned, he started telling lame, annoying jokes about Mexicans' fascination with death and rituals between bites of his fajitas and sips of soda.

With Zamora occasionally peeking out the window while eating his burrito, Sierra began to talk about her father again, after sensing my impatience.

She weaved her way, slowly, and soon gave Francisco some details about how her brother Emilio had died in the violent car explosion.

A flash of rage passed through her eyes when she talked about why they had to keep Emilio's coffin closed. The explosion tore up his body, Sierra told Francisco.

"My brother had nothing to do with any of this," she said. "*Nada.*"

"*Pobrecito*," Francisco said.

Sierra pushed the envelope and went for the kill.

"You and my father, the last time you went to my house, he was furious about what you told him. Why? What was that about? What did you tell him?"

"A big misunderstanding," he said, finishing the remainder of the tequila in his cup.

"A misunderstanding?" Sierra pressed him. "He was very angry at you."

"It's the past," he said, dismissing the question. "He got upset and felt I was charging him too much for one of my paintings. I wanted five-thousand dollars."

We both knew he was lying. Mickey Madrid spent money like water. A five-thousand-dollar painting was nothing to him.

"Who killed my brother?" Sierra said, burrowing her eyes into red-faced Francisco.

"I don't know. I really don't," he said.

Fearful of the daughter of a big-time drug dealer, Francisco took a swallow of the tequila.

"Tell me," she demanded. "What do you know?"

"Some things, especially in Mexico, shouldn't be repeated. Shouldn't be questioned. It can be very dangerous. The wrong word, the wrong question, in certain circles, can get a person killed."

"My father would have gone to the ends of the earth to find out who killed my brother. He isn't here. I am."

"Okay, I will tell you only what I know. You can draw your own conclusions. Late one evening, I got a message from Nino, your father's bodyguard," Francisco said.

"What message?" She said.

I said nothing, sat comfortably on the bench and listened.

Francisco gave me a suspicious glance.

"He's my fiancée. I trust him, and so did my father. He's family," she told Francisco.

Francisco nodded and poured more tequila into his cup. He sat on a small stool, scratched his beard, and straightened his hat. He shifted his eyes from me to Sierra.

"One day, a boy came knocking," he said. "He had a message. Nino sent word that he wanted to talk to me and wanted to meet at *La Palmera*, a cantina in Zacatecas. I thought your father wanted another painting. I was excited."

Francisco briefly stared at the cement floor as though the words were surfacing from the cracks, and he was reading them as they rose.

"It wasn't about a painting," Francisco said. "When I got to the bar, Nino told me about Los Zetas. He said they had told him that the Colombians were going to try and make a move to take over your father's drug business. Los Zetas had an offer. They asked me to approach your father with their offer."

"Offer? What offer?" Sierra said angrily. "What plans?"

"Los Zetas would help protect your father's business from the Sinaloa Cartel and the Colombians. But I later learned that they had other plans too. They wanted to muscle out the Juarez Cartel."

Francisco had a worrisome look. He paused before he finished explaining the nefarious plan that was unfurled by the Zetas.

"In exchange for their protection, Los Zetas would collect ten percent of the profits," he said. "That would get them inside your father's drug routes."

"Why did Nino come to you?" she asked.

"I learned later that Nino was working a fat deal with Los Zetas. Nino was the Zeta's *rata*."

"Who killed my brother?"

He paused and slowly shook his head.

"Like I said, 'I don't know,'" Francisco said. "A week before he died, I went across the border to look for your brother. I thought like everybody else, that he was helping run your father's business. So I tried to set up a meeting between him and Los Zetas, hoping to find a more sympathetic ear to negotiate with them. Then, I found out he had been killed."

Francisco drank the remaining tequila from his cup.

"The Colombians, I suspect, had him killed. I became afraid that they would come for me next," he said. "So, I hired Zamora. He came with as many problems as a dog has fleas. He was a bodyguard in Guadalajara. Protected a businessman. But he drank too much and stole from him."

"What did my father say about Los Zetas' offer?"

"It was an insult to him," Francisco said. "He thought I was involved *con* Los Zetas. He told me, 'don't ever come back to my house with these insults or I'll kill you.' I left quickly. He said he wasn't going to get involved with savages who kill women and children."

"Who's running my father's drug business?" Sierra asked.

"*Quien sabe?*" he replied. "I heard different things, rumors and mostly *chisme*. I don't really know. But I heard it's some Mexican in Juarez who they call *El Gusano*."

When Francisco looked up, there was a smile, almost angelic, as though he had just left a confessional booth, as though he had just rid himself of some evil spirit who released the choke-hold on his soul.

"That's all I know," he said. "Nothing more."

I knew there was much more to all this, much more. I detected insincerity in his voice and saw through his bogus, mournful eyes.

It got quiet, a long drawn out and awkward quiet.

We left as the sunlight stretched the late afternoon shadows in Calera. Francisco walked beside us as we ambled to the car.

Zamora was several feet behind. His eyes shifted from one end of the street to the other, a hand close to his waistband.

As I slowly drove off, I glanced in the rearview mirror and saw Zamora lean close to Francisco's ear. Zamora said something that made the old painter grimace and wipe sweat from his forehead with a red handkerchief. Francisco put his hand into his pocket. He stared down the street at an old white car with tinted windows two blocks away with two people inside. The car made a U-turn, slowly turned the corner, and disappeared.

Francisco and Zamora hurriedly walked into the studio. Zamora looked over his shoulder a few times, with his handgun now in the open, by his side. I didn't say anything to Sierra about the white car or anything I had seen in the rearview mirror as we left Calera.

When we left the city limits, Sierra turned to me and said, "We can pump him for more information tomorrow."

"I don't know if he knows anything else."

I didn't tell her that I saw Francisco stand on the bucket and hide something in the ceiling when I peeped inside his house. I didn't want that to be in the back of her mind when she questioned Francisco, resulting in Sierra saying something about the white car and him clamming up.

I glanced at Sierra who stared at the mountain range as a blanket of clouds hovered just above the horizon.

"Look, I going to lay this all out, right now," I said. "I don't trust Francisco. He's a snake, and he's hiding something, and he's lying."

"I know. I don't trust him either," she said to my surprise, not taking her eyes off the mountains.

After we left the city limits of Calera and were several miles down the highway, Sierra turned off the air conditioner and rolled down her window. The cool, evening air teased my hair.

I turned the knob until I found a Mexican news station. The music was soon interrupted by breaking news. The country's oil fields were under attack, the news announcer said in Spanish.

Two major roads were closed after six Pemex pipelines were blown up in Veracruz and Tlaxcala early today, the announcer said. A leftist guerilla group claimed responsibility, vowing to continue their attacks until half of the revenue from the oil fields is given to the poor. Mexico is the world's sixth largest oil producer and second major oil supplier to the United States.

I clicked off the radio.

"If the peasants get enough guns, this country is going to collapse under the weight of corruption, drugs and Third World poverty," I said.

Later, I started sending notes through my cell phone to my desk at the newsroom. She read a magazine that she had bought at the airport in LA and an hour later, she fell asleep.

After I transferred my notes from my head to my cell phone, I copied and pasted them in an email. I immediately deleted the emails I had sent from my cell phone. I then erased all my notes I had made on the phone.

A few seconds after I hit the log off button, Sierra jolted up in the bed. She gasped for air, looking around the room with wide eyes.

"Are you okay?" I asked.

She nodded, "A bad dream."

Within minutes, Sierra was asleep again. Her breathing was light, chest hardly rising. I sat at the edge of my bed. My eyes weighed heavy. I yawned.

Footsteps, footsteps in the hallway headed in our direction. I clicked off the light. The footsteps stopped in front of our door before continuing and fading away.

My heart raced. I slowly rose, walked over and gently put my ear against door. It was quiet. I waited, opened the door and looked both ways down the hallway. Nothing.

I grabbed a pillow and a chair. I pushed the chair near the door, turned off the lamplight, and waited, hoping the footsteps didn't return.

Moon rays slipped into the room through the top of an arched glass-stained window above some curtain-clothed French doors that led to a fourth-floor balcony. I lay my head on my pillow on the chair and looked at the moonlight scrape, the ceiling. I could see a bright blur of stars, twirling in the sky.

My fingertips followed the chain around my neck, followed it until my thumb and forefinger rubbed the imprint on the St. Michael the Archangel medallion. I held it as though it had some magical powers. I mumbled a short prayer, asking God to get us out of Mexico safely, get us out quick, feeling insecure about our safety.

I had never had this strong feeling before of impending danger, never.

An hour went by before a deep sleep swallowed me. When I woke up, I was in my bed. Sierra was taking an early morning shower and humming. I vaguely recalled getting up in the middle of the night, pushing the chair back to where it was before I moved it and getting into bed.

I reached for my watch on the nightstand. I was 7:00 a.m.

I waited for Sierra to come out of the bathroom with all but a flimsy towel holding her curves together, barely hiding all the good parts, another towel twisted around her hair like a turban.

Thick traces of hot steam crept out from between her vanilla-colored breasts.

My fantasy was quickly snuffed out.

She bolted out of the bathroom with a hair dryer going full blast, wearing tight jeans and a blue blouse, of course, giving orders as though I was one of her servants.

"Get up. Pack up the clothes we need and let's go," she said.

I nodded. I didn't tell her about the footsteps and the person who briefly stopped outside our door during the night. Maybe it was an honest mistake, somebody on the wrong floor, wrong room, and maybe, not.

We went down and had a light breakfast and were on the road, back to Francisco's place. It would be the last day to try and milk more information from him, try to convince him to tell us more.

"We need more, more details, more names of people and places," I said.

"It's not easy. When the animal instincts of these people kick up and they suspect anything, they go into self-preservation mode. That's dangerous, very dangerous."

"We need to get in and get out quickly without arousing any suspicion. Zamora is giving the creeps, and I believe Francisco is on to us," I said.

"Yeah. I am getting the same vibes."

CHAPTER 31

An eerie quiet engulfed me after I pulled up in front up Francisco's studio. It was too quiet. Zamora was nowhere in sight. Something wasn't right. Sierra didn't get the same feelings. She used the rear-view mirror to brush her hair, got out of the car, and headed toward the studio with a purposeful stride.

Near the end of the block, a dog that heard the doors of our rental car slam shut and started barking. Sierra started to open the six-foot wrought-iron gate to Francisco's yard.

"Wait," I said.

"What?"

"Just wait a minute. Stay put."

"Why?"

"Something is not right."

My eyes swept across the windows and house. Nothing. There was no sign of Zamora or Francisco. The curtains didn't move ever so slightly, signaling that Zamora was peeking out the window.

Nothing happened, nothing moved.

I told her to stay. She dismissed my suspicions as unfounded fears with an eye roll and by shaking her head. She started to walk toward the studio again.

"Don't move," I said. "I'm dead serious."

"What's wrong?" she said, agitated.

"Get in the car," I ordered her. "Now."

"What?" She said, hanging up a quizzical look. "But —"

"Go."

After she was inside the car, I went to the side of the house. My heart pounded faster. The studio door was wide open. I called out for Francisco, then Zamora a few times.

Nada.

I cautiously walked toward the studio. If someone were standing around the corner with a gun, he'd fire before I could blink. Worse, someone could run up and bury a knife in my chest. I took a few steps, stopped and listened.

Finally, I entered the short hallway. I stood there. I called Francisco's name again and swallowed hard. Nobody replied. I called Zamora's name a few more times.

Nothing, but flies buzzing.

I look down. A trail of bloody footprints came out of Francisco's large studio room. The footsteps went down the hallway, out the door. I walked slowly down the damp, bloody hallway, now sweating, heart thumping. Every fiber in my body screamed for me to leave, run like hell and not look back. But hardedge, reporter's curiosity kept me going, uneasily and slowly taking each step, stopping and listening along the way.

"Francisco. Zamora." I called out.

No response. A few flies landed on my face. I shook my head. I kept walking.

At the end of the hallway, I looked inside the room where Francisco did his artwork. I froze.

Images, horrific images bombarded my mind.

Blood splattered everywhere, on the walls, floor. Two headless bodies were there, one was propped up. It was Francisco's torso, slumped on a chair. His swollen, beaten head, as big as a pumpkin, sat on his lap.

Francisco's head had a Z sliced on his forehead and on his chest. Los Zetas, I thought. The grotesque handiwork of Los Zetas.

Legions of flies were all over the room. I was breathing erratically.

Eyes reflecting excruciating pain mixed with horror, mouth opened wide. Bloody handprints were everywhere, signs of a violent struggle, of rage. The smell of blood and alcohol was thick.

The fly buzzing got louder. Some feasted on blood and saliva around his mouth. The stench of blood, alcohol, feces and bodies starting to decompose choked the air.

Fear gave my body an adrenaline jolt. My legs stiffened, then became wobbly. I put my hand against the wall to keep from falling down.

The crime scene looked like a butcher shop from Dante's Inferno.

Heaving, I slowly turned my head across the room. Zamora's body was against the wall disemboweled, his head stuffed inside his belly. His intestines around his neck and coiled around his hand as though he had ripped them out of his body. His mouth contorted and lips sliced up and dangling.

Zamora's rifle was leaning against a wall, which told me that Francisco and Zamora knew their killers. Zamora didn't bother to grab his weapon, and probably let the assassins inside, believing that they had nothing to fear.

My lower jaw twitched. I couldn't move. My brain shut down, overwhelmed, trying to process the monstrous crime scene. The blood, pools of dark blood, butchered body parts strewn here and there. I groaned in horror, putting my palms on my forehead with my back against the wall.

I wanted to vomit as the stench gripped my nostrils. I was sick, shaking. Nauseated.

My thoughts were all over the map.

These brutes, these demons that were responsible for the macabre human sculptures could still be inside the house, lurking and waiting to strike. My mouth struggled to gulp down some air. I turned away, shaking uncontrollably.

The bottle of Tequila that Sierra had given Francisco was near the coffee pot. It was half full. I grabbed the bottle, opened it and took several gulps to steady my shaking hands and slow down the erratic circuitry inside my brain. It was on overloaded. Mental fuses were popping, sparking. My psyche couldn't process what I was seeing.

I turned around, moving toward the door. As I made my way out, Sierra appeared in the doorway and called out my name. I opened my mouth. Nothing came out.

"Are you okay?" she said and hurried over to help me. "Jack. What's wrong?"

I shook and emptied my lungs.

"They're dead," I said.

"Who?"

Before I could stop her, she looked inside the large room. She screamed so loud that it ignited a stray dog's bark in the alley. Stunned, Sierra wrapped her arms tightly around my chest. She buried her head inside my shoulder. She started crying, trembling and could barely speak.

"I want to go. I want to go. Please, let's go," she said frantically. "Please, let's go now. Please."

"Okay, okay, okay," I said, gently stroking her hair and kissing the side of her head. "It's okay."

With her head pressing against my chest, I led her out the door to the back yard. I had her sit on a large patch of dirt surrounded by high weeds, a few yards from the house. She held my hand tightly.

"I've got to get back inside," I said.

"No. Don't go. Please don't go, Jack," she pleaded with fervor. "Please, don't leave me here alone."

"I got to go back inside. I forgot something," I said.

I knelt beside Sierra. She clutched my hand and put it against her breasts, held it tightly, panting.

"Don't leave, please," she whimpered. "I am scared, Jack."

"I'll go get it, and we'll leave. I promise."

I took off my Saint Michael's medallion and slipped it around her neck. She wiped some tears away and gripped the medallion.

"Here, it's good luck. It wards off evil. I'll be back," I said, half believing it.

She rocked slightly back and forth. I went back inside. My eyes felt as though they were walking a visual tightrope, avoiding the pools of blood, headless corpses, protruding intestines, and severed heads with terror-filled eyes open and looking straight up.

I couldn't sidestep these images. I had to look at the bodies one more time so I could describe it all in my newspaper story.

Goosebumps surfaced, the hair on my arms and in the back of my head rose.

A blood trail indicated that the bullet-ridden bodies of Francisco and Zamora were dragged to a small bathroom where the smell of piss weighed heavily.

I looked down. My foot nearly touched the tip of a bloody butcher knife. A hatchet lay close to the sink was also used to slice, dice, and carve up the remains.

I went to the other room used to store paintings, searching for the large metal bucket, the one I saw Francisco stand on when I had peeked inside the studio through the window. I found it, turned it over and placed the metal bucket directly under the spot where I saw Francisco put it. I took off a ceiling panel. My hands were twitched.

My fingertips felt around the surface. I felt a cold large plastic cover wrapped around a machine. I grabbed it. Unwrapping it, I found a small laptop. Francisco was computer savvy. I was surprised. I carefully brought it down, sat on the bucket, got a butter knife from the next room that was beside the coffee pot, came back and began to frantically turn the two screws on the laptop as fast as possible.

The Tequila started to calm me down a bit, steadying my hands.

I opened the computer panel. I took out the hard drive and slipped it into my pocket. I screwed the panel back on, wrapped the laptop in plastic again, and put it back where it had been on the ceiling. I put the bucket in the exact spot where I had found it.

I got a rusty kitchen knife that Francisco used to open coffee bags. Four slices from the knife took the half-finished portrait of Sierra and me out of its wooden frame. I folded the portrait several times and crammed it into my waistband.

I didn't want our face plastered on wanted leaflets all over Mexico. I hurried out the door, snatching the neck of the Tequila bottle on my way out. The bright sun hit my face as I stepped out the door. I squinted and suck up as much fresh air as I could.

Outside, I shook my head violently, believing that this might help shake out some of the grisly images from my head. I glanced at Sierra. She was sitting in a fetal position trying to ride out what she had seen, still slowly rocking back and forth and quietly invoking a higher power. Lips moved rapidly. I stood over her. She looked up. I offered her some Tequila to calm her nerves. She politely refused.

"I'll be okay," she said, sobbing.

"Take a few swallows. It'll stop the shakes. Drink."

She took a long gulp.

I took another gulp of the Tequila to chase away the horror my eyes had seen. I put the bottle to one side, flopped down beside her, and stared into the distance.

Sierra scooted near me and tightly hugged my arm, occasionally wiping away a tear or two. She leaned her head against the crux of my neck. Her hair smelled like a strawberry patch. Its fragrance had a calming effect, briefly holding my soul in its arms and gently rocking it.

A few minutes later, her breathing slowed down. She eased the grip on my arm, and the shivering had subsided.

"Jack," she whispered.

"What?"

"Please, let's just go home. Just leave here. I don't want to be here anymore. I want to go home."

"Just sit still for a minute. Wait until you get a buzz."

Chirping birds interrupted the long quiet. A passing breeze ruffled the leaves of trees that lined both sides of the house.

I could feel Sierra's heart beat as her chest rose and gently collapsed. Then, a thought pierced my brain like a dart. I got to move the car before it was spotted.

Just as her heartbeat was slowing down, we heard a vehicle brake hard. The sound made Sierra twitch. I put my finger against my lips. She nodded. I went and poked my head up from behind a fence on the side of the house.

Two men, big men with cowboy hats and long sideburns, quickly got out of the mysterious white car with dark windows. We had seen the car at the end of the block as we left Francisco's studio yesterday.

The two men looked inside the rental car and immediately headed for the car trunk and took out a shotgun. Voices, deep and very upset, cursed in Spanish. They muttered and mumbled. Cursed and spat.

One of them racked a round into the shotgun. The car trunk slammed shut. I hurried and grabbed Sierra. Her eyes got big. She had heard the noises. She stood and started to say something. I picked and put the Tequila bottle behind a tree, put my hand over her mouth tightly and the other hand on the back of her neck at the same time to seal off any sound or frightful utterance.

"Run," I said above a whisper. "Run like hell. They're here."

Like two thoroughbred horses leaving the starting gate, we bolted. We held hands and ran, heading for the five-foot cinder block wall a few feet away. I helped her hump over the wall as though she was a rag doll. Then, I climbed over it. I nearly landed on Sierra.

Seconds after we scaled the wall, the two men walked into the back yard. When I felt that the two were inside the house, I peered over the wall and caught the backs of two burly shadows armed with what appeared to be a shotgun and a pistol cautiously making their way deeper into the house.

As they knocked things over with their fists, broke glass and kicked closet doors open, they spewed out curse words and threats.

They were looking for something.

I motioned to Sierra with my hands to keep her head down, seal her lips, and follow me.

We took off, doubled over, making sure that nobody on the other side of the wall would spot our heads. After we ran past the wall, we lifted our upper bodies and ran as fast as we could. Sierra ran a few steps behind. Adrenaline fueled out legs.

The male voices moved outside the house and approached the cinder block wall we had just scaled over. I figured that they were searching for the owners of the car parked near the front of Francisco's studio. They probably spotted our fresh bloody footprints.

I would hear their movements - fast approaching the wall. I could hear glass being smashed against a wall. I figured it was probably the bottle of Tequila.

We ran four blocks and cut in and out of some small alleyways between two brick houses, and then suddenly stopped. We were both out of breath. Sierra nearly fell on me. With one arm, I pushed her against the wall. I popped my head around the corner.

The men in white shirts and dark pants walked fast in our direction, half a mile away and closing. One pointed in my direction. The other fired his handgun. The bullets clipped the top of a cinderblock fence, and one ricocheted off a wrought iron gate.

I peeked out from behind a large, rusty barrel and saw the two break into a stride in our direction. I grabbed Sierra's hand. We took off running, again.

We dashed by crumbling houses and crooked fences, running on dented roads, cracked sidewalks and onto dirt alleys, past junked cars, and around old bicycles. Barking and fenced in dogs along the way were alerting the two men of the direction we were heading. Sierra held on to my hand with a vise-like grip. She was now keeping up with me, our legs fueled by a mixture of fear and pure adrenaline.

We went into another alley that ran deep into a neighborhood a mile from a large city park. We ran until we got to a wooden door. Ducking inside, we found ourselves in a backyard.

We startled a middle-aged woman with a round face, flabby dark-brown arms, and a ragged green apron. She hung clothes on a clothesline. The startled woman started to speak, but Sierra, trying to catch her breath, begged her to help us before she said a word.

"Help us. Assassins. They want to kill us. Please help us," Sierra hurriedly said in Spanish. *"Por favor, senora."*

Big-eyed, the woman looked at Sierra and me and didn't move an inch. I knew she was weighing the cost she might bear for helping us.

"Por favor," a tearful Sierra pleaded. *"Por Dios santo los quieren matar."*

The woman snapped out of her trance, and went to the side of the house. She stacked up an old wooden box and put another one on top. Pointing to the boxes and a flat roof, she said, *"Al techo, pronto"*

I climbed onto the boxes and got on top of the roof, careful to stay as low as possible to keep from being detected. Once on top of the roof, I waved for Sierra to climb up.

As she stepped on the boxes, the men with booming voices walked quickly down the alley. I put my hands around both Sierra's wrists like clamps. I tightened my muscles and used all my strength, every ounce of energy, to whisk her up high enough so she was able to put one foot on the roof.

The Mexican woman rapidly removed the boxes. I could hear her opening the back screen door to her house, going inside and the sound of a broom. I surmised that she covering our footprints with a broom. She went back to hanging clothes.

A minute later, the two-armed men burst through the wooden backyard door.

The woman screamed, *"Por favor. No tengo dinero."*

The two men cursed.

"Cayate," one said.

One man asked whether she had seen two young people, a man and a woman, running through the alley. She said with a frantic voice that she had not. She put on a good acting job.

"Why? Who are you?" She asked meekly.

The man with a heavy lisp and deep lungs lied.

"*Federales*. We're looking for these two," he said. "They killed two people."

Nobody said anything. There was a long pause. I thought the woman had believed them and now was motioning that we were up on the roof. If she did, Sierra and I would soon be dead.

"What do they look like? Show me photographs," the woman said. "Do you have badges, *senores*?"

"Shut your mouth. We ask the question," he barked. "Have you seen them?"

"No, *senor. No, Nadien ha passado por aqui.*"

I closed my eyes and swallowed hard. The woman believed our story. I was relieved. We lay still, squinting with our faces toward the sun. I slowly turned my head and saw Sierra with tears streaming from the side of her eyes, lips moving fast from one prayer to another. There was a terrifying silence before one of the men coughed. I assumed their eyes scanned the yard, perhaps looking for footsteps on the ground to see if they could trace our movements. One of the men stood in the alley.

"*Quieren unos cafécitos, jefes?*" the old woman said softly, trying to distract their attention with coffee.

The woman was also poor, and it was her humble way of showing them they were in charge along with cutting the tension that was as thick as mud. If they found us on the roof, she knew she'd probably end up dead along with whoever else was in the house.

"*Vamonos*," one of the men said loudly.

His voice startled Sierra. She twitched, held my hand tightly with her fingernails digging into my flesh. I put my mouth within centimeters of her ear and barely whispered.

"It's okay. It's okay. They're leaving. Don't move. It's okay," I told her.

She eased her grip.

Just as they were about to leave, they asked the woman if anyone was inside the house? She told them her husband was bedridden in the bedroom.

"He is sick with diabetes. Almost blind," she replied with vocal chords now tainted with fear.

I prayed that she wouldn't change her mind and give us up. Her voice indicated that the two goons were terrorizing her with guns and intimidating looks.

"Go inside, *senores, por favor,* if you don't believe me. Please," she said humbly. "My husband is there. Please, come inside, *senor.*"

They walked into the house and woke up her sleeping husband. He moaned with pain.

"Who are these men?" he asked his wife in Spanish.

"La Cruz Roja," one joked, and the other laughed.

The woman humored the two men.

"These gentlemen are looking for two dangerous suspects. A woman and a man. They're *federales.*"

From atop the roof, we heard the two men opening a closet door and checking another room. One used his cell phone, talking to somebody named Pantejas. Moments later, they went out the door. As soon as their heavy footsteps began to fade in the direction of the studio and our rented car, I raised my head just enough to see two burly brutes walking down the middle of the street.

While one spoke on a cell phone, the one with a white cowboy hat made sweeping movements with his head to try to find his human quarry. He even looked under parked cars. Two blocks away, he spotted a group of neighborhood youngsters in a semi-circle around two beat-up bicycles. He walked toward them, whistling and motioning for them to come to him. They did. Whipping out his wallet, he pulled out some American money and waved it in the air.

He raised his arm and pointed toward Francisco's studio. As soon as he finished speaking, the four boys, one barefooted, eagerly scattered like bloodhounds throughout the neighborhood unknowingly playing a deadly game of hide-and-go-seek.

I dipped my head when one of the men and the children turned in my direction. My glasses slipped off my face. I picked them up and pushed them against my face, hoping that I hadn't been spotted. I felt Sierra's pounding heart, her body locked by terror.

"Let's go," she said. "Let's get out of here."

"We leave now, we're dead. It's not safe, yet," I said.

"I want to go," she insisted.

"Do you want to end up like Francisco and Zamora?"

"No."

"Then shut up," I said angrily. "Quit bitching. We will be here until it is safe to come down."

She sighed.

I told her some youngsters were now hunting for us. We had to let things cool down. Minutes later, I heard two youngsters going by the house, stopping briefly, then continuing to walk. They talked about canvassing downtown streets, and one suggested that we might have taken refuge in the downtown church. They ran like young, eager hunting dogs after two foxes.

Seconds later, the middle-aged woman's words jolted us.

"*Senor*," she said in a low voice. "*Senor*, they're gone."

I told her that we were going to stay up on her roof until we felt it was safe to come down. She said she understood and left.

The sun blazed straight over our faces. We were soaked with sweat. The red tiles on the roof were beginning to cook our bodies. I didn't know how long we would be able to stay in the hot sun.

A few minutes later, we heard the old woman return, stand underneath close to the house and near to where we lay on the roof. She flung a rope tied to a rock.

"*Jalale*," she said in Spanish. "Pull hard."

I pried loose from Sierra, crawled over, and slowly pulled the rope. At the end of the rope was a plastic milk container filled with water. We quenched our thirst. Sierra took long, hard swallows. A few minutes later, another rope tied to a rock was flung up to the roof. I crawled over, grabbed, and began to pull it up.

Just as I pulled the makeshift fishing line over the edge of the roof, I heard more young boys walk quickly through the alley. They were upset because the police were also out looking for us. If they found us first, they'd lose the finder's fee. One of the boys swore at the police for showing up and spoiling their chances of earning some serious cash.

The boys playfully laughed and yelled to other youngsters at the end of the alley. A shrill whistle, and they took off running. The search now became a youthful sport, a contest. One that would cost us our lives.

I finally reeled in the plastic bucket. Inside were a sheet and a blanket. While on my elbows with my head as low as possible, I spread one blanket over the red tiles. I motioned for Sierra to roll over and lay on the blanket. I dragged myself over and lay next to her. I covered our upper bodies with the sheet to bend the direct sunrays.

We waited. It was the safest place to be, on top of a Mexican rooftop that belonged to a poor family in Calera.

We were exhausted and fell asleep. When I woke up, we were drenched in perspiration. Sierra stirred, opened her eyes, gasped for air, and was about to scream. I put my hand over her mouth.

"Shhhhh," I said. "It's okay. It's okay."

Ten minutes later, the woman told us that she had walked to the store four blocks away.

"The boys are gone," she said. "Police are everywhere. The neighbors said they found Don Francisco and his guard dead inside the studio."

"We need to get down." I said.

The old woman immediately got the smaller box on top of the larger one so we could climb down. Slowly, we descended from the roof, trying to make ourselves as inconspicuous as possible. Our bodies clung to the top of the roof so we wouldn't be spotted from a distance.

As soon as we got down and were inside the woman's house, I told her what had happened, saying that we were there to get our portrait painted.

"We didn't kill anybody. They were dead when we got there," I said. "You've got to believe us. I swear, we're not killers."

Without hesitation, she said, "I believe you. Those men, *son demonios*. I could see the flames of hell in their eyes."

Her name was Lydia. She motioned us to come inside. We walked into her husband's bedroom. The smell of vinegar and old sweat filled the room. Her husband's name was Eloy. He worked in the bean fields before diabetes ravished his body. His skin was a hard brown tan. He wore a graying beard with a few crumbs of food on it, and his face was badly cracked by time and toiling in the sun.

Lydia told him who we were and why we were hiding.

"Be careful," Eloy said in Spanish. "These men have no consciences."

"*La gente de Mexico*, most are good, humble and hardworking people who are tired of these drug devils who ravage *nuestra tierra*, *nustra gente*," Lydia. "We pray that God, one day, rids this country of this scourge, and lets us live in peace."

Then, they talked about their son, Alberto, who worked at the beer brewing plant on the outskirts of Calera.

"He works hard and is planning his wedding to a girl from a good family," said Lydia, puffed up with pride. *"Mijo, es muy honesto, muy inteligente."*

Eloy told us to wait until it gets dark so his son could sneak us out with his truck.

"Police are all over the streets. It's not safe," Lydia said.

Lydia let Sierra and I clean up. She served up caldo de res with corn tortillas and coffee. We were hungry, and it was delicious. By the time their lanky son Alberto, with the long sideburns and large hands arrived, a light sprinkle was cooling down the evening.

Alberto was at first suspicious of why we were there, asking some questions. But he was a listener and did what his mother told him to do. Lydia said she believed us. That we had good hearts. Alberto nodded and grinned. He made sure his father was okay before we drove off. As we walked out the door, we hugged the old woman and her husband. Sierra swatted a tear. She promised to come back one day and repay them for helping us.

"God repays. Don't worry," said Lydia. "Go. *Que Dios los bendiga.* Be very careful."

Alberto's plan was to drive along the side streets and enter the main road once we got close to the city limits so we wouldn't have to slow down for the weekend traffic.

He had told us about a makeshift checkpoint near the town square as a result of the murders and extra police cars patrolling the streets.

Sierra and I bunched up on the floor of the front passenger side of the large truck. He threw a blanket and an old saddle on top of us, just in case we had to stop or slow down next to one of the tractor-trailer rigs with high seats that frequently go through

Calera. The high seats let those inside the large trucks look down and see what was inside other vehicles.

Alberto reassured us not to worry because most in Calera recognized his truck, including the cops. It was unlikely that anyone would be suspicious and stop him. The rain was now coming down hard. We could hear the windshield wiper swaying back and forth.

As we drove, Alberto kept telling us where we were going, saying that, if we were caught, we'd be taken to the police station.

"They'd let you go before anybody ever knows you were there," said Alberto. "Some calls are made, you'll step out of the station and get kidnapped. Nobody will ever see you again."

Alberto told us that it was hard to be a good cop in Mexico.

"The claws of the cartels are dug deep into Mexico's belly," he said. "You either take their bribes or you wind up dead."

When we turned a corner, a police car's red light went up and lit the inside of the truck. It startled Sierra who stiffened up. It followed Albert a couple of blocks. The patrol car flicked on its lights and briefly turned on its siren. Alberto pulled over.

"Don't move. Don't say a word," he said, rolling down the truck's window.

The police car suddenly pulled up beside him. The patrol car window went down. The rain made it hard to see who was inside, but he recognized the voice.

"*Oyes buey,*" a male in the patrol car said. "*Que onda?*"

"*Julian, que pues?* What's going on?" Alberto said in Spanish.

"*Estamos buscando un cabron y una muchacha. Mataron a Francisco y su bofo Zamora,*" said Julian.

"I heard," said Alberto in Spanish. "A man and a woman killed them?"

"Yes, two strangers. They're not from Calera. Seen any strangers on the streets?" said Julian, speaking Spanish.

Alberto replied, "No, *nadien. Ni touristas.*"

"*Orale*," he said. "*Oyes*, Myrna asks about you all the time."

"The secretary with the big ass and nice tits?"

"Yeah," Julian said and laughed. "She told me she likes your truck. So take her for a long ride and show her your stick shift."

"She's too wild." Alberto chuckled. "If Elizabeth ever found out about it, she'd never talk to me again."

"When is the *boda?*" Julian said.

"We plan to marry next summer. I will send you an invitation," Alberto said.

"Gracias. Elizabeth is a good girl. Too old-fashioned for my tastes," said Julian. "Know what I mean? Good girls, you marry. *Putas*, like Myrna, you use until you find a good girl like Elizabeth."

Alberto laughed heartily to ward off any suspicion from Julian. The patrol car radio squawked, possibly suspects spotted near an intersection. Julian quickly said goodbye and sped off.

As he drove, he told us that he and Julian were boyhood friends and both had been altar boys at the church. Alberto said he suspected that Julian, who came from a good family, was taking bribes. Making it clear, however, that Julian had once helped him in school to fight off some schoolyard toughs who were about to give him a good beating and steal his shoeshine money.

"Julian is a very good friend," said Alberto. "He knows too much. Too much about the drugs in this city. About the drug cartel money going through Calera and about the crooked bankers in Zacatecas. The cartel has the police chief on its payroll but nobody can prove it. Julian keeps his mouth shut and lives on his wits."

Alberto told us not to worry, that we were almost out of town.

"Pack your things up in a hurry and get out of Mexico," he said. "They will be hunting you relentlessly, like dogs. You are not safe anywhere in Mexico."

CHAPTER 32

I told Alberto to drive me to mail delivery service before he took us to the hotel.

First, we stopped at a convenience store and bought a prepaid telephone card. Calls would be untraceable.

I used the pay phone outside the store to call a good friend, a computer wiz, Simon Del Rio, whose nickname was Geek. The 26-year-old with his long nimble fingers could take a computer apart and put it back together again inside a bat cave. Years ago, he hacked into some insurance companies' web sites and scored an easy $25,000. It cost him three years in prison.

The name "Geek" stuck with him after a federal judge told him at his sentencing that he despised computer Geeks who hack into business websites.

The phone rang six times before the Geek picked it up. He immediately recognized my voice.

"Jack, what's up?"

"It's deep. I'm in deep shit man."

Long pause.

"Where are you?"

"In Mexico. Zacatecas, Mexico."

"Where?"

"Zacatecas, Mexico."

"Locked up? In need of cash?"

"No, just listen. This is important. I need for you to do something."

"What?"

"I'm shipping a computer hard drive to your house. It's probably encrypted, maybe a sophisticated firewall. I don't know. It belonged to a Mexican artist. So everything in there is in Spanish. This artist was murdered."

A long silence followed by a clearing of his throat.

"What? Murdered? By who?"

"Forget that. It's a long, complicated story, and I don't have time. I need you to crack the hard drive. How long will it take?"

He waited a moment before revealing his uncertainty.

"Depends. What's this about?"

"I can't say on the phone. How long will it take to get everything out of the hard drive?"

"I don't know. Hard to say. Hours, days, weeks. Who knows. I need to see what's in there."

"This is a rush job."

He snickered.

"You're kidding, right?"

"I'm serious. Heart-attack serious."

"Is this going to send me back to prison?"

"No. Trust me. I had nothing to do with the murder, and nobody is going to report the hard drive lost or stolen. Just trust me."

Silence, followed by a deep breath before he spoke.

"A rush job, huh?"

"Yeah, I need to know what's on the hard drive. This is some heavy-duty, mind-boggling shit. Completely off the mental Richter scale. That's all I can say, right now. It's big. Really big."

Now, a bit frustrated, he said, "Okay, send it."

"Thanks, man. Thanks."

"Wait. I'm not done. I get to use your new deer rifle on our next hunting trip."

"Whatever, sure, no problem," I said impatiently. "Listen, if you don't hear from me within two days, take the stuff to Tommy Rubio. He's an undercover cop. C.J. has his cell number. Tell Tommy how you got it."

"Right."

"I got to go."

"Wait a minute. I'm not done yet."

"What!?"

"Introduce me to Amy Van Alstein."

"The weather girl on Channel 4?"

"Yeah, she's a beautiful lady."

"Oh, man. Hey, I've got to go. I don't have time."

"You want a rush job? Introduce me," he said emphatically.

"Alright, alright. I'll take you to the next press club meeting, make the introduction, and you take it from there."

"Slam dunk," Geek said.

Alberto drove us to La Zona Postal, a mail delivery services, and parked three blocks away. I told Sierra I had to mail some stuff to the newsroom. She was too tired to question what I was sending, and I didn't want to tell her about the laptop, not just yet.

I mailed the hard drive overnight express to the Geek's house.

When I returned to the hotel, we thanked Alberto profusely. Sierra kissed him on the cheek and promised to repay him and his family for their help.

"Don't worry about none of that. Just take care. Both of you. Be safe," he said with a half smile. "*Adios. Que Dios los bendigan.*"

He drove away.

I told Sierra to stay put and wait near an alley. I would go into our room, pack a couple of suitcases, my notebooks, and computer laptop, and some of her things. We would pay a cab driver to take us to Torreon and from there, and we'd ride the train to Chihuahua and take a bus to Juarez.

Sierra begged not to be left there on her own, but I insisted that she stay put.

"I'm just going in, grabbing our passports and a few of our things and leaving," I said. "If I don't return in 20 minutes, go to Torreon by yourself and take a bus back home."

I made her repeat my instructions, and she did so reluctantly.

"Stay put. I'll be back," I said with a stern voice.

I dashed across the street, dodged into an alley and climbed over a brick wall. I was in the back parking lot of the hotel. I walked into the servants' entrance of the hotel and bumped into a man emptying trash. He immediately wanted to know what I was doing. I fed him a bogus line. I showed him my room key, saying that my wife was walking into the front lobby, and I had to run up the stairs to get my girlfriend out of my room before she caught us together. Before he said another word, I quickly took out $20 from my wallet and gave it to him. The ends of his lips went upward, and he told me how to get to my room the fastest way possible.

"*Pronto, senor*," he said. "*Rapido.*"

I ran up the stairs, went down a short hallway and up the stairs to the eighth floor.

I stopped at a steel door on the eighth floor, cracked it, and poked my head out. The hallway was eerily empty. I went into the long hallway leading to rows of rooms. A bell dinged. The elevator stopped on the eighth floor. I hid behind the steel door, observed and waited, swallowing hard.

The elevator door opened. It spat out an older man with a neatly pressed gray suit, several diamond rings, graying temples, a dour look on a badly pockmarked face, and a folded newspaper tucked in his armpit.

He walked at the end of the hallway, fumbled for the room card key to open the door.

After a couple of attempts to unlock the door, he finally opened it. He walked inside and was greeted by a woman's high-pitched voice. They began bickering. The door closed.

As I walked down the hallway, I noticed that the elevator was coming up. I opened our hotel room, catching a glimpse of two men with brown leather jackets as they stepped out of the elevator. I hoped they didn't see me.

I hurriedly put our two suitcases on the bed and began putting things inside them, grabbing the passports, as many of our clothes, notebooks and laptop. I went into to the bathroom to splash some water on my face.

A clicking sound was coming from the doorway. I froze staring at the mirror. Water dripped from my hair. It ran to the side of my head. The door creaked opened.

I swallowed hard and stuck my head out. It was Sierra. She stood under the doorway, sobbing, her hair partially covering her face. I was livid. She had ignored what I told her. I walked toward her and stopped a few feet from the doorway

"What are you doing? I told you to wait. Are you crazy?"

She opened her mouth. The words didn't come out. I got close. There was a red bruise on her upper left cheek.

"What happened?" I said with furrowed eyebrows. "Who did this?"

"They found me," she whimpered.

"What?"

A man with protruding teeth and a black overcoat appeared. He stood behind Sierra and pushed her inside the room. He had a gun. He put his large arm around her neck and put the gun against her temple.

"*Cayate*," he told her.

Sierra was breathing heavily.

"Gordo," he said to another man waiting in the hallway.

The other man, with eyes that looked like saucers, a large mouth, and a bloated neck, pushed his way between me, Sierra.

"My boss wants to meet with you *y tu puta*," he said, pointing a gun to my head and standing a few feet in front of me.

He looked back at Sierra who had tears running down her cheeks.

"He's going to love bouncing on your fine, tight little ass," he told Sierra.

He pulled her dress up and grabbed her thigh. She screamed, went into a rage, and scratched his face. He smacked her hard. She went limp. I lunged at him, swung and struck his jaw. Gordo sidestepped my next punch. He slammed the butt of his gun over my head twice.

I was out cold.

CHAPTER 33

I woke up, in front of me, a fireplace with a blazing fire. I was in a bedroom sitting on the marble floor, looking at some French windows. My hands tied behind my back. Sierra was nowhere to be found. My head was throbbing from Gordo's blow with his gun to the side of my head.

I sat up and slowly moved my jaw. I felt some pain.

A thudding of heavy footsteps headed my way. They stopped in front of the door. The key opened the door. A squat man with collar-length hair, a patch on his eye, a loose-fitting gray suit and powerful forearms kneeled close to me. He snarled and patted my cheek.

"*Soy* Cortez," he said, sounding like an owner of a bed and breakfast inn. "Please forgive, Gordo. He has a propensity for violence. He's got what you American's say, 'a chip on his shoulder' and gets carried away sometimes."

He laughed, booming laughter.

"Well, you've seen his handiwork at Francisco's house," Cortez said. "*Es cuelero* but very passionate about his work."

He stroked my hair and sighed.

"You're *senor* Jack, no?"

"Yeah. Where is Sierra?"

"You have something we want, *senor* Jack."

"I don't know what you're talking about. I don't have shit. Where is Sierra?"

Cortez curled his fingers and used them like pliers to latch onto my nose, squeeze, and twisted it. My eyes wanted to pop out. The pain was excruciating. It bloodied my nose. I moaned loudly.

"Let's start over, Senor Jack. The hard drive. You have it. We want it. Where is it?"

"Lost."

Cortez barely laughed.

"Not good. Lost is not good," he said.

He calmly pulled out a switchblade. He pushed the button; a big, shiny blade sprang out. His eyes were like red-hot coals.

"Maybe, you can search for it inside your head and find it," he said. "Lost is not good."

I cringed. He put the blade near my cheek. I prepared myself to see my blood flowing on the carpet as he sliced bits of flesh from my face, and then, probably, cut my throat. Instead, he turned me to the side and cut the rope binding my hands.

"Relax," he said. "Make yourself at home. Your girlfriend will be here in a minute. She is upstairs talking to *El Pac Man*, Pantejas, about your visit to Mexico. My boss is a charming man who is very good with a blowtorch and a chainsaw."

As he was leaving, he saw me glance at the windows, laughed, haughty laughter. He waved his finger.

"No, no, no. Don't think about it. There are people outside who'd love to carve you up and feed you to the coyotes."

He turned and left.

A few minutes later, Sierra was shoved into the room.

"They're going to kill us," she said, sobbing.

She burrowed her head on my shoulder.

"What happened?" I whispered in her ear.

"They're threatening to rape me," she said. "They were going through your notebooks. Laptop. Everything. Asking me questions."

"What did you tell them?"

"Everything. They know who we are."

"Oh, my God, we need to get out of here."

"God?" she said, angrily mocking me. "What? Have you given up on the tooth fairy or Zorro, huh? Or, will they show up with God and the Cisco Kid?"

"Calm down, okay? Let me think."

"Think? Here!"

She reached inside her blouse, took off the Archangel medallion dangling from her neck and threw it at me. It landed on the floor.

"So much for your religious voodoo," she said.

I picked it up, gently put it back on her, and kissed her cheek.

"We'll get out. Somehow, we'll get out of here," I said

"Bullshit. We're going to die."

An hour later, Cortez walked into the room. He said we would be moved early in the morning to a ranch in the mountains.

"There, we'll have a piñata party," Cortez said and chuckled. "You two are the piñatas. We provide the music, whores and liquor. You'll provide the entertainment. The screams."

Abruptly, his face became distorted, a nefarious torturous look. Then, he scratched the palm of his hand while he glared at us. He closed his eyes for a few moments.

"Oh, by the way, you have a visitor," Cortez said "Gordo! Bring Alberto."

Gordo opened the door. He walked into the room holding up Alberto's badly beaten and swollen head by the hair. All the oxygen was sucked out of my lungs. My brain shut down. I couldn't yell or utter a word.

Sierra let out a blood-curdling scream. Terror filled her brain with riot.

Gordo's eyes unleashed a cold blast of pure evil that burned through my skull and went down my spine. My leg twitched hard, as Sierra cried, shook her head uncontrollably and tried to shake the hellish image. Gordo rolled the head across the wooden floor like a bowling ball until it landed near us.

I grabbed Sierra to calm her down. She had a bear hug around my chest. Her head turned away. My head was bowed. Sierra whimpered and shivered.

Cortez's and Gordo's cackling rattled my psyche.

As they were leaving, Cortez turned around and said, "Gordo will be just outside the door. If you need ice cubes, clean towels, or mints or condoms, please dial room service."

They burst out laughing. The door was slammed shut.

I reached over, grabbed the top of the bedspread and flung it over the head. Sierra curled up tightly on the floor, covered her head with her arms and kept sobbing, gasping for air.

Leaning forward, I sat with elbows on my knees and my head dropped in resignation. I had never felt so desperate and helpless in all my life. Never.

CHAPTER 34

A couple of hours went by before Gordo ambled into the room and removed the head, said nothing and left. He came back a few minutes later and turned the lights off.

"Sleep tight, *con los angelitos*," the cartel ghoul chimed.

Gordo left. If I had a gun, I would have emptied the clip on him.

The evening was fading fast. Its orange hue made the room glow. It made a surreal day, more disoriented. Staring at the walls, I wondered if this would be the last sunset of my life as I watched the shadows stretch across the large room.

Exhausted, Sierra and I took a few catnaps on the floor. Our sleep was restless, interrupted by the slightest noise. In the hallway, voices faded in and out. Sierra woke up a few times, wet from perspiration and trembling.

"I'm so scared," she said. "I don't want to die."

"Just stay try to stay calm, we'll figure something out," I remarked, scantily believing a word I said.

Sierra pleaded and made me swear that I would try to grab a gun from one of our captors so we could try to escape, escape or kill two or three of them before we died. I told her I had a pen in my pocket. I planned to jam it through the eye of one of them and try and snatch his weapon and start shooting, hoping Sierra would grab a gun from a dead thug and fire away too.

It all seemed so desperate and crazy. There would be too many of them. But there was nothing else, nothing, and we were running out of time.

We anxiously waited for traces of daylight to arrive, for others to decide our fate. Sierra snuggled next to me. I felt like her guardian angel but I knew I was her last hope in getting us out alive. I went through another escape plan I thought about throughout the night.

I checked my watch. It was almost 4 a.m.

The silhouettes of a man's pair of shoes were visible under a slit of hallway light beneath the door. The man stood near the door. But he took several steps down the hallway every ten minutes or so and returning to the same spot in 30 seconds, always to the same spot near the door. He cleared his throat, hummed, yawn or used a handheld device every twenty or thirty minutes to try to talk to someone named Rios.

Outside, the leaves rustled and shook hard when a strong, unexpected wind blew by. A tree branch scraped the window. I pulled back the edge of a curtain and peeked out the window. There was nobody outside. Two cars were parked near the house.

I nudged Sierra.

"Wake up," I whispered.

She was wide-awake.

"What?"

"We can't just wait. We need to get out of here before daylight. There are two parked cars. I think I can hotwire one. If not, we run like hell toward the mountain. Either way, we need to put as much distance as we can from this place before the sun comes up."

"I'm ready."

"I've been watching the shadow on the other side of the door. I thought of something," I said. "The guy leaves for 30 seconds and walks down the hallway."

"I noticed that too."

"Okay, this is what we are going to do. When I point to you, slowly, go and try to quietly open the door. Gordo or someone else is on the other side of the door. He will get angry when he hears you turning the doorknob. He will open the door. When he does, look startled, frighten. Don't scream."

I stopped talking for a few second to emphasis that she must not scream.

"Whatever you do, don't scream or it will wake the others up. Then, just quickly, back up. When he comes into the room, I'll bust him in the head with the lamp."

"Okay."

"Wait until I give you a signal."

She nodded.

I put pillows that were on the bed on the floor and put a blanket over them to make it look as though I was sleeping there. I took off my shoes, socks and placed them carefully near the blanket, tipping one shoe over with a sock barely visible. Everything had to be staged perfectly.

I stopped and watched the shadow underneath the door.

The person walked away, I slowly grabbed a lamp and yanked the electrical cord out of the lamp. I tied the cord around my wrist. When the person walked back to the door, I froze.

Twenty minutes later, he walked away. I slowly lifted a small chair and put it next to the door. Drops of sweat fell on the chair's seat. I stood on it, closed my eyes, took a deep breath and exhaled. He came back to his spot and talked to someone on the radio about a soccer game.

I was ready. I'd hit him hard on the head, hopefully, crush his skull or knock him out. If he were still breathing, I'd wrap the electric cord around his neck and squeeze as hard as I could until he was dead.

I locked eyes with Sierra, nodded and pointed toward the doorknob.

Sierra walked to the door, grabbed the knob and turned it. It didn't open. She turned it again. The turning knob made a little more noise. Nothing. The door didn't open. She tried again, nothing. I swallowed hard.

She gave the knob another turn and gently tugged on the doorknob. She was about to turn the knob again but a key was rammed into the keyhole. Sierra stepped back. The door opened.

"Donde vas?"

It was Gordo. He snorted like an enraged bull. Sierra raised her shaking hands to her chest and took a step back, trying to lure Gordo into the room. It didn't work.

His switchblade click. His radio briefly crackled and went silent.

"Rios, *donde andas*?" Gordo said.

There was no response.

I waited for him to take a step inside the room. My hands trembled. The sweaty grip on the lamp tightened. Heart racing. Mouth begging God to get us out of this place.

Gordo didn't move. His fat shadow was cast halfway inside the room.

He grunted with displeasure.

"Rios, *bien pronto*," Gordo said. "Rios."

"Let me go, and I will give you anything you want. *Por favor*," Sierra whimpered. "Anything."

"*Cayate,*" Gordo said and spat out curse words.

In the middle of a curse word, a muffled, pop sound. Gordo fell forward, face first. A thud. His barrel chest was halfway inside the room. I raised the lamp to bust it over his head. My raised hand stopped in mid-air. My jaw dropped when I saw blood squirt out from the side of his head. Sierra and I stood motionless staring at Gordo. I snapped out of the trance, let go of the lamp and grabbed her hand.

"Let's go," I said.

Before we could step through the door, a burst of bullets flew in the hallway. More gunfire outside. I yanked Sierra to the floor. She squeezed my neck hard and screamed. I covered her mouth with my hand, squeezing her cheeks hard. She whimpered.

"Shut up," I said, in a very low voice. "Whoever it is probably doesn't know that we are here. Don't open your mouth, whimper or twitch."

I grabbed the pillows and blanket on the floor and flung them on the bed. I toss the shoes and socks under the bed. We crawled under the bed and held each other tight.

Breaking glass.

A stun grenade exploded. The explosion left us in a daze, disoriented. I barely heard commands in Spanish, sharp, crisp commands from someone who left no doubt that he was in charge.

We didn't move an inch. Everything was in a fog. Boots thudding, a quick burst of gunfire, and more loud commands.

Men in military boots trampled everywhere. They searched the rooms and closets. Outside the room, a couple of explosions shook the house's foundation. More gunshots.

Silence, an eerie quiet smothered the noise. A gun smoke smell filled the room.

The gunmen who burst into the house spoke Spanish.

"Target cleared!" one man shouted.

"Clear two," another with a thick accent yelled from downstairs.

"Three clear," a distant voice screamed.

It was bizarre. The men moved as though they had one mind. Sierra hadn't moved. I thought she'd been hit by a stray bullet and was dead.

"You okay?" I whispered. "Sierra. Hey. Sierra."

She nodded.

"Don't breathe hard," I said. My lips touched her earlobe.

Trying to regain all my hearing, I moved my jaws from side to side and tugged on my ear to try and stop the ringing from the stun grenade. I prayed that these men wouldn't find us. But a man with black boots kicked the bed. Kicked it hard.

"Get out! Now! Out! Both of you. Out, let's go!" He said in English. "Now! Up!"

Who was this English-speaking man?

We crawled out from under the bed. Two men in military uniforms, black ski masks, and clutching automatic weapons stood in front of us. Ferocious eyes bore down on us.

Los Zetas had finally surfaced from the narco-world shadows, I thought. As soon as they find out I'm a journalist, I'm dead. They'd rape Sierra and kill her too.

The American-trained killers who were helping drug lords were all over the house, I surmised. I could hear more short, military commands and was sure that they were also looking for the hard drive. We'd be interrogated and if we were lucky, quickly killed.

I stood and helped Sierra off the floor.

"*Quines son?*" she asked one of them.

The man replied: "Mexican Marines. *Vamonos.*"

"Mexican Special Forces?" I asked in Spanish. "How did you find us?"

"Shut up. Move out! Move!" said an English-speaking soldier.

One dragged Gordo's body into the hallway and searched his pockets.

"Don't touch anything or step on the blood," the English-speaking gunman said.

"Where are we going?" I said, insisting that he tell me.

He came and got right in my face.

"Far," he barked. "You want to go or do you want to stay? Your choice."

"Go. We'll go. We'll go," Sierra said without hesitation.

We were ushered into the hallway. Sierra yelped after she nearly stepped on Gordo's body. A trail of blood brushed across the carpet. Gordo's dead face had a look of total shock, as though he was still trying to size up what had hit him so hard on the side of his head. Fragments of glass and wood splinters from the bullets were all over the floor.

Sierra covered her face as she walked past Gordo. I felt like kicking him in the head. I was so damn pissed by what he and the others had put us through, what they did to Alberto. I was glad rigor mortis and worms would soon be devouring this fat piece of shit.

Outside, there were short bursts of gunfire. A short time later, more assault rifles and black ski masks appeared.

It freaked out Sierra.

"I don't want to go with them," she whispered, panting hard. "I don't. Please, I want to go home. I can walk. I can."

"Shhhhh, it's okay," I said. "We'll be all right."

We walked down the stairs into the large den with the earth-red fireplace and salmon-colored terra cotta front. The wealthy owner had spent a lot of thought and detail on its ranch-style construction. All built with drug money.

There were men searching the place, taking files, computers on desks and cell phones from some of the dead bodies and putting them inside backpacks. A body lay near the steps and another behind the couch.

The ranch sat on the side of a mountain, overlooking the city whose lights in the distance looked like clusters of stars.

Outside, two dead bodies were in the front of the ranch near two large oak trees. We were taken to an old van with a cracked windshield and a crooked and bent Zacatecas license plates held together by chicken wire. As soon as we were inside, six men with automatic weapons and two boxes of confiscated files got inside, one drove and the other sat in the passenger seat. Sierra and I and the other four-armed soldiers sat on the floor. The soldiers sat straight with rifles between their legs, both hands on their weapons.

Under a half moon, the van sped away with its lights off.

Nobody said a word.

A sea of uncertainty and darkness suddenly swallowed Sierra and I. The driver used night-vision goggles to maneuver down the narrow road. A bumpy ride. A few times, bushes by the side of the road scratched the side of the van.

Smells of army canvas and fresh sweat edged out the trace of gasoline fumes coming from the old engine. Sierra mumbled. All I could think about was home, anywhere else but here.

I longed to see my family and Dexter. I wanted to go see Dana, talk to Emily. I'd even find solace in the newsroom. The sound of people pecking away on the computer keys and a police radio squelching and squawking would be a symphony to my ears.

But I was somewhere in the middle of Mexico on a dark, dirt road and on my way to only God knows where. The vehicle rattled more. It picked up speed going down hill.

We hit a hole, and everybody flew up a few inches. Sierra clung to my arm for dear life. Both my hands were in my pockets to keep them warm.

"Who are they?" she whispered. "Where are we going?"

"I don't know."

Ten minutes later, we stopped. The van's doors slid wide open. All of us stepped out and waited. A minute later, a second van rounded the base of the mountain. Its lights went on and off to signal that it was close by. The second van stopped a few yards away.

Everybody jumped out and ran.

Sierra and I swung our arms. Kicked our legs as wildly as they would go.

Weak sunrays began to peek out from behind the spiked silhouette of a stretch of mountains. The light, a soft orange, sprawled across the distant horizon. A film of dust from a brisk breeze lingered in the air.

The group leader motioned to stop. We all stopped. It gave us time to catch our breath after running alongside the mountain base for what seemed like forever.

A hand signal flashed. Everybody went to flat on the ground. Sierra and I dropped to the prone position when everybody else did. A large dirt clod nipped my nose. We heard nothing but the leaves from a juniper tree shake as a strong, gust of wind slipped past us and into the canyon.

Seconds later, an explosion rocked the canyon, followed by another.

Sierra and I flinched. "What the hell," I said. The men around us didn't twitch or move a muscle.

Dead silence. I glanced up. The vans that had brought us there were in a thousand pieces and on fire. These men seemed resistant, almost immune, to powerful and loud blasts. Immune to fear, it seemed. These hard, tested bodies were programmed to obey the slightest command in seconds.

"Take a knee," the deep-voiced man said.

The soldiers obeyed. We obeyed.

Kneeling, our rescuers set up another tight, makeshift perimeter again, with eyes and rifles aimed at the four corners of the earth. Their ears were also pointed in every direction, rigid stances ready to take on anyone who might dare to venture into where we were.

The soldier giving the orders took out a tiny radio, clicked it on, paused, looked around, and said in a flat Spanish voice, "Sun is up. Ready to go home."

I asked an armed man nearby.

"Where are we going?"

"*Silencio*," he replied.

Five minutes later, the whooping sounds of a helicopter approaching over the towering mountain peaks could be heard. Soon the helicopter was directly overhead. The leader of the group went out into the middle of the clearing. He put a small, blinking flashlight on the ground to guide the chopper and ran back. The Black Hawk helicopter swooped down. It landed.

We rushed toward the helicopter.

As soon as the last armed man was on board, the helicopter's powerful rotors took us up like a giant metal eagle that had just dived down, snatched up a fat fish and zoomed up into the heavens again.

Suddenly, our altitude dropped. We were practically hugging the terrain and heading toward a distant mountain range. I sat near Sierra, who clutched Michael the Archangel medallion with a tight fist.

The helicopter slashed across the sky and then, cut sharply to the right.

Sierra gasped to catch her breath as our stomachs went into our chests.

One by one, the men slowly took off their black ski masks. A funnel of sunlight hit a blur of camouflaged painted faces streaked with thick black and green tiger lines.

The men had brown or black hair. The one who gave the orders to about a dozen men had a shaved head and piercing green eyes.

Stoic faces kept tight hold on their upright automatic weapons. My attention cautiously shifted from one face to another as I studied each one.

"If these are Mexican Marines, why do two speak English?" Sierra whispered.

"Maybe, DEA agents. Who knows?"

The Black Hawk gained altitude, hovering along the mountainside. We wondered where we were going, and how these men found us?

CHAPTER 35

The high-flying helicopter circled, dipped suddenly, and landed in a Mexican valley buried deep inside some mammoth mountains with primordial, whimsical jagged edges, sandstone slabs, and a boulder-choked gully.

A lanky man took long steps toward us as soon as we got out.

"Where is the hard drive?" he said.

"Who are you?" I asked.

"I'm a Captain," he said with a somber face. "Call me Ramsey."

"We're so glad to see you guys," I said.

"Oh, God, yes," Sierra said. "Thank you so much. I'm Sierra. This is Jack."

"I know," he said flatly. "So, where is the hard drive?"

Sierra knitted her eyebrows and stared at me. I blushed. I was so busted.

"What hard drive?" Sierra asked me. "What's he talking about?"

"I took a hard drive from Francisco's laptop computer. The laptop was hidden in the ceiling," I said and turned toward Ramsey. "I don't have it anymore."

"You never said anything about a hard drive," Sierra said.

"I was going to tell you," I said.

"So where is it?" she said.

"Can't say, right now."

"Why?" Sierra asked.

Ramsey immediately lost his cool and raised his voice.

"Shut up, both of you, right now and listen. That hard drive is ours. We knew Francisco was keeping records. We were going to seize the laptop before you two came along and snatched it up."

"What's on the hard drive?" I asked.

"Information. A lot of information that is vital to national security," he said sternly.

"Like what?"

"Look, if I don't get my hard drive, you're going to wind up in a federal pen for theft of government property."

I scoffed at his threats.

"That's a joke, right?" I said.

"I'll put your ass in jail!" Ramsey said, stabbing his finger in front of my face.

"Really? You bust me, throw me in jail and the story will be on front pages quicker than a cheetah on fucking steroids."

"What story is that?"

"That Mexican Marines and DEA are teaming up in Mexico to do drug raids in an American Blackhawk helicopter. Once the story goes viral, and you lockup the reporter who wrote it, you'll be lucky to end up being assigned to some ancient Middle East shithole that predates the Bible. Do you want that? Then, do it. Bust my ass and put me behind bars."

He scoffed, "Is that the story. Mexican Marines and DEA? We're not DEA."

Ramsey's fiery eyes went from me to Sierra and back to me. He probably is wondering whether he could trust us. But he had no choice.

The hard drive was a treasure trove of narco-trafficking secrets, and God only knows what else. I could tell that he was desperate to get it back by how he began shifting his eyes from us to his men who were spread throughout the canyon.

Ramsey had a deep voice, a round, crooked nose and wore a black jungle hat. His uniform had no patches, rank, or nametag sewn on it. His dark brown beard was well groomed. He wasn't quite six-feet tall and emitted an aura of self-confidence and indestructibility that a Roman gladiator would envy.

"Who are you with?" I said.

"Delta Force," he said flatly.

Stunned, I wondered what Delta Force was doing in Mexico of all places?

"American Special Ops forces?" I said, ashen-faced.

"Correct," he said.

"Seriously?" I said.

"Drop-dead serious."

There was no doubt that he'd probably been on secret missions at several goat-herding, hot spots around the world that aren't on anybody's GPS yet.

Delta Force is similar to SEAL teams but much more classified. They operate in teams of four or five men. Delta Force recruits from Army Rangers and Green Beret outfits. They work closely with the CIA.

Before I could ask the most obvious question, Ramsey said, "This whole thing. It never happened. We were never here, and you two were never rescued. This is a top-secret operation in Mexico."

"What is Delta Force doing in Mexico?"

"Basically, dumpster diving. We're helping Mexico take out its two-legged, drug-dealing garbage. The cartels."

"If there was no demand, there'd be no supply," I said. "Simple economics."

"You must have gone to an Ivy League School. Let me guess. Harvard?" He said sarcastically.

Stories about the Mexican Marines linked them to the tracking and capture of major drug cartel kingpins. They are tough, loyal soldiers who will eat nails for breakfast, march 50 miles without complaining and jump out of planes and into any hotspots in Mexico, anytime, anywhere, unannounced and uninvited.

Sierra ran her fingers through her untidy hair, raking bits and pieces of tiny twigs, leaves and old carpet fiber from the bedroom where we were held hostage.

"How did you find us?" I said.

"Our satellite did," Ramsey said, raising a stiff thumb toward the heavens. "It zeroed in on your whereabouts. At first, we thought you two were drug couriers."

"How were we being tracked?" I said.

"The medallion of Michael the Archangel. Where is it?" said Ramsey.

"The one I got from the musician?" I said with a puzzled expression.

He nodded. I glanced at Sierra who pulled it out from under her shirt and held it up.

"That?" I said.

Ramsey stuck his hand out.

"It's ours. I'll take it."

"What?" Sierra said.

"Give it to me." He demanded.

Sierra slipped the medallion off her neck and slapped it on the palm of his hand. He put it in his pocket.

"It's mine," I half-heartedly protested. "It was a gift from a Mexican musician."

"It's government property. It's a tiny and very expensive GPS tracking device that saved your asses. It's still experimental. It's a solar-powered, microchip-tracking device. A human dog collar, and you two were one of our first guinea pigs. Those musicians at the restaurant were our two Mexican operatives in Calera."

"The medallion emits a signal?" I asked.

"Linked to a satellite," He said.

"And, you hang it on unsuspecting people like tracking collars on animals," Sierra said with a voice laced with cynicism. "Right?"

"Yep. But don't get your self-righteous ass in a tizzy, Ms. Madrid. In the end, it saved you and your pal's asses," he said. "We lost the signal when you two left Calera. So the chip has a few kinks."

"Who is Francisco working for?" I asked.

"Francisco spent five years in prison. Years ago, he stole tens of thousands pesos from Bancomex. He knows the Mexican economy backwards and forwards. Painting is his cover story. He does money laundering for the Juarez Cartel."

"Who killed Francisco and Zamora?" I said.

"We believe Zeta gunmen sent by the Juarez Cartel. The Juarez Cartel believed Francisco was skimming hundreds of thousands of dollars from them. The Zetas returned for the laptop after they were told where it was. Apparently, they saw your bloody footprints, and the laptop was gone. They weren't happy."

"The laptop is where he did his bookkeeping?" I said.

"Bookkeeping and made a lot of notes," said Ramsey. "Notes that we need to see."

"When did cartel money laundering become vital to national security?"

A long pause. He looked around before his words got weighty, robotic.

"What I tell you is classified information, not for print. You print it and it'll endanger lives, including the lives of American soldiers. You got that?"

Sierra and I nodded.

"I told you all that to repeat, 'Delta Force was never in Mexico.' Got that?" he said. "We were never here."

"Yeah, yeah, we got it, okay," I said.

He took a deep breath. His hard expression softened a bit.

"Our intelligence indicates that terrorists are setting shop in Central America and southern Mexico, moving weapons and jihadists into the Western Hemisphere in small groups."

"ISIS?"

"Not yet. Sympathetic Muslim businessmen in Central America are bankrolling Al Qaeda, fragments of Hezbollah and a Syrian terrorist splinter group. Iran is kicking in some money."

"Sleeper cells in Central America and Mexico?" I asked.

"Right, but it is bigger than that. They're using MS-13, Mara Salvatrucha for muscle. The North Koreans and Iran are supplying some of the heavy weapons, a lot of weapons including RPGs."

"Weapons for what?"

"Jihad. The plan is to light up the U.S. and Mexico. These weapons are gradually being smuggled into Mexican cities and into the U.S. through commercial trucks, boats or tunnels along the border dug by the cartels. Arsenals are stockpiled in houses and warehouses."

Sierra and I looked at each other in total disbelief.

"That's what got our interest into Francisco the artist. MS-13 gang members are getting laundered drug money through Francisco. Homeland Security deported thousands MS-13, LA and Southern California gang members who were in the country illegally," Ramsey said.

" Most were dumped in Central America," I said.

"Right. Some, desperate, unemployed and angry, were recruited into these terrorists' groups. Career criminals are brainwashed, sold on the holy war bullshit. Many end up in jungle camps in Southern Mexico where they are trained in guerilla warfare. We know of a few who were supplied with cash, fake documents and quietly slip back into the United States. They easily blend into cities. They know the language, the people and the streets. Most don't even get as much as a parking ticket. And, as soon as the word comes down, they start hitting targets, malls, parks, schools, and police stations. Blowing shit up."

"Why?"

"Unleash a holy war in America and Mexico, hoping to spark a race war too."

"Fear will paralyze the country," I said. "The economy will collapse."

"Yeah. This is bigger than the DEA. Much bigger, and we're trying to shut this down fast before it spills across the border and thousands are hurt or killed," Ramsey said. "That's it. That's all I can say. This conversation is over, and it never happened. Got it."

We nodded and were floored by what he said. He walked away. Sierra turned to me with eyes dilated by Ramsey's words.

"This could be really catastrophic," she said in a low voice. "Wow."

Later, Ramsey, Sierra and I had breakfast while sitting on some rocks. Ramsey served up MRE rations. He said very little at first. Then, Sierra and him talked briefly about horses and the best fishing holes in New Mexico.

We didn't utter another word about Ramsey's doomsday conversation. The silence soon turned awkward. I was still trying to wrap my head around this looming terrorist threat that, so far, very few people know existed.

Nearby, the black-uniformed soldiers ate MRE rations while standing, sitting, or squatting in a circle in high and low ground around the helicopter and us. The beauty of the unspoiled mountains was a serene and perfect backdrop of a rather quiet meal.

"You can have the hard drive but I get first crack at it," I told Ramsey.

He kept his cool, staring into oblivion.

"I can't negotiate any of that. Talk to my superiors," he said, paused and solemnly shook his head. "All this bullshit so people can get their recreational dope to get high."

Ramsey checked his watch, rose, gave some commands, and we were all in the helicopters in less than ten minutes. But before we left, Ramsey told Sierra and I that it was too dangerous to stay in Mexico.

"They'll be looking for both of you. The Zetas want the hard drive. They know it exists. It probably has the names of corrupt politicians on cartel payrolls," Ramsey said. "So every Mexican bus station, airport, and taxicab stand is being monitored by the cartel's henchmen or corrupt cops. If you two are picked up, you'll be tortured and killed. So you can't stay in Mexico."

We didn't argue and were anxious to get out.

An hour later, the low-flying helicopter with everyone on board meandered out of the valley before it raised its nose and hurled over the mountains peaks, heading west.

CHAPTER 36

The Black Hawk helicopter zoomed at top speed across Mexican hard blue skies toward the Pacific Ocean to a waiting U.S. Navy aircraft carrier hundreds of miles away.

An hour into flight, the helicopter refueled by a U.S. Air Force aircraft tanker that extended its refueling probe to the helicopter. We landed on the aircraft carrier and were rushed into a conference room filled with lights from telephones, computers, computer screens and a large weather satellite screen hanging on the wall. The American and Mexican soldiers were escorted to another part of the ship.

Inside the conference room, two men immediately greeted Sierra, Captain Ramsey and I. There was disdain in both of their eyes. We shook hands with them and exchanged a few niceties before they cut to the chase.

A lanky man with a clipped baritone voice said he was Agent McBride. Another man named Wesley who had thinning hair, weak chin and large ears was with him.

"We're CIA," McBride said.

"The hard drive where is it?" Wesley said.

"He said he doesn't have it," Ramsey said.

Sierra squirmed and looked at me along with the others.

McBride had thick arms, a handlebar mustache, sandy wavy hair, and intense, weather-beaten skin.

Both were expert interrogators by the way they immediately positioned themselves while asking us questions, standing and cautiously hovering around us, slowly setting up dominance poses as a prelude to some intense questioning.

"Where is the hard drive?" McBride said.

"Safe," I said.

Wesley upped the ante before talking to Captain Ramsey who hung up a half smile. Ramsey knew this wasn't going to work but Wesley or McBride were now in charge.

"I can get some Justice Department legal hack to get a judge to sign a piece of paper, and we can warehouse both of you in some federal shithole until the hard drive turns up," said Wesley.

"We'll do it in a heartbeat if we have to," McBride said.

I didn't flinch. I was enraged.

"Let's cut the bullshit, okay? I'm not impressed."

Smirking, Sierra interjected, "Wow."

"Lock them up," McBride said flatly, jabbing his finger in our faces. "I'm done."

"Go ahead," I said. "We get locked up, and flocks of reporters will land on the White House's doorstep wanting to know why Delta Force and Blackhawk are in Mexico with the Mexican Marines. So, please, stop this interrogation cluster fuck."

I paused long enough to let what I said sink into their psyches.

"Tell them what you want," Ramsey said.

McBride's face turned crimson. He was furious, muttering curse words. Wesley raised an eyebrow. Captain Ramsey had an uneasy smile, and wide-eyed, Sierra nodded

I reached into my pocket, took out my wallet, lifted out a business card, and wrote my cell phone number down on the back of it. I handed it to McBride.

"That's my cell phone number. Here's what we're going to do. After all this goes down, the big climax, I expect a call," I said. "Even if it happens in the middle of the night or high noon or I'm dead and in the morgue. I expect a call. Got it?"

"That's bullshit," Wesley said.

"I'm not negotiating," I said.

After they looked at each other with resignation, McBride and Wesley agreed to my terms.

"Okay, we'll call you," McBride said unenthusiastically.

"Good, and I expect decent quotes, solid quotes, and plenty of details. Nothing sanitized. No military jargon or the usual PR babble you guys sling, either."

"Where's the hard drive?" McBride said, eyes burrowing through my skull, nose flaring.

"You'll get it in 48 hours. That's the other part of the deal."

"You're crazy," said Wesley.

"But we're serious," Sierra interjected.

McBride paused, shot a cold look at Wesley, his subordinate, telling him to back off.

"Fine, 48 hours. That's it," said McBride. "Forty-eight hours, and it better be intact."

"It will," I said.

I made it clear, however, what would happen if I looked over my shoulder and saw one of their agents on my tail.

"Kiss the hard drive goodbye. I push the send button and everything will be sent to a dozen newspapers across the country," I paused so they could think about what I had just said. "Is everybody here on the same page?"

"We'll give you 48 hours. Not a minute more. Compromise national security and every federal agent I can round up will be looking for both of your asses," McBride said. "This isn't a fucking game. Got it?"

"Deal," I said.

"This is important," McBride said. "Nothing gets published until we give you the word or it'll compromise our mission and endanger lives. And most of all, Delta Force was never in Mexico. We should wrap things up in a few days."

"We got that. No problem. What are you wrapping up?"

"It's big. That's all you have to know." McBride said.

Wesley wrote down a telephone number on a blank piece of paper and a name too.

"That's FBI Agent Frank Garza in El Paso. Take the hard drive to him."

The agents sat down. More questions followed, this time without the angry chest thumping or threats. Sierra told them about her conversation with Francisco when I was at the restaurant. She talked about her father. Much of what she told them, I had already written about. She told the truth, however.

Later, Sierra came to my cabin. She was about to say something.

I immediately held my finger against my lips. I motioned by touching my ear, pointed to the ceiling, and swirled my forefinger, indicating that there could be listening devices in the cabin.

She nodded, indicating that she understood.

Sierra left the cabin, but not before writing on a piece of paper that there were armed Navy security guards nearby. I wrote back that I knew this. She wanted to know where the laptop's hard drive was. I scribbled: In the mail.

She wrote a question mark and underscored it. I shook my head and wrote: Memorize this number.

I wrote down C.J.'s home telephone number with a note beside it: In case something happens to me, call the newsroom and ask for Editor C.J. Cortez and tell him to go to Geek and get hard copies of what's in the hard drive. Also give copies to Tommy Rubio, the cop.

She stared at the telephone number for nearly a minute.

"I got it," she whispered and left.

I took the piece of paper, put it in my mouth, chewed and washed it down with some water. I turned off the lights after I took the notes about my conversation with Ramsey and the two agents, along with other observations, folded them tightly and put them inside my sock.

Exhausted, I fell asleep.

CHAPTER 37

The early morning sound of the pneumatic hiss of the Greyhound bus door opening in El Paso sounded sweet.

We finally made it to the city.

Outside, a starless night filled the bleak sky. Inside, a few people were scattered throughout the bus terminal. A rail-thin man with a slightly arched back hummed and pushed a broom around the passenger loading area.

Sierra made a trip straight to the vending machines. I found a payphone and called Geek who was half asleep. He yawned.

"What?" He said.

"It's me."

He perked up when he heard my voice.

"Holy shit. It's a treasure trove," he said. "There were passwords everywhere. I had to dive deep into the file vault and go around some passwords and —"

"Save it. Save it for later. Big ears everywhere," I said, trying not to sound excited that Geek cracked the hard drive. "Come get us. We're at San Jacinto Park downtown."

"I'm on my way," he said.

After I hung up, I told Sierra that I had sent the hard drive to a guy nicknamed Geek. I said he was a computer hacker and cracked the laptop's password and retrieved some information from it.

"He's on his way to pick us up," I said.

"Fantastic. Good. Let's get out of here. Downtown, this late at night, creeps me out," she said.

We walk three blocks down the street and past the park; turned left, crossed the street and walked two more blocks. We doubled back, crossed the street, again, and walked back toward the park. There, we wait.

Tommy Rubio had schooled me well on how to lose a tail on the streets.

As we walked, a red van slowed when the driver saw us. It was too early in the morning for the work traffic to crowd the downtown streets. But the tweakers, methamphetamine junkies, roamed some of the dark roads on the edges of town aimlessly like robots, always up, always scheming, sometimes for days, looking to consume more drugs or rob 24-7 prostitutes with heroin-collapsed veins. Or, stick a gun in some poor soul's face.

However, I didn't rule out a hired assassin. Someone who had been tipped off that we were on the way back to El Paso, who had been staking out the bus station and had spotted us.

When the van turned, we hid in the alley for a few minutes and waited to see if it would return. The driver went slowly by the second time before speeding up and heading toward the freeway.

We stayed in the alley another five minutes. After I poked my head out to see if the red van was anywhere near. We dashed to the park and sat behind a bench, near a tree.

Twenty minutes later, I spotted Geek driving slowly by the park. I popped up, waved him over and told him to let me drive.

Sierra and I hopped into the car.

I exited the freeway, doubled back, and got back on it. I did this twice. Geek said I was paranoid. Sierra understood why. She looked back a couple of times but didn't utter a word.

An hour later, after taking a number of other detours, we got to Geek's apartment. He had the hard drive on a large table hooked up to his computer that was connected to a printer. A stack of papers about two inches high near the printer.

"There are hundreds of pages in that stack. There is a ton of information in that hard drive," Geek said. "I transferred a lot of it to my computer."

I immediately went to the table and began combing through the papers. Sierra went into the bathroom to take a shower. She came out with a towel around her head and flopped down on the couch and tossed her head all the way back. Geek offered her some hot tea and gave me a cup of coffee.

After blow-drying her hair, she ambled over to the kitchen table, sat rigidly on a chair, and slowly revolved a stiff neck before sticking out a limp, palm-up hand. Not taking my eyes off the paper I was reading, I handed her half my stack of papers and a yellow BIC Brite Liner.

"What?" she said. "It's late."

"Mark key words, sentences, phrases," I said. "Mark things that stick out at you. Code words, slang words, names and numbers. We have a lot of work to do."

She nodded half-heartedly and began reading. I glanced up and saw Geek staring at Sierra, probably wondering how the world I teamed up with Mickey Madrid's beautiful daughter and why.

"Hey," I said to him.

"What?" he said after I yanked him out of his gaze.

"Crank out some more stuff," I said.

"It's not that easy. Some of this stuff is encrypted," he protested. "I've been doing this for hours. I'm tired, dog tired."

"I appreciate that but we need to get this done," I said. "I've got to give the hard drive to the FBI."

"FBI!? Man, I'm not going back to prison, am I?" he said. "This is bullshit. You never said the laptop belonged to the FBI. You never said anything about the FBI."

"Chill. It doesn't belong to them, and beside the feds are cool with it but I'm on the clock," I said. "So, nobody's going to prison."

"The FBI is cool with hacking into someone else's computer?"

"It's really complicated," Sierra told Geek.

"Just keep tapping the hard drive and don't worry about the FBI," I said.

He nodded after looking at the two of us. Sierra nodded to reassure him that what I had said was true.

Our collective eyes and markers went full throttle.

Geek was right. The hard drive was proving to be a gold mine, and we were milking it for every document or record it had. It gave the names of the shot-callers in the finance world that is linked up with narco-traffickers. It soon became apparent that Mickey's pseudo name was El Gato.

My eyes got wide when I saw the name "El Pescado," the Fisherman, a vague reference, perhaps, to Sheriff Ward. I read that El Pescado was getting hundreds of thousands of dollars in kickbacks, money washed at a bank in Zacatecas.

"Oh, my God," I said stunned and barely moving my lips.

Sierra didn't hear me. She was busily working the yellow marker, eyes moving from side to side like old typewriter rollers. Geek pecked on the computer keys, stacking up information in neat piles.

He was excited about the electronic mineshaft that was pumping out one priceless gem of information after another.

"Bingo" or "great," he would say every now and then, "beautiful."

After eating take-out burgers, the three of us worked for six more hours before exhaustion took its toll. Sierra fell into a dead sleep in Geek's bedroom. Geek snored on the couch. I lay on the floor with a pillow to prop up my head, stared at the ceiling for a few minutes as countless of thoughts flashed, bounced and tumbled inside my head.

I finally shut my eyes and fell sleep a few minutes later.

CHAPTER 38

I woke up a few hours later, left Geek's apartment and headed for the newsroom after dropping Sierra off at her apartment. As I walked into the newsroom, I felt pelted by a sea of smiles all tainted with sarcasm.

Everybody knew about the fake great-grandmother funeral. One reporter grinned and winked. Another cynically waved good-bye to indicate that I was going to get canned.

"Did you interview the Mexican president?" asked a business reporter. "The CEO of the Sinaloa Drug Cartel?"

I ignored the ribbing.

"How did it go?" said another in a more serious tone.

"Better than expected," I said dismissively.

I knew I was in deep shit. Everybody knew I lied to go to Mexico. I headed for the corner office where I was about to be cast into the outer darkness as soon as I walked into Ricardo's lair. There would be dragon flames shooting out of his eyes.

Faking a funeral was the easy part but trying to explain the death defying roller coaster ride through the belly of the Mexican drug beast was going to be a bitch. I was glad that I had taken Sierra with me to verify what I was about to say.

But I was mentally exhausted and had reached an emotional saturation point where I didn't care what happened to me. It was 4 p.m. I was emotionally numb, and the hot sun was not letting up. If I got fired, I was ready to go quietly out the door.

As I got near Ricardo's office, I made a quick pit stop at C.J.'s desk, which was at the end of a row of computers manned by other assistant editors whose pinched faces looked like they were being pulled into computer screens.

A couple of copy editors snuck peeks at me as I walked by. One was bold and put his forefinger on the side of his head, simulating a gun and grinned. Boom, he mouthed. His eyebrows flashed up and down.

C.J. was on the phone and in foul mood, berating a young reporter.

He motioned with his hand to wait while he continued the tongue lashing of the rookie journalist.

"Just because the guys says it, doesn't mean you believe it," C.J. told the rookie. "Seriously, just shut the fuck up and listen, okay. This work is sloppy and unacceptable. You need to find out how this money is being spent. Go through the invoices, records and the rest of the pile of shit that they keep at City Hall and find out. I'm looking at your story, and it has holes. I talking about enough holes to drive a semi-truck through it. So, fix it and get back to me. I don't give a damn if it takes a few more calls to fix it. Do it, okay, and never send me this crap, again. Yeah, bye."

He hung up, bellowed and turned toward me.

"Some of these clueless twits with notebooks lack the passion and balls for this job. It's astounding. Where do they find these people?"

A few years ago, the recession hit newsrooms, and there was a pink-slip epidemic that resulted in job cuts. A lot of experienced reporters who got big paychecks were given buyouts and let go. Fresh faces straight out of college were hired for peanuts. Power and people in powerful positions intimidated most of them.

But corporate likes them because they don't bitch as much as the older curmudgeons with notebooks. C.J., however, found some redeeming qualities in the reporter he had just chewed out.

"Actually, this kid, he is a good reporter. He just needs to grow a pair," he said.

He leaned back in his chair and sized me up.

"Why the bullshit about a dead grandmother?"

"It's a long story. Trust me, I got a gold mine of shit."

"It better be some mind-boggling, earth-shattering stuff," C.J. said. "Humor me."

"A Hollywood screenwriter couldn't dream this up."

"Awesome. Great. Start banging out the story. Let me finish editing this story and we'll talk."

"Okay. What's the mood *de jure* at the corner office?" I asked.

"Pissed. Pissed at you. Pissed at me. Pissed at the world," C.J. said. "Just pissed."

"How did Ricardo find out about the Mexico trip?"

"Benny shot off his mouth by accident at the Painted Lady. Bruce and Lisa were with him. Two days later, it made it back to the newsroom, and gradually, it got back to Hannibal Lector at the corner office," C.J. said.

"*Pinche* Benny," I said angrily. "Can't keep his mouth shut."

"It wasn't his fault. He was worried about you with all the shit happening in Mexico. The kid looks up to you, and the beer loosened his tongue."

I quickly told C.J. that we needed to hold the story for at least a week.

"What!?" he said. "Are you fucking serious? Don't tell me that."

"We can't print anything until some major busts go down," I said. "If we do, it can jeopardize people's lives."

"Ohhhh, man," he exclaimed, tossing his hands into the air. "We're all screwed. Go tell the deadline god at the corner office. He expects to publish your story in four days. So now, you go deal with his red-eyed rage. I'm not going in there with you. Good luck, *carnal*. I'm out."

" I don't need you holding my hand or luck," I said.

After taking a deep breath in front of Ricardo Scott's office door, I knocked twice and swallowed hard.

"Come in," Ricardo said.

Ricardo was typing on his computer screen and sucking his pipe. A cherry blend tobacco filled the air. He had his back toward me. He turned around and frowned. He put his pipe on an ashtray, elbows resting on the arms of his executive chair before he leaned back. He snarled. I could almost feel his look ripping me apart.

Before he said a word, I said, "Wait, okay, just listen for a minute."

I reached into my sports coat pocket and pulled out the hard drive. It was inside a clear plastic bag, and I tossed it onto his over-sized, cluttered oak desk. His eyes bounced from the hard drive to my stoic expression.

"The CIA wants that," I said with a rigid forefinger tapping at the hard drive a few times. "So does the FBI. It's a computer hard drive. And I've got it. I went through hell to get it. Pure *pinche* hell."

"What are you talking about?"

"The hard drive contains a list of the who's who of the narco-trafficking world and how drug money is being laundered, names of banks and other businesses involved. That's the easy part. There is terrorist plan to blow the hinges off America's front door, which means targeting malls, railroad tracks, water supplies, police stations and other institutions."

There was no appeasing, Ricardo.

"I'm supposed to be impressed?" he said. "Let's just publish this science fiction novel. You lied to the editors about why you went to Mexico. Why should anyone believe this bullshit, now?"

"Look, I'll save you the trouble," I said. "I went to Mexico on my dime and my time to chase this story. I went with Sierra Madrid. Mickey Madrid's daughter. And, in the last few days, we've been shot at, chased and threatened. My house bugged."

I stood up and grabbed the hard drive.

"You want to fire me, fine, fire me. No problem. As soon as I walk out, I will find a magazine to freelance this story. And you'll end up having to explain why you passed on it," I said in a flat, icy voice.

Red-faced, Ricardo paused, leaned forward, interlocked his fingers, and rested them on his desk.

"Close the door," he said, a bit flustered. "And sit down."

After closing the door, I sat on a chair facing him with my legs crossed, I boldly zeroed in on his face.

"What pisses me off about you is that you seem to be in your own time zone, your own world, and you seem to delight thumbing your nose at anybody with authority," he said. "We set deadlines, and you find ways to go around them. We have staff meetings, and you make excuses and weasel your way out of attending. You just don't seem to give a shit about anything that goes on in the newsroom unless it revolves around you."

He paused, huffed and continued.

"Now, you come in here and drop this hard drive on my desk, and this wild story, and we are supposed to listen to your every word with bated breath?"

I leaned forward, put my elbows on his desk and looked right into his still smoldering eyes.

"What I'm telling you is the truth. Look, it's not about me. There is stuff in that hard drive that will stun the world," I said. "Send shivers down a lot of spines who believe that hundreds of Middle East terrorists aren't capable of causing havoc in this country because there is an ocean and thousands of miles between us and them. Well, they're wrong, dead wrong."

"Tell me what you've got," he said. "Every detail, don't leave anything out."

I leaned back in my seat and did just that, including why I went to Mexico with Mickey Madrid's daughter. Half an hour into our conversation, and after telling him about Delta Force's secret mission, Ricardo, mouth open slightly, was still asking probing questions, slowly shaking his head in disbelief.

"You're serious? Delta Force?" He said.

"Yes, they saved my ass and Sierra's."

"Who is going on the record with all this? This is all incredible."

"The CIA, after Delta Force and Mexican Marines wrap up their operations. I expect arrests in dozens of cities throughout the United States," I said. "The newspaper get first crack after it all goes down."

"Where is the stuff you guys pulled out of the hard drive? I want to see it."

"No problem."

Ricardo stopped briefly to tell his secretary to hold his calls and called C.J. and managing editor, Tom Westbrook, into his office.

Nearly half an hour went by and the questions were still coming from Ricardo, C.J. and Westbrook. I told them there was still more to do, more digging, more pieces to the puzzle were scattered out there, somewhere.

"The raids are going down soon in Mexico and in this country," I said.

I didn't tell him about one fat piece of the puzzle that, so far, I had been unable to nail down, the part about Sheriff Rick Ward. That would have been a big bombshell, and right now, I couldn't tie the sheriff into anything I had gathered.

I told Ricardo about the trade off for getting quotes from the CIA, DEA, and Homeland Security.

"We can't publish the story right now or we jeopardize American and Mexican lives and compromise this secret operation. I won't do that. Ever."

"We can't hold this story forever," said Ricardo.

"Not forever, but until we get a call, get the okay," I said. "We'll have the story and quotes first while every newspaper in the nation is scrambling to catch up."

C.J. and Tom looked at Ricardo, who was pensive like some Pentagon general mulling over a big battlefield decision.

"We need to get ahead of the game," He told Michael and C.J. "I want a three-day package, four if necessary, that includes the Mickey's bio and downfall of his empire."

Michael Westbrook nodded. C.J. grinned. I still had a somber expression.

"One more thing," I said.

C.J. held his breath and locked his jaw.

"No mention of Delta Force, none," I said emphatically. "I gave them my word."

"That's a huge part of the story," Michael Westbrook protested.

"No way I give them up. No way in hell. Only a handful of people in the White House and Mexico City know Delta Force is in Mexico," I said.

"That's a bit of an exaggeration," Ricardo said.

"I'm risking my career, everything on that," I said.

They all looked at each other before turning their eyes on me.

"It's that serious," I said. "I gave them my word."

CHAPTER 39

I needed a car so I took a taxicab ride to Rodrigo's Restaurant to get a beer and a burger, and of course, to see Dana. She had taken care of Dexter, while I was in Mexico. I wanted to thank her, ask her for a small favor and give her a box of chocolates and flowers.

When I arrived half the restaurant was full. The lunchtime crowd had come and gone. Vicky Briggs, who owned the restaurant, said Dana had gone to the gym to instruct an aerobics class. I guzzled down the beer, ate half the burger, barely touched the fries, and took another cab ride to Body Builders Gym on the Westside with the chocolates and flowers.

There were a few people working out at the gym. Dana's class was inside a large room near the rear of the gym. The room was packed with odd-shaped, mostly middle-aged bodies in yoga pants and spandex. The women were sweating, jumping, swaying, and humping to the high-powered boom, boom, boom music. Dana effortlessly bellowed out exercise commands like a tightly wound Marine Corps drill instructor.

A young receptionist with manicured fingernails and bleached dirty blonde hair, who had Crystal written on the top of the left breast pocket of her gym-issued, blue uniform, sat on a chair at the front desk.

She chatted on a cell phone with a boyfriend who was making sexual demands. While her lips moved, she tapped on computer keys.

"Jonathan, well, yeah, I did say on Facebook that I wasn't in a serious relationship," she said. "Having casual sex with someone isn't serious unless both partners aren't having casual sex with someone else. And you're screwing around too."

She lifted her eyes. Smiling, she held up her finger, motioning for me to wait while she quickly ended her telephone conversation, promising to call Jonathan back.

"Hi," Crystal said, gingerly.

"Hello. I'm here to see Dana."

"She's instructing an aerobics class."

"I know. When does the class end?"

Crystal glanced up at the large clock, looked at the log on her clipboard and replied, "In about ten minutes. She's got a training session with a client at three."

"I'll wait."

"You want to schedule a training session with her?"

"No."

Crystal leaned forward slightly and peered over the front-desk counter. She noticed the chocolates and flowers after I sat on one of the leather couches in the lobby with giant windows and six-foot tall plants.

"She never mentioned a boyfriend," Crystal said with a sly smile.

"We're friends. Good friends," I replied.

"Were you at the party? I didn't see you there."

"What party?" I asked.

"Graduation party. She got her Masters last week."

My heart sank. I felt bad that I hadn't even bought a graduation card or gift. She never forgot my birthday, even came over to my house once with a cake and a gift, a gold pen inscribed: Jack, Here is your magic pen, go and kick ass, love Dana.

Crystal wasn't tired of probing, trying to find out whether I was for real or some nut-job who was infatuated with Dana and her sculptured thighs.

To defuse her annoying perusing, I told her about Dexter.

"Did you see a bird at the party?"

"Dexter the cockatiel?"

I nodded. "My bird. Dana takes care of Dexter when I'm away."

"She loves the bird. He's cute," said Crystal. "Loves to whistle."

"Especially at hot ladies," I said, grinning.

Ten minutes later, Dana walked toward us. A swath of perspiration extended along the top of her tight-fitting workout outfit. She toweled herself and paused to answer a question from one of her aerobic students, an older woman whose backside looked like an old thrift-store loveseat.

I walked over, kissed Dana cheek and handed her the chocolates and flowers.

"It's from Dexter and me," I said.

"Ohhh, that's so sweet. Thank you," she said.

She smelled the flowers and smiled.

"I'm sorry, huh, I forgot your graduation," I said. "Didn't even send a card or anything."

"Don't worry about it," she said, quickly changing the subject. "Got a couple of good job prospects, so far, in Seattle and of all places, Augusta."

"In Georgia?"

"No," she said and chuckled. "In Maine."

"Way up there? It's cold up there."

She sadly nodded.

My heart sank. I knew I'd miss Dana if she moved. I only shared my personal problems with her and my sister Susan. They knew the names of all the ladies who I had loved and had dumped me. I'd miss talking to Dana.

I'd deal with that later. There were other more pressing thoughts going on inside my head. I asked her to step outside for a minute. She hesitated briefly, and then walked out the door, sensing my urgency. I scanned the parking lot from one end of the street to the other.

"I need a small favor," I said, almost whispering.

She frowned, and her sweet temperament turned bitter.

"No. There's no way in hell that I'll ever lend you my car. Not in this lifetime or the next, not ever," she said. "No."

"Look. I can't use my own car. It might have a tracking device on it. GPS. I'm in trouble. Deep shit. Taxis take forever. So, I need your help. Please."

"Is this more of your bullshit?"

"I swear it's not."

"Why can't you rent a car? Or get your pals, C.J. or Geek to rent one for you?"

"They have bad credit, C.J. has a DUI and if I use my credit card, they might find me. Plus my credit also sucks."

"Who are they?" she said, irritated.

"I can't say," I said. "Can you at least rent a car for me using your credit card? I'll pay you for it. I swear. I'm desperate."

She glanced out the large window facing the parking lot.

"Somebody tailing you, Jack?"

"Not that I am aware of. Why?"

"Holy shit. Who'd you piss off this time?"

I was about to say something but she stopped me.

"No. Don't tell me. I don't want to know. Wait here," she said, and muttered, "*Idiota*."

A short time later, we drove to the airport. While I stayed in her parked car, she went into the airport lobby and rented a car. She flung the keys at me, which bounced off my chest. I picked them up from the sidewalk.

"One more thing," I said.

"What!?" she said.

"Could you keep Dexter a couple of days?"

"Sure. That'll be no problem," she said. "Is that it?"

"Yeah."

As I was about to drive away after dropping her off at the gym, Dana shouted my name. I turned around.

"I forgot to tell you, this guy, Tommy Rubio, is looking for you. Said it was really important that you call him. Urgent," she said. "Came by the restaurant yesterday."

That was so odd.

Tommy Rubio, the undercover cop, had never left a message with anybody for me to call him, much less tell them it was on an important matter, urgent no less.

CHAPTER 40

It was late when I walked into Geek's apartment. The TV mute button was on.

On the flat screen was a cop show rerun. On the iPod, the singer Pit Bull could barely be heard. Usually, Geek's stereo system was loud enough to greet someone coming up the stairs.

I was certain that Sierra had reeled in any loud music.

She sat near Geek at the kitchen table next to a stack of papers that had grown larger. Half-eaten chicken salads were inside a small box beside an unfinished Romanian salad and a freshly ordered pizza.

The two glanced up when I walked into the door, said nothing and continued reading papers drawn from two piles.

Sierra's face was wary and sullen. Geek, who held a half-eaten candy bar, looked up. He smiled, the corners of his lips touching the end of tomorrow.

"This is a treasure trove, a load of good shit!" he said. "Contacts and code names. Dirty deeds. Hits. Payoffs. Surveillance. Bank information. Documents and drug money trails. It's all here."

He held a bunch of papers high in the air like a trophy.

"Drug dealers, desperados, and dead men," he said. "All in the hard drive."

Geek looked at the stacks of papers with a smug look, one of satisfaction and pride in his work.

"This guy Francisco, one meticulous bookkeeper," he said. "Two thumbs up."

"Great," I said.

Sierra gave me a long look brimming with exhaustion.

"Grab some pizza. Help us sort through this," Geek said.

I shook my head. "I'm not hungry."

My complete attention shifted to Sierra who intensely marked up the papers with a yellow felt pen. I couldn't take my eyes off her for the longest time. She looked stunning, wearing white pants with a drawstring set low on the waist and a soft yellow blouse. A riotous mane flowed over her petite shoulders, head tilted to one side.

She abruptly interrupted my gaze with a question.

"Who's Ruy Lopez?"

I turned pale. My blood dropped to my ankles. A chill zapped my body. I knew exactly who he was, but found it hard to come to terms with what I had just heard.

"I don't know. Google the name."

"I did. Ruy Lopez Sigura was a Fifteenth Century chess master. He's credited with improving the game. Had a passion for cigars," she said.

Tommy Rubio admired this chess master and studied the way he moved the chess pieces. He used it as a code name when he sent a text message to me. He also bragged about being able to score Cuban cigars from a source he nicknamed Ruy.

Geek said the name appeared several times on a few pages.

"It's a code name for someone," said Geek.

I was hoping Geek's remark would satisfy Sierra's curiosity.

It didn't.

"This Ruy guy got paid $25,000. Two days after my brother was killed," she said. "Francisco made a note. It states, 'Payment dead prince. Madrid Down. *El Pescador* green lighted hit."

She glared at me.

"What does that mean?" Sierra said.

"I don't know." I said.

I flopped down in the middle of the sofa, grabbed the TV remote and moved my head backwards and sideways, pretending to unwind. I tried to change the conversation.

"A friend rented a car for me. A good friend. I need to go places fast."

It didn't work.

Sierra walked over and sat beside me. I could feel her cold, hard stare boring into the side of my face. I ignored her, turned up the sound and went channel surfing.

After a minute, I became agitated, turned toward her, and blurted out, "What?"

"You know exactly what this means," she snapped, yanked the remote from my hand and turned off the television. "Don't bullshit me."

"Hey!" I protested.

"Who the hell is it?" She demanded to know.

Red faced, I gave Geek a dirty look. He seemed to be enjoying the verbal fracas, but pretended like he wasn't even there. I reached into my pocket, took out my wallet, pulled out a $10 bill, and tossed it onto the table.

"Hey man," I said to Geek. "Go get us some beer."

"What, you're an invalid?" he replied.

Geek glared at me, scooped up the money, fished the keys out of his pocket, and huffed out of the apartment. He slammed the door. The building shook. The heavy thudding of angry footsteps went down a flight of stairs. A car door opened and closed as I looked toward an open window, organizing my thoughts and hoping Sierra wouldn't say a word for a few minutes while the shock of what I had just learned gradually subsided.

"Ruy Lopez. Who is this guy?" She said.

"All this shit didn't come with instructions or code decoders. How would I know?"

"Don't bullshit me. I can tell that you're lying!" she said. "You know damn well who killed my brother. You know this Ruy Lopez is the moniker for the person involved with my brother's death?"

"Maybe, I have an idea who it might be and maybe not," I said. "I can't say for sure. It might be the name of an undercover cop."

"A cop? A cop killed my brother! I told you everything. I trusted you, and you sit there lying to me about not knowing anything," she said. "You never said a word about the hard drive."

"I have my reasons."

"Yeah, you're a liar. Period. I can't trust you! What else aren't you telling me?"

"I just want to write this story and be done with all this."

"Story? There wouldn't be any story worth printing if I hadn't taken you to Calera," she said. "Without the hard drive, you had nothing."

She was right, but I was upset.

"You don't run this show. I do. Got it? This isn't your father's drug circus."

"You bastard!" Sierra shot back. "It's about my brother. Finding my brother's killer! I could care less about your damn story. I just want one thing, the name of my brother's killer."

"I can't say anything right now," I said.

She jumped up, picked up her purse and stormed out of the apartment in tears.

"Asshole," she muttered. "This is not over."

I watched her go. I thought about saying something that would placate her hurt feelings and perhaps keep her from leaving. But I didn't. She slammed the door hard but not before telling me that she never wanted to hear my lies again, emphasizing never.

CHAPTER 41

By the time Geek got back with the beer, I bore through a pile of papers that he had churned out from Francisco's hard drive. He walked into the door with a frown. I flashed a smile, hoping to disarm his hurt feelings. He would have none of it. I quickly walked over, offered a heartfelt apology and stuck my hand out as he put the beer into the refrigerator. He mumbled his discontent and squeezed my hand.

"Are we still tight?" I said.

"I guess."

"Look, I knew the conversation between Sierra and I was going to get heated. I didn't want you to be in the middle of it. I trust you or I wouldn't be here."

"Where did she go?"

"She is pissed and tired. She'll be back."

For several hours, Geek and I pored through every page, every word, every tiny detail in the electronic sludge pile. They helped me design an outline on a poster-size sheet of paper I taped on the dining room wall.

Like some corporate general, I drew a chart with a diagram marked with arrows, dashes, words underscored and circled after we carefully went over papers spitting out from the printer. The dots started to connect. Then, a pattern emerged, and as I had suspected the scheme was detailed and very organized.

The chart would help me understand what I was looking at and write a much better story.

A cadre of drug cartel assassins prompted another chart listing all the aliases and monikers in addition to the goons and brutes along with crooked doctors, arms dealers, lawyers, people in the finance world, and people with Arab names.

It became clear that they were running a terrorist operation with the precision of Mobil Oil executives, using bank expertise to transfer bundles of cash by wire. This group wielded a lot of influence with a stable of high-powered politicians, cops, Mexican prosecutors, overseas banking officials and South American contacts.

We read how a wicked, invisible, and budding empire was put together in several Mexican cities that stretched into Nuevo Laredo, Juarez and Tijuana, and even the capital itself.

We kept reading, and kept writing.

Code names, bank accounts, and addresses were strewn all over the charts. We wrote everything on three, large pieces of paper on the wall.

There were banks, plenty of banks, some overseas. Laundered money was sent to offshore banking accounts in the Cayman Islands, where it would go to Europe, then get transferred to shell companies in Bolivia and Venezuela businesses. From there, the money made its way back to Mexican banks.

I had scribbled arrows that pointed at other arrows that pointed at boxes, and the boxes linked to other boxes, mapping out the illegal transfer of money, activities.

All of the money laundering began right after Francisco got cash, which probably arrived in suitcases or electronic money transfers. He'd take his cut and take tons of cash to three banks, one in Calera, and the other two in Zacatecas and Chihuahua.

Francisco made copious notations of a financial inventory of North Korean and Chinese weapons being smuggled from South America through commercial trucks heading to some American cities.

We kept writing, adding another large blank piece of paper to the wall to help us understand the whole, complex and intricate scheme.

The drug cartels' and terrorists' arsenal included rocket-propelled grenade launchers, anti-tank weapons, armor piercing bullets and C-4 plastic explosives. There were plans to use the firepower and a mountain of money to protect drug routes from cops and to hunt down and eliminate rivals.

My exhausted eyes finally screeched to a cold stop on words written in Spanish by Francisco on some of the last entries: Mission: Topple the Beast.

I stepped back, rubbed my forehead and stared at the charts as though it was the Wailing Wall and I was a prophet on some a sacred pilgrimage.

"Wow," I said softly. "Incredible."

In short, the nefarious plan to topple the so-called beast was simple: launch a jihad and ignite a race war in America using terror, hardcore gang members and heavy weapons and explosives.

Weapons were being stockpiled at a several places throughout Mexico for nearly a decade, mostly in the Southern Mexican states of Chiapas, Guerrero and Oaxaca.

The staging points were Zeta guerilla training camps all located at Mexico's three poorest states, all located in the jungles near Guatemala. One of the camps was in Chiapas where there had been an Indian uprising that lasted twelve days and killed a few hundred people.

I walked to the table and slowly trudged through the last pages of a stack of papers, expecting to find nothing new. I was wrong. I stopped. My pupils widened. I found a gem, a big piece of the puzzle. I spotted the code name: Chihuahua Charlie.

"Chihuahua Charlie?" I mumbled.

"What?" Geek said, yawning and barely looking up.

"It states that Chihuahua Charlie desert landings are made twice a day."

"So what's Chihuahua Charlie?"

"An airfield, I guess, used to smuggle drugs in from Mexico."

"Where?"

"Who knows."

I wrote the name Chihuahua Charlie on the yellow notepad, put a question mark at the end, and circled it with several exclamation marks after the two words. Tore the piece of paper and put it in my shirt pocket.

Half an hour later, Geek was in a dead sleep with an arm and leg dangling over the edge of the couch. He snored with his face down and burrowed deep into the meaty well of his triangle-shaped arm. I got up from the table, stretched, yawned, and slowly moved my neck form side to side to keep any soreness at bay.

The TV was still on with the volume off. There were some disturbing images, an early morning CNN breaking news story from Los Angeles. Police and ICE agents, some with shotguns and rifles, swarmed all over a gang-infested neighborhood with several dogs as a helicopter thudded overhead.

I found the remote and turned the volume up a bit.

"Police and federal agents encircled a Los Angeles neighborhood where four police officers were ambushed and killed a few hours ago by unknown group of assailants after they responded to a 'shots fired' call. Two other officers are in critical condition. A massive but cautious search is underway for suspects who might still be in the area," the news reporter said.

The television showed a helicopter swooping down low with its bright lights shining in the alleys and illuminating obscure crevices, looking for any movement in and around the area.

Neighbors, who didn't want to go on camera, told a reporter they heard many short bursts of machine-gun fire, followed by two loud explosions. Two police cars were totally destroyed and caught on fire.

Four fire trucks also responded to the scene to help knock down the flames from the police cars. But they weren't allowed in the area until the police secured it.

The newsroom anchor said one man who lived near the crime scene and didn't want his identity revealed for fear of retaliation. He also didn't want his face shown while he was being interviewed.

He said, "I woke up. There was shooting going on everywhere. It lasted maybe, two or three minutes. My wife and I went to our daughters' bedroom after bullets went through of the windows. My children were screaming and crying. We all got under the bed. After it was over, it got quiet and I could hear screeching tires. It sounded like two cars. I heard someone shout, 'It's on. We were all shaking under the bed. A few seconds after the two cars got out of there, I heard one voice screaming, 'Officers down. Officers down. Need help now.' A few minutes later, dozens of police cars were all over the neighborhood.

The eerie images on TV looked like they had been lifted from Iraq, dying smoke still coming from the two police cars, red and blue emergency lights flashing like Christmas tree ornaments, and men with weapons and badges trying to make sense of the pandemonium, police dogs everywhere, trying to find a scent.

A small crowd of people, apparently awakened by the gunfire, lights, and racket emitted by the police, emergency crews, and fire trucks, stood a couple of blocks away.

I turned up the volume a bit as a TV reporter using the burned police car for a backdrop said, "One Vietnam veteran who lives near here described what he heard as similar to a firefight in the streets of Saigon during the Tet Offensive of 1968. Neighbors said the two explosions, automatic weapons followed by screams not only rattled windows, but also fragile nerves."

My spine stiffened.

"Damn!" I muttered under my breath.

After taking out the hard drive out of the computer, I dropped it inside a plastic bag, walked to the car, and drove to the FBI office downtown. I parked a few blocks away from the building. Getting off the elevator on the fourth floor, I walked up to the receptionist and put the hard drive on the counter.

I still had nearly an hour to spare before the 48-hour deadline set by the CIA agent, McBride.

"Give this to Agent Garza," I said. "My name is Jack Fuentes. He knows what it's about."

"Should I tell him you're here?" she said, reaching for the phone.

"No," I said as I walked out the door. "I can't wait."

I walked outside the building, hurriedly walked to my car, and drove off. I didn't want to be found after the FBI cracked open the hard drive, found out what was in it and what I knew and searched for me.

They would probably trump up some criminal charge and lock me up until after the raids and busts went down.

CHAPTER 42

Right after I went inside Geek's apartment, I sat in front of the computer. I frantically searched the Internet for a few hours, made dozens of phone calls to sources on the streets that might have had contact with Tommy Rubio.

No luck.

I asked questions and more questions, writing down every bit of information about Tommy, especially about his past with the Special Forces in the early 1990s.

Still, I had no luck.

Geek was at work and I felt safe at his apartment. It was spotless. The smell of lemon oil and Pine Sol mixed in the air. Geek had cleaned the apartment before going to work. I felt secure there, away from my house where there might be a hidden listening device or federal agents parked on the street waiting for me to return. Or, worse, someone hiding inside.

A computer search spat out a list of Special Forces units that served in the Persian Gulf in 1991, the time that Tommy Rubio said he was there.

Tommy said little about what he did. But I remembered the name, Andy Foxman.

Another search of obituaries in Boston and bingo: Charles Foxman, an architect and Korea War veteran, had died in 1995.

He was preceded in death by his wife, Marjorie, and survived by his son Andrew Foxman, a daughter, Michelle Hill and a brother Gregory Foxman.

Yesss, I found Andy Fox man's family.

I called the funeral home in Boston to see if there were any records of where Andy Foxman or Michelle Hill lived.

A funeral director Henry Hanover, who had a deep voice and a lisp, answered the phone and said they had destroyed all those records.

"We keep them for seven years. After that, we shredded them," he said, taking a deep breath. "Sorry."

"Who's this?" he then demanded to know.

I told him that I was a newspaper reporter doing a story about a local cop, Tommy Rubio, who served in the Special Forces with Charles Foxman's son, Andy, during the Iraq war.

A half-truth, but nonetheless, a truth, I surmised.

"Do you remember the funeral?" I asked.

He chuckled.

"No. What's to remember? There have been hundreds of funerals and many grieving survivors," he said. "A lot of faces, stories."

Henry was about to hang up when I urged him to help me out.

"Please, I need to find Mr. Foxman. This guy might have shown up in a military uniform, wearing a green beret. He was in Special Forces," I said to jump-start his memory.

Henry spoke. This time in a voice tinged with excitement. It was as though I awakened a deep-seated memory.

"Yes, yes, I remember that fellow," he said. "How can I forget? He had an airborne badge."

He described how Andy had walked into the funeral home after the place was empty, sat in a back row, stared straight ahead before he went and stood over the coffin.

"Yeah, three rows of medals on his chest. Special Forces. He mumbled something. Then, he reached into his pocket, pinned something on his dead father's suit and saluted," said Henry. "I watched from the back for a few minutes. I thought it was odd and walked over to him."

Henry said Andy slowly turned around and smiled.

"Sir, I'm sorry but it's nearly closing time," Henry said he told him. "He just nodded. Tears were welling up in his eyes. I recall. He stepped away, and I thought he was going to walk away."

Henry said he noticed that Andy Foxman had put an airborne badge on his father's lapel.

"He turned around and said his father and him had unresolved issues," said Henry. "He wanted to make his father proud of him. Apparently, his father didn't approve of what he did, tracking people and killing them."

"He was a hero," I said.

"Yeah," said Henry. "Well, his father and him never patched things up. The family didn't expect him to show up. But he did. Came in right after everyone left. The whole thing was pretty sad."

He paused before clearing of his throat.

"Could you please check your records?" I pleaded. "Please, I'm desperate. I really need to find Andy Foxman. I need your help. If you can come up with anything, I'd appreciate it."

"The old records were kept in files back then. What remains is down in the basement. It'll take hours, there are boxes and boxes of financial and some business records."

'It's important. I would appreciate it."

He groaned and said. "I'll see what I can do."

"Thank you, so much."

After I hung up, I realized that this was a very, long shot. Andy Foxman could be anywhere in the United States, or for that matter, the world. His sister also was somewhere in the fifty states.

I tossed my pen on the table and pinched the bridge of my nose to fend off a headache creeping into the middle of my forehead, boring through the middle of my brain.

I went back to work, going through piles of paper with red and yellow markers.

Two hours later, the phone rang. Caller ID showed that it was an unknown telephone number with an equally unknown area code.

It was Henry.

"You didn't get this from me. Michelle Hill lives in Chicago. Do you have a pen?"

Henry gave me Michelle Hill's last known telephone number and hung up before I could ask a question or thank him.

I punched the phone numbers. The phone rang once, twice, before a child picked up the phone on the third ring.

"Hello?" said the boy, sounding like he was about six years old.

"Can I speak to your mom, please?"

"Yeah," the child said, and at the top of his lungs hollered, "Mooooom!"

I could hear footsteps descending from the stairs. A woman grabbed the phone and scolded the child. "Jason, don't yell. I can hear you. I'm not deaf."

"Okay," the boy casually dismissed his mother's chiding.

"Hello?" she said.

"Michelle Hill?"

"Yes, who is this?"

I introduced myself, told her that I was a reporter doing a story about a former Special Forces unit, her brother's unit. I needed to find her brother. She asked questions, probing whether I was a bill collector, lawman, or worse, a foreign assassin tracking down her sibling. She wasn't about to give up her brother's cell phone number that easily.

When I had a gut feeling that she was going to say that she didn't know where her brother was, I said, "Please. Just give him the message. I would really appreciate it."

"All right," she said. "I guess I can do that."

For hours while I waited for a call from Andy, I read and reread stacks of pages that Geek milked from the laptop's hard drive and took notes. My puffy eyes were dead tired.

I closed them, fell asleep and was consumed by deep sleep void of faces, images and monsters. I woke up two hours later and went to the bathroom to wash my face and continue reading more pages.

As I stared at the exhaustion stamped on my face, the cell phone rang. I rushed to the kitchen table and grabbed it.

"Hello?" I said.

"Jack Fuentes?"

"Yeah."

"Andy Foxman."

"Wow, yeah, thanks. I appreciate you calling back."

"No problem. What can I do for you?"

I was anxious to talk to him, yet afraid of what he would say, afraid he would tell me what I didn't want to hear about Tommy Rubio, whom I had trusted with my life. I didn't want to call Tommy for fear I would alert him as to what I had found on the hard drive. What were the chances that the name Ruy Lopez would pop up on a hard drive that belonged to Francisco? If Tommy knew what I had found out, my life could be in danger. Was it a coincidence that a gunman tried to kill me at the cemetery while I waited for Tommy?

"I'm doing an investigative piece on international terrorism, and Tommy Rubio is part of the story. What kind of soldier was he? Were you two close?"

"Tommy Rubio and I were like brothers. He's a good dude. Knew his stuff and had a pair of brass balls. Fearless."

Surprisingly, Andy didn't know that much about Tommy's life before he joined the Army. He said Tommy seldom talked about his family or a girlfriend or a sibling. He said they both were with the 5th Special Forces Group in Riyadh, Saudi Arabia, just before the start of the Gulf War in 1991.

"I haven't seen him in ages," he said. "All I know about what he is up to is by a few Christmas cards that he mailed to my sister's house."

Andy Foxman said Tommy Rubio graduated from the Special Forces training school at Fort Bragg with high marks.

"Hell of a chess player. I love the game. So I gave him a run for his money. Then, he started reading every chess book he could get his hands on," Foxman said. "He studied the game like some astronomers study the stars. Then, he blew everybody out of the water with his mastery of the game."

"Did he ever mention a medieval chess master who he admired?"

"Naw. Not that I recall."

"A Spanish chess master, perhaps."

Silence. Then, I could hear a clicking of fingers.

"Oh, yeah, yeah," said Andy. "It was a guy named Lopez. Rory or Roman Lopez. No, no wait. Roy, I think. Roy Lopez. Yeah."

"Do you mean, Ruy? Ruy Lopez?"

"Yeah. Yeah. Ruy. Ruy Lopez."

"Are you sure?"

"Absolutely, I told Tommy to study some of Lopez's moves. Lopez was a medieval chess player, a genius who revolutionized the game. Even back then."

I cut to the chase.

"The Special Forces unit that both of you were assigned to during the war; I understand that you guys hunted down and destroy Scud missile sites?"

"Correct. But a lot of what we did, to this day, is still classified."

I could hear a short breath during a long pause.

"I just want to know the basics, no details," I said.

"Right. Well, many of Saddam's Scud missiles contained chemical and biological warheads," said Andy. "Some were pointed toward Israel. We knew that one hit by a Scud on Tel Aviv early in the war, and Israel would enter the fighting. That would have pissed off the Saudis and broken up the fragile Arab coalition that we'd been putting together against Iraq."

"What was Tommy Rubio's job?" I said.

"Blowing things up."

"Scuds?"

"Mostly."

The oxygen was sucked from my lungs. I turned pale.

"So, Tommy Rubio is an expert bomb maker?"

"The best. I've never seen better. He can blow open a four-inch-thick steel door or take down the MGM Grand in Vegas with C4 explosives."

"That good?" I said, recalling what happened to Sierra's brother.

"I saw him put a bomb together in a thick sand storm. The next night we took out a truck towing a Scud with it," Andy said.

Andy explained that Special Forces units, including the British Special Air Service, had problems finding mobile Scuds throughout the 29,000 square-miles of desert. It was hard because the Iraqis hid them in gullies, culverts, and underpasses in the daytime and fired most of them at night, he said.

"Our team was dropped off by a Blackhawk copter at night," he said. "We searched for Scuds."

Immediately, he said there were more problems attached to the mission.

"When we'd pin-point the locations, the Scuds would be rapidly moved by the time an air strike could hit them with bombs and take them out," Andy said. "So our unit rigged the roads with explosives, and when the Scuds were moved by armed convoys to another location, the explosives would go off and take out the Scuds along with armored personnel carriers."

"So, Tommy did a lot of damage."

"Yeah, and he was a good teacher too. We swapped skills. He showed me how to rig bombs, and I showed him how to take targets out from a thousand yards," Andy said.

"He's good with a sniper rifle?"

Andy nodded.

"He's a natural. He knew the basics. I taught him all the fine points," he sighed. "So, when is your newspaper article coming out?"

"In a few weeks," I said.

Andy asked for Tommy's cell phone number. I hoped that he didn't call Tommy after I hung up and let him know that I was probing, asking questions about his bomb-making days in the Special Forces.

Right after I ended my conversation with Andy, I called Daniel Apodaca, a U.S. Marshal. I asked him to meet me in an hour at a truck stop on the east side of town, off Interstate 10.

He said he was coaching his teenage son's basketball team.

"Can it wait until tomorrow?"

"It's important, Dan. I really need to talk to you about the Emilio Madrid murder."

He said he'd meet me there after the game.

CHAPTER 43

Daniel Apodaca sat at a far corner booth at the busy Petro truck stop, which hugged Interstate 10 on the east side of town. He seemed pensive with thoughts that seemed to burrow into the darkness outside. His reflection on the window stared back at him as he held his coffee cup near his mouth.

It was nearly 10 p.m. The restaurant was busy, mostly red-eyed truckers, a few sporting cowboy hats or baseball caps. A couple with two children sat at a corner booth. One of them, a fussy youngster, insisted that he wanted pancakes with a happy face on top that was made with a whipped-cream smile, chocolate eyes, and a bucket of red strawberry syrup.

An ebb and flow of Spanish-speaking conversations came out of the restaurant's kitchen.

Daniel was a patient man. It served him well as a headhunter with the U.S. Marshal's office. A husky man with a cinnamon crew cut and a few freckles to match, he was an expert tracker of wanted felons. Occasionally, he teamed up with other marshals to track fugitives around the country. He became a source after I wrote a story about how his team of U.S. Marshals and others found a local fugitive who had made the FBI's Most Wanted list. The wanted drug trafficker was caught in Panama living on a fishing boat on the Chepo River.

In that case, Daniel and the other marshals meticulously put smidgens of clues together, mostly by locating the fugitive's high school buddies and old neighbors and bombarding them with questions.

So, Daniel's hunches were solid, and most importantly, professionally tweaked. He could also tap into intelligence tentacles that stretched across the Mexican border and beyond. He was someone I trusted and sometimes ran my own hunches past. He soon became a close friend, and we both talked about our families, our lives, and sometimes, our dreams.

After I arrived at the truck stop, he gave me a bear hug.

Dan and I never talked business until we briefly traded stories about our families. This night was no different.

Dan said he was still coaching his son's basketball team. A divorcee, he told me that he had just met a woman named Carmen in San Antonio who owned a floral shop. They met at a Baptism while he was visiting relatives there

He sounded happy with the relationship.

"How is the family?" He said.

"My mom is still teaching at the college. Susan is good. Opened a dental practice in Santa Fe. My niece is growing like a weed."

"Patched things up with your dad?"

I shook my head.

"So, you two haven't gone hunting?" He asked.

"My dad and I haven't talked in months. I just don't get him. He was in the Gulf War with a Marine rifle company, came home got a master's degree in electrical engineering, works at a corporation for three years, making gobs of money. He resigns and opens up a barbershop."

Daniel grinned.

"Happiness to him is a pair of scissors. That's his passion. It's in his blood. His love. With you, it's a notebook or a pool stick in your hand."

Halfway through my second cup of coffee, the caffeine chitchat abruptly stopped and Daniel's face turned somber after I asked, "Any DNA or fingerprints found on the car bomb that took out Emilio?"

Daniel glanced out the window as two tractor-trailer trucks slowly drove by, heading past the gas pumps and toward I-10.

"Off the record, right?" He said.

"Absolutely."

"No prints or DNA were found. Nothing. But my guy at ATF said an expert rigged it. A C-4 explosives expert. It wasn't a pipe bomb."

"A Colombian, maybe?" I said.

Daniel slowly shook his head.

"No, C-4 is not part of their game plan," Daniel said. "The wire splices were perfect. It was a nice, neat, tidy little device. Rigged to go off in a small confined area. This was the work of a pro, an explosives expert. "

The conversation with Andy Foxman about Tommy Rubio's bomb-making skills with C-4 flashed across my mind.

I had to be wrong. It couldn't have been Tommy. No way.

"The Colombians could have hired a bomb maker, an expert, right?" I said.

"No way," he replied. "If the Colombians or cartels start blowing things up in this country, killing innocent people. There would be outrage. It'll shut down the border, put an army of federal agents and army reserves near the fence. The cartels won't even be able to hide balloons of coke up keisters to get them across the border. Explosions are bad for business. Somebody was sending a very personal message."

Daniel finished his coffee and wiped his mouth with a napkin. The waitress returned with the cheesecake and the donut that I ordered. She glared at me while sliding my plate with the donut in front of me and poured more coffee into our cups. She was upset because I refused the cheesecake special. I bit my lip. Daniel had a smirk. She left after slapping the bill on the table and insincerely wishing us a nice night.

"Some people push pies. Others dope," Daniel said and laughed.

"Supply and demand," I said sarcastically.

He nodded. "Most of the world's coke goes up American noses."

I took a bite of my donut and washed it down with coffee.

"So, what's the word on the streets? Who took out Emilio?" I said.

"Someone who felt Emilio was going to inherit the keys to the Madrid kingdom. Beyond that, your guess is as good as mine."

It was hard to swallow the second mouthful of the donut after hearing those words. Seconds later, my cell phone popped out a text message from Tommy Rubio.

"Need to meet. Urgent," the message read. "Heard you talked to Andy Foxman."

Blood drained from my head, a reaction that didn't go unnoticed.

"Something wrong?" Daniel said

He could see that I had been rattled by the text message.

"Naaw, just a source," I said.

"You've got my cell phone number, okay?" he said. "Some of the people you write about are vicious, violent criminals. If it becomes a serious issue and you can't handle it, call me."

"I'll be fine. Really," I said.

We said our goodbyes, and I tried to masquerade my growing concern behind a fragile smile.

"Remember, call if you need me," Daniel said as I walked away. "I mean it."

I turned around.

"If it hits the fan, you'll get a call," I said as I left. "I promise."

CHAPTER 44

Minutes after Daniel and I left the restaurant and I was driving down the highway, another text message flashed. It was Tommy, again. He sent a five-number message - 35845. It meant that he wanted to me to meet him in an hour at a roadside bar called Slim Jim's located at the end of the Westside.

Slim Jim's was at the end of a poorly lit, winding road and close to an industrial park.

We met there a few times, drank a few beers, played pool, and talked about drug busts. While sucking on expensive cigars, Tommy would give me tips on drug busts and interesting insights and tidbits about cops including the dirty little secrets, the station-house rumors, the backstabbing, womanizing, and the alcoholism in the police department, from the chief to the cop on the streets.

It seemed odd. Tommy's text message stated that he would be there in an hour. Why did he want to meet at Slim Jim's when two weeks earlier he was involved in a large drug bust there?

I messaged back. "Can't make it. On my way to newsroom. Working late. Get back to U later."

It was just after 10 p.m. when I got to the newspaper building.

Inside the newsroom, a few reporters sat in front of computer screens, mostly late-night copy editors who were correcting, changing and modifying stories for the next day's newspaper.

The police radio traffic was sluggish. Some of the newsroom lights were dim on one side of the large room where desks were empty. Nobody noticed that I was there except the cop reporter Preston whom everybody nicknamed Harpo because of his striking resemblance to one of the Marx brothers with his gigantic, mushroom explosion of curls on his head.

I walked by him as he bickered with someone on the phone. He looked up and motioned for me to stop. I did, and he rapidly scrawled a note on his notebook, ripped it out, handed it to me and continued his telephone conversation.

I read the message as I walked away. It stated: An FBI guy Garza looking for you. Call him. Very important.

"Thanks," I said.

He nodded. I slipped Garza's message and phone number into my shirt pocket. As I sat in front of my computer, I thought about calling Garza, but immediately scoffed at the idea. The last thing I wanted to do was get bogged down by a myriad of questions from FBI agents about the laptop and Mexico and God knows what else.

I didn't have time.

No doubt, they wanted to know how much I was able to retrieve from the computer. I was certain that the FBI and Homeland Security did a rush job on the laptop's hard drive and squeezed every bit of information out of it.

Now, they know what I know. We're all on the same page.

I stared at a blank computer, an intense, almost hypnotic stare as though I was reading electronic tealeaves.

But it was clear and cataclysmic. The plan would trigger a bloodbath in Mexico, if not an all out revolution, capable of turning Mexico into a narco-terrorist country with much of the bloodshed exported to America.

The airwaves would be filled with rightwing talk show hosts, stirring the cauldron of hatred, fear, racism and contempt against Mexicans, foreigners, or anybody with brown or dark skin. Gun sales would go up, national anxiety and rumors would skyrocket, and paranoia would make people do crazy things.

A tempest of terror would rock the country.

The computer finally logged into the Internet. I snapped out of a Nostradamus-like trance and went to work. My fingers, mind, and eyes whipped across the computer screen. I typed as fast as I could.

Nearly an hour after putting pages of notes, including names, places and dates, onto the computer, I attached everything to an e-mail. I hit the send button. Everything went to my sister, Susan. I told her that if anything happened to me, to forward all this stuff to C.J. He'd know what to do with it. I told her not to say anything to anyone receiving my e-mail or open my e-mail attachments.

"Don't reply," I emphasized by capitalizing the words "Don't Reply."

It was nearly 11 a.m. when I finished.

Everybody in the newsroom was long gone. Other reporters and copy editors had trickled out the door. The police radio had gone nearly flat.

A cleaning woman finished applying furniture polish atop Ricardo's desk, her counterpart with his headphones on his head swayed to the music as he collected the trashcans. They finished, smiled, politely said good night, and left.

I got up to put on my coat and head out the door when the phone on my desk rang loudly. Startled, I checked the Caller ID. It was an unknown number.

"Newsroom."

No reply.

"Hello. This is the newsroom. Hello."

The person hung up. The number was unknown. The silence bothered me but it was probably the wrong number.

I stared across a sea of empty desks, stacks of paper, newspapers and books. I took a deep breath and let it out. As I interlocked my fingers and put them behind the back of my head, leaned back on my chair, and tossed my head back to relax, the cell phone bleeped. Another message: "Look out window. Ruy Lopez."

It was Tommy Rubio.

My face turned pale.

It was from an unknown cell phone number. My heartbeat picked up speed as I walked toward the window. I glanced out from the second floor window, as though I expected him to be there hanging up in midair like a ghost, glaring and waving.

Fear at first shook my being, then, I just got angry, very angry. I cursed, cursed some more.

I was tired and in no mood to be intimidated or pushed around by Tommy Rubio, the FBI, DEA, CIA, Ricardo or anyone else. I was sick of the cat and mouse game. I was sick of being afraid. I refused to be the mouse in a house full of alley cats.

Frustrated, I threw my shoulders back, raised my chin, and stood in a defiant stance with arms spread, palms up, as I stared out the window.

"What!?" I yelled.

Downtown had a yellowish, surreal glow from the streetlights. The light bounced from building windows and pavement. Occasionally, a car would go by the street below as it made its way to the exit to get on the highway. The newspaper's parking lot was empty. The two cars that had been parked there were gone. I figured they belonged to the cleaning crew.

I wondered whether this was a joke, and Tommy was sitting at a table at Slim Jim's playing head games with me.

Nothing was going on outside. The darkness and the bright lights seemed undisturbed. Then, a rapid flash of headlights. Lights from a slow moving car two blocks away, turning on and off several times. The car stopped.

My cell phone bleeped a few times. I went over, picked it up, and looked at the blinking name "Tommy Rubio" on my ID caller. I stood in front of the large window. I couldn't see his car.

"What's up, Tommy?" I said.

"So, you're working late, huh?" he said.

Long pause.

"Yeah."

He groaned.

"Did Andy Foxman give you some good quotes? About my background with the Special Forces? Ruy Lopez? Heard you found a laptop in Mexico."

He laughed, chilling laughter that sent goose bumps across my arms. Abruptly, he stopped and snorted. I swallowed hard before unloading a nuke.

"Why did you kill Emilio?"

He grunted and didn't deny it.

"I picked up the contract. Emilio was too close to Mickey and Bazooka. They took him to Mexico on business trips a few times."

"Who gave the green light?"

"The Juarez Drug Cartel. Word got back to Sheriff Rick. I picked up the contract."

"Emilio had nothing to do with any of this shit," I said. "Nothing. They went on fishing trips on the Gulf of Mexico. That's it."

"Well, the cartel had him pegged as the heir apparent to Mickey's kingdom," he said coldly.

"They were wrong. Dead wrong, and you killed him. For nothing. He was innocent."

"In this business, mistakes are made," he said coldly.

"Let me get this straight. Sheriff Rick hired you?"

"Correct. He also hired prison gang members as muscle for the Juarez Cartel. After they do a hit or two, they're taken out. No more witnesses or snitches."

I wanted to scream at him and curse some more. I had put all this trust in him. How could I have been so stupid? I decided to remain calm. I knew there was more, and I needed to get it from him. Losing my cool would just botch things up.

"So Rick and Mickey used Chihuahua Charlie to smuggle in drugs?"

"Who told you about Chihuahua Charlie?"

"The hard drive. The named popped up. Everything is there, even the name Ruy Lopez," I said, wondering if he knew that the FBI had the hard drive.

He didn't.

"Where is the hard drive?"

"In a safe place. Where is this Chihuahua Charlie airfield?"

He chuckled.

"It ain't an airfield. It's the nickname of a glider pilot."

"What?"

"Gliders."

"They're using gliders to smuggle drugs?"

"Bingo," he said and groaned. "Sheriff Rick and Mickey hired Chihuahua Charlie more than a decade ago. The Juarez Cartel loads up the gliders in Mexico. Charlie flies them into Marfa, landing just over three or four miles from the airport. Tons of cocaine have gone through. Once in awhile, a bundle or two of weed is lost so it can keep Rick legitimate in the eyes of law. The cartel sits back and signs off on the whole thing."

"Meanwhile, Chihuahua Charlie's gliders loaded with coke quietly cross the border and land in some secluded, little desert airstrip in Marfa, right?" I said.

"You catch on quick," he said, goading me. "Sharp as a tack." He laughed.

I was pissed. My eyes were set on the streetlight that bounced off car windshields below. I couldn't see Tommy or his car or anyone else below.

"Who killed Francisco the painter?" I asked.

"The Zetas. Francisco got greedy. Started skimming drug money," he said. "That's all I know."

As I scanned the cars parked on the streets and underneath the bright streetlights below, the headlights of one turned on and off several times to let me know where he was.

"I'm here," he said, taunting me.

"What now, Tommy?" I asked. "Huh? What now?"

There was a brief pause before he replied.

"Now, the ball is in your court. I laid all my cards on the table. Everything."

"The ball is in my court? How's that?"

"Forget all this. Forget Ruy Lopez. Forget what happened. Keep my name out of the newspaper. Write a lame little story. One with a few details, drop a few names and walk away."

"Why? Why would I ever do that?"

"Half a million dollars," he said.

Half-a-million dollars. Wow, a lot of bucks, I thought.

Tommy didn't say a word. I figured he was letting me savor the thought of all that money and think about how much it would change my life.

"Write your lame little story and walk away with a bundle of cash. Enough to set you up in some cozy little Caribbean Island somewhere. Sit on the beach, sip beer and play pool all day. You can buy a nice little sailboat, cruise the islands and bang the rich European tourists and college chicks."

I swallowed hard, glanced over my shoulder at the rows of computers. The police radio was dead, nothing going on.

"And if I don't go along with the program?" I said.

He cracked up, sinister laughter.

"Look, if I had wanted you dead, it would have happened in the cemetery."

I was astonished, then my blood began to boil.

"You? You sent that prick to the cemetery? That bastard with the gun who shot at me?"

"Yeah," he said. "Sheriff Ward wanted you dead. I told him that killing a reporter would bring a lot of heat to our business. I convinced him to just put the fear of God in you. When that didn't work, the listening devices helped me keep tabs on where you were. An electronic dog collar, so to speak."

He chortled and stopped.

"So, I saved your ass, buddy," he said.

Angrily, I pounded the large glass window hard twice with the palm of my hand.

"You son of a bitch," I said. "I trusted you."

"Get over it," he said. "I gave you more shit than you knew what to do with. A lot of front-page stories. But, hey, I admit that to your credit you've got more balls than most. A lot of heart too."

I locked my jaw and swore under my breath.

"So what about it?" he said.

"I'm not interested."

"Tell you what, pal. I'll sweeten the pot to a million. One million dollars. Write a bullshit story, give me the hard drive, and as soon as you do, you'll get suitcases full of cash. There are a lot of heavy-duty players who want that hard drive."

Sailboats, beaches, and beautiful ladies in bikinis zoomed across my mind, eased the outrage brewing in my heart. But there were internal forces much stronger than that, powerful things that had kept me grounded throughout my life, things that I couldn't shake off, that would haunt me throughout my life if I did. Things that no amount of money could buy.

"Can't do it, pal" I said emphatically with a tinge of sarcasm.

"So, for the rest of your life, you're satisfied with being this nosy, dipshit reporter who keeps a sad little notebook in your back pocket and has problems paying the rent?"

"My family is everything. I'm not letting them down, especially my father. I'd never accept a bribe, not now, not ever."

A long silence, long enough to clear my throat and sigh.

"My dignity and self-respect have never had a for-sale sign hanging on them," I said. "Oh, and the hard drive that you and the rest of your playmates are looking for, they're just going to have to talk to the FBI, pal. They have it. And, they'll soon figure out who Ruy Lopez is. I know now who he is, though. He's a conniving, scumbag drug dealer who spreads poison on the streets, destroys families and inflicts pain and suffering on people. Simply put, Ruy

Lopez, a.k.a. Tommy Rubio, is a greedy parasite who lives off the misery of others."

"You little bitch."

I chuckled, knowing I had stirred up plenty of bile. It felt so good.

"Checkmate, motherfucker," I said.

Then, the sound. The crude sound of metal, cold steel. A familiar sound I'd heard countless times when my father and I went hunting came across my cell phone.

Holy shit!

A round being chambered into a rifle, I thought.

I was a target.

Before I could jump out of the way, a bullet took out the newsroom window.

I felt the hot lead graze and sting the side of my cheek like someone had sliced me with a hot box-cutter.

A powerful explosion rocked downtown.

I dove and hit the side of a desk. The blast sent a hailstorm of broken window glass on the streets. A smaller secondary explosion followed. A bright orange and yellow fireball swirled and hurled itself high, lighting up the night as though it were day.

My breaths were deep and long as I shook the glass from my hair, some of it falling from my shirt. The glass cut my forefinger and the side of my head just above my left eye. The tiny cuts felt like bee stings. My lip was also tender from hitting the desk. I lowered my upper torso as far as I could, reached up, and flipped off the light switches.

The room was a dark. The streetlights were out.

I waited a few seconds for another shot that never came. My back was against the wall. I didn't dare poke my head up. The computer screen lights lit up the shards of glass on the floor.

It looked like someone had spilled millions of diamonds on the floor.

Outside, there were frantic voices coming from the street below as I struggled to piece together what happened. Then, somebody, a man's voice, shouted. "Get an ambulance!"

The police radio erupted in frantic squawking and bleeping. Emergency vehicles were on the way. I could hear distant sirens. I made my way to a window and took a quick peek at the streets below, careful to keep my head low. Tommy Rubio's car was on fire. Flames consumed the inside and were roaring from the back of the car.

There was no sign of Tommy. The sirens were getting closer.

My cell phone flashed. Was it Tommy?

The phone was halfway across the newsroom. The explosion and my momentum had sent it sliding across the floor. The phone kept flashing. I ducked and dashed over to pick it up. It was Sierra's cell phone number on my phone screen. I answered it.

"He's dead," she said coldly. "Payback. Just like he did my brother."

"Are you fucking crazy?" I shouted.

"You're the fool. Your cop friend just tried to kill you. He had a rifle with a scope's crosshairs aimed at you. Who's the crazy one?"

After she said that, it felt as though scales from my eyes had dropped.

I then saw Tommy Rubio for what he was, a drug dealer and cold-blooded killer, a rogue cop who had probably shaken down or killed small-time drug dealers. Any slim chance that I was wrong about Tommy Rubio vaporized. The truth, however, didn't pack less of a punch. I felt sad, angry, and confused.

"Where are you?" I said in a low voice.

"I'm beside a red car parked in the alley. Near your car."

"You set off that bomb?" I said, incredulously.

"No. That is all you need to know."

"Stay put. I'll be there in minute."

I hurriedly walked out of the newspaper building and slipped into an alley a block away just as a fire engine raced by, followed by a police car, then another police car. Picking up the pace, I didn't want to run the risk of being seen by a witness who would describe the person running away right after the blast.

As I got near my car, which was parked next to a large commercial truck next to a warehouse, I slowed down. A red Mazda was parked half a block away near two other cars.

Nobody was inside. I stopped for a moment before taking some slow steps toward her car. I wondered whether I was walking into a trap where Sierra or someone of her choosing would open up with gunfire. She would avenge her brother's killer, and now she'd get rid of the witness.

I wondered if detectives would also be collecting fragments from a second bomb blast after I opened the door to my car and turned on the ignition.

Another fire truck went by the alley, followed by an ambulance. No sirens, just red lights splashing across large store windows as the emergency vehicles drove down the street. The alley was dark and empty. Sweat trickled down my forehead.

"Sierra," I called out. "Sierra."

"I'm here." She stood behind me.

I stiffened hard, breathing heavily.

"If I wanted you dead, that would have happened seconds ago," she said. "I have a score to settle with Rick Ward."

"Let's get out of here," I said. "This place is going to be crawling with cops."

We got into my car and pulled out of the alley.

"Where are we going?"

I slowly zigzagged our way out of downtown driving through some alleys, across an empty parking lot, going the wrong way on a one-way street for a couple of blocks, then, turning in and out of side streets before we got on Interstate 10.

Ironically, it was Tommy Rubio who taught me the intricate ins and outs of dodging police dragnets and perimeters set up to catch suspect vehicles.

"You'll probably never use this," Tommy had once told me. "But who knows. Things change like the weather."

I didn't realize then how prophetic Tommy's words would be about things changing like the weather until we drove down the highway as police car lights and sirens passed us by, going in the opposite direction.

CHAPTER 45

We drove to Geek's apartment. I hopped out.

"Wait here," I told Sierra.

I rushed up the stairs to the apartment. Geek was asleep on the couch with the television on. I shook him.

"What's up," he said and yawned.

"I need your hunting gear, rifle, sleeping bag. Also binoculars and a coat, a heavy coat," I said.

"In the closet," he said, weakly pointing to the bedroom. "All in the closet. Everything you need. Take what you need. The ammo is on the top shelf."

I snatched a backpack, Winchester rifle, a sleeping bag and other stuff. I looked up at the closet and grabbed a box of ammo in the corner of the shelf.

"Where's your camera?" I shouted to Geek.

"Middle shelf on the bookend," he shouted.

"Thanks."

I walked out of the bedroom past Geek who was now sitting up, struggling to keep his eyes open.

"You're going deer hunting?" Geek said.

"Glider hunting."

I started toward the door. Geek lazily scratched the back of his head.

"Get a glider-hunting license," he teased.

I smiled, stopped, and patted my coat pocket, "Got one. Right here."

"Good," he said.

"Oh, I need to borrow your laptop."

"Take it."

"What's the password?"

"Stud Horse. One word."

"Are you serious? Stud Horse?"

Sleepy-eyed, he nodded. "One word."

"Got it. Thanks."

His head fell onto the pillow, and he pulled the covers over his body.

I went downstairs. Sierra got out of the car and went to the back of my car where I was loading everything in the trunk. She stood there for a while before asking the obvious.

"What's the gun for?"

"Marfa," I said. "There are mountain lions and coyotes out there. Who knows what I'll bump into."

"The camera?"

"Photograph gliders. Drug smugglers. I've got a deadline. I need proof that there is a landing site out there. That Rick Ward is involved."

"There is a lot of desert out there. "Why don't you just call the cops and let them handle it?" She said.

"He is a cop, and so was Tommy Rubio. So why would I trust any of them?"

I closed the trunk of the car and locked eyes with Sierra.

"This whole thing with Ward is personal now, very god-damn personal. I want to nail that arrogant sonna-va-bitch. He's hurt a lot of people, including killing a good man who trusted him because he was the sheriff. A migrant worker who simply wanted a job to feed his family. His wife and daughter were devastated. And, Ward wanted me dead. But I'm still here. So, it's game on."

"I'm going," she said.

"Where?"

"With you."

"No way in hell. I'm dropping you off at your house."

"I'm going with you. Period," she said, fiery eyed.

"You got what you came for. Tommy Rubio is dead."

"Rick Ward hired Tommy Rubio to kill my brother. I've come this far. And, you owe me. I saved your ass. I'm going. End of conversation."

"You know what's out there in the desert besides the wild animals?"

"Yes, I know. I was with you in Mexico or did you forget?" she said.

We drove fast, heading east down Interstate 10 toward Marfa. I drove for an hour. Sierra was asleep, her head against the passenger door.

The sun was barely making a slow crawl from behind the West Texas Mountains. We had driven nearly two hours. The summer air was light, cool and crisp. The numbing stillness of the desert beckoned a grayish-blue sky. The lone highway with its neat white lines and endless asphalt sliced up the desert floor. Ancient rows of barbwire set man-made boundaries.

I scanned the sky dome above the high plateau and across the highest mountain peaks at the edge of this, Big Bend Country. It was all surreal. Yet Marfa was the perfect spot, isolated and halfway between a lonely stretch of Interstate 10 and the Mexican border.

"It's perfect," I said.

With a puzzled look, she looked at the dry vastness.

"Perfect for what?"

I told her everything that Tommy Rubio had said about the gliders. I said cocaine would be an easy ride on hot air currents and land at thousands of isolated places hidden inside canyons, behind mountain ranges.

"The whole thing. It's brilliant plan," I said. "Bringing dope from Mexico on gliders, landing them on a secluded spot near Marfa. Almost undetectable and protected by Rick Ward."

"Gliders? Here?"

"Oh, yeah."

"Strong thermal updrafts found under cumulus clouds are legendary in Marfa. So strong that they attract gliding enthusiasts," I said. "In these conditions, gliders can quietly soar more than 500 miles. They can fly in from Mexico almost undetected. They are made out of wood and have no motors. So they can fly under radar and over electronic trip wires, audio recorders."

I told her that Marfa holds an annual Glider Rally at the airport, and ten state soaring records have been set there. The hot winds are so powerful that nearly 40 years ago, Marfa hosted the World Soaring Championship.

"So what's another glider in the desert skies over Marfa? Who would notice?" I said. "It's in Rick Ward's neighborhood. So who would care?"

Half an hour later, we pulled on the side of the road at a rest stop. I stretched my legs and arms. I woke up Sierra, who was taking another catnap, reclining her seat all the way back. I took out Geek's laptop from the trunk, attached the Wi-Fi mobile device to it that belonged to the newspaper and logged in. I gave it to Sierra.

"Here."

"What?" she said, sitting up and staring at the laptop.

"Search for an airfield. It'll be tiny. About two miles or so from Marfa's airport. Use the Google map."

"You can't be serious?"

"Just look, look closely. Follow the highway close to Marfa, and look for places close to a mountain range but far from the road. Take your time. Look for a dirt road. One that looks like a path that hunters might use that leads to a large, narrow clearing. One that might be used to land an aircraft."

"You know how hard —"

"Just look," I said.

She yawned, brought her seat back up, hooked up the laptop to the cigarette lighter, and tapped into cyberspace. As I drove, she worked the laptop, clicking onto web sites, discarding others. Twenty minutes later, I asked if she found any trace of an airfield.

"A few dirt roads off Highway 17, two to five miles south of the Marfa."

"Great," I said. "We'll start there."

We made a quick stop at a convenience-souvenir shop in Marfa. I bought a backpack, canteens, large bottles of drinking water, power bars, two desert camouflage hats, and dozens of bags of packaged nuts, apple, and orange slices. Also I bought beef jerky, sun tan lotion, a flashlight, batteries, and toilet paper.

I put everything inside the backpack, and tossed the desert hat to Sierra, who was already outside, sitting in the car, munching on a granola bar that she had bought along with a <u>Vanity Fair</u> magazine, which she flipped through the pages.

"Put it on. It'll shield you from the desert heat," I told her. "It'll be brutal."

After I got a tank of gas, we drove south of the airport. Miles of barbwire lined the highway and streaked like crooked pencil lines through the carpeting of vivid yellow grass, piles of sand dunes and broom weeds.

After checking out a few roads that cut through the desert, we stopped in front of a dirt road with a rusty metal gate. It was about six miles from the Marfa airport and blocked by a cattle guard with metal wings.

A large rusty sign on the fence with bullet holes and big, fading white letters read: Keep Out. Private Road. No Trespassing. A padlocked chain was wrapped around the cattle gate and post. Whoever owned the property made it clear that intruders weren't welcomed.

The sun's hot breath landed on my face as soon as I got out of the air-conditioned car. Heading into noon, the day already promised to be a scorcher, very hot and sweaty.

"This has to be the road," I said. "I have a gut feeling. This is it."

"Why?"

"Close to the airport but not close enough to arouse suspicion. A glider would only be another aircraft in the sky. Most people would either conclude that it was either landing or taking off from the airport."

I walked up to the gate. There were fresh tire marks. Crap, I thought, as I stared at the palm-size padlock. Now, I'd have to drive several miles down the road and turn into a dirt road that hunters might use, go deep inside the desert and hide the car behind a sand dune.

We'd have to turn around and walk back, climb over the cattle crossing and walk two or three miles down the dirt road and head toward a canyon.

I'd do this on a hunch.

Upset, I grabbed the lock, tugged on it in frustration and uttered a curse word.

The latch on the lock opened when I yanked on it.

Beautiful.

I grinned, raised the lock and waved it at Sierra who grinned and shot a rigid thumb up. She whipped her neck toward the two-lane asphalt when she heard a truck approaching fast on the opposite side of the road.

"Truck!" she yelled.

Sierra pointed into the distance. The vehicle was minutes away.

"Open the driver's door," I said loudly.

She did.

An open driver's door would make someone believe that this was a brief stop in front of the gate.

"Pretend to be reading the magazine," I told her.

She picked up a magazine, reclined the car seat, took her shoes off and put her bare feet on the dashboard. I put the lock back on the cattle gate, making sure it looked like it was latched.

I pretended to take a leak a few yards from the gate, away from the lock. My back faced the highway. My face tilted up as though I was looking at the mountain peaks.

The vehicle slowed down as it passed us. I looked over my shoulder.

A young, bearded man with long sideburns, tattooed forearms and wearing a black cowboy hat was inside a banged-up brown Jeep Grand Cherokee SUV. The SUV had Lone Star flag mud flaps and large tires. Heavy metal music spewed out of large speakers. The SUV slowed down even more as he passed close to us. I glanced over my shoulder. His twisted face looked like some wild animal protecting a dead rodent he had just killed. He mouthed a curse word when our eyes briefly locked.

I had to defuse his suspicion quickly.

"Hi, there. Had to drain my weasel," I said gingerly, pointing at my crotch and looked around. "Beautiful country you folks have out here. Just drove up from Big Bend Park, heading to Vegas."

"Have a nice trip," he said in a gruff, flat voice.

I zipped up my pants, and walked toward Sierra. A bold walk as though I would tangle with him, a bear or any one if he was entertaining any thoughts about getting off the vehicle and walking toward us.

I got inside the car and watched the SUV get smaller on my rearview mirror. I drove five miles down the highway in the opposite the direction, stopping on the shoulder around a bend. We waited for twenty minutes in case the stranger in the SUV decided to return. I got Sierra to drive back to the cattle guard. We stopped at the entrance of the private road, again.

I jumped out, took off the lock and opened the gate. The car rattled over the cattle guard as Sierra drove it onto the property. I made sure I left the unlatched lock exactly as I found it.

We drove into the desert and toward the mountain. Some shallow ruts beside the gravel-topped road appeared to be made by big trucks or heavy jeeps or perhaps an SUV loaded with something heavy, maybe drug dealers with bundles of weed or packages of cocaine or other stuff as well.

Less than a mile away, the old mountains punctured through the desert floor with sawed-tooth tops like a coarse eruption of prehistoric daggers.

The volcanic mountains stood like deformed sand castles. At one time, the rock formation stood like proud, giant guards along the main road. In a crude way, the mammoth pile of boulders protected the land by discouraging the hordes of new-world Spanish invaders searching for gold, fortunes, and lost souls from penetrating deeper into the desert.

I went off the road and hid the car behind a mammoth outcrop of large rocks. We both got out. She straightened her sunglasses and tugged on the legs of her blue jeans to straighten them too. I took the stuff we had bought at the store out of the trunk, starting putting the supplies into both backpacks.

Sierra shook her head and ran her fingers through her hair. We rubbed sun tan lotion on ourselves.

After strapping on my backpack, I looked at Sierra who had a somber look.

"Ready?" I said, grabbing the rifle.

She nodded.

I led the way. Sierra had her hat bill low over a dark pair of sunglasses.

"Where are we going?" she said while walking.

"Toward the mountain along the cliff, get on the ridge along the road, find a good, high spot, and wait. Hopefully, the gliders will descend. And then, we converge."

I expected Sierra to whine and gripe about the sizzling sun and argue and second-guess my plan, then, complain that she should have stayed in El Paso. I wondered what I would do if she started getting scared or paranoid from being traumatized during the trip to Mexico.

A half-hour of walking past the desert candelilla and scrub cat claw, she hadn't said a word. We stopped to briefly rest on some small cluster of rocks and drank some water.

"How are you doing?" I said.

"I'm okay," she said.

A short time later, she went around a large stack of rocks to take a leak. A minute or so later, she screamed. I raced around the boulder just as she was finishing pulling up her jeans. A scared lizard nimbly dashed on its hind legs a few feet from Sierra's legs and vanished under some tall yellow grass.

Blood boiling and flabbergasted, she said, "The damn thing moved, I saw its tail and thought it was a snake."

My smirk turned into a playful grin.

"Nice," I said.

"Leave. I wasn't finished."

"Don't get too close to the rocks. There are holes with snakes," I said. "Rat-fed rattlers."

I went around the boulder, chuckled softly and sat a few yards away on at the edge of a hardened sand dune, quietly drank water and swept the skies to see a hawk circling as though it spotted a dead jackrabbit or maybe an old dead coyote or a rotting human corpse.

I could hear Sierra urinating.

"Do snakes come out during the day?" she said. "Jack. Jack did you hear me? Jack!"

I purposely delayed my response just to freak her out.

"What?"

"I heard snakes are nocturnal."

"Yeah, but if they're hungry and want to snack on a mouse, they crawl out of their holes," I said. "But if I were a snake, this is just me, and I knew you were there peeing, wearing a yellow thong with a white floral pattern, I'd tuck my fangs and poke my head from under a large cool rock and enjoy the scenery."

"Shut up," she said. "Jerk."

Two miles later, I felt Sierra starting to slow down. I turned around and saw that she was wet with sweat. We stopped again, drank more water while hugging the shadows of two scrawny juniper trees that formed an arch beside a large rock.

"Drink more water," I said.

"I'm not thirsty," she said with dry lips.

"Drink before you get thirsty. We're losing a lot of water. You get dehydrated out here, and you can die."

After gulping down another bottled water, she reached into her shirt pocket, took out her cell phone, and started to punch numbers as she walked. I looked up and my blood began to boil.

"Put the phone away!" I said. "Turn it off!"

"Why?" She winced.

I pointed my forefinger toward the sky.

"Aircraft. If the feds have something in the sky like radar or other electronic equipment, they can monitor cell phone conversations and track vehicle engines. If we're detected in the middle of nowhere, they will alert Sheriff Rick and he'll come calling."

"I'm just letting a friend know where we are. Just in case something happens. I'll only be on the phone for a minute or so."

"No! Stay off the phone. Got it?" I said angrily. "Turn it off. Now."

"What's the big deal?"

"Turn it off!"

"Okay," she said reluctantly.

I groaned and started to have serious second thoughts about my decision to let Sierra tag along with me. I got up and picked up the pace. We got closer to the road, staying within a stone's throw from it.

We got to a mountain, hiked up, and found a cliff that gave us a hazy view of a distant mountain range that split the horizon. A large carpet of sand reflected heat waves, strong powerful waves that dissipated as they went up into the cloudless sky.

I took my binoculars out from my backpack, sat Indian style on the edge of the cliff, and glassed the area. I carefully combed the road and the highway, which was barely visible with the naked eye.

Nothing.

Perfect weather for gliders to hover above for hours, travel long distances quietly, undetected or ignored by West Texas residents who are aware that gliders were as commonplace as hawks, quail and wild doves, especially near the small airport.

Sierra found shelter from the sun under a flat rock that shot out from the rocky ledge like an Apache hatchet. She barely moved her jaw as she chewed on a package of trail mix nuts.

Her eyes told me that she was exhausted.

"What now?" she said.

"We wait."

"For how long?"

"For as long as it takes. We've got enough water, dried fruit and trail mix for three days."

Sierra moaned her displeasure. I glanced back at her with a disapproving look, and she quickly flashed a perky grin, sat up straight and raised a stiff thumb.

"Good plan," she said.

I lifted the binoculars, keeping my eyes on the sky, on the road. I wonder if I was in the right spot.

CHAPTER 46

We waited the rest of the day. Nothing was up in the sky except for an odd collection of birds that for millions of years had laid claim to the vast desert sky and the plentiful pickings of quarry below.

The desert danced beneath the heat haze. For the most part, except for with occasional rabbit hopping from one hole to another, the desert's prickly and craggy floor was empty. Sierra sat legs crossed and read the magazine she bought at the store.

Just before dusk, I handed Sierra the binoculars and told her I was going to go down a pathway and into some narrow rock passages within the mountain to gather wood for a fire.

A short time later as I gathered wood between two towering faults less than a mile from where we had set up camp. I turned the corner of a rocky outcrop and discovered a large pool of recent rainwater made by late summer thunderstorms.

The clear water protected from sunrays by mammoth rock formations was cool from the previous night's temperature drop. I took off my shirt, dunked it into the water a few times, and twisted it to remove the access water and sweat before throwing it on my hot head. In an instant, the day's heat seemed to dissipate from my body, and I felt energized, refreshed.

When I returned with an armful of firewood, I told Sierra about the rainwater. Before it got dark, we walked back to the water hole but first, I took out my video camera, set it on a flat rock and pointed toward the horizon and pushed the on button. I wanted to make sure that if any aircraft flew into our area while we were gone, I would record it.

Sierra kept up with my hurried pace and smiled when she saw the rainwater pond. She took off her T-shirt. I waited for her to unfasten her bra and was bummed out when she didn't.

We waded into the water until it was waist high, standing in the middle of the hole. She used her shirt and used it like a washcloth to remove the desert sweat and dust from her upper body.

I did the same thing with my wet T-shirt, trying to avoid eye contact with a pair of robust breasts, wondering what they looked like without the white bra and with her long hair touching her nipples.

She caught me taking glances, daydreaming.

"It's not going to happen," she said, a smirk.

"I can live with that," I said.

We cooled down in our shady oasis.

"Jack, you struck gold here," she said, cupping her hands to pour water down her head.

"I figured you'd like it," I said.

I submerged myself into the water; Giggling, Sierra followed suit.

Soon, we were playing like two children, laughing and beating back the heat like being inside a plastic backyard pool, splashing water on each other. Our laughter, and her joyful laughter bounced off the tall rock formations. I gleefully picked her up and tossed her into the deeper water while she laughed and yelled for me to stop.

I lost track of time, about where we were and why we were there in the middle of nowhere.

I could have stayed there another hour but we had to go back before it got dark, getting stuck near rain-filled hole would be dangerous. A sudden summer rain could bring a flood of water rushing down the mountain. Worse, thirsty wolves, coyotes and mountain lions might decided to drop by and quench their thirst after it got dark.

"We need to go," I said, not telling her about the wild animals that come out to hunt at night.

I started to get out of the water. She smiled, tilted her head, and ran her fingers through her wet hair as water dripped from her head. She fixed her somber eyes on mine.

For what seemed like forever, we didn't say a word. I couldn't stop staring at her eyes, beautiful and elusive like butterflies as they scanned my face. I was puzzled by her somber expression that turned into a big smile.

She took a couple of steps toward me, put both hands on my cheeks and kissed my lips, a long and hard kiss. Surprised, I slowly closed my eyes while our lips pressed against each other. She eased back, a lazy smile that filled the silence with unsaid feelings.

"Thank you for bringing me here," she said.

"You're welcome," I said.

I moved forward to kiss her, again. She pulled her head back.

"We better go," she said.

My stare dissolved as disappointment dropped its anchor on my flighty heart.

"Yeah. It's starting to get dark," I said.

We walked back to our campsite and put on some dry clothes. I tossed her a football jersey and a pair of my gym shorts to wear while the sun dried our clothes, which were lying on some rock.

We ate trail mix, dates, dried fruit and a couple of power granola bars for dinner, washing it all down with four bottles of water.

In the distance, a reddish-gold sunset that lingered on the horizon was nearly gone. I prepared a small fire deep inside a crevice on the side of a rocky ridge I had found. I made sure the fire wouldn't be spotted from the road or in the air. We unraveled our sleeping bags on the soft sand. Sierra was already in her sleeping bag. Her back was facing me. She was motionless. It had been a long day.

The desert temperatures were dropping fast. It would be cold soon.

I changed into dry clothes and wrapped Geek's thick wool coat that I had taken from his apartment. My rifle was within easy reach in case a Mexican Gray wolf or mountain lion wandered into our campsite.

Heat from the fire reflected from the rocks and warmed our spot quickly. I had gathered enough dry mesquite branches to keep the flames going until the early morning hours.

The dying sunset held, caressed and stroked my thoughts. Sometimes conjuring up images of the Mexican mountain ranges of incredible beauty. I wondered how we made it out of Mexico alive. Where all this was going, and where I would end up?

I missed my family, and thought about Emily, wondering what she was doing. She had probably moved on with her life and had found someone to love, again. I blamed myself for being selfish, for not appreciating what I had, for not spending more time with those I love.

Some of these thoughts were sweet. Others pierced my mind like thorns.

The first stars of the night began to appear, strung in the sky, each one in its place, spinning like they had been doing for billions of years.

I turned around when I heard Sierra's body stir a bit before she sat up, glanced at my direction and started sobbing. I walked over and sat beside her, gently put my hand on her shoulder.

"Hey, you okay?"

She nodded, barely, and swiped away some tears.

"Are you sure?" I said.

"Yeah."

Watery eyed, she turned and brought her legs up to her chest. She scanned the stars and slowly rocked back and forth.

"It's been a long day. Were you having a bad dream?" I said. "What happened in Mexico will be hard to shake off."

She shook her head.

"I am just angry, very angry and sad," she said.

"Why?"

"That world is so cruel and cold. So dark and ugly world. So evil. It makes men worse than animals. And, my father was part of it," she said. "I can't stop thinking about Alberto and his family."

"They were good people who saved our lives," I said.

"I should hate my father for being involved in all this. But I can't. I'll always love him, and I knew who he was. I knew exactly what he did. But I choose to ignore his dark side. The evil world that he was a part of."

She sobbed.

"Learn to forgive him, to forgive yourself. Put it all behind. Mexico, it changed our lives forever. When I thought I was going to die and never see those I love again, my heart ached, ached really bad. There were so many words I had yet to say, so much to tell those I love. But I realized that I'd probably never see them again. My heart. It felt like a cold stone."

I turned my head and scanned the diamond-studded sky.

"When I'm alone and think about it, it bust me up inside," I said, my voice cracking with emotion. "Family is everything, everything in this world. These are the people who love you no matter what. Come rain or shine, they are there."

She kissed my cheek.

"I know how you feel," she said.

"Sometimes, I wish I'd never gone up to the third floor that night. Never talked to your father, just left town and not looked back," I said. "But I'm glad I did because I would have never seen the sweet and tender side of his daughter, the side that I never thought I'd see."

"Thank you," she said. "I'm sorry about your friend, Tommy."

"Friend?" I said with an incredulous throb in my voice. "Tommy Rubio wasn't a friend. He wanted to take a head shot. He came close to splattering my brains all over the newsroom. And, he played me like a fool. He was never a friend, never."

I look into her eyes with intensity.

"I need to know," I said. "The pipe bomb. If it wasn't you, who put it under Tommy's car?"

"Bazooka."

"Bazooka," I said with half-breathless murmur of amazement and incredulity.

"Yeah," she said. "I told him who killed Emilio. Bazooka went into a rage."

"Why?"

"Emilio was like his son. Bazooka and Emilio went hunting together in New Mexico. They loved to fish in the Gulf of Mexico.

Ride horses. My father tagged along a few times. Bazooka knew that Tommy was a dirty cop."

"How'd he know that Tommy would drive to the newspaper building?"

"He didn't. He put a GPS device on Tommy's car to keep track of him," she said. "Bazooka set Tommy up. He had someone tell Tommy to pick up ten-thousand-dollars from a petty drug dealer who wanted to sell cocaine in Tommy's neighborhood. Tommy collected street taxes from drug dealers. Ten thousand was the entry fee."

"Tommy is too streetwise to pick up cash from a drug dealer he never met, didn't know."

"Yeah, but he knew the person who Bazooka was sending with the money. It was Bazooka's relative."

"A relative? Who?"

"His cousin, Tecolote."

"Tecolote? I thought he was dead. Buried out in the desert."

."No, he was in Cancun driving a cab when Bazooka called him," said Sierra.

"Wow, my source was right," I chuckled. "A cab driver, huh?"

"Yeah. After he got out of prison, he left the drug business. Bazooka told him that he was going to kill Tommy. Tecolote owed Bazooka a big favor, and agreed to help his cousin. So he briefly came out of a retirement this one last time."

"What was the plan?"

"Tecolote was to wait in the parking lot of a warehouse near the railroad tracks that night with a briefcase. There was ten-thousand-dollars and a five-pounds of weed inside," she said.

"There was no money in the suitcase?"

"Yeah. As soon as Tommy drove up to the parking lot, Bazooka would be a block away, waiting. Once Tecolote gave him the briefcase and Tommy checked it and drove away; Bazooka would detonate a pipe bomb. Police would find the briefcase, the marijuana and the ten-thousand-dollars all over the place. An investigation would show that Tommy was a dirty cop. So, it wouldn't bring heat on drug dealers," she said. "Tommy also had other plans. He stopped by the newspaper building. Bazooka called you and hung up after you picked up the phone. He then called me and said you were there, and Tommy was waiting outside. He said he didn't trust Tommy. I drove down there. Right before I got there, I heard the explosion."

"Tommy offered me a bribe. I didn't accept it. He shot at me, and I heard an explosion," I said. "I guess he planned to kill me. Pick up the briefcase from Tecolote, and then go back to the crime scene and help search for the killer. That would give him an alibi."

"I believe so," she said. "Bazooka detonated the bomb after he saw Tommy fired the rifle."

"Wow, why would Bazooka do that? Why would he care if I got shot?"

"When we returned from Mexico, I told him everything and that you weren't such a bad guy. That I was starting to have some feelings for you."

"Feeling?" I said.

"Some."

"I'll take some. I can work with that."

It got quiet before I put my hand under her chin, leaned toward her and kissed her lips. I got my lips close to her ear and whispered.

"Sierra Madrid. I'm off-the-charts falling in love with you, and I can't help it. I'm beyond having some feelings, and I'm not making any apologizes for that either. I'm simply telling you what's going on in my heart."

She kissed my lips, softly first. I smiled and gently pulled her toward me. I kissed her neck with fervor. She lifted her neck, breathing heavily.

"Jack, we can't. Jack, Please," she said softly.

We couldn't stop kissing. I unbuttoned her shirt, pulled up her bra and kissed her nipples on hard breasts. She panted. Eyes closed. Head tilted back. Then, she suddenly pushed me away.

"Wait, wait, wait. Jack, wait," she whined. "I can't do this."

"Why?" I said, breathing hard and frustrated. "The Catholic thing? The strict up bringing. The nuns told you 'it was a sin.' What?"

"No, the hair thing."

"What?" I said.

"Look at my hair, look at me. No makeup. I'm a mess. I don't feel pretty or sexy. We are out here in the desert, and I feel so yucky."

"You look gorgeous. I promise. Twigs in hair and all."

Puzzled, she ran her fingers through her hair.

"Really? Twigs?" She said with a sense of insecurity. "I look awful."

"Two twigs, just two little bitty ones. Really. I'm serious. You look beautiful. I swear." I said, haphazardly raising my right hand. "Two. Two, tiny twigs."

"You're just saying that to get laid," she said with a smirk on her face. "Pig."

After a mischievous smile followed by a serious expression, Sierra kissed and pulled me toward her as she laid back on the sleeping bag.

We made love beside a fire that crackled, releasing its mystic yellow energy in spirals and twists. As the flames danced, swirling wildly, Sierra moaned as the rhythm of our lovemaking reached its crescendo. We were both exhausted and afterwards snuggled up inside the same sleeping bag.

The next morning, we sat under some juniper trees near the ledge of a cliff, watched the sunrise, and ate more trail mix nuts, slices of apples, oranges, beef jerky, and potted meat on crackers. For the next three hours, we waited for a glider to appear.

We had conversations going in every direction.

She insisted that I take her fishing, camping, and on a long hike someday.

"I hope Dexter gets to know me," she said. "Sees the good side too."

"He will. He loves the ladies," I said.

She told me about the Copper Canyon in Mexico and Cancun, too, and horseback riding on the family's cattle ranch in Chihuahua.

"You'd love Pepe, my horse," she said. "Is your family close?"

"Very close. On Thanksgiving Day, everybody shows up. I mean everybody. Aunts, uncles, my niece and cousins. After we eat turkey, my dad and my *tios*, Jesse and Pablo, start strumming the guitars, sipping Cognac. The evening becomes Mexican Karaoke. The kids, and even my grandmother dance. The house is filled with old memories. Laughter. The fireplace is going strong."

"I'd love all that."

"Next Thanksgiving, go home with me."

"Really?"

"Oh yeah, my family would love to meet you. My mom, she's sweet. My dad, well, we sort of had a falling out. He's hard to please, and I stopped trying. But I've got to patch things up. I just don't know how."

"Are you two close?"

"We used to go hunting together. Sometimes, Geek tagged along. Then, everything changed when he finally realized that I

wasn't going to drop everything I was doing and manage his prop-
erties after he retired."

"So, he had plans for you?"

"Yeah. Crazy stuff. He also thinks I drink too much, play too
much pool and looks down at what I do, write for a newspaper.
And, my mom wants me to get married, settle down, have kids and
live in this world of a quiet, middle-class existence."

"It's not so bad. What's wrong with all that if you're happy?"

"Nothing. It's all just too premature," I said. "I had a girlfriend
named Emily, and we drew up those blueprints. Plans to get married,
and years later, have two kids. But first, we planned to travel, just the
two of us. Go places we didn't even know existed."

"So what happened?"

"Newsrooms, deadlines, and pool halls got in the way. She felt I
never had time for her. Felt alone. So, one day, she packed up and left.
And, I don't blame her. I screwed up, and I still kick myself in the ass
when I think about it."

"That's too bad. You miss her?"

I slowly nodded.

" You know, there is this switch in our brains that life sometimes
flips on when you least expect it. This light floods the dark corners
of your mind. Suddenly, you realize what really matters, what's important. What's not, and what you should fight for with every ounce
of your being to keep. I can honestly say that this switch was flipped
on in Mexico."

"Mine too," she said softly, putting her head on my shoulder
and hugging my arm.

"Check this out," I said. "It's a waterfall in a jungle in Peru."

I unfolded the grainy photo and handed it to her.

"It's beautiful."

"I want to go there someday, just to stand under it. It's way up in the mountains. There are so many things, so places like this to see. It's all out there."

"You're going by yourself?"

"Yeah, I guess," I said, plucking a twig out of her hair and kissing her lips.

"I'd like to tag along."

"Sure. Of, course," I said. "Hey, want to go to the West Coast with me?"

With much enthusiasm, she shook her head and grinned, a toothy grin.

"I mean we'd go up to California. If we get bored there, head up to Portland or Seattle," I said.

"I'd like that."

"But we have to leave soon."

"Sure, I'm in."

"Fantastic."

I raised my binoculars and spotted two objects far away that looked like gigantic eagles soaring across the dry southern sky. I sat on a flat rock to get a better view. I squatted and steadied my arms on my elbows as I glassed the sky.

The two gliders were making a slow-circling descent near the mountain base about three miles out.

"Bingo," I said. "Gliders. Two gliders."

I stood, got the video camera, and turned it on. I took some photographs, too.

"Let's go," I said.

I latched onto my rifle, put a box of bullets in my shirt pocket, and grabbed the cameras and other stuff. We began climbing down the mountain, going toward where the gliders descended.

As soon as the gliders disappeared into a rocky valley, we spotted a banged up pickup truck in the distance driving down the dirt road. It snaked and rattled its way through the desert road, kicking up a long funnel of dust that hung in the dry air. It raced toward the direction where the gliders touched down.

We found a safe slope to get off the mountain and headed toward the airfield, meandering around sand dunes, yucca and agave lechuguilla plants, and tumbleweeds lying across the desert floor like giant popcorn. The road curved into the valley. We continued to follow it.

Just as we turned into the valley, we heard another vehicle coming down the road. We were in the open, too late to hide behind some boulders. I yanked Sierra and pulled her down behind a mound of sand and some scrub brush.

"Keep your head down," I said.

I put the palm of my hand on her back and put my forefinger against my lips while we faced each other. Her eyes were the size of pie pans. We hugged the sand and didn't move. The vehicle, which was less than a 100 yards away, flew by.

After it passed, I lifted my head and snapped more photographs. It was a sheriff's patrol car with two men inside.

One man was in the back seat and the other, wearing a cowboy hat, was driving with hands gripping the top of the steering wheel. The cloud of dust stopped about two miles down the road. I pulled Sierra up, grabbed her by her shoulder, and we dashed for the large rocks before the dust cloud settled, and we were spotted on side or rear-view mirrors.

"That was close," she said.

"Too close."

We made our way toward the airfield by staying close to the large rocks near the mountain's edge. When we were less than a mile away from the airfield, we could see two gliders being unloaded. Bundles of cocaine were put inside the van. Three men, including the glider pilots, drank beer and stood near the aircraft as two other men unloaded the glider.

I clicked more photographs, used the video camera, too.

I got the binoculars and kept them on the patrol car a few hundred yards away. Two men were still in the car. The driver with the cowboy hat opened the car door and stepped out.

When he stood, there was no doubt that it was Sheriff Rick Ward with a beer in his hand, barking orders.

The sheriff's badge and sunglasses reflected the sunlight. He put the beer on top of the patrol car, lifted his cowboy hat and wiped the sweat with his arm sleeve, spat, and scanned the mountains.

The sheriff walked behind the patrol car, opened the trunk, and casually leaned inside. He reached in and took out a sawed-off shotgun. He lowered the weapon to the side of his body and whistled, a shrill whistle. His hand motion quickly brought two Mexicans, who were unloading packaged bundles from the gliders, running to him.

The sheriff said something and pointed to the car.

"*Vajen el cabron,*" he said.

One of the Mexicans nodded. Both went into the back seat of the patrol car.

Inside, a frantic man who was handcuffed, began yelling obscenities in Spanish. The shirtless, sunburned and barefooted man started kicking as the two Mexicans reached into the car and tried to grab him by the legs to drag him out.

The sheriff stood close to the hood of the car, laughing, bellowing laughter echoed through the canyon.

"Paquito, *afuera*, get your ass out here," the sheriff said. "*Adale.*"

As I watched, my finger kept pressing the button on the camera. One of the Mexicans ran to the other side of the car, opened the car door and began walloping Paquito with his fists.

Paquito was screaming like a banshee, bucking like a rodeo horse. He wasn't going down easy.

A few minutes later, one of the Mexicans finally grabbed a handful of Paquito's shirt, dragged him out of the car, and flung him on the dirt like a sack of potatoes. The handcuffed Paquito kicked his legs high, rolled on the ground and was hysterical, begging for his life.

The two Mexicans kicked and boot stomped him for about a minute. The sheriff went over and stood over the badly battered and timorous quarry that was now begging for his life.

The Mexicans dragged him to a large mound of sand a few yards away. On his back, slobbering and slowly twisting like a vanquished worm, Paquito looked up at the sheriff who had his head bowed and sunglasses near the end of his nose.

Glaring at the prisoner, the sheriff calmly reached into his pocket, took out shotgun shells and loaded the weapon. He racked a round, the clacking of a round rose before falling hard.

The sheriff stood straight, chest out and waved his hand for the Mexicans to back away. He ordered the beaten man to kneel. The terrified prisoner shook his body uncontrollably and refused to kneel.

"*Perdites el cargo, Paquito. Aqui no se perde nada,*" the sheriff said loudly. "Nobody loses loads. *Tu sabes, eso.*"

"*Por favor, no me mates, viejito. Por favor,*" Paquito whimpered. "*Por Dios santo. Tengo familia, senor. No me mates.*"

The two Mexicans chortled.

"Incate, cabron," the sheriff said. "Kneel and say a prayer, and maybe, *La Virgincita* will come down in a chariot or drive up in a gold Chevy pickup and scoop up your worthless ass."

The sheriff took two steps forward. Nobody uttered another word.

By this time, two glider pilots had walked up. All eyes were on the sheriff, who took a few swallows from his beer and placed the beer on top of the car's trunk.

The man hollered for mercy, promising again to pay what he owed for the lost load of dope the Border Patrol had intercepted. He promised to do contract hits for free, anything, if his life was spared, if he could see his family in Mexico again.

"Mi familia. Por favor. Mis ninos. No me mates, senor. Por favor," he screamed.

"Time's up," the sheriff said. *"Vete a la chingada, culero."*

He fired and blew a hole in the man's chest, spraying his blood and guts across a mound of desert.

The sheriff tossed his head back, laughed and went over and stood close to Paquito. He jolted once like he was trying to un-saddle death before he went still. His blood soaked the desert sand. The others watched with dropped jaws.

"Paquito ya esta con los angelitos," the sheriff said and went over and spat at the body. "Nobody loses loads. Nobody steals from me. *Nadien.*"

A strong gust of wind picked up the sand and flung it across everyone's eyes as though a death angel had arrived to claim its trophy, a human soul and wanted to cloak its arrival. Sierra and I put our heads near large boulders to protect our eyes from the sand.

The hot surge of wind died down. There was a semi-circle around Paquito's body.

One of the Mexicans walked up to the sheriff, nervously handed him his beer, and patted him in the back. The sheriff pointed to the trunk of the car, and the two Mexicans quickly walked in back of the car. One of them leaned into the trunk and struggled to get a dirt-caked body wrapped in a blanket out of the car. The other helped him pull it out and throw it on the ground.

They grabbed and dragged the body near the handcuffed dead prisoner.

The sheriff leaned over and closely examined the two corpses. He rapidly cocked the shotgun blew the face off Paquito and shot the other in the head area.

Blood, brains and bones sprayed the desert floor.

"*Sus cajas ya estan ceradas*," he said and laughed. "No viewing of the dearly departed at the rosary service. Lose a load and lose your life."

He went around the car. A glider pilot paced near the bodies in disbelief, jittery and brushing his fingers across his hair before squatting on the dirt with his head lowered.

The two other men kept looking at the bodies and at the sheriff. The sheriff finished his beer, tossed the bottle, clicked and waved his fingers, ordering the Mexicans to pick up everything and bury the bodies, telling them to dig a deep, wide hole.

I turned pale, put the camera away and slowly reached for my backpack. Before I could grab it, Sierra's hand latched on my shoulder.

I turned to look at Sierra, following her line of sight. A few feet away, a rattlesnake had finished coiling itself. It rattled. Rattled hard. Ready to spring, showing its fangs.

Oh, shit, I thought.

Without taking my eyes off the snake, I whispered.

"Don't move. Or twitch."

She yelped.

"Shhhh," I said.

Very slowly, my hand inched its way to my backpack. I took out a large hunting knife, my eyes fixated on the rattler. I dropped the knife as I brought it closer to me. It slipped out of my hand, hit a rock and clanged loudly.

It startled Sierra. She twitched. The snake raised its head, showing its fangs and lunged a few feet in the air toward Sierra.

She screamed. I quickly put my hand on her mouth.

A flash of snake's fangs grazed the top of her boot. I grabbed a large rock and struck the snake, partially crushing its head. It rolled over and slithered several times. I pinned the head down with a stick. With a quick slashing motion, I sliced off its head with one stroke of the knife. Sierra, rolled up into a tight ball, trembled.

The snake continued its death throes near her feet.

I slowly poked my head from around a boulder to see the two Mexicans pointing in our direction. I grabbed the backpack, cameras, the rifle, and Sierra and we bolted out of there.

We dashed for higher ground. As we climbed to a high ridge, shots zinged past us, ricocheting off the rocks. We heard engines starting, men swearing and voices hurrying in our direction. We ran up a rocky slope, following the ridgeline to a higher spot. Sierra squeezed my hand as we struggled up the mountain. Bullets whizzed by. I heard Sierra groan and fall to one knee.

"Get up, up, up!" I said. "Run!"

I looked back and saw the sheriff taking aim with his rifle. He fired a few times as two of his men ran up the gravel slope. I grabbed Sierra, tossed her to the ground and we rolled behind a boulder. Bits of rock and dust nicked by a barrage of bullets flew up and sprayed the air.

I low crawled to the side of a rock pile and stuck my head out. The two men near the foot of the mountain, about 100 yards away. Seconds later, I got on my knees and behind a large rock and squeezed the trigger several times.

One of the Mexicans went down. Another, frightened, retreated, stumbled, and rolled down the hill. The sheriff took cover behind his patrol car. As he did, I fired a few more shots and took out the patrol car's side windows, side-view mirror, and a tire. It was my way of telling the sheriff and his minions to back off.

I shot at the other Mexican who had scrambled behind a truck, shattering the truck's windshield and taking out a headlight. He didn't move, covering his head with his arms.

I crouched down, turned and looked at Sierra. She appeared numb with a blank look. She put her hand behind her back, pulled it out and it was red with blood.

"I'm hit," she said.

Heavily breathing and still shaking, I reloaded my rifle.

"Hold on, sweetheart. I'll get us out. I promise," I said. "Just hold on."

I went to the opposite side of a cluster of boulders and fired six more shots. I took out the patrol car's passenger window before turning my attention to Sierra.

"Can you roll over?" I asked her.

She nodded, turned to the side, and moaned. Her shirt was soaked with blood. I raised the shirt and there was a hole the size of a dime in her back, blood leaking.

"Don't move."

"It hurts so much."

"I know. Be still."

I took off my shirt and put it on Sierra to stop the bleeding. I took my coat out of my backpack, rolled it up, and put it under her head. I crawled several yards on the desert floor behind a wall of large rocks. My scope picked up one of the glider pilots loading his rifle behind the left front tire of the van. I pulled the trigger and hit him in the shoulder. He dropped the weapon like it was a hot skillet.

With a new burst of energy, they returned fire.

Another swarm of bullets pinged over my head as the sheriff yelled commands to keep shooting. When they stopped shooting, I fired, hitting the vehicles, shattering glass and flatting two tires.

I crawled back to Sierra, satisfied that I had kept them pinned down and at bay for now.

A strange softness encircled Sierra's eyes, creating this awkward calm. She whimpered when I checked the wound. Satisfied that the bleeding had stopped, I peeked and saw the sheriff crouched behind the patrol car wheel, talking on his car radio. I fired and took out the patrol car's emergency lights. The sheriff flattened his body to the ground.

The others returned fire with several shotgun blasts that stirred up the dust, sending bits of rock sputtering in the air around us.

Sierra didn't move. She gave me an odd half-smile, an unresisting acceptance of something inescapable. I needed to get her out of here as fast as possible.

"I should have never brought you here," I said.

"I want to be here. We're a team."

"They'll be bringing others up here, more men with guns. Where's your cell phone?"

"In the backpack."

I took out the cell phone, turned it on, stabbed at the phone numbers, and waited. A message flashed on the telephone screen: Signal not available. The large mountain rocks were blocking the satellite signal. I tried several times.

Zilch.

"I've got to go higher to pick up a signal. Sit tight."

I dashed from behind a boulder, slinging my rifle, zigzagging along the ridgeline, working my way up the mountain. Darts of hot lead bounced off the mountain, coming close to my head and legs, ripping up the sides of rocks that flew like fragments of glass.

When I got to a high plateau, I squeezed several rounds off and momentarily silenced the shooters. I punched the telephone number, again and waited. Nothing. I tried again and again. Still nothing. The signal was still unavailable.

I went a little higher. I tried to get a signal, and finally, on the third try, I got a dial tone. I called my friend Daniel, the U.S. Marshal.

Pick up, pick up, pick up, I kept saying. It rang several times.

"Pick up, damn it! Pick up!"

A voice recording: "Hello, this is Daniel I am not in —"

Then, Daniel picked up the phone in the middle of the recording.

"Hello?"

"Daniel," I said.

There was silence. He didn't recognize my voice that struggled to get past the heavy breathing and adrenaline.

"Daniel, it's me. Jack."

"Jack," he said in a cheerful voice. "How are you? Where are you at, the gym?"

"No, No, listen. I found the airfield. The one that Mickey used."

"The what field?"

I rapidly spewed out what had happened, where we were, who was firing at us, and how Sierra and I ended up being pinned down on the side of a mountain by the sheriff and his men.

"Sierra Madrid is wounded. Shot in the back. It's bad. She needs help," I said.

"Mickey Madrid's daughter?"

"Yeah, man. She's bleeding bad."

"Oooh, man."

"Please. I need your help. Are there any copters in this area?"

"Stay put. Hang in there," he said. "I believe there is a Black Hawk helicopter used by the Border Patrol."

"Please hurry. Sierra needs to get out of here, and I'm almost out of bullets," I implored him.

"Where are you?"

"About three miles from the Marfa Airport, northwest. Off a dirt road on the highway, near the base of the mountain. There are several vehicles near us."

"That's a big desert."

"I know. But that's the best I can do."

Daniel said he'd call back in a few minutes to let me know whether the chopper was available. I waited for what seemed to be an eternity.

The phone finally rang four minutes later. The longest four minutes of my life. I answered it.

"Yes."

"Jack, they're on their way. A Black Hawk loaded with federal agents. They should be there shortly. Sit tight."

"Great. Tell them to hurry."

"Yeah, yeah. Leave the cell phone up high on so they can pick up the signal."

"Thanks, Daniel. I owe you big time."

"You don't owe me anything. Just hang tough."

I left the phone high up on a mountain. Two shots cracked in the air and zinged by my head.

I made a slow descent, lost my grip on my way down, fell four feet, and lost my rifle. I had the wind knocked out of me. As soon as I was spotted, the guns took aim again and peppered the area with bullets that bit into the dirt. I got up and crawled behind a large rock mass, reached, and recovered my rifle.

I banged the side of my face hard on a flat rock. It began to bleed and swell.

In the distance and on the highway, I saw two pickup trucks rapidly approaching and kicking up trails of dusts.

Oh, God, more men with rifles.

I made it back to Sierra. Her eyes were barely open.

"Hey," I said softly.

"What?" she said with a weak voice.

"I got a signal. Called a friend. A U.S. Marshal. They've got a helicopter on the way."

Sierra didn't say a word. Her eyes barely opened. I kissed her lips and face.

"Hang on, okay, hang on."

"Jack?" she said softly.

"What?"

"It hurts so much. I'm so sleepy."

"I know. You're a tough lady, a very tough lady. Just stay awake."

"I want to stop hurting, Jack."

"I know, I know."

A stream of blood trickled from Sierra's nose. She raised her hand and gently stroked my face. I clutched her hand with both my hands, squeezed, and kissed it. She sighed and barely raised her eyes, a limp, yet peaceful smile.

"Jack Fuentes."

"What?"

"I love you, okay. No matter what. I do."

"I love you too," I said. "Hey, after this is over, we're going places, me and you. I promise. First, to go see my folks, and then, we're going up to this Colorado lake to do some fishing. There are plenty of fat fish up there. The mountain sky in the evening turns purple and gold. You're going to love it. Then, we head west."

I kissed her, a long, deep kiss. She didn't say anything, fighting to keep her eyes open. She labored to breath. I sobbed. My fingertips slowly traced her nose and lips.

"Stay with me, sweetheart," I said. "Please, stay awake."

The gunfire stopped while loud commands were given to flank us. A volley of gunfire to suppress return fire pinned me down. I crawled and quickly poked my head out from the side of a rock pile. Two pickups with four men inside pulled into the dirt road. Doors slammed. More voices and rifles had arrived. Seconds later, all hell broke loose. The firepower increased as men rushed from the trucks. Bullets ripped up the jagged rocks.

I could barely move. Sierra's eyes were closed.

I crawled to the mountain ledge. There, I reloaded my rifle, repositioned myself and cracked back one shot after another, shattering more windows, sending people scattering for cover.

They were trying to encircle me. I crawled from one large rock to another and fired.

I stopped them from coming up the mountain. But I was running out of ammo, running out of time, and I knew that it would be a matter of time before they would be on top of us.

I had a few bullets left. I decided to save my last three bullets and pick off someone who got too close, hoping fear would slow down their advance.

Squinting, I scanned the sky. The sun blazed. Nothing was in sight except some stratus clouds.

"Please, hurry. Please," I said and inhaled.

I looked at Sierra. She looked like she was peacefully sleeping. Sweat streaked down my face. I leaned against a boulder and bowed my head, praying hard.

"God, please, help us. Don't let Sierra die. Oh, Jesus, I beg you."

Just then, Sierra's cell phone beeped wildly. It stopped and went dead. The bullets were nipping at the dirt my feet. I curled up to avoid getting hit. Then, the firing stopped, an eerie silence as the dust kicked up by bullets settled. The voices were nearly on top of us. They were very close. I stared at the pale, blue sky. It was empty and quiet.

"God, get us out," I said, squinting. "Come on, come on. Where in the hell are you guys?"

Then I heard the sweet and muffled sound of helicopter blades slicing up the hot air from a distance. I looked at the nearby mountain range. A black helicopter magically popped up from the top of a mountain. Rounding the mountain, it headed our way, slicing the hot air with its large blades. The helicopter dipped its nose as it flew in our direction.

It circled the sky, just above us. Someone using a loudspeaker ordered everyone below to drop their weapons. One man fired a few shots at the chopper. A burst of gunfire from the Black Hawk shredded him up.

"It's over. It's all over," I said sobbing. "We're going home, sweetheart."

Sierra didn't say a word. A film of dust right underneath her nose barely moved.

CHAPTER 47

Thud.

The familiar dull sound of a fat newspaper landing on my driveway nudged me from a light sleep. Tires from the car used to deliver my paper sloshed down the wet street. Then, the very feint sounds of two more newspaper thuds several houses down.

It sounded sweet. But I wasn't anxious to go outside. I knew the stories backwards and forwards.

It had been days since the shootout, and finally, the stores of an incredible and evil international plot were in print. The stories had been through the normal labyrinth of editing, reworking and fine tuning sentences and shifting paragraphs around.

The editors always had questions, dozens of them. It is the nature of the beast, the deadlines, the questions and the editing process.

Throughout the night, everything swirled inside my head. I relived the conversations, recalling the names and lifting the descriptions of places, much of it from memory, or a flash of faces, good and evil faces, that appeared, sometimes like a bad storm, and just as quickly vanished.

My feet touched the cold floor. An explosion of butterflies fluttered inside my stomach. I nervously yawned, rubbed my eyes and waited for the remaining blur to leave. I glanced at the clock.

It was 5:35 a.m. I sat in the dark room, wondering how long it was going to take to pack up my things and leave town.

I wrote about the shootout and arrest of Sheriff Rick Ward and his henchmen. The following day, I banged out another story about the eight dead bodies that were buried in the secret airfield near Marfa.

Chihuahua Charlie turned out to be a national glider champion pilot named Charles Bates, a 36-year-old, smallish man with a stutter, a long prison sentence for drug smuggling, gun running. His back arched after a gliding accident. His bony fingers stood out at Indian gaming casinos where he gambled away a lot of his drug profits.

Bates, who lived in Chihuahua, and another glider pilot got a bundle of cash for every load they flew into the United States from Mexico. He'd made millions working for Mickey Madrid. He now worked exclusively for Sheriff Ward. Occasionally, he'd do some freelance work for the Juarez Cartel.

My investigative series tied everything together, except who killed rogue cop Tommy Rubio. Reporter Mark West wrote about his death. I didn't want to go near it.

Strangely, I felt a bit sad about the demise of the man who tried to kill me, concluding that his own greed got him killed by someone who he never saw coming, Bazooka.

"There's an ongoing investigation," the article stated, quoting the head of the El Paso DEA who suspected Tommy of being a dirty, rogue cop. The sniper rifle was found near Tommy Rubio's body along with cocaine and money scattered around the car.

I doubted that anyone would really want to know the truth. Maybe, it's best that it was left that way. By now, the FBI figured out who Ruy Lopez was, just like I did.

Mickey Madrid's daughter was rushed from the West Texas desert to the hospital by helicopter. She died a few hours later in the emergency room. There were no family members there. She died alone. The doctors said they tried frantically to save her life.

I was in the hospital's waiting room when a doctor told me that she didn't make it. It busted me up inside, really bad.

The doctor said I could go to her bedside and say goodbye.

I kissed her lips a couple of times, stroked her soft hair. Cried and told her I loved her and would miss her. I hugged her, kissed her lips and said goodbye when two guys dressed in hospital garb quietly came into the room to take her body away.

That night, I went out, bought a six-pack, went deep into the desert, sat on the hood of my car, got drunk, sobbed, screamed and cursed at drug users and dealers, at the world, at God. I searched for answers, trying to figure out why life flings its callous and cold cruelty on those closest to our hearts.

Three days later, Sierra Angelica Madrid was laid to rest. Hundreds attended her funeral. Bazooka sat rigidly four rows from the front.

I sat in the back of the room, the second to the last row. I was certain that nobody would know I was there or even cared who I was. I preferred it that way. I wanted to make myself as small as possible, so I sat staring straight ahead.

People started to line up to view Sierra's body, lying inside a white coffin with polished brass handles. I struggled as to whether I should get in that line. But I couldn't bring myself to see her lifeless body. She would be cold and stiff with a white rosary probably wrapped around her hands that were pressed against her chest.

Maybe, she looked like a beautiful bride or a pretty princess sleeping, waiting for her prince or some knight in shining armor from a faraway land to kiss her lips so she could wake up and live happily ever after.

Even so, I didn't want to see her lying there like a frigid, marble statue.

My thoughts went back to that small pond in the desert. I could still see her splashing, hear her laughing and giggling. I could hear her voice. It was clear, strong and confident. Her eyes were eager and vivacious.

I lowered my head, said a short prayer, walked out and headed to the parking lot. The evening was being gently edged out by night. I went down the steps and just as I was about to turn the corner, someone shouted my name. I turned. It was Bazooka.

As Bazooka walked up, a ghastly sensation crawled up my spine. I swallowed hard as he approached. I braced myself for a snarl, a subtle threat or a tacit warning to forget the Tommy Rubio bombing or stay away from the Madrid family. Or, maybe, he would just ram his fist upside my head for being there.

I still wasn't convinced that this man, this monster, who would have taken a bullet for Mickey Madrid, had any feelings.

But there was a smile, a Sunday morning smile on his face like a rainbow busting through some ominous dark cloud. He stuck out his large, beefy hand. I shook it and spread the corners of my lips as high as they could go.

We were eye to eye.

"I thought you'd like to know. Sierra spoke about you, about Mexico. She said 'you weren't such a bad guy.' I could tell that she was in love. She looked happy," he said. "Sierra was like a daughter, Emilio like a son. I loved them both. They were good kids. They were my family. All the family I ever had."

I took a deep breath and let it out slowly and looked away as my eyes watered up. I nodded, stared into the distance.

"I appreciate what you did. *Gracias*, Bazooka."

"Sierra would have wanted it that way."

He nodded, patted his chest and hung his heart on every word he said.

"She'll always live in here, *siempre*," he said. "Her and Emilio, always, *aqui*."

Wiping away a tear, he cleared his throat, turned his head sideways and glanced at the centipede of car headlights trudging down the long street.

"*Bueno, hasta luego.*" Bazooka said.

"*Que Dios mi lo cuide, mucho,*" I said.

"*Gracias, joven. Igualmente.*"

"Where are you going from here?"

"*Quien sabe?* Somewhere south, somewhere near a river, a jungle, where I can fish in peace," he said.

Bazooka looked back at the funeral home as though he expected Sierra to be standing on the top step, beckoning him to come over.

"There is nothing here, anymore. I know the cartel has long tentacles and even a longer memory. Someday, they might catch up to me. I don't care. Their people will go for theirs, and I will go for mine, and we'll see what happens."

Bazooka thought about what he said and nodded

"Mickey. He held everything together. *Era cabron*, but he had a good side, *tambien*. Now, *es un desmadre*. The cartel beasts are killing women and children. They're brutes who don't give a damn. Say what you want about Mickey but he was never about that. *Nunca*."

Bazooka slowly shook his head. Almost immediately, he turned and started to walk away.

"Bazooka." I said.

He turned around.

"*Que?*"

"I have to ask. I need to know. That story about the two Colombians, Fernando and Topo."

"Yeah, what about it?"

"*Era verdad?*"

"Is what true?"

"Were the heads of Fernando and Topo FedExed to their boss in Bogota?" I asked.

A faint and wistful expression lightened Bazooka's brooding face.

"It's not true," he said.

As if by reflex, he cautiously gazed over his shoulder to make sure he wasn't within earshot of anyone else.

"The heads were put in an ice chest, hauled down to Bogota in a freight truck and dropped on the steps of Alvarez Cantu's house along with a dozen roses and a Hallmark card," Bazooka whispered. "There was no FedEx service to Bogota at that time."

"A Hallmark card?"

"Yeah."

"What did the card say?"

"As I recall, 'may the comfort of God help you during this difficult time' or something like that. It was signed Miguel."

"Mickey."

"Right. He had a sense of humor like his daughter."

He winked, chuckled, ambled around the corner and disappeared. I knew I would never see him again.

Early the next morning, I packed a bag and drove toward the Sangre de Cristo Mountains in southern Colorado, stopping only to fill the gasoline tank. Once I arrived at the rented cabin, I took out my belongings out, including some fishing gear. I turned off my cell phone and tossed it inside the trunk of my car.

I told C.J. I need a few days off. I didn't want to be found or talk to anyone on the Internet about anything, about what they thought might be important, about the weather, about deadlines or pool halls or anything else. None of that seemed to matter. Much of the time, I thought about Sierra.

It rained the next two days. The rain came suddenly and brought heavy thundershowers. I stayed inside the cabin, read books and worked on a novel that I started writing years ago and never got around to finishing it.

When the sun finally broke through the clouds for the better part of the day, I rented a boat and put a fishing line into the lake as clouds slid across the glass surface of the water like large balls of cotton. One evening, the horizon was brushed with a swirling purple and gold sunset. I sat on a hill and watched it, wishing Sierra was sitting beside me. Her head on my shoulder.

Sometimes, especially when I walked into the woods, I also thought about Emily and Knuckles and realized how much I missed them. How I'd love to toss a ball and beg Knuckles to chase it. I would have loved to walk alone with Emily down this lone, trail running next to the river. I'd tell her everything that happened, including how I fell in love with Sierra without even meaning to go there. That it all just happened, and Emily, I know, would understand.

During the night, I'd sit on a chair on the cabin's porch, sip on a beer and watch a sheet of rain gush down from the roof and onto the dirt road, creating a muddy torrent.

Sunday morning, I woke up and reluctantly logged onto the Internet. There it was the email. It had arrived a few hours earlier. I cracked it open.

It was from a Delta Force operative named Quinton, just as CIA agent McBride promised.

Showtime, the email stated: Big Mac will call Monday.

That was it. It simply let me know that the newspaper could run the final story on Tuesday morning.

I stared at the wooden floor for the longest time. Then, I dashed outside, danced barefoot with joy and screamed.

"Yesssssss! It's over! It's over!"

I immediately sent an email to C.J: Run first batch of stories on the Internet, late Monday afternoon. I hit the send key. Minutes later, an email reply.

"Great!" C.J. stated. "Where are you at?"

"Out of town. See you soon," I emailed back and clicked off the computer.

After the newspaper published everything, I'd pack up my stuff, get on Interstate 10 and head west until I hit the Pacific Ocean, turn north and drive 100 miles to my cousin Michael's place in Santa Barbara. I sent him an email: Should be there in a few days. I'll call when I leave El Paso.

Driving home from southern Colorado, I knew that thousands of miles away, plans were underway to raid guerilla-training camps in Mexico. Mexican troops would make incursions deep into the jungle, ambushing and killing Mexican and South American terrorists, gang members and drug dealers.

Somewhere, federal prosecutors prepared indictments that would later result in doors being busted down and hundreds of arrests across the nation and in Mexico.

Monday, 5 a.m., I went straight to the newsroom and contacted CIA agent McBride, who came through with a lot of great, lively, and detailed quotes describing the pre-dawn operation, the raids and areas hit by Mexican Special Forces. McBride spoke under the cloak of anonymity.

Not a word was written about Delta Force secretly operating in Mexico. I kept the promise that Delta Force would never make its way into my stories.

By late afternoon after the stories were published on the Internet, I knew that millions of eyes would read about the secret plan to funnel guns and terrorists into the United States through Central America and Mexico.

A series on drugs, terrorists, drug cartels and weapons would pack a wallop that would shock and awe the senses. The Associated Press, CNN, New York Times and the other media heavyweights picked up these jaw-dropping stories.

A press conference would be held in Washington D.C. followed by walls of denial by suspects' lawyers. People would run for cover behind them. There would be a lot of dead bodies south of the border.

When I walked outside my house to get the newspaper, the sun's fingertips were beginning their primordial climb over the Franklin Mountains, I scooped up the paper and tucked it under my arm. A cold breeze hit my skin like tiny razors as I walked inside.

I tossed the newspaper on the kitchen table looked with a grin and walked away. I would read it later and savor every word. But right now, there was no rush to do so.

I filled a bowl with Wheaties, poured milk into the bowl and tasted it.

I gagged. Spat the cereal into the bowl. The milk had turned sour. I opened the refrigerator. No more milk. I grabbed the last beer from a six-pack of Corona. I poured cereal and beer into a new bowl.

I walked into the bedroom, sat at the edge of my bed with my bowl of cereal. Soon my eyes were transfixed on the portrait I duct-taped on the wall. The portrait that Francisco painted of Sierra and me. I planned to frame it someday. Or maybe, I'd just leave it up for awhile before putting it inside a box and storing it in a closet shelf until my hair turned gray, and I rummaged through those memories.

The portrait was beautiful, even if it would never be completed.

Shoving a spoonful of cereal and beer into my mouth, I turned on my cell phone and checked my messages. I hit the play arrow on the phone and tapped the phone speaker.

The first message was from the car rental company.

"Mr. Fuentes, this is Joseph from Avis Rent-A-Car. I've got the price quotes on the rental truck. When will you be leaving town? Give me a call, please. Thank you, sir."

The next message surprised me. It was my father. His voice laced with emotion.

"*Mijo*, Susan showed me your stories on the Internet. I am very proud of you. Hope you can come and visit us. I miss you. We all miss you. Love you, son."

I replayed his message two more times.

Glassy-eyed, I said, "I love you too, Dad."

The next message was from Emily. Her upbeat tone made my heart flutter.

"Hi stranger. Just called to wish you a Happy Birthday. Knuckles says, hi. Okay, I know your birthday is next week. But I thought I'd get a jumpstart on everybody else in wishing you a happy birthday."

There was a brief pause.

"And, I miss you. Miss you a lot. So, if you are ever down this way, drop by and say, 'hi.' Bye, and take care."

The last message was from my landlady.

"Rent is overdue. So pay up," she said with her grumpy voice and hung up.

I grinned, stared at the cell phone and played Emily's message again.

A smile, the size of a cantaloupe, appeared on my face.

Then, I gathered my thoughts and punched some numbers. Nobody answered. So, I left a message: "Brother Andrew, it's Jack. Just called to tell you that we nailed them. Nailed all of them, including Rick Ward. Thanks, for all your help."

I was about to end the call when I thought about Emily.

"Oh, one more thing. I'm thinking about going to Chicago around Christmas to visit a very close friend. We have so much to talk about. There are so many things to say. I have a lot of fences to mend in a lot of places. Well, you've worked in this profession so you'd understand. I'm just asking, please keep me in your prayers. *Gracias.*"

I called the rental company and left a message.

"Hey, Joseph. Jack Fuentes here. Change of plans. Cancel the truck. But I will need a convertible. Going up to New Mexico to see my family. I'll be returning Sunday night. Got to get back to work. The newsroom monster needs stories, quotes."

I ended the call and looked up at Sierra's portrait. Her eyes radiated as though she approved of what I just did. Her mischievous smile that could have been lifted from a wayward buccaneer filled the silence like bubbling speech.

I shoved another spoonful of cereal into my mouth, chewed, gazed at her portrait and grinned, a toothy grin. No doubt, if Sierra was sitting beside me she'd look at my Breakfast Of Champions beer concoction playfully crinkle her nose and twist her lips in disgust.

"*Estas loco?* That's so disgusting. Seriously, Jack? Really? Beer and cereal?" she'd probably say.

"It's good. Want some?" I'd reply through a mouthful of cereal. "Try it."

"No," she'd say, frowning. "No way, absolutely not."

There would be an awkward silence, and then, she'd crack up.

"You're crazy!" She'd say.

"Yeah, so what's your point?"

"Is crazy contagious?"

"Like the Swine Flu. But it fine tunes the day. Gives it sparkle, clarity. Pretty soon, you start seeing newsrooms, pigeons, and people in a totally different light. And before long, the whole world is wearing a clown suit."

"I doubt that."

"Doubt all you want. Would I lie to you?" I'd say and put the spoonful of cereal near her lips. "Here."

"Jack, no."

"Here, just a spoonful."

"I said, stop! No!"

"Here!"

"Jack! No!"

"Watch," I'd say shoving more cereal in my mouth and making ugly, silly faces.

Sierra would pause and take a deep breath.

"Okay, okay."

She'd cautiously put a spoonful of cereal in her mouth, slowly chew and gulp it down.

"Not bad," she'd say and grin. "Not bad at all."

"Now, you're certified crazy, just like me."

"Yep," she'd say, wide-eyed, pause and giggle.

"I love you, Jack Fuentes."

"I love you too."

And just like that, her vibrant voice slowly drifted away until it was no more.

THE END

www.ingramcontent.com/pod-product-compliance
Lightning Source LLC
Chambersburg PA
CBHW070630180626
46817CB00006B/2088